UNFORGETTABLE

By the same author

Sugar and Spice
Fortune's Child
Eyes of Jade

UNFORGETTABLE

William Gill

HarperCollins*Publishers*

HarperCollinsPublishers
77–85 Fulham Palace Road,
Hammersmith, London W6 8JB

Published by HarperCollins*Publishers* 1995
1 3 5 7 9 8 6 4 2

A catalogue record for this book is
available from the British Library

ISBN 0 224592 2

Set in Linotron Sabon by
Rowland Phototypesetting Ltd
Bury St Edmunds, Suffolk

Printed in Great Britain by
HarperCollinsManufacturing Glasgow

To Carmen and Julian

ACKNOWLEDGEMENTS

I am very grateful to Martín Cullen, Robert Hancock, María Marta Sanchez Elía de Nuñez, Luis Ramirez Bosco, and Yves Osmu for their help with my research. My special thanks to Mark Lucas for his good advice.

NOW

PEOPLE SAY I HAVE PLENTY of reasons to be pleased with myself. I wouldn't disagree openly, because tempting fate is a dangerous habit we forgo as we get older. Here in America, getting older is considered a dangerous habit in itself, and it would be hypocritical of me to pretend that I am any different to most of my friends and acquaintances. I use my swimming pool and my tennis court regularly, at least when I'm not away, and my personal trainer comes to the house early in the morning, three times a week. I gave up saturated fats and fried food almost as long ago as I gave up tempting fate, and I was among the first for whom mineral water became a necessity. Unusually for my business, I've never done drugs, other than the occasional joint at parties, before they went out of style. I have affairs, which I call 'relationships' to avoid complications with my therapist.

The result is that I look pretty good for my fifty-four years. More important, I feel good, too. I have learned to overlook, to ignore. Both are skills as essential to survival as being alert, although much less often discussed. They need good PR, like everything in this town.

I feel proud of my career. Predictably, I am also proud of my daughter, although I can't claim sole credit for her. My ex-wife would be justly angry, and I have no reason to hurt her now. At a lesser level, I feel proud of my home, particularly when someone recognizes it as a building by Neutra, or asks me about a picture or a piece in my collection. I have become adept at distinguishing genuine interest from politeness, and tailor my explanation accordingly.

This was a consideration when my guests of honour asked for a tour of the house after dinner one night. They were a New York couple, a Wall Street banker who might put money into my next project, and his Upper East Side wife. The lights were on in all the rooms facing the garden, so that the house would look its best from the terrace. Like my clothes, my car, my vacations or my art collection, my home is both a source of pleasure and a tool of my trade, and I know how to maximize its effect. Guadalupe, my housekeeper, had turned off most of the hidden lights behind shrubs or trees while we were in the dining room; she knows the routine by now. The garden fading into darkness heightened the contrast between the dark sky, the blue-white incandescence of the illuminated pool at the far end of the dark lawn, and the city lights beyond the edge of the cliff.

Although my guests' request fitted my own inclination, I still felt uncertain about how genuine their interest was as we moved from room to room. I was trying to please the banker, who had suggested the tour; the banker was trying to please his wife by pretending to be interested in art, and his wife was the type who gets on in life by never showing when they are pleased. She looked carefully at everything but didn't say anything, he had nothing to say, and I was saying too much to fill the silence. As we were about to leave the small sitting room that overlooked the lily pond to join the other guests, she stood in front of my Dunand lacquer screen in the far corner of the room.

'*Le Mariage d'Atalante*. You bought it at Christie's five years ago,' she said.

'How did you know?' I asked.

'I was the underbidder. You paid too much,' she replied.

I smiled. I could understand the need to justify the loss of something one had wanted very badly. She went behind the screen, to inspect its back, and her husband glanced at his watch.

'It's getting late, darling,' he said.

There was no reply, then we heard the clicking of her heels on the short flight of stone steps concealed by the screen. I began to feel anxious. Technically, my guest wasn't snooping; but she was in my study, my own space, and I don't like people going in there. It is more private to me than my bedroom or my bathroom. I followed her; she was standing in front of one of the many framed prints on the wall. I keep my collection of photographs there.

'Amazing face. God, that woman is stunning,' the banker's wife said. She had a good eye. 'Who is she?'

'I don't know,' I lied. After a lifetime of self-deception, deceiving others wasn't difficult. 'I bought it years ago. I'm very fond of Avedon's portraits of the fifties.'

We stood in silence, my guest staring at the picture. I didn't need to look at it, because I knew every grain of that particular print. The sitter faces the camera in close-up, her left hand raised, her delicate fingers running through her short hair. Her head is tilted back slightly, so that light falls on her upturned face and her long, beautiful neck. The sight of her had never lost its power to move me.

'I've never seen a face like that,' the banker's wife said finally. 'It's unforgettable.'

Although it is customary among polite people to pay each other overblown compliments on their possessions, my guest's admiration was genuine. She was more right than she knew. I had been trying to forget that face for thirty years.

THEN

One

I will always remember the first time I saw Delia. I had not been in Paris for long. I was just enjoying myself, trying not to seem too young, pretending to be blasé. I had arrived with some phone numbers, names that meant little to me, and a lot of hope. One of the phone numbers belonged to somebody at the Argentine embassy. I can't remember who, and they wouldn't remember me now. It doesn't matter; whoever gave me the number must have been significant enough for me to receive an invitation to a party there. I think it was either for the National Day, or in honour of some dignitary visiting France.

Embassies are curious places. They conjure reminiscences of Marco Polo, *My Fair Lady*, statesmanship and decorations. At least for me. Then. The building was one of those solemn houses in the *Seizième Arrondissement*. I went in, awed by the marble, the gilt and the chandeliers, and hoped it didn't show. I wasn't expecting a receiving line, and they weren't expecting me: I mumbled something, they mumbled back, and I walked away, following the other guests, and feeling unsure of myself. I came to a huge reception room, which led onto another one, all full of people I didn't know. A waiter offered me a drink. The trivial gesture of acceptance made me feel more at ease, and I considered my options. I could try to find my unknown host, or watch the scene. I watched.

Even then, when I knew so little about anything – myself included – I could tell that I had not walked into a fairy tale. The laughter was too harsh, the blondes too blonde, the men too too. The setting had lived up to my expectations, but not the guests.

I scanned the room. I was a sucker for splendour in those days. Not because of greed; my life would have been different otherwise. But I still had a romantic notion of splendour, and I had found it. Then I caught sight of three people in a corner, a man and two women. They were older – in their late thirties or early forties – and glamorous. The man was the genuine version of the many pin-striped, double-breasted types among the crowd. One of the women was blonde, a real blonde, and wore diamonds as if she had been born in them, but it was the other woman who really caught my eye. She wasn't wearing diamonds: baroque pearls and old gold glinted at her neck instead. It was clear from the fur-lined coat casually slung around her shoulders that she had not given up money, and yet she was not showing off. She wore it as if it was an old raincoat, a useful barrier between her and an environment not to her liking.

There was great beauty about her. In every gesture, in every movement, and most of all in her face. She had been born beautiful, and she had lived beautifully. It was beauty beyond sex, beyond gain, beauty for the sake of it. As it should be.

I was entranced. I thought I had seen that face before, but maybe it was just the instinctive recognition of perfection when we stumble across it, a void in our imagination waiting to be filled. I wondered how everybody else in the room could carry on nibbling at canapés and talking nonsense rather than look at her. A minute before I would have prayed for anyone to speak to me; now someone did, and it annoyed me. It broke the spell.

'Isn't she wonderful? Delia Lagos is the best we have.'

I can't remember now if the voice was a man's or a woman's. But I am grateful to that voice, because it allowed me to put a name to the face.

I had heard of Delia through my mother, her friends, and gossip in that small world we lived in in Buenos Aires. She was always referred to as one of us, even though she had lived in France most of her life and had never been back. They wanted her to be one of them, although I don't know if the feeling was reciprocated. Delia had become well known as a writer, but writers are seldom famous enough for people to remember their faces. I had vaguely recognized hers only because one of my mother's favourite pastimes was to sit with old photograph albums, and show us the mementoes of her early years, a time so significant to her and so meaningless to us, her children. The occasional glimpses of Delia in those fading group photographs had been stunning enough to momentarily overcome my boredom, and now I was confronted with the real person. Time had only added interest to her face.

If I had not known who she was, maybe I would have managed to introduce myself, to make conversation. I didn't want a polite greeting and an equally polite dismissal, though. I wanted more than that. I wanted to know her. I paused, and then it was too late. The man she was with said something, some remark about being late perhaps, because they made their way to the door. Delia's arm brushed mine as she walked past, and she gave me a small smile in apology. There was what I thought was a flicker of recognition in her eyes, as if she expected me to greet her, but I was staring at her so intently that she might have assumed we had met before. Then she must have realized that mine was merely a look of anonymous admiration, something she must have been used to, and she moved on. A second later she was gone.

'You know why she still looks like that?' the voice asked me. It wasn't a question really, since I was given no time to answer.

'It's because she had it so easy. All her life she had it easy.'

At the time, I believed it.

I had told everybody at home that I would stay in Paris for three or four weeks at most, and then I would return to Buenos Aires. It is easier to lie when you believe your own fabrication, if only in part, and it was the most likely outcome anyway. The truth was I did not want to go back to Buenos Aires: I didn't want what waited for me there, although I did not know yet how to avoid it. One way to protect an uncertain hope is not to think too much about the future. I just lived for the moment, enjoying myself.

I was offered a studio apartment near Montparnasse by a friend of a friend before she left for God knows where, and I moved in. First one month, then another went by, until my book of traveller's cheques became alarmingly thin. Odd jobs came my way, and I took them. The prospect of becoming an illegal immigrant soon didn't worry me. I still believed that things sort themselves out in the end.

I was having a good time, bobbing and ebbing with the tide, caught in a never-never world of expatriates, enjoying a sense of freedom I had never felt at home. Sometimes there were bottle parties, sometimes endless nights moving in shifting groups from one café to another, brief flirtations that bleached my already fading memory of Patricia and our brief time together in Buenos Aires. There was always something, even formal dinners with *placement* and candlesticks on the table. I went to only one, but it was enough.

My hostess, a Venezuelan, was one of those old, vague acquaintances my mother struggled to keep in spite of her changed circumstances. I had phoned her some time after my arrival; we exchanged a few pleasantries, and she took my number. I was too flattered by her completely unexpected invitation to consider that it was likely to be due to a last-minute cancellation: a formal dinner was not a frequent event in my life. I preened myself and went.

The party was in one of those grand Avenue Foch apartments. I'm not very punctual in any case, and my knowledge of the Métro didn't stand up to three changes of line, so by the time I arrived, everybody was there. My hostess hurriedly introduced me to some of the other guests just before dinner was announced, and we were led into the dining room. There were two round tables seating ten each. Mine was not the hostess's table: my dinner companions were a sprinkling of Cuban exiles, a Brazilian couple and some French people, presumably asked to add local colour to this evening of South American expatriates. The main point in common seemed to be that everybody was rich – except for me. Half-way through the soufflé I realized that the conversation was about people I didn't know, or places I couldn't afford. I didn't belong here, an all-too-familiar feeling for me, and one I saw as my own fault because of my lack of worldliness. I didn't want to be like my dinner companions, and yet I felt handicapped by the fact that I wasn't.

I found myself looking at the mirrored wall facing me, as if the general scene interested me more than my neighbours, when they were too interested in each other to bother about a silent young newcomer who knew nothing. The mirror gave me a good view of the other table, and there I saw Delia. From this angle, her face was framed by two tall candles, like ivory bars isolating her from the rest. The soft light enhanced the red glow in her hair, short enough to reveal the grace of her neck. Her grey eyes were brighter than the opals in her long necklace. Beautiful as she was, I was once again struck most by the elegance of her movements. She moved as if time had no bearing on her, although there was nothing languid about her attitude. On the contrary: hers was the calm of someone who does only as she pleases.

I felt an embarrassing rush of blood to my face as soon as I saw her. It was tantalizing to have such a good view of Delia, and yet it was a reflection, an illusion, when I wanted the true image. For that I would have to wait until dinner was over, but now I had found a purpose to my being here, compelling enough to make me overcome my inhibitions. I made small-talk as best I could, and pretended to listen, until we moved to the drawing room for coffee.

Delia sat on a sofa at the far end of the room, where she was joined by other guests. As people redistributed themselves, I moved closer to her. I told myself I was waiting for the right opportunity to join her circle, when in fact I was gathering my courage to approach her, searching frantically for words that would make me interesting, and pierce through the intimidating aura of self-possession around her.

Eventually my hostess came up to me, probably eager to eliminate the offending sight of a lonely guest. 'You must meet Delia,' she said, leading me by the arm. 'You are compatriots, after all.'

Our hostess introduced me as a promising young artist, although I didn't know I was one. Her lie didn't bother me much; it made me sound interesting, which suited us both. Delia nodded in automatic acknowledgement, then fixed her eyes on me.

'Are you any relation of Francis's?' she asked. Her voice didn't let her down. It rose and fell, from velvet to silk.

'He was my father.'

Delia's hand slid over her necklace. Her slim fingers toyed with the beads.

'You look like him. How old are you?'

'I'm twenty-four.' My birthday was a few months away, in fact, but if my hostess could lie to improve my standing, so could I.

'You're lucky to be so young,' she said. There was a brief shift of expression in her eyes, half-way between an ironic smile and a glint of wistfulness.

I felt lucky at that moment, and not because of my age. Delia seemed interested in me.

'Are you staying in Paris for long?' she asked.

'I don't know. Not as long as I'd like, probably.'

I counted on my vagueness to make me appear exciting and mysterious, a misjudgement soon rectified when she turned away abruptly and began to talk to the man beside her. I stayed there, until I felt silly. I had had my encounter, my moment of grace and, after all, she was of my parents' generation. There were plenty of reasons for me to find Delia fascinating, but none whatsoever for her to give me more than a minute or two of her time. I turned, ready to move away, when I felt her hand on my arm.

'Come for a drink next Monday. Seven o'clock.' She gave me her address, then continued with her conversation without paying any further attention to me.

I forced myself to move away, and left the party as soon as I could thank my hostess and make an excuse. I didn't want to run the risk of Delia changing her mind.

Her address was one of those buildings in the Rue de Grenelle, offering only a huge wall and massive wooden gates to the street. Chastened by the dinner party experience, I made a point of being there on time. Then I decided it was gauche to arrive on the dot, so I paced up and down the street, from the Square des Invalides to the Rue de Bac. It seemed like an eternity, although it was only fifteen minutes. I really didn't know then what the Rue de Grenelle meant on the Paris scale of things, but I could guess. I wasn't my mother's son for nothing. This was the life she and my father had had when they were my age, and sometimes my mother made it sound as if he had been lucky to die so young, when things were still good for them, as if sudden death when you are thirty amounted to divine mercy.

Finally I walked into the building. I addressed the concierge with a voice which I hoped wasn't shaking, and she nodded towards the end of the courtyard, at the row of glazed doors flanked by orange trees in tubs. A manservant let me in. I remember the tentative sheen of faded velvet on the walls of the hall, glimpsed through an accumulation of gilt frames, paintings old and new, and ornate mirrors. Now people pay fortunes to interior designers to elegantly clutter their rooms, but not then.

After the riot of the entrance, the drawing room was a surprise. Bare parquet floor, off-white walls, another row of tall glazed doors leading to a small garden, a few pieces of very good antique furniture and only one painting. It was an abstract, big enough for the room, its mosaic of dappled greens mirroring the hues of the garden under the fading light. I could describe every brush-stroke of that painting, every detail of the furniture; my vagueness is only because I'm trying to be accurate about how it seemed to me then, when they weren't yet imprinted in my memory. Like Delia herself, her drawing room awed me in its elegant perfection. It seemed a dreamscape rather than anything real.

I walked around the room, then I tried to make myself comfortable in one of the armchairs. After a while I wondered if I shouldn't move to the sofa instead, to look more at ease than in this straight-backed antique made for people with shorter legs and arms than mine. I was about to do so, when I thought it would be awkward if Delia arrived half-way through my change of seat. My restlessness had little to do with physical comfort.

At last she walked in, late enough to make me feel uneasy, but not so late as to make me feel unwanted. Delia was wearing trousers and a shirt. It could have been silk or wool, a petty detail. I only mention it because Delia could make one look like the other, and she did. Her entrance had the polish of an actress in a play she knows by heart. She didn't pause on her way to the sofa, explaining that she had been on the phone. This resolved a dilemma that had occupied me while I waited. I had wondered whether I should shake her hand – too formal – or kiss her cheek – too familiar. Delia hadn't given me the chance to do either, and I was glad of that. Those gestures, so trivial as to be second-nature in everyday life, would have become impossible for me once I was confronted with Delia in the flesh. The notion of physical contact – however casual – became ludicrous: I could barely bring myself to hold her gaze for a second. My awareness of how painfully conscious of her I was, while she remained so at ease, felt as confining as a glass case around me, a restraint I could neither see nor break.

She asked me what I wanted to drink and then pointed towards a drinks tray – no, she didn't point. Delia never pointed at anything. Her gesture was precise enough to be clear, and yet not as abrupt as a blunt direction. I was granted the illusion of being in charge.

I think she asked me why I was in Paris, and what I wanted to do. I told her that I had come to Europe after I had finished studying law in Buenos Aires, the only part of her question I was in a position to answer. She must have sensed it was a subject best left alone, because then she quickly asked me about my mother, whom she said she had met a long time ago. I didn't tell her the truth, and I don't think she cared enough to expect it.

She shifted the conversation to my trip, and I managed to relax a little now we were into small talk. I told her about Madrid and Barcelona, and my overland journey to Paris. I tried to sound observant, erudite, and she listened as attentively as if she hadn't lived in Europe most of her life, as if my comments really interested her. Perhaps they did. Hers was a Europe of chateaux and schlosses, while mine was Europe on Eurailpass and student hostels. She could have been patronizing me, but that's not how it felt at the time, particularly once the conversation focused on her. A welcome change; she had much to tell, and I didn't. Not that she revelled in details; Delia combined the self-assurance of someone who knows her life to be public property with a narrator's skill at hinting rather than explaining.

We had another round of drinks, maybe a third; I honestly can't remember. I was spellbound by her story, because it was so vivid, so neat, such a seamless progression. Bored with her life in Buenos Aires, she had moved to New York. She did mention her affair with a famous American writer. It would have been shameless not to do so: everybody knew about it. Her casual reference to the relationship made it clear it had been an incident, a distraction in her rise. Was rise the right word? Probably not. Delia's life had started at the top, and she had never moved from there. She made the affair sound like a circumstantial event, a happening. Her life had been one we all aspire to, a succession of delicious moments inexorably leading towards a happy ending.

She didn't dwell on anything in particular; it was banter after all, not a confession. But she made me feel like a confidant, and it would be unfair to say she was deceitful. I asked about her writing, and she told me she was facing some difficulties at the moment. She didn't call it writer's block, and the possibility didn't cross my mind.

At some point she must have looked at the clock (Delia never wore a watch, she found them vulgar) and made some noises about how late it was. I didn't want to leave. I wanted to make the evening as long as possible, badly enough to forget my situation and suggest taking her out to dinner. She smiled at me, a smile that seemed so guileless that ulterior motives were unimaginable, and told me that she would choose the restaurant. I had a few francs in my pocket, and a lot of Scotch inside me. I hoped for the best, and followed her.

She led me to a place nearby. It was a local haunt, with gingham table-cloths and candles stuck in bottles. I can't remember the food, and I have a dim recollection of the wine, constantly poured by a knowledgeable owner from an inexhaustible demijohn. Unlike me, he was sober, and yet he seemed equally unconcerned about my ability to pay for what he provided in abundance. He was a wise man; although I didn't know it, Delia had an account there. The check never appeared.

I can't even remember what we talked about: having obliterated from my mind the spectre of the check, I must have forgotten about the differences between us, let alone what we discussed. I remember her laugh though, the magical moment when it ceased to be a chatelaine's polite bell to become a woman's laugh, laughter beyond control, like mine. She looked at me, and wiped her eyes with her napkin. Then she spoke, and I can still hear her voice, because she used her drawing-room tone. It would not have jarred a couple of hours earlier; now it did.

'You know, Martín,' she told me, 'if you were older, or if I were younger, we . . .' She stopped, but I knew what she meant.

Sometimes you say something that changes everything, something so reckless that later you can't imagine how you could have done it. Being drunk must have helped me. I was drunk as much from the wine as from the fact that I was with the most beautiful, the most fascinating woman I had ever met.

'Why not, anyway?' I asked without a pause. My timing was perfect, as good as in those replies you make up long after the event. She looked at me. Her smile was gone, and the mask too. What was left were her magnificent, smoky-grey eyes locked onto mine.

'Why not?' she repeated, like an echo, and I took her hand. I remember my heart beating very fast, my giddiness at a moment that reduced every other experience I had had so far into insignificance. I couldn't know that it would also shape the rest of my life.

Two

The next morning, when I woke up and stared at Delia asleep, my first thought wasn't that I was in love. I knew it immediately, but it wasn't a possibility I wanted to confront yet. A beam of sunlight came through a chink in the curtains and turned the dust in the air to gold. The crumpled sheet veiled Delia's legs, leaving her back free for my eyes to take in slowly, from the soft dimples below her waist to the smooth roundness of her shoulders. The taste of her skin was still in my mouth – or in my mind, far more powerful than a mere sensation. I looked at her in the rapt pride of possession. In wonder too, not least because I had *slept* with a woman for the first time.

I wasn't a twenty-three-year-old virgin. Like all my friends, I had lost my virginity to a maid at home when I was fifteen (my mother fired her when she found me coming out of the maid's room late at night), and there had been a few willing girlfriends since then. But this was 1963, and I had grown up in Buenos Aires, where only married couples or older single people slept together. For the young, who lived at home with their parents until they married, sex was a hazardous prize to be had briefly, in dubious hotels that rented rooms by the hour, tawdry establishments with names like 'Acapulco' or 'Waikiki', perhaps to justify the fact that their customers wore sun-glasses when they went in or came out, regardless of the season or the time of the day.

It was very different this time. There was no hurry, no need to watch the clock to ward off some girl's suspicious parents. I should have found it relaxing, if an equally powerful fear hadn't shattered my all-too-brief contentment. The morning after was unknown territory to me. I didn't know the rules, what I should do, what was expected of me. Ignorance was too close to loss of control, and I hated the idea of Delia seeing me floundering. Perhaps she didn't want me to be here when she woke up, and the thought of being found in bed with her by one of her servants was enough to overcome any inclination to stay – a new twist on the principle of '*Pas devant les domestiques*', which I had heard spoken often during my childhood. I forced myself to get out of bed quietly, gathered up my clothes and left the room, planning to make a speedy, discreet exit. I was wise (or insecure) enough not to take anything for granted regarding Delia. I felt too vulnerable, too hooked on her now to run the risk of face-to-face rejection. Better to call her later and find out if she had plans for the evening, shielding myself with the safe impersonality of the phone.

Delia's bathroom was beyond the mirrored maze of her dressing room. I wasn't sure the noise of the shower wouldn't wake her, so I opened a door at the end of a corridor and found myself in another bedroom. Although the décor was as personal, as expensively simple as in her rooms, there was a stillness in the air, and in the arrangement of books and objects, indicating that nobody lived here. It had to be a guest room, a place for temporary visitors – like me.

I found everything I could need in the bathroom nearby: fresh towels laid out on polished brass rails, untouched bars of soap piled up on a silver dish, and a toothbrush and shaving kit in a china bowl, still in their wrappings. The sight of a bottle of after-shave was enough to cause a stab of jealousy, until I noticed that it was sealed, as were the bottles of scent next to it. I was staring at the evidence of luxurious hospitality, not betrayal. I felt helpless, at the mercy of my too-quick assumptions based on my inflated expectations. I had no claim on Delia, beyond whatever fraction of her time she was prepared to grant me. All that had happened was that I had spent the night with a very beautiful woman – who was much older and more knowing than me. I told myself to expect nothing, and yearned to be proved wrong.

I lingered under the steaming shower, then rubbed myself dry with a thick, shroud-like bath sheet. After months of hostels and seedy apartments, where a tepid trickle of water would turn to cold without warning, and the ends of the coarse towels barely met around my waist, this was the ablutionary equivalent of Nirvana. The blurred sight of my own naked body in the misted-up mirror reminded me of Delia, lying just a few steps away from me, and my blood rushed to my prick. Only my intention of leaving as soon as possible, my attempt at playing it cool, forced me to get dressed and abandon my temporary haven instead of going back to her.

I was walking down the curving marble steps to the hall when I heard a vacuum cleaner somewhere nearby, and remembered the dour-faced manservant. I tightened the muscles in my neck and held my head high, my lips ready for a fleeting '*Bonjour*' on the final stretch towards the door.

The man wasn't in the hall; he must have been in some other room. Delia was there instead, wrapped in an old Chinese silk dressing gown, standing by a side table and checking the post. I realized then that her beauty had nothing to do with soft lighting or evening make-up.

'There you are,' she said. 'I wondered where you had gone.'

Later I would learn that Delia wasn't an early riser. She must have heard me in the guest bathroom, realized my discomfort, and gone downstairs to stand by the door, forestalling my plan of escape. But I could only rely on what I felt or heard, and words are like dice at that age: you add up their face value, and that appears to be the score. Delia seemed no more pleased by the fact that I was still there than the mild delight we feel at good weather when we open the curtains. Although preferable to the alternative, it makes no real difference to our plans for the day.

'I didn't want to wake you. I was going to call you later,' I said, aware of the absurdity of the situation. We had been having unembarrassed sex not long ago, and now we were making stiltedly casual conversation. The first time is usually like that, and even then I knew it; the occasion wasn't different to previous experiences. The situation was, though. I didn't know quite what to do.

'Wouldn't you like to have breakfast before you go?' Delia

suggested, as she continued to sort through her mail. Before I had time to reply, she raised her head towards the open drawing-room doors.

'Américo,' she called, loud enough to be heard over the din of the vacuum cleaner. A second later, the butler appeared.

'We'll be having breakfast in the study,' Delia told him in Spanish. The butler's glance said everything. He knew why I was there, and he left me in no doubt that I shouldn't be. As for Delia, she had taken my reply for granted.

'I can't stay, I have something to do,' I said, astonished at my own words. I wanted nothing more than to stay with her, and yet I was trying to save face, not to admit that Delia had seen through my stupid fears. I wanted her to see me as self-possessed, in control, because that's how I wanted to feel myself. I wanted her to see me as a man, not as a floundering juvenile.

'It can't be so urgent that you can't stay for a cup of coffee at nine o'clock in the morning,' she smiled, calling my bluff, then she walked towards a door. I followed her into her study. The early spring sunshine came through the tall windows, bringing out honey-coloured highlights in the mahogany bookcases around the room. The walls were as cluttered as the hall's, but not with paintings or mirrors. There were books from floor to ceiling here, and the library steps indicated that they weren't just for decoration. There was little of that: only one painting, a large oil above the fireplace. The picture was good enough to deserve a closer look. It also gave me the chance to keep my back to the butler as he laid breakfast on a corner table.

It was a family portrait. A tall man stood to the left of the canvas, next to a woman sitting on an ornate French armchair, and there were two small children. The boy was about two years old, and he wore a sailor suit; the girl wasn't much older. She sat at her mother's feet on a velvet cushion, almost concealed by her spreading white dress. The painting was very accomplished: its fluid brushwork conveyed the man's power, the woman's languid elegance, the innocent beauty of the children, and the subdued opulence of the half-seen interior behind them. I guessed from the clothes that it had been painted in the 1920s.

'It's one of the last pictures Sargent did before he died,' Delia explained. 'My father used to boast that he managed to convince him to paint us, even though Sargent had given up portraits by then. He was a very persuasive man.'

I hadn't heard of Sargent, but I had heard a lot about Ambrosio Lagos. Even long after his death, he was the kind of person my mother's guests would discuss over dinner as if they were passing on legends of the past to my brother and me, like nomads instructing the young around the camp fire. Ambrosio had done all the right things: he multiplied his father's fortune in Argentina and then abroad, married a French aristocrat's daughter, and eventually entered politics in the grand manner. A wistful mention of 'how different things would have been in this country if he had lived longer', used to be the closing remark of those evocations, as if the titanic Ambrosio would have been able to stem the Peronist tide, like that English king sitting in front of the sea.

After a moment, I joined Delia at the table. The painting, and the recollections it had triggered, disturbed me. They referred to a past that wouldn't seem so distant to me now. Then I thought it to be almost prehistoric, and Delia was part of it. I knew she had to be in her early forties: there were twenty years between us. The notion seemed meaningless, since my memory didn't stretch back that far, and was as irrelevant when I stared at her smiling face in the sunlight now as when I had made love to her the previous night. But the portrait was there. The little girl who looked like pre-war royalty, and the woman I wanted so much, were one and the same.

'It's a beautiful picture,' I said, avoiding Delia's eyes as she handed me my cup across the table. I didn't succeed entirely.

'I'm glad you like it. I'm fond of that picture now, but I didn't care for it for a long time. It was in storage for years,' she said. Her repeated reference to time made me wonder if Delia had read my thoughts.

'There's a very good portrait by Sargent at the museum in Versailles. If you are interested, we could go and see it today or tomorrow,' she went on. Her offer, her veiled reassurance that she was including me in her plans, was enough to sweep away my lingering doubts. The morning light reflected off her smooth skin; my eyes followed the line of her neck and throat, and the shadowed edges of the silk covering her breasts. Delia saw me, and she smiled.

'What are your plans?' she asked.

'I don't have any plans. Why?' I decided to give up pretence. She could have meant that morning or that month; my answer truly covered both.

'It's a beautiful day, so I thought we could drive somewhere nearby. Versailles is full of tourists during the summer, so Fontainebleau might be better. It's the best time of the year for the forest, and we could have lunch at Barbizon. I have pictures of the village somewhere, you'll love it . . .'

She stood up, and went to one of the bookcases. 'Yes, here it is. It hasn't changed much,' she said, opening a large picture book. I went to stand beside her, aware of her particular scent for the first time. It was the smell of jasmine, without the heady tang of manufactured perfume. Delia seemed to exude the light, fresh fragrance of a cool, shaded courtyard in summer.

'This is the house where Rousseau used to paint . . .'

I glanced at the old sepia photograph, and struggled to listen to her explanation. I was far more aware of her physical presence, of the feel of the skin of her arm against mine, than of her voice. I put the book away, and turned her to face me. It was a long kiss. Afterwards I held her, Delia's head resting on my shoulder. I saw our long shadows on the Persian rug. My hand slid under her dressing gown, and her fingers undid the buttons of my shirt. I remember her touch, because it felt as tentative, as uncertain as my own, as if the hesitation that should have been there last night had made a tardy appearance. We fell to our knees. The carpet pattern grew larger in my eyes. Then I closed them, because I felt her lips on mine. Any hesitancy vanished: Delia wanted me as much as I wanted her.

Everything seems easy with hindsight, and I make allowances for that. Even so, I know that our first days together *were* easy. We lived for the moment, without worries; or it could be that I ignored them, like letters left unopened in case they contain bad news. I don't remember worries. Instead I remember walks arm in arm along the Seine, when silence was as sweet as words, or sitting on the grass at the Jardin du Luxembourg, under the big chestnut trees. Most of my memories are not complete. I recall fragments, isolated snapshots, Delia's hand as she picked up her cup in a particular café, her profile as I stared at her while we crossed the Pont Neuf, clothes she wore or things she said, details that are irrelevant in themselves and yet add to an all-important whole, like an alphabet turned into coherent words by some corner of my mind that is neither my memory nor my imagination.

Those daytime memories are so powerful because they preceded our nights together, when Delia stopped being an icon, a perfect image, and became herself. That contrast in her between complete control and utter abandonment haunted and excited me as much or more than the beauty of her face or her body. These I could take for granted, and they were for everybody to see. Her surrender was mine alone.

I moved into her house, or rather I stopped going back to my dusty studio, that uniquely French denomination for tiny one-room apartments which endows penury with the mantle of artistry. It just happened, without me really noticing it, probably because Delia made it seem inevitable by never saying anything or betraying any thought that would make me feel uncomfortable about it. She had a knack for that. After a few days with her, I even managed not to mind the occasional steely glance from Américo, her butler. I had fallen in love, and I felt at home with her.

I had been in love before, but I had never experienced anything comparable to my feelings then. I thought about Delia all the time. I only wanted to be with her. I couldn't tell if it was because this was a dimension of love I had missed so far, or the very different fact that, for the first time in my life, I was with a woman who could have any man she wanted, and yet she had chosen me.

I was frightened too, which was the reason I couldn't bring myself to mention or use the word 'love' at a time when no other emotion mattered to me. Love implies commitment, although I doubt I thought that far ahead. My fear was of a more immediate risk, the possibility that, once I acknowledged my love in so many words, I could find out that it meant much more for me than for her. My love for Delia was all I had, while she had so much besides. I don't mean just money, although that was a factor I couldn't ignore. It was there all the time, even that first morning.

We had lunch at some country restaurant by a river, not far from the village. The food was very good and we lingered afterwards, talking, laughing, and holding hands, perhaps teasing ourselves by delaying our return to Paris to shed our clothes and fall into bed. Eventually the waiter brought our check. I hadn't thought about it, perhaps because I counted on Delia also having an account in this place. I glanced at the folded piece of paper, as white and unwelcome as the proverbial ghost at the banquet, my nightmare of the previous evening now materializing in broad daylight. Delia reached for her bag. I expected her to produce her wallet and pick up the bill, but she didn't. She pulled out her lipstick and compact instead, and retouched her make-up. My fingers were approaching the dreaded plate, as tentatively as if what sat on it was an angry scorpion, when I saw her slip her napkin across the table towards me, the corner of a bank note just visible under it. Delia was helping me in the most discreet way possible, but her gesture made me feel humbled and angry. I thought I had to put up some token masculine resistance.

'That's –' I started, but she cut me short.

'You're not going to be ridiculous, I hope,' she said with an amused glimmer in her eyes. She had turned the situation into a humorous irrelevance, and she knew what she was doing. Appearing ridiculous in her eyes was even worse to me than being broke.

I took her money, and paid.

We didn't see anyone else the following days, or at least I didn't. There were times when Delia had to visit her lawyer, or her brokers, or her tax advisers, or deal with correspondence, and I forced myself to wander around Paris or visit sights that would have interested me if I hadn't seen them as a kind of penance until I could be with her again. Otherwise she gave me all her time; we lingered in bed in the mornings, or listened to music in the evenings, huddled together on one of the sofas downstairs. It was during one of those evenings when Delia told me that some friends of hers were coming for a drink the next day.

'They are very boring. Unfortunately I've cancelled them once before. I can't do it again,' she explained.

'Don't worry, I'll find myself something to do,' I said. I understood her hesitation at my being there, at having to explain me, and yet it hurt me.

'Are you mad? *They* are boring, not you.' Delia sounded half-astonished, half-perplexed by my suggestion. 'I'm just warning you, so you don't blame me for a dreary evening later.'

The next day, we were still in her bedroom when the clock struck seven. I was dressed but she wasn't. Her guests might arrive at any time, and I didn't want to walk down the stairs with Delia to greet them. The situation was awkward enough already. I went straight to the drawing room; the guests could assume I had arrived a few minutes earlier when they found me there.

'You don't need to stand by the door. They don't expect a guard of honour,' Delia said lightly as she came in. She went around the room briskly, checking cigarette boxes, turning off one light and switching on another, crushing a cushion here or moving one there, pushing a chair slightly out of place. 'Américo always leaves the room looking too perfect,' she commented. 'Pour me a whisky, please, darling, and help yourself to whatever you want.'

The bell rang, and I heard Américo open the door. A moment later he showed the guests in.

There was a flurry of kisses and compliments on everybody's appearance, then Delia turned to me. 'This is Martín,' she said, before introducing the newcomers. They gave me a slightly surprised look; I guessed they expected some explanation of my presence there, something like 'my nephew', or 'Martín is so-and-so's son,' but Delia didn't offer one. She offered drinks instead, and the man suggested he would pour them himself. Delia replied that I was in charge, in a tone that conveyed that it was my privilege, not my duty.

She had been right. Her guests were rather stiff and formal. It became apparent fairly soon that the main link between them was a friend with a house in the French Caribbean, where they had all stayed that winter. The conversation drifted around their memories of the holiday, places or houses they had been to, the visitors mentioning a number of people they had met again since.

'I feel rather chilly,' Delia said suddenly, turning towards me. 'Would you mind bringing me a shawl from my bedroom, *chéri*?

You know where they are, don't you? It's the cupboard next to yours.'

The explanation was unnecessary, and she could have called Américo to fetch it. She was letting her friends know that I was her lover, making them accept me on her terms. At first it was deeply embarrassing, but as soon as I left the room I felt strangely elated, my feet gliding up the stairs with an almost proprietorial spring to them. When I came back, and she sat by my side after I had wrapped the shawl around her shoulders, I didn't feel embarrassed at all.

I couldn't see Delia's home as *my* home, but soon familiarity masked that unease behind the new pleasures of our shared life – or the small, but more immediately noticeable adjustments it demanded. Waiting for her in the mornings was one of these.

Eventually I made it easier by going to her study to read the newspaper once I was dressed, but not during our early days together. Then the feeling of entitlement I got from sharing her privacy was more than enough compensation for the seemingly endless time Delia needed after her bath to find something in her closets to wear. The faint clicking of hangers as they slid along metal rails was followed by long silences while she held one dress or other against herself and inspected the effect in the mirror. My intuition that I could be the reason for so much effort, the expectation I saw in her eyes when she came back into the bedroom, made those long waits almost enjoyable for me.

It must have been during one of those very first mornings together, when the contents of her bedroom hadn't yet become imprinted on my memory, that I looked at the photographs in silver frames cramming so many surfaces. Some were portraits of friends, others were group shots. One in particular caught my attention, perhaps because it had been taken at a costume party. Delia was sitting at a table, wearing an eighteenth-century dress. The carriage of her head and neck was as relaxedly elegant as usual, as if her enormous wig and the frondage of feathers, ribbons and jewels crowning it were weightless. She and the man on her left were looking at each other. He was in period costume too. His three-cornered hat was casually pushed aside, and rested rakishly on the stiff white curls to the side of his head. The anachronistic formality of their costumes made the warmth in their eyes and their smiles even more striking. The sharpness of the man's profile, the strength of his face, didn't please me either. He looked like a man for whom the morning after with a woman held no mysteries, and the photograph was a black-and-white reminder that Delia lived in a world I had no place in. I felt both angry and humiliated. I took the picture and went into the dressing room. Delia was standing in front of an open closet. Under the soft silk of her slip, the straps of a garter belt formed faint ridges along her thighs.

'This looks as if you were having fun. Where were you?' I asked, forcing myself to sound casual, almost indifferent, while feeling unaccountably miserable. She glanced at the photograph.

'That was at the Beistegui ball in Venice. It was quite a party,' she replied casually, her attention fully focused on her clothes again. Close to, the metal-on-metal noise of the hangers as she pushed them aside irritated me.

'You look as if you were having a great time. Who is he?' The photograph was in place of honour in her bedroom for a reason. That man had meant something to her – probably a lot, judging from the look on their faces, and there was no reason other than my idiotic naïveté to assume that 'had meant' was the right tense to use.

'An Austrian friend of mine.'

'Doesn't he have a name?'

'Yes. He's Karl . . . Karl . . . Oh, it's so annoying. I can't remember his surname. I'm sure it'll come back to me in a second.'

'So you keep his photograph, but you have forgotten his name . . .'

Delia looked at me now.

'What on earth is this about?' She seemed at a loss at first, then her eyes lit with amusement.

'Don't tell me you're jealous!' she laughed. 'There was nothing between us, and anyway that picture was taken more than ten years ago.'

I looked at the photo again. Although the costumes made it impossible to date, it was true that Delia's face looked slightly younger.

'That's stupid; of course I'm not jealous. I was only asking,' I snapped, as if I were still angry with her, when in fact I was angrier at myself for being so clumsy, so uncool, for jumping to conclusions.

'Perhaps you'd like me to ask you about *your* friends? I'd rather you told me whether this doesn't look too dull,' she went on, heading for the mirror with a dress held up to her body.

'It looks fantastic,' I said without paying the slightest attention. My eyes were on her naked shoulders, on the play of light and shadow on the silken sheen of her slip as it followed the curves of her hips and her bottom, which stirred my pride – and my renewed insecurity.

It wasn't because of any sense of discretion that the prospect of Delia asking me about my past troubled me. I didn't want her to know how little of it there was.

'*Martín!*'

It was a male voice behind me, pronouncing my name in the French way. Delia and I were having coffee in Les Deux Magots, on our way back to her house from one of our walks, and I was glad for the unexpected interruption. After a few weeks of living together, I was becoming more and more conscious of the fact that every phone call, every letter, was for her. The people we saw, the chance encounters on the street, were always with Delia's friends. I existed through her, in a world where I only belonged because of her.

I turned round. Standing next to me was the boyfriend of the girl whose studio I was renting.

'Where have you been?' he asked. 'I've been calling you, but there's no answer.'

'I've been away,' I replied. 'Sorry, this is Yves Dufour. Delia Lagos.' They exchanged smiles, and I could immediately sense Yves figuring out the true reason behind my disappearance.

'Are you planning to stay in Vivianne's apartment?' he asked. 'I know someone who might want it, if you don't.'

Although the rent was low, the saving would make a difference to my slim resources. I would be able to stay in Paris for longer, without having to ask Delia for money. I was about to tell him he could have the studio back, when I thought again. Even if I didn't use it, a place of my own gave me a sense of security, an illusion of independence. To give it up would mean accepting my complete reliance on Delia.

'I'll keep it for the time being. I'll let you know in plenty of time before I go back, so you can find somebody else,' I said. Yves gave Delia an appreciative smile as he bade us *au revoir*.

'You hadn't said anything about going,' Delia said, too casually. I knew her well enough by now to pick up minute signals in her manner, faint clues in the pattern of her speech, that hinted at her true feelings. The mention of my leaving unsettled her. I might have found pleasure in that, in the evidence that I mattered to Delia, if I had been able to believe that I was free to decide whether to stay or go for myself.

'I'm not leaving yet. But I can't stay forever.' I was being ambiguous because of my own fear, not because I meant to alarm her. The probability that I would have to give Delia up and go back was too terrifying for me to confront squarely.

The prospect became real much sooner than I had anticipated. I've never been good at bureaucracy, and being with Delia, in our own little world, made me forget about my visa. One morning, as I took a traveller's cheque and my passport out of a drawer before going to the bank, some second sense made me check the immigration stamp. I was to become an illegal alien in forty-eight hours' time.

I had heard enough stories during my early days in Paris to know that it was no small matter. If found, I would be deported immediately, and I wouldn't be allowed to come back to France. Even if I were to apply for an extension that very day, I would have to show either a reason for the request, or enough money to prove that I could support myself for the length of the extension. The inevitable outcome was that I would be on a plane to Buenos Aires before the end of the week.

Delia was downstairs, in her study. She was reading her post when I burst in.

'Do you have a dinner jacket?' she asked, holding a stiff white card in her hand. 'The Mandevilles are giving a party, and it's black tie. You'll like their place, it's one of the most beautiful houses in Paris.'

'I won't be there,' I blurted out in panic. 'I have to leave. Now.'

'Why? What on earth is wrong?' She jumped to her feet and came to me. I told her at once.

'I thought it was something serious,' she said, almost laughing. 'My lawyers can deal with that. Américo will take your passport to them while we are out. Now, do you have a dinner jacket or not?'

I was as stunned by the immediate solution as by her attitude, the fact that Delia didn't even see it as a problem. Hers was the self-assurance of deep-rooted privilege, almost innocent in its presumption that things always turn out right.

'No, I don't. And you're not buying me one either,' I grumbled, in an attempt to forestall further tokens of generosity from her. 'But thanks for the visa,' I said in conciliation.

'Now, don't be silly,' she replied. 'And I'll ask Américo to have a look in the trunks in the attic. There might be an old dinner jacket there.'

It was only later, once I was on my way to the bank, that I realized something that would have seemed unthinkable until now. For the first time, Delia had helped me beyond trivial matters like small expenses or using her car, and I had let her. My terror at the prospect of having to leave her had weakened any abstract, self-imposed rules. I wanted to stay with her, in Paris. I wanted it more than anything. It could only be possible through her help.

I remember one particular evening, when Delia and I had dinner at a cheap Chinese restaurant off the Boulevard Saint Germain. I took her out that night, at my own expense, which accounted for the choice of venue. On our way back, we walked past a cinema showing *Le Mépris*; we were in time for the late screening, so we went in. It wasn't an unusual occurrence. Movies had always been my passion, and one that I indulged on my own if a friend was not available to join me. I never felt lonely in a cinema, even if it was empty. Delia liked the theatre better, but she was sporting enough to adapt to my preference.

Half-way through the movie I began to lose interest, something that had never happened to me before. It could be that my French wasn't sufficiently good to follow dialogue on a sound-track. It could also be that my lack of concentration grew as I became more and more aware of Delia's arm pressed against me, the warmth of her thigh touching mine. I looked at her face, lit in the glow from the screen, and put my arm around her shoulders. She moved closer within my embrace. A second later we were kissing, slowly at first, then more eagerly.

The cinema was nearly empty. I took Delia's hand, leading her to the foyer. We weren't far from her house, perhaps ten or fifteen minutes on foot at most, but as soon as I saw the traffic outside, and heard the noise from the boulevard, it felt too long. I didn't want to walk through that. I didn't want to pay attention to other people, to be forced to watch the traffic, to wait for traffic lights. I wanted Delia now. I looked around. The varnish on the door marked '*Toilette*' glistened like caramel.

'Not there,' Delia murmured. 'There must be some old woman keeping an eye on the place.'

The movie was well into its second half; I could hear the usherette and the ticket seller chatting inside the box-office. We ran up some stairs to the circle like children, trying not to giggle. There was nobody there. We tore at each other's clothes, our bodies and our faces glowing in the eerie light from the screen, then we lowered ourselves into the soft, carpeted darkness. Our sex was so urgent it couldn't be called making love, and yet I had never loved her more.

It was during one of those early summer months when Delia suggested we go away for the weekend. Some Italian friends had offered her their yacht, which was anchored in Naples.

'We can sail to Capri and Ischia, and you'll love the Costa Amalfitana,' she enthused, adding that we would leave on Thursday and be back by Monday – if it suited me. She might have had a reason for coming back then, but it was more likely that she was being careful not to make it too obvious that my time was free, at her disposal. She was aware of my sensitivity in that respect. Unusually, I didn't mind it this time, because I was so excited by the prospect of just the two of us sailing on what was likely to be a stunning yacht, visiting places like Positano or Anacapri which I had seen only on postcards sent to my mother by travelling friends.

We went directly to the harbour from the airport. Delia said Naples was one of the most depressing cities she had ever been to, and that there was no point in wasting time there. The view from the taxi made me agree with her. Nothing countered the ugliness of the concrete blocks piling up the hillsides, because the bay and the coastline were shrouded under a veil of heat haze.

My excitement resurfaced once we reached the port. The air here didn't smell of damp heat and traffic fumes; it felt clean, easy to breathe. Seagulls hovered in the breeze. We found the yacht towards the end of a pier: it was as big, as white and as gleaming as in my fantasies. The skipper gave me a once-over, followed by a knowing look, and then greeted Delia with the mixture of politeness, respect and awe spawned by the certainty of a big tip in due course. We were shown to the main cabin, where the furniture was covered in the same soft green leather as the walls, which were punctuated by circular light fittings in white frosted glass.

It was the kind of room and situation where Antonioni characters would nurture their ennui, but Delia and I were wrong for the parts. We were too excited, too eager to enjoy ourselves. We felt the vibration of the engines, then the boat began to move, and soon we could see through the windows that we were outside the harbour. Our attempts at unpacking didn't last long, because we ended up falling on the huge bed, our fingers undoing buttons and zippers with the ease of experience not yet dulled by familiarity.

We didn't linger in bed. After a shower, we changed into fresh clothes and went outside. The deck felt warm under my bare feet. From the bow, where we leaned over the rail like figureheads, the sun on our backs, Delia showed me the outline of Capri on the horizon. The yacht was cruising fast, cutting across the gentle swell, which added to my feeling of adventure. We watched the white cliffs of the island grow larger until we saw the harbour, and the village on the heights. By now the yacht had veered to the left, and we were sailing along the coast.

'I asked him to take us to the Faraglioni,' Delia said. 'I want you to see Curzio Malaparte's place. I went there years ago, and I've never seen a more beautiful house.'

Since I hadn't heard of the Faraglioni or Curzio Malaparte, I opted to appear knowledgeable, and didn't ask Delia for a further explanation. In any case, I was too absorbed by the landscape of sheer cliffs rising from the vibrant blue water. I put my arm around her waist, and pulled Delia close to me. After a while the yacht turned the corner of the island.

'Tiberius's villa is at the top of that mountain,' Delia explained when she noticed my eyes focusing on the peak.

'He chose a good place. It must have been great to live there,' I said.

'Not if you were one of his guests. They say he used to throw them down the cliff for fun.'

A few minutes later I saw a pair of rocky outcrops ahead, emerging from the sea like fantastic towers, dwarfing a couple of yachts that bobbed in the water near them.

'Let's go and change,' Delia suggested. 'I feel like going for a swim.'

I didn't follow her, because I didn't want to give up on a perfect moment: the sun was high in the sky, bleaching the grey rocks and gilding the water. We dropped anchor. My eyes followed it below the surface, through the transparent sea, until it disappeared. I raised my face towards the sun and remained there, still, enjoying the warmth on my cheeks.

'What are you doing? Don't be a bore, go and get changed.'

Delia was behind me, wearing a white swimsuit. The suntan oil made her skin shimmer.

'We have all the time in the world,' I countered. I didn't feel like being pushed into anything.

'Perhaps I can make you change your mind,' she said, coming close. I felt the rail press into my back as she leaned on me, her chest against mine. I closed my eyes when I felt the tip of her tongue part my lips.

'Look into my eyes and tell me you don't feel like having a swim now,' she said, then she kissed me again.

'Not yet,' I insisted.

'Let's make a deal,' she said, holding my face. 'You stay just as you are, but you move at least a yard towards our cabin every time I kiss you. Once we are by the door, you have to go in and change.'

We were about ten yards away from the door.

'Sounds good,' I said. 'I won't promise anything though.'

'We'll see,' she replied, kissing me. I moved along. She kissed me again. After a few seconds, I didn't pay attention to anything other than the feel of her mouth, and her body against mine as we slid down the rail. Suddenly there was nothing behind me, and Delia's hands pushed me hard. My arms flapped in the air as I fell backwards, the sound of her laughter drowned by the splash as I hit the water.

When I came up to the surface, Delia was still on deck, laughing by the gate she had opened without me noticing it. A second later she dived in, feigning fear at my fury as I tried to chase her. My soaked clothes were too heavy; I couldn't make any headway. Delia came back to me, and helped me reach the ladder.

'Take them off,' she instructed, removing her swimsuit and throwing it onto the bottom step. It took only a short while for my clothes to join it there, then I swam after Delia in the brilliant, cool water, my anger forgotten, the sun on our naked backs.

Once we were back in Paris, Delia mentioned the party again. I wasn't too keen on going and I sensed she didn't care that much for the party itself, but I thought she found pleasure in daring her world to comment, because how others see us matters terribly when you are young. Even if I didn't feel any need to justify our affair to myself, I was too aware of how others might judge it – or me. Unable to see beyond myself, I interpreted Delia's attitude as the mirror image of my own. It did not occur to me then that she was merely doing what she wanted to do.

In any case, my best line of defence collapsed when I saw a dinner jacket hanging in Delia's room. She claimed that Américo had found it in the attic that morning. The smell of mothballs was convincing enough, and yet the clothes looked quite new.

'You didn't buy it for me then?' I asked. I didn't like Delia to buy me things, and she knew it.

'Of course not. I was pretty sure there had to be one in the attic. There's no point in throwing money away,' Delia replied. Young as I was, an extraordinarily wealthy and indulged person making academic claims to thrift seemed preposterous to me, and the clothes fitted me perfectly, although I'm taller than most men. But if Delia hadn't bought them for me, I didn't need much encouragement to suspect alternative explanations.

'How did you know there was a dinner jacket there? Whose was it?' I fired at her.

Delia frowned. 'I wish you weren't so prone to groundless suspicion,' she sighed. 'A lot of people have stayed here at one time or other, and they often leave things behind . . .'

I couldn't believe a temporary visitor would have left a dinner jacket behind and never claimed it, as if it were a toothbrush. The thought that Delia could be making me wear clothes some lover had discarded before she discarded *him* seemed more logical, and much more distressing.

'The party will be terrific. There'll be hundreds of people, and Victoire told me they're bringing a disc-jockey from London,' Delia added as I was about to make a dramatic announcement of my irrevocable intention never to set foot in the damned place. I inspected the dinner jacket again. It seemed virtually new. An ex-lover of Delia's was no more likely to be its previous owner than a transient guest. She must have bought the outfit for me.

'I don't have a bow tie anyway, and you're not going to buy me one,' I mumbled.

'Oh, that's easy. Américo can lend you one of his,' Delia suggested breezily, and at last her enthusiasm began to infect me. I would be going to a grand party, with Delia, in Paris. I was young, I was in love with a ravishing woman, and this was 1963. Fun was in the air.

Not only for me, as I discovered one afternoon that week when I returned to the house. Delia had declined to come to a movie with me because she said she wanted to write. To my surprise, I heard music in the drawing room. I recognized the sound immediately: it was 'Hitch Hike' by Marvin Gaye. I had bought the American single some days before, at some *disquaire* on the Boulevard Saint Michel which specialized in hot novelties. It was the last thing I would have expected Delia to listen to, and I peeked through the half-open door. Delia wasn't writing. She was dancing on her own, watching herself in a mirror, checking the movements of her shoulders and arms as she practised the new style.

I stood there, watching her. She didn't get it wrong, but she was too graceful to get it right. Delia cut an elegant figure even when she danced to pop music, with the grace of someone who had learned to dance on marble floors to Cole Porter songs. She was dancing to *my* music now, a beautiful, touching sight, and yet there was something melancholy in her face that contradicted the vigour of her movements. I stepped back a little, so she couldn't see me. I went in only after the music stopped.

'Oh, you're back!' Delia said cheerfully, her cheeks slightly flushed. She put the record back on.

'I'm glad you are here. I want to learn this before the party, and it's much more fun to practise with you,' she said. She started to dance again, and this time so did I. For once it was Delia who was trying to fit into my world, not the other way round. It should have pleased me, but there was something forced, self-conscious, about the whole thing. I was glad when we stopped.

On the night of the party, I waited for Delia downstairs. And waited. Eventually I went to her bedroom, where I found her sitting at her dressing table, applying the finishing touches to her make-up. Her hair was pulled back from her face, and dense black eyeliner made the grey of her irises take on the luminous tint of a sea mist at dawn. Her outfit for the evening was carefully laid on the bed, a Raj-like trouser suit in embossed, heavy silk. The rich material had the colour and lustre of thick fresh cream.

As she leaned forward towards the mirror, holding a mascara brush with the concentration of a miniature painter, her bra dug into the smooth skin of her back. Our eyes met in the mirror. I saw the top of her breasts bulge against the wave-like pattern of the lace edge; my hands rested on her shoulders, then they moved down as I kissed her neck and unfastened the hooks.

'I don't want you to change your mind, but don't mess up my hair too much, will you? I spent hours under the drier in this heat,' Delia murmured.

'I wasn't planning to do anything to your hair,' I replied, my hands cupping her breasts. Delia stood up and faced me. Her arms were around my waist, then she took my hand as I was about to undo my black tie.

'Don't,' she said. 'I've never made love to a man in evening clothes.'

I could see her back in the mirror, and I was excited by the sight of her naked body pressed against my clothed figure. She looked vulnerable, and I looked powerful. Delia's hands slipped under my jacket; she untucked my shirt. I felt her nails and the cold hardness of her bracelet scratch gently against my ribs as she sat on the edge of the dressing table, her thighs holding my sides. We made love quickly, with the thrilling urgency of unnecessary impatience, as if we ran the risk of being caught. Afterwards we held each other for a while, then she raised her head from my shoulder and checked herself in the triple mirror.

'Full marks for hair care,' she smiled.

'Only that?'

'You don't need to fish for compliments,' she said, kissing me. 'Wait a minute, I have to do something about my lipstick – and yours.' Delia took a tissue from the box on the table and wiped my lips. 'You'd better leave me now. Your staying here won't help me to get dressed quickly.'

I went to the spare bedroom and made myself presentable again, then waited for Delia at the foot of the stairs. Eventually she appeared, looking immaculate, perfect in her cool, elegant way, so at odds with the naked woman who had clawed at my back moments before. I felt the thrill of possession.

'You look great. Really great,' I said, without any need to exaggerate. Delia's smile acknowledged my compliment – and the hint of astonishment she must have read in my voice. Our urgent sex upstairs made our appearance now seem wonderful and absurd at once, as if we had acquired gleaming carapaces when nakedness was our natural state.

'Let's go,' she said. 'We'll be more than fashionably late.'

As far as spectacle is concerned, the party didn't let me down from the moment we arrived. There were torches along the tree-lined drive, and the floodlit chateau rose from the surrounding moat, its edges as crisp as the curlicued yew hedges in the parterres. Inside, people were as densely packed as the gods, warriors and nymphs on the frescoed ceilings. After dinner in a candle-lit long gallery, we moved to another cavernous space, where silver plastic, coloured lights, and deafeningly amplified music reclaimed the party for the space age we were supposed to be living in.

The crowd began to thin out at around three o'clock. By then Delia and I had finally stopped dancing, hot and exhausted, and we had moved to a room in one of the corner towers. We were in a group, listening to an amusing raconteur in full flow, when Delia turned her head. There was a tall man standing behind her, his hand on her shoulder.

'I saw you dancing earlier, but I didn't want to interrupt you,' he said. 'You seemed very busy.'

The man was in his fifties, with thick silver-grey hair and a suntanned face that creased into lines in all the right places. He was the type French people describe as *un vieux beau.*

'It's nice to see you again. You're looking so young and so delicious, Delia,' he went on. The man addressed her in a sort of barbed intimacy that turned compliments into arrows. I guessed immediately that they had been lovers.

'Your eyesight is as good as ever, Jean-Marc. I don't think you've met Martín,' she added.

I began to puff myself up for some sort of confrontation, hoping that he might turn his smooth sarcasm on me next, giving me a chance to put him in his place. He looked at Delia instead, as if I simply wasn't there.

'I'd better move on. I might call you though,' he said, kissing her lightly on the cheek before he walked away.

Delia looked unbothered by this encounter, while I tried to ignore the fact that it had disturbed me, and not because of the man's silken animosity. It boiled down to jealousy, and the jealousy of someone like him was flattering to me. The encounter bothered me because it was a flash of reality into our life. That man had been Delia's lover too, but he was what I could never be: Delia's equal.

Eventually the group broke up, and we sat on a sofa by the windows. We had been there for a short while, talking about anything without mentioning Jean-Marc at all, when a woman joined us.

'Oh, *Deliá*, you're looking so well!' she cooed. 'I loved that suit at the Saint Laurent show. Unfortunately I'm too fat to wear all that white . . .'

I left them to their conversation. A thin old man was watching us from a corner. After a moment he came and sat down – too close – next to me.

'I haven't seen you before, I think. My loss, of course,' he said, adjusting his rather absurd monocle. 'It's a wonderful party, isn't it?'

I said it was, and we made innocuous conversation for a while, then he rested his hand on my arm. 'You're not French, are you? How charming . . .'

'No,' I replied, moving my arm away.

'Are you here on your own?' he asked.

'No, he's here with me, Michel,' Delia cut in before I could reply.

'That's your luck then, *chérie*. How are you?'

'I'm very well. How are you?'

'Oh, I'm fine. Dying slowly, of course, but that's the best time to go to a party, don't you think? I take it that this handsome young man must be the son of a friend of yours.'

Anger had been bubbling quietly in me ever since the encounter with Delia's old flame, prickling me like the stiff, starched collar round my neck. Now it burst out.

'This *handsome young man* doesn't like gossipy old faggots. Beat it,' I snapped, rising to my feet. 'Come on, let's get out of here,' I said to Delia. She sat back instead. The woman next to her edged forwards, to avoid missing anything.

'Martín is a friend of mine. Is there anything else you want to know?' Delia asked sharply. The old man stood up, keeping some distance between himself and me.

'No, no,' he replied. 'I hope you are not taking my interest as criticism, Delia. Going to bed with my friends' sons is what I've been doing all my life, darling.'

Three

The old man's bitchiness lingered in my mind, although not in the way he had intended. He had mocked Delia about her age, but I was aware of that already, and I was almost used to it. Instead, his indirect reference to my parents made me realize something else. Ever since I had been in Paris, I hadn't thought about my father. I hadn't thought much about my mother either, which was a welcome relief.

My father had died of a burst aneurysm when he was thirty years old. I was two at the time, so I didn't remember him at all. Or I shouldn't be able to, if years of looking at photographs around our home or listening to my mother reminisce over old picture albums, my brother and I sitting by her side, hadn't invested those fading prints with a life of their own for me, changing two-dimensional images into the illusory reality of a man.

Nonetheless my quasi-memories were as flat as their source. If a photograph showed him in jodhpurs and boots, my mother would tell us about his brilliance at polo, or the country estate where they were staying at the time. If the picture showed them together in evening clothes, she would mention what a great dancer he had been – followed by the details of the particular ball where the picture had been taken, mentioned with equal enthusiasm. She mourned his death, but no more than she mourned the simultaneous disappearance of that golden life. Only when it came to money did he stand on his own, because it had been his strength and wisdom that had protected my mother's inheritance through the perils of the thirties, and she had lost virtually everything she owned as soon as she had had to fend for herself. The sale of their great house and the auction of its contents, some time after his death, was a tragic event comparable to Wounded Knee or the Charge of the Light Brigade in my mother's account of our family history.

Once I reached my teens, when I began to realize how different her expectations of me were to my own, how genuinely incapable she was of understanding anything other than what she believed in or cared about, I began to wonder. I wanted to know my father as a man, not as a storybook figure. I couldn't blame my mother for being superficial any more than I could blame her for being left-handed, or loving us in her well-meaning though overbearing way. It was her nature.

But I knew I wasn't like her, and I needed allies to balance our unequal powers. I enrolled my father to my cause, or at least the character I imagined him to be. It was an alliance my mother herself encouraged, as discussions about my plans for the future became more frequent. 'You are a dreamer, like your father. At least he knew when to be practical though,' she would say. I took her at her word, not so much about practicality (she had no lessons to teach on that score), but in making me see my father as a validation of the many aspects of my personality which were so unlike hers.

It isn't easy to love a phantom. I needed a notion of the real man, his beliefs and his predilections; his prejudices even. Since I couldn't get that from my mother, I turned to relations or friends of his. My attempts weren't very successful. Their descriptions were filtered through the benevolent condescension people use when talking to someone much younger than they are, and their eulogies only made me more aware of my own shortcomings. In the end, I put together a patchy image of him as best I could, and one that had more to do with my own aspirations than anything else. I wanted a different life. His memory became both the justification for this need, and the talisman that would make it possible.

Once I started university, and my life seemed to settle in a particular direction, I thought less about him – only when I came across people who had known him, or places he had been. Perhaps there was a reason why I had not thought about him since coming to Paris. Delia belonged to my parents' generation, and I didn't want to remind myself of the fact too often. 'Suspension of disbelief' has entered the language, unlike that far more common occurrence in anybody's life: suspension of knowledge. I would have found my early days with Delia much harder without it.

The old man's jibe had brought out into the open the matter of our ages. He had made us face it squarely. Neither Delia nor I made any reference to it afterwards, and yet something changed for me because nothing had changed between us. We *knew*. To pretend Delia wasn't much older than me was as ludicrous as to dwell on the fact we couldn't change. Gradually, day by day, I was tantalized by the thought that I could ask Delia about my father; unlike my mother or her friends, she could tell me about him in a way that would interest me.

Soon I realized it wouldn't be as easy as I thought. Delia seemed not to care about Argentina, or her old life there. She never spoke about it, so I couldn't count on her to give me the opportunity: I had to find it myself. One evening, while we were watching *Spellbound* on television in her study, I decided to raise the subject. Gregory Peck and Ingrid Bergman had been dubbed into French, which made them sound slightly ridiculous, so I left the sofa and stood up to examine the family portrait by Sargent. The flickering blue-white glow from the television gave a ghost-like aura to the figures.

'You seem a lot like your mother, you know,' I said.

'Only as far as looks are concerned, I hope,' she replied. 'Madness was quite common in her family.'

Her comment made me momentarily curious, but I wanted to talk about *my* family, not hers.

'You said I looked like my father, when we first met.'

'Did I? I was making party conversation, probably,' she said, her eyes fixed on the screen.

'But do I look like him?' I insisted.

She turned her face towards me. 'You might. I don't remember him that clearly, though. Francis was one of many people I used to see. It's a long time ago.'

Delia reached for her cup of coffee, took a sip, and sat back, her face blank of expression other than total absorption in the movie. After a moment, I joined her. We didn't speak again until it ended.

Perhaps I had made too much of a passing remark. It had been party talk, as Delia said, and my scepticism at her words now was probably due to my own disappointment. I had no reason to assume she knew my parents well. My mother had always mentioned Delia's name in passing, and the photographs in her album showed Delia in group pictures, none of which included my father. It could be that Delia and my mother had met at parties, both members of a tribe-like group, and their casual friendship had petered out before my parents met. In any case, Delia managed to focus my mind on the present again later that evening. We were in bed, silent and contented in each other's arms.

'What are you planning to do after the summer?' she asked.

By then it was early June. We were supposed to go and stay with some friends of hers in Cap d'Antibes for a long weekend towards the end of the month. That was as far as I had considered the future, and not because of lack of concern. The opposite, rather. I couldn't work as a lawyer in Paris, and I couldn't plan my life on the basis of casual work as a waiter. Being kept by Delia was equally out of the question as a long-term plan.

'I don't know. I can't practise law here,' I replied.

'I don't think that's what you want, anyway,' she said, and I was stung by the implication that I didn't want to work.

'You're drawing the wrong conclusion. I'm not counting on you to keep me,' I retorted.

'Don't be so touchy,' she sighed. 'You haven't mentioned your career once since we've been together. You don't read books about the law in your spare time, you just go to the cinema. You love films, not the law.'

Delia wasn't telling me something I didn't know. If I had had the choice, I would much rather have been a movie director than a lawyer, but there wasn't a film school in Buenos Aires; going abroad to study was almost unheard of in those days, and it was financially impossible in my case. I couldn't choose what I really wanted, and I knew I didn't like sciences; this left me with a few options – all equally possible, none especially attractive. Like many people with an uncertain vocation, I had settled for the law. The choice had pleased my mother, who made much of the sacrifice involved in putting two sons through university on her limited resources.

'It's too late to start again now,' I said.

'No, it's not – there's no point in putting up with past mistakes. You can find out about film schools here. I'll help you. I can ask friends in the film business about the best places, if you like.'

Delia was offering me the opportunity I had always wanted, and I noticed her clever blurring of the matter of 'help' through her reference to friends. I couldn't refuse her financial support straightaway, because she would say she hadn't ever mentioned money. I was reacting out of habit anyway; as soon as I thought about it, I found myself willing to accept her help. This was something completely different from clothes or a sports car, and I would pay her back one day. I knew in my heart that she wouldn't take my money, nor could I count on the possibility of earning quickly enough, but I needed to give myself an excuse.

'Yes, please,' I said. Delia's face lit up in relief. She must have been worried about the likelihood that I would turn down her suggestion. She hadn't taken my response for granted. Flattered by the thought, and tingling with excitement at the double prospect of staying with her and fulfilling my true vocation, I wanted her to share my mood.

'What about *your* plans? Are you going to write another book?' I asked.

'Maybe. I haven't thought about it. I'm busy enough now,' she smiled.

'You never talk about your books. I'd like to read them.' It was true, and I thought that my interest would please her.

'I don't think I have any copies left, and I wouldn't know where to begin to look,' she said. 'There might be some downstairs. If you come across them, of course you can read them.'

The Rue de Vaugirard is divided into two sections by the Boulevard Raspail. Most of the first half skirts the Palais du Luxembourg and its gardens, where tourists congregate; there is nothing special about the section that runs towards Montparnasse. However, as

I walked down the short flight of steps to the entrance of the École Louis Lumière, the narrow perspective of apartment buildings, a brick depot and the blank wall of a chapel opposite seemed as inspiring to me in the summer morning light as any of the grand vistas of Paris.

Everything was working in my favour. My secondary education was considered equivalent to the French baccalaureate, and my age was not a problem.

'You are not the first one to change his mind after finishing university,' said the jovial Monsieur Golbin, the man behind the information counter who handed me the registration forms once I had explained my case. School started in early October; the entrance exam was in September, and Golbin made it sound simple enough. I would hear the result by the end of the month. Monsieur Golbin suggested I look in the café down the road, where the names and addresses of private tutors who crammed students for the exam could be found on a notice-board.

Even the fact that the school was only half a mile away from Delia's house worked to my advantage. I felt light-hearted, light-footed, and light-headed all at once. I would be able to do what I had always wanted; everything that had seemed transient or uncertain until now had become secure and real here in Paris. I wouldn't have to worry about next week, or next month. I would be with Delia, and I would study cinematography for the next three years. I didn't want anything more.

We opened a bottle of champagne that evening. Although exuberance was not part of Delia's character, she was as delighted by the outcome as I was – in her way. Unlike me, during the following days she did not behave as if celestial music was ringing in her ears all the time. On the contrary; up until now she had seemed to share my feeling of being on an extended holiday, as if normal life was on hold. Now she set her mornings aside to write in her study, and there were appointments in the afternoon. Life was becoming real again for both of us.

As our trip to the Côte d'Azur approached, we were caught up in the usual excitement of imminent departure. Delia had booked a cabin on the Train Bleu to Cannes, and we sat in the evenings discussing whether to visit Menton, or Vence, or Roquebrune. Delia would make suggestions, since she knew the area and I didn't, but she was careful to stress that the choice was mine.

After months in Europe planning nothing beyond the next day, I liked this new organizational mood. I called Yves one morning, to tell him I would be giving up the studio at the end of the month. Yves seemed happy enough to see the termination of my phantom tenancy.

I realized also that I hadn't told my mother about my new arrangements. I had written to her once I got my extended visa, saying that I would be hitchhiking around France, so she shouldn't worry if she didn't hear from me for a while, and left it at that. Another letter now, or a phone call, was out of the question. I would have to explain my plans in some detail, and she would wonder how I'd manage to pay for my studies. I didn't want to tell my mother about Delia, but I would have to give her my new address. She knew the city well: the Rue de Grenelle hardly sounded a credible place for student accommodation.

I took the easy option by sending her a telegram: *Career opportunity here. Might have to stay. Love, Martín.* I wrote the address of my studio on the form, and gave it to the clerk. I felt my message was rather shabby, a half-lie disguised as a half-truth.

I heard Delia's voice as soon as I let myself into the house. She was talking in Spanish, in her study. I assumed she was with Américo.

'. . . I know it's hard, it's hard for me too. Don't think I've forgotten you . . .' I heard her say as I came in. She was on the phone. Her face froze when she saw me. '. . . I'm sorry, but I have to go now,' she added. 'I'll call you again. Goodbye.'

Delia hung up, and gave me a beaming smile. 'Thank God you appeared, I needed an excuse to get rid of that pest. I thought she'd never stop,' she said.

'Who was it?'

'The housekeeper at the *estancia*. I have to keep in touch and check how things are there, but that woman goes *on* and *on*.'

Her exaggerated emphasis was out of character, and I knew the voice Delia used when she spoke to servants other than Américo.

This had been different. She hadn't sounded like someone eager to finish the call either.

The episode bothered me for the rest of the day. I didn't believe what Delia had said. Her conversation hadn't been about trivial everyday matters. She could have been speaking to a man who meant enough to her to justify her words and her concerned tone. I searched in my mind for other clues or indications of duplicity: I couldn't find any. We had been together most of the time during the day, and every night. I couldn't be sure though. I had had no reason to question her references to business meetings until now. It could well be that there was somebody else, a married man who wasn't free in the evenings or at weekends, and that I was nothing more than a distraction, Delia's protection against a long, established relationship leading nowhere but that she couldn't break.

I didn't mention my suspicions during the rest of the day or during dinner, not because I didn't want to, but because I didn't trust her not to lie again. It was only late that night, in bed, after sex brought back my faith in her, that I asked her again.

'Who was the person on the phone this afternoon?'

Delia propped herself up, her elbow nestled in the pillow, and gave me a baffled look.

'I told you. Why are you so concerned about it?'

'Because I thought it was somebody else . . . a man.' My words sounded strained, hesitant in my ears.

'You're crazy. Worse than that, you're being silly. How can you imagine something so ridiculous?'

I didn't feel jealous any more. Her casual dismissal irritated me only because of her condescending manner.

'Be more precise then, if you don't want me to be silly. Who is this housekeeper? Doesn't she have a name? And where is this *estancia* she looks after? Doesn't the place have a name either?'

Delia sighed. 'There's something you must understand, Martín. I own many things, and a lot of people work for me. If I were to give you a detailed account of every conversation, every person I see because of business, we wouldn't have time for much else, leaving aside the fact that I don't see why I should.'

'Oh, sure! *I know it's hard. It's hard for me too. Don't think*

I've forgotten you . . . Do you have that kind of conversation with all your employees?' We were naked, and yet there was a distance between us now, as if we had our clothes on.

'You are going to make our life very difficult if you jump to absurd conclusions over things that don't concern you in any way,' she said. 'Her name is Angela Gómez, she has worked for me for nearly twenty years, and she says she wants to leave because she is bored. She wants a pay rise, in fact, but sometimes you have to sound terribly concerned if you want them to do what you want. It's human nature.'

Her explanation mollified me, although Delia had never sounded cynical before. I didn't like it. Then she smiled and leaned over me, slowly running her finger over my lips, her hair brushing my cheeks.

'You look even more handsome when you're jealous, though. Let me prove how wrong you are,' she murmured as she came closer.

Some friends of Delia's came to dinner the day before we were due to leave for Antibes. They didn't stay late, because they knew we were going away in the morning. After they left, Delia and I went back to the drawing room to finish our brandies.

'You look very happy,' Delia said.

'I am happy. I'm with you, we're going away tomorrow, and then I'll start school in October. I couldn't ask for more.' I pulled Delia close to me. 'You made it all possible. I'll never forget that,' I added.

'You don't owe me anything, and "never" is too big a word,' she smiled. 'I am glad to be able to help. Let's leave it at that.'

It was unlike Delia to be humble, but she was gracious; perhaps she feared also that gratitude in our unequal circumstances would come between us. Either way, her words pleased me.

'Have you told your . . . family?' she asked. Delia had never mentioned or asked me about them, and I wondered why she should concern herself now.

'I told my mother I'm staying on, but I didn't tell her about going to film school. Whenever I mentioned the possibility before, she used to say that I was as impractical as my father. She was terrified of me doing anything "artistic", as she would put it.'

'She made the wrong comparison. There was nothing artistic about Francis,' Delia said dismissively, and I was dumbfounded. At last she had acknowledged that she had known my father, although I hadn't expected a slighting remark.

'Why? What was he like?'

'I have no idea. He was like all the other men in our group, I suppose. They were interested in horses or cars, not the arts.'

I had asked her a specific question, and Delia had given me a general answer. Something in her attitude reminded me of our argument a few nights ago, when I had questioned her about her conversation on the phone with the housekeeper. I saw her point then, because it was true that I couldn't expect Delia to tell me everything that concerned her businesses. It was different now, though. We were talking about someone who concerned me very much.

'I'm interested in my father, not the others. What was he like?' I insisted.

Delia stood up. 'I've told you I knew him very superficially, as one knows people one meets at parties. I don't know what he was *like*, and anyway, it's getting late. We'd better go to bed now.'

Delia was upset, or at least uneasy. I was perplexed by her claims of a vague acquaintance with my parents, when she had questioned the accuracy of my mother's comment about my father. Now I understood: my parents weren't the problem, it was us. Perhaps to talk about them reminded her of the gap between our ages. I had assumed that, like me, Delia saw it as a problem only in relation to others, hence her flaunting of our relationship to her friends. I had thought she was too sure of her own position in the world to care, when clearly she was worried about how I saw her, not about anybody else. I felt proud of my detection of her unspoken fear, and glad for the opportunity to be worldly about it, to defuse it rather than sweep it away.

'Look, this is crazy,' I said. 'I can't see what's so awkward about my asking what you thought of my father.'

One of the many things I admired in Delia was her ability to cut people short with an icy look. Now I found it less admirable.

'It's not up to you to decide what we might or might not discuss,' she said slowly.

Her words were a reminder of her superior standing in our relationship, and it made me furious. I could have been completely open about her worry concerning our ages, and yet I chose not to be; I didn't want to hurt her through what she saw as her weakness. Now Delia was using mine to shut me up, and her cutting remark made plain what I had tried to ignore from the beginning. I had joined Delia's world; my life had changed totally as a result, while hers remained the same. I depended on her, no matter how much I tried to disguise or minimize the fact. There was no balance between us. She had the power to lay down rules and conditions; I had none.

'In that case, you'd better go to Antibes on your own,' I snapped back.

'You're overreacting,' she said.

'I'm not, and I'm not your pet either. I've had enough of your friends giving me amused looks. Take Américo with you instead; they'd hardly notice the difference.' I enjoyed my anger. It gave me the chance to hurt her, to pay her back.

'Martín, stop this now. I'm sorry if I sounded cross. I'm just tired, and so are you. Let's go to bed.'

For once, I didn't want to go to bed with her.

'I'm not tired, and I'm not staying here. Good night,' I said.

Delia came after me; once we were in the hall, she moved in front of the main door.

'Don't do this,' she pleaded, and I almost relented.

'You're making too much of it. It's only a few days, and it's better this way.' I had to stand my ground. I needed to prove to myself, and to Delia, that it wouldn't be her way all the time.

Her face relaxed and she smiled. 'You might be right. I can't cancel now, so I'll see you when I get back.' She held my face and kissed me gently.

'I'll miss you,' she said softly.

'I'll miss you too.'

We looked at each other, then Delia took my hand.

'May I ask you a favour? Américo and the cook are taking their holidays now. I don't like the house to be empty.' She sounded completely calm now, her usual self discussing some small detail of everyday life. 'Why don't you stay here while I'm away, and keep an eye on the place?'

Now that I had calmed down, I remembered that I only had the studio for a couple more days, until the end of the month. Although Delia didn't know it, I wouldn't have anywhere to live after that. In any case, I wanted to make a point, not to leave her.

'Sure, no problem,' I agreed. Having said it, I realized that it was farcical to leave tonight only to come back the following morning, and I expected Delia to say so. She didn't; we kissed again, then I heard the door close behind me. Either the thought didn't cross her mind, or she was allowing me my small victory.

I should have felt pleased with myself. I had made my point. I had stood my ground. Delia wouldn't have everything her way. And yet, once I found myself outside, alone in the dark, empty street, I wondered. Only sleep would stop me from thinking about her now, from deliberating on whether I shouldn't have relented and gone away with Delia. I could see her in my mind as clearly as if I was still there, going through her bed-time routine I knew so well. She would have gone upstairs after bolting the front door, sat down at her dressing table, and started to remove her make-up. Then she would undress and pick up her nightgown, carefully folded by Américo and placed on the turned-down sheet. She might take a sip from the iced water on her bedside table, her fingers smearing the cold dew on the glass, before she got into bed, rearranged the pillows behind her, and opened the novel she was reading, carefully putting aside the leather page-marker beside the glass. I could predict every movement she would make – but I couldn't know if she was thinking about me.

I tried to enjoy my first day on my own, forcing myself into a driven routine of sight-seeing, as if the city was new to my eyes, only to notice how slowly time went without company. Around five o'clock I was back in my studio, where I started to call people I had met during my first days in Paris. I managed to find one of them, who said there was a party that night at the apartment of some Mexican students near Bastille. I wrote down the address.

I thought of having a shower, but the sight of the filthy bathroom made me reconsider, and all my clothes were at Delia's in any case. I was hungry by then. There was nothing in the refrigerator other than a bottle of curdled milk and a rancid pat of butter. Breakfast and a quick lunch at a café had taken care of my draconian budget for the day; I still had to buy a bottle of wine for the party, and there would be no food there. I couldn't delay going back to Delia's house any longer. I emptied the refrigerator, put my few remaining possessions in a bag, switched off the electricity at the mains, took one last look at the miserable room, and set off on foot.

The first thing that struck me as I walked into Delia's home was the stillness of the place. On the few occasions I had been on my own in the house before, there had been distant noises from the kitchen, the ringing of the telephone, or the creaking of the parquet under Américo's shoes. The silence now was so total, so deep, that it made me nervous. A light had been left on in the hall; this misleading hint of a human presence only heightened the sense of emptiness.

I was even hungrier after my walk, so I headed for the kitchen. For a second, I felt like an intruder among the polished copper pots lined up on wooden shelves over the thick marble tops, half-expecting Marie, the cook, to appear and give me one of the looks she fired at anyone – Delia included – if they encroached on her territory unexpectedly. She had gone though; I had the place to myself. I helped myself to cold meats, and a tin of peas I found in the larder. Afterwards I washed my plate and cutlery scrupulously and put them away, making sure that everything looked exactly as I had found it. Back in the hall, I wondered if Delia had left me a note somewhere in the house. A quick check of the drawing room, the dining room, and her study proved unsuccessful, so I picked up my bag and went upstairs.

I knew Delia's bedroom better than any other room in the house. I was familiar with every ornament, every picture, the painted flowers on the panelling, the tortoiseshell brushes and lacquer boxes on her table, and yet it seemed different to me now, almost forbidding, as if I had no right to be there. I went to the nearest spare bedroom, the one I had been into on my first morning in the house, and I settled there instead. I watched television for a while, then had a shower, changed clothes, and left.

I spent only a couple of hours at the party. The atmosphere was raucous, and I joined in the general chorus as we all danced to 'La Bamba', but I didn't enjoy myself. My heart wasn't in it.

I didn't go out much the next day. I couldn't be bothered. Leaving the radio or the television on to defeat the silence in the house only made me more aware of it, and the sultry weather added to my increasing discomfort. Telling myself that Delia was probably as unhappy without me as I was without her made little difference, because I knew she wasn't alone. I could imagine her, lying by a pristine pool edged by exuberant geraniums in terracotta tubs, or sitting under white awnings for long, leisurely lunches or dinners, the tinkle of witty conversation leaving her no time to think about me.

I had plenty of time to think about Delia though, and everything around reminded me of her. Her monogram was on the sheets I slept in, on the towels I used; her scent lingered in her cupboards, although I didn't discover that immediately, having purposely avoided going into her rooms. It takes time and a reason to overcome scruples.

I began to wonder why Delia had been so sympathetic to my change of mind. I knew nothing about the other guests at the villa, and I remembered the dashing Jean-Marc at the party. Perhaps she had discovered that he, or someone else like him, would be there. The ghost of the man whom I suspected had been on the phone to her came alive again. I had trusted her explanation because I trusted her, and yet I knew so little about her life before we met. I had assumed she was free then only because I was. Delia hadn't told me anything about her private life. Now I had a chance to find out.

This is the excuse I gave myself in retrospect to justify my actions, once guilt and regret made me wish I hadn't been so keen to discover what I didn't need to know. Perhaps it was just that I was idle, bored, uncertain, and curious: a dangerous combination. I started my search by flicking through the engagements diary on her desk. I couldn't find anything of interest in it; there were plenty of names and events entered in Delia's strong, angular handwriting, but not a particular name that kept reappearing regularly. Then I tried her telephone book, as if I might expect lovers to be listed in any way that would differentiate them from her other friends, work contacts, or the shops she frequented. I failed there too.

Shame wears away more quickly than unsatisfied curiosity. I found no evidence of infidelity, but I still hadn't found anything of consequence about her life either. My constant thoughts of her made me desperate for information. I wanted to know more, and it was all within reach, somewhere in this house. I went back to her desk, where I checked her papers without removing them from the drawers. I didn't find much of real interest other than an album of newspaper clippings, which were the reviews of her novels. Her first novel, a surreal love story set in some unspecified corner of South America, had been very well received in 1952, and her promising debut was confirmed by her next two books. Her latest novel had appeared in 1960, three years ago, but by then the praise was faint. Although the reviewers acknowledged her professionalism, they also pointed out the vacuum at the heart of the book. They called it an exercise in style.

Perhaps her books would give me the insight into her life I couldn't find in her papers. Delia had done nothing to encourage me to read them when I said I'd like to, or she had done as little as she could without sounding evasive enough to incite my curiosity. I went to the bookcases. The authors were arranged in alphabetical order. I scanned the 'L' shelf: none of Delia's books was there.

I tried every possible hiding place in her study, without success. There were a couple of bookcases in her bedroom, but I didn't find her novels there either, or in her chests of drawers. By the time I moved to her dressing room, my search for her books had become a justification for a far more immediate need. I convinced myself that Delia might keep her books among her personal effects, rather than admit that the combination of her jasmine scent with glimpses of fabric and colours I had seen on her was the only consolation I could find for the sheer fact that I needed her presence so desperately. I ran my fingers along the rows of suits and dresses, over the warmth of wools or the coolness of silks, as if by miracle one of those limp, inert materials would replicate the feel of her skin.

I closed the wardrobes and went back to the bedroom. On my way out, I noticed a low door flush in the wall of the corridor leading to the hallway, half-concealed by a small gilded table. I moved the table aside, and opened the door. As I poked my head through the opening, I found myself staring into a triangular-shaped cupboard, occupying the space under a secondary staircase on the other side of the wall. The smell of jasmine was replaced here by the pungency of camphor; there were old leather suitcases and trunks inside, stamped with yellowing labels from navigation lines. The size of the trunks and the awkward shape of the cupboard deterred me from opening them. There was a hat box on the floor, and for no very good reason I raised the lid. It was full of letters.

I will not attempt to justify myself. Ever since I have wished that I hadn't done it, but I pulled the hat box out, sat on the floor, and began to read. I wasn't methodical about it; I chose letters at random, and glanced at the contents, my feelings of guilt increasing in proportion to the banality of the correspondence. The reference to family events identified letters from relations, the others were from friends. There seemed to be none from boyfriends, admirers, or lovers, as if Delia had not bothered to keep those. Perhaps they were in another hiding place, but I was ashamed enough by my intrusion not to begin further searches.

I was about to give up and put the box back when I came across something I wasn't expecting at all: letters from my mother to Delia. I recognized the handwriting immediately, with its childish untidiness that the years hadn't changed. There were several of them, all written in the early thirties, during vacations, when they had been in different places. I learned that Delia and my mother had been at school together, and it was evident that they had been best friends during those years. I read them with more care than they deserved, because there was something immediate, timeless, about their warm banality. Those letters wouldn't have been much different if my mother had written them now. However, my find gave me a dubious excuse for my intrusion, and

I continued with my search through the old papers with renewed curiosity.

One of the letters was from Ambrosio Lagos to Delia, dated May 1943. She had moved to New York by then, and he asked her to reconsider her decision to leave. Ambrosio was sad about his daughter's departure and he missed her, although he kept his emotions under control through a combination of patriarchal sententiousness and elegant manners. I can't remember his exact words other than the closing paragraph, because it mentioned guilt, a feeling I was experiencing so acutely at that moment. It was guilt, not excitement, that made my heart pound while I read Delia's papers, as if I expected her to burst through the door and catch me here, red-handed.

In his letter, Ambrosio asked Delia not to let misplaced guilt influence her judgement. Neither of them should feel guilty about anything that had happened, he said, and he hoped that Delia would return soon. There must have been some rift between them before Delia's departure, or perhaps because of it. I had never thought about how unusual, how scandalous it must have been for a young woman to leave Buenos Aires in the early 1940s to live abroad on her own. By the time I started to hear about her, once my brother and I were allowed to sit at table with my mother and her guests, Delia's departure had been a fact of life for several years. Her latest picture in some social feature in *Paris-Match*, alongside some handsome man or other who might or might not be her lover, or the latest gossip from someone who had just been to Paris, were far more topical.

From my perspective, time had blunted the shock value of her action. Influenced by the immediacy of Ambrosio Lagos's letter in my hand, I saw it differently now, and I could imagine how much she must have scandalized her world – and her father too. It was hard to say whether the dominant emotion rising from his writing was repressed anger or grief – it was so contained, so understated, and yet so overwhelming, like Delia's scent in her closets. Ambrosio must have loved his daughter very much to be so accommodating. Even now, it was most unlikely that girls my age would travel alone, let alone move abroad. It must have seemed an outrageously impossible notion in 1943.

The paper felt brittle in my hand, and the ink had faded into a watery paleness. Other letters I had read were equally damaged by the passage of time, but I couldn't distance myself from this one so easily: Delia had been more or less my age when it was written. I folded the sheet before I dropped it back into the box.

Closer to the bottom, I found another packet of letters, still in their envelopes. Unlike the others, they were tied together with a ribbon instead of an elastic band. I opened the first one, written in 1938. Although Delia must have been seventeen or eighteen at the time, the writer addressed her as '*usted*', the formal pronoun in Spanish, and I assumed that he or she had to be an older relation of Delia's. However, the following paragraph referred to his delight in meeting her, and his hope that he would see her again soon. I remembered conversations at home between older people, about how much the world had changed since they were young. It was customary then for boys and girls to address each other formally, at least during the early stages of friendship. In line with the required solemnity, the letter was signed in the writer's full name, a bold, florid, and incomprehensible squiggle.

His second letter was longer. He made much of his joy at seeing Delia again, how lucky he felt that she had danced with him more than once, and asked for her permission to address her as '*vos*', the familiar pronoun, next time they met. He signed himself formally – and illegibly – again.

The third letter was much less stilted in tone, and Delia's admirer must have been granted the privilege of addressing her informally, as he did now. He made it plain that he was smitten with her, and was much encouraged by the fact that, although she had called him bold, she hadn't rejected him. In the final paragraph, he said that any word from Delia was precious to him, so he would sign himself 'Bold' from then on.

It was touching to read the remaining letters, once Delia and the writer had fallen in love with each other. I couldn't feel jealous about something that had happened twenty-five years ago, before I was born. The letters were nearly history from my point of view, other than the fact that I felt as if I was reading about myself. Like the writer, I was experiencing the wonderful obsession of love, the inability to think about anything else, the simultaneous certainty about one's own feelings and the fear that the woman I loved might change her mind. He wasn't particularly gifted with words, which made his efforts to explain his emotions even more poignant. I could understand his ambivalence, his cocky assurance in one sentence, followed by the evidence of doubt in the next.

However, subsequent letters made clear that his predicament was quite different to mine. At some point he must have proposed marriage and Delia must have mentioned her parents' opposition, because in one of his letters he accused her of using it as an excuse. If the problem was her parents, 'Bold' was prepared to wait. Once Delia came of age, her father would not be able to stop her from doing what she really wanted. She must make up her own mind, he beseeched her.

The last letter, nearly a year after the first, was quite different in tone. The writer didn't revert to formal language, but it was almost as if he had. He told Delia that although she could never doubt the love he had offered her, it was unfair to bind him with vague promises she had no intention of honouring. In any case, he was releasing her. The purpose of the letter was to tell her about what she would hear, or read in the paper, the next day. He had proposed marriage to Isabel, and his offer of marriage had been accepted. This time he signed himself with his Christian name: Francisco.

Francisco and Isabel were my parents' names. The man who loved Delia then was my father.

I didn't bother to put the hat box away. I left it on the floor, its contents as disordered as my thoughts. I had to be wrong. It couldn't be. I would have recognized my father's handwriting on sight, as I had recognized my mother's. There were other Franciscos and many Isabels among their contemporaries. If I thought hard enough, I would find at least another couple with the same Christian names. My mother had never mentioned Delia as a friend. She hardly mentioned her at all, in fact, except to gossip about her occasionally with her cronies. If my father was the author of the letters in my hands, it was inconceivable that Delia would have denied knowing him well.

But even during those first moments of shock, when incredulity still held some degree of fractured control over my emotions, like a defeated general over his disbanding army, I doubted my own justifications. If my father had left Delia for her best friend, the break between them must have been grievous enough to justify my mother's silence – or Delia's denial. As for the handwriting, I had only seen my father's in captions beneath photographs in our albums at home. I didn't remember it well enough to be certain either way.

Anger struck me suddenly from nowhere. It was a rage so pure, so incandescent, that for a moment I lost any awareness of my immediate surroundings, or my senses. I was blind to anything other than the images inside my head, deaf to sounds except those I imagined. My father, the man I knew from photographs, suddenly broke free from that two-dimensional paralysis and came alive. I could see him with Delia, not as she would have been then, but as she was now, with me. That was the Delia I knew. My vision of her face blurred into images of us making love. Memories that my imagination had invested with the mellow half-light of perfection acquired the sharp, atrocious quality of pornographic photographs once my father took my place in them.

Delia *knew*. Every second of our time together, she knew. She had held me in her arms, she had whispered in my ear, she had kissed me, she had fucked me, and all the time she *knew*. She had lied to me. I remembered her smooth, unperturbed expression whenever I asked her about my father, as if my questions had nothing to do with her. I kicked the box hard, its contents spilling onto the floor. My father's letters were still in my hand; I crumpled them, and went to the bathroom. There I dropped the ball of crushed sheets of paper into the washbasin, my fingers fumbling in my pocket to grip my lighter. I held the small flame against the letters and kept it there, watching the paper turn brown and crack under the heat. The metal began to burn my skin, but only when smouldering became flames did I move my hand away. After a while I turned over the burning mass, to make sure that every bit of paper was consumed by the fire. Although the smoke made me cough, I felt better for it; the acrid smell obliterated the nauseating aroma of Delia's scent in the small room, as if the fire was cleansing me too. Once every scrap had become black ash, I turned the faucets on full blast and watched the cinders swirl away down the drain, then rubbed off the oily, dirty yellow smudge on the white porcelain until there was no trace left. I wanted to obliterate every particle of those letters from my sight, in the hopeless expectation that they would vanish from my mind too.

My overwhelming feeling now was an urge to run away. I went into my room, and threw my things into my suitcase. As I walked past Delia's bedroom, I saw the papers lying on the floor in the corridor, scattered around like the confetti of her past. I imagined her reaction when she came back – her horror at the sight, at the evidence that I had discovered about my father and her – only to realize that my revenge illustrated the very fact I wanted to deny so fervently: that she had mattered so much to me that I had read her private correspondence. I didn't want to give her the excuse of my own behaviour to justify hers. I dropped the letters back into the box as if I was conjuring an evil genie back into its bottle, put the box back in the cupboard, and moved the table into place.

I rushed down the stairs, and out of the house. The only thought that brought some comfort to me was the idea that I'd never see this place again. I hated Delia. I hated her because she had lied to me, and because she'd made me ashamed of myself for the rest of my life.

I wished her dead.

Four

Solitary confinement in jail is said to be a punishment akin to physical torture. I wouldn't know, although I found the studio as stifling as a prison cell that night. The skin on my fingers had blistered over the burns from the lighter, but that was a clean, minor pain that would heal itself. I almost cherished those burns because I saw them as a form of expiation, even if they were too small in proportion to my remorse.

I left the place as soon as the sun rose the next morning. It was Sunday. After a while, the oppressive atmosphere of my studio began to seem less stifling than a deserted city where I remained a stranger. Being with Delia had not only given me the illusion of love, it had also deceived me into a false sense of being at home here. Now I found myself idling along empty streets and shuttered shops.

Thoughts about Delia and my father churned obsessively in my head, like the water of the Seine in the wake of the *bateaux-mouches* and barges. Leaning on stone or iron balustrades, I stared at the boats as I drifted from bridge to bridge. By now, nearly a day after the initial shock, my pain seemed greater, more unbearable than ever, because the explosive fury of discovery had given way to the slow, choking grip of despondency. The idea of jumping into the river came to me. It was an obvious, traditional solution; the water was right there, swirling below me. I could do it. Yet I didn't want to die. I didn't want to give up my life: I only wanted to efface the last few months. I wanted to forget. I wanted to be able to go to sleep, and wake up the next morning free of any memories of Delia or those letters. It should have been so easy, so sensible a cure to my pain compared to the brutal, irreversible emptiness of death, and yet it was impossible.

Despair was followed by slow, rolling waves of feeble hope. It would have been impossible for my father and Delia to make love. I had heard many times how closely watched unmarried girls had been when Delia was very young, how the restricted freedoms available to people my age seemed like a libertine's charter to the previous generation. Although never too detailed, my mother's occasional comments made it plain that she and all her girlfriends had been virgins until they married. Delia and my father couldn't have been lovers, I assured myself.

But Delia wasn't like everybody else. She had lived as she pleased. She had left Buenos Aires against her father's wish. She had never married. It could be that Delia had been so closely watched that she and my father could never be alone for any length of time, that her leaving had been a final rejection of rules she found impossible to abide. I wasn't unfamiliar with the situation myself. Things hadn't changed *that* much from her day to mine; I had had my fair share of quick, desperate fumblings in dark corners or the back seat of cars, the struggle with frothy petticoats, or unyielding hooks and elastics as effective as barbed wire. Those fumblings could be more binding or more carnal in their frustration than being naked in a bed.

Delia had kissed my father, wanted him, as she had wanted me. Probably more. She didn't need to want me. She had me. Jealousy shook me, like iced water trickling down my back. Delia was mine. I didn't want anybody else to have mattered in her life – least of all my own father. He was an ideal, unreachable and unquestionable. I hated Delia for loving my father, but I couldn't hate him: I felt jealous instead. Worse than jealous, I was envious. My father had had Delia's love at the right time in their lives, when everything was possible for them. Even if it hadn't worked out in the end, he had had a chance denied to me, because Delia and I could never have a future together. She would be old long before me. It was so starkly obvious, and yet I had fooled myself into blind ignorance. I should have known better from the very beginning.

Why? Why should I have known? I had no reason to suspect. Delia knew her past. I didn't. She had started everything. She had led me on. I couldn't imagine the emotional callousness, the depth of detachment that made it possible for her to be with me, and deny her memories of my father at the same time. Perhaps she had been comparing me all the time . . .

At that point I reached rock bottom, the final stop of guilt. I couldn't go on snaring myself in my own thoughts. Maybe the letters weren't from my father. Maybe Delia wasn't a monster of deceit. Maybe she could explain everything. I had planned never to see her again, but that had been yesterday. I felt different now – I was prepared to give myself the chance of being proven wrong.

A second later I despised myself. I was trying to excuse Delia. I didn't want to accept that she could be a monster, so focused on whatever suited her whim that any other consideration was irrelevant. I had to see her again. I wouldn't give her the chance of easy justifications once she found out that I was gone. I wanted her to share in my revulsion, a feeling that should be hers more than mine because she didn't have the excuse of ignorance. In anticipation I relished the sight of her shocked face once she heard what I had discovered, and my enjoyment of her humiliation.

She should be back at the house that evening. I didn't have too long to wait.

It was dark and silent when I let myself in. The servants would be back the next morning, but Delia had to be here. I knew it because I had kept watch on the place that afternoon, standing in the recess of a portal down the road, until she arrived in a taxi, wearing a white sleeveless dress that showed off the new tan on her arms and legs. Even from where I was standing, I could see her gracious smile when she tipped the driver after he took her suitcase out of the trunk. There was no reason why she shouldn't be her usual self, other than I expected her to sense that I had found out. It seemed inconceivable to me that she could have no hint, no premonition of the change in my feelings for her. When she rang the bell, the *concierge* came out and picked up the luggage. Delia said something to her as they walked into the building. I wondered if she had asked whether I was home.

I didn't follow her into the house, because I didn't want Delia to know I had been waiting for her, that I could think only of her. Better for her to notice that I had taken away my things, and wonder why, to fret in her uncertainty, to feel rejected. I wanted to hurt Delia in every possible way, to spare her nothing.

I forced myself not to check the hour or count the minutes. I walked all the way to Montmartre and spent time there moving from café to café, drinking glasses of rough red wine and pretending to be interested in the bad renderings of the Place du Tertre offered to tourists by local artists with the smiling insistence of the desperate. I left after the bells of Sacré Coeur had struck eleven, and I headed for the Métro. My earlier wish to delay our confrontation was replaced now by an overwhelming sense of urgency.

As I reached the top of the stairs, the chink of light under Delia's bedroom door distracted me from the beating of my own heart. I didn't bother to knock. A sense of privacy had not been part of our life before, and seemed ludicrous now.

'Martín, is that you?' Delia called. She must have heard the parquet creak under my feet, and the ring of fear in her voice pleased me. Her shadow moved across the drawn curtains on the other side of the room as she got out of bed. Then I saw her standing in front of her bedside light, the outline of her body visible beneath the flimsy silk of her nightgown.

'God, you frightened me,' she laughed. I could tell she was expecting me to move towards her, to embrace her as I would have done before – until she noticed my face.

'Is there anything wrong? I didn't know where you'd gone. I was worried about you.'

'Were you? Maybe you have reason to be.'

'I don't know what you mean . . .' The look of incomprehension in her eyes was too intense to be real. Delia knew something was wrong. She had to know. Her attempt at simulation enraged me more. I grabbed her arms, ready to shake that vacuous grin off her face, but she held me around my waist, gripping me tightly.

'I'm so glad you're here. I missed you,' she murmured, her head on my shoulder. I smelled the jasmine scent warmed by her skin, and a part of me reacted to it, as if I still could love her.

I pushed her away. She fell on the bed, on her back, the satin of her skirt riding up her legs as fluidly as wet paint. She raised her head slightly, stretching that long neck of hers that seemed almost too slender to carry any weight, so easy to snap under the slightest pressure. I leaned over her. She grabbed my wrists and pulled me down, on top of her, our faces nearly touching. She bit my lip, playfully at first, then hard, until I felt the faintest taste of blood in my mouth.

My thighs straddled hers, pinning her down, and I tore my wrists free from her grip. She raised her arms to protect herself – or to embrace me, but I didn't let her. My left hand caught hers like a manacle, and pushed her bent arms upwards, until they encircled her head. I thought of slapping her face, but my hand went to her neck instead. She struggled under my weight until she heard the silk of her nightdress rip under the pull of my fingers. Delia lay there, breathing fast, her skin soft and lustrous against the matt inside of the torn satin, her breasts thrust upwards by the pull of her captive arms. Fear or incomprehension darkened her eyes. She was my hostage. I could do whatever I wanted to her. I could tell her why I hated her. I could hit her. Or I could fuck her.

I had to have Delia to appease my anger, to humiliate her, to restore my own power. I stretched my back upwards, to bring my face away from hers, and my hands gripped the sheet to avoid touching her, to deny her whatever might please her. I didn't make love to her, because love didn't come into it in any way. I did nothing to make it enjoyable for Delia, to acknowledge she was anything but flesh I was fucking for my own sake. She had used me, and now it was my turn to use her. Unexpectedly, anger began to lose its grip on me, gradually replaced by the anaesthetizing effect of concentration on my own satisfaction. I heard Delia moan. It could be pain, or it could be pleasure too, and I wasn't going to grant her that. I thrust hard into her, and then it was over for me. I stood up; Delia lay still, her arms and legs outstretched on the bed.

My anger was spent. All that was left was a sickening feeling of revulsion. I straightened my clothes, purposely avoided looking at her, and headed for the door. I was about to reach the top of the stairs when I heard Delia's bare footsteps behind me.

'What's this all about? What have I done?' she asked.

I could have ignored her question, walked down the stairs and got out of the house, but the opportunity of humiliating her further was too tempting. I turned, and gave her a slow, blistering look from head to toe. For once, Delia wasn't such a glorious sight to behold. The shreds of her tattered nightdress hung from her shoulders; her face was flushed, and her hair clung lankly to her temples.

'Nothing much. I just want to know if I was better than him.'

Alertness hardened her features now. 'Who are you talking about?'

'My father. You must know if I'm a better fuck than he was,' I said.

Delia's eyes turned to blind discs of fury. Her hands rammed my chest, and sent me flying backwards down the stairs. My arms flapped wildly, searching for a hold in the air. I managed to grab the handrail and break my fall, but I was falling too fast to keep my grip. I tripped, and rolled down to the bottom.

'Get out. Get out of here *now*.' Her voice reached me from the heights of the hall as I lay sprawled on the floor at the bottom of the stairs. A shrill scream would have sounded less startling, less dangerous than her slow, spiteful hiss. 'I'll call the police if you aren't out of that door in ten seconds.'

It was only after I stood up and stumbled to the door, once I was in the calm of the courtyard, that I felt a sharp pain down my left side.

It must have been after two in the morning when I reached my apartment building. I had slept there the night before, I had been through that hall at the start of that miserable day, and yet I felt as if I had reached home at last after an interminable absence.

Almost anywhere I could shut myself in, away from everybody, would have felt like home. I felt tired beyond tiredness, drained of strength. My legs and arms felt heavy and clumsy, as if the bandages binding my torso also restrained them. Once I left Delia's house, it took only a couple of minutes for me to realize that the pain was more than just a bad fall. I persevered on my way towards the Boulevard des Invalides, but after a hundred yards or so I had to stop. I remembered the big hospital at the bottom of the Rue

Vaneau, along the Rue de Sèvres. There had to be an emergency room there.

The brutally eerie atmosphere of the hospital at night and the see-saw changes in mood in the waiting room, where long silences or whispered conversations were interrupted by the commotion of moaning or bleeding patients on stretchers being brought in by ambulance staff, the bustle of nurses or doctors rushing past in their pale green coats, helped me go through the next couple of hours. In that grim ambience, so at one with my emotions, I felt less isolated, less of an outcast, than in the 'normal' world outside. My estrangement from that world had been brought home to me swiftly when I had to fill in my registration form. I paused when I reached the dotted line headed 'Next of Kin'. My mother and my brother were thousands of miles away; they couldn't help me here, or be of any use to the hospital in an emergency. Eventually I wrote 'Argentine Consulate'. The sight of the words made me feel so lonely, so at the mercy of others, so *small*.

When my name was called, I explained to a nurse that I had slipped, and fallen down the stairs. Eventually a young doctor came into the cubicle and read the notes. He rotated my arm gently, felt my side, and then sent me for an X-ray.

'Nothing to worry about,' he said once he came back, half an hour later, examining the X-ray on a light box while he lit a Gitane. 'You've cracked a rib. The nurse will bandage you. Keep the bandages on for ten days. You'll have to be careful over the next three weeks, but otherwise you can carry on with your life as usual.'

I bit my lip. I felt tears come to my eyes, but I don't think the doctor noticed. What was my usual life? I had lost the life I wanted, and I didn't want the life I could have.

By the time I left the hospital, the painkiller the nurse gave me before she swaddled my chest had taken effect. My eyes began to itch with tiredness. All I wanted was to go back to my studio, in the hope that I would be able to sleep for a while, that I wouldn't carry on replaying the scenes at Delia's house in my head again and again.

I could hear the elevator approaching, then light from the cabin spilled through the open ironwork into the hall. I saw my suitcase standing nearby. There were a couple of envelopes under the handle. I picked them up. The first one was a note from Yves, who hadn't wasted time in letting the studio: his new tenant had moved in that morning. He had put my things in my suitcase, because he had no telephone number or forwarding address for me. Only then did I notice that it was July 1st. I opened the case, and checked that my passport and my return ticket to Buenos Aires were there. Once again they had become my most important possessions.

The second envelope was a telegram from my mother: *Lucas Marquez has offered you job. Come back immediately.*

Lucas Marquez was a senior partner in one of Buenos Aires' largest law firms, founded by his father. They had been my grandfather's business lawyers and then my mother's, although by now the fiction that she was a client worth having was maintained only because Lucas and his wife were friends from her youth. My mother had not been idle after my message; she had used whatever influence she had to entice me back home. If I wanted an opportunity to start my career as a lawyer, this was as good as any I could expect, and better than most.

I had lost Delia, and now I had lost my studio too. I left the building and sat on my suitcase, staring vacantly at the empty boulevard. People walked past every now and then, solitary figures on their way back home, eyeing me with a mixture of curiosity and suspicion, as if I didn't belong. They were right. I had nothing to do in Paris, and I wished I could forget every minute of my stay here. I had deluded myself into loving Delia, in the stupid conceit that time didn't matter, like a novice rider heady with the excitement of galloping at full speed across open country, only to realize that he has no control over his runaway horse. Now I was lying flat on the ground, battered and broken. I hated Delia. She had poisoned everything between us – even the thought of my father had become poisonous. All I could do was find a cheap hotel for the night, and book myself onto the first flight home the next morning.

I knew I had screamed in my sleep, bringing my dream to an end. The sheets and the bandages were damp with my sweat. I could smell the dust ingrained in the pile of the velvet headboard, more lasting than the faint traces of scent left by dozens of anonymous heads. I had opened the window before I went to bed, in the hope that it would make the tiny hotel room cooler, but there was no breeze; all that came through it was the noise of buses and cars outside Montparnasse station.

I sat up carefully and leaned against the dusty velvet. The painkiller had begun to wear off, and my chest and side ached as if hammers had pounded over me in my sleep. The weak first light of day spared me the full picture of the squalor around me, or perhaps the memory of my dream was still so sharp, so vivid, that it blurred the surroundings. Those eyes were as real an image as if they were in front of me, burning bright with rage. I couldn't remember anything about the rest of the face, only the eyes. I was looking at them from below, as I had stared up at Delia's when she pushed me down the stairs. I had seen that same rage in her eyes, but those in my dream weren't hers. They were brown, and I knew they weren't a woman's eyes. I couldn't tell why, but I knew that. I was sure.

It was too early to check out of the hotel. I would have to drag my suitcase from café to café, waiting for the office of *Aerolineas Argentinas* to open. I also knew there was no chance of falling asleep again. Perhaps I was beginning to learn to live without Delia – or at least I had begun to grasp just how painful it would be.

Five

Something in my mother's eyes made me wonder if she knew, if she had heard about Delia and me. The possibility had bothered me ever since I had arrived in Buenos Aires a week ago, and was fostered by the fact that she had asked me in great detail about virtually every aspect of my trip but my stay in Paris. She seemed almost as unconcerned about it as I was unwilling to volunteer anything but the sketchiest details. Her critical gaze as I sat down to breakfast with her made me nervous, until I realized she was inspecting my appearance, not trying to decipher my expression.

'You ought to cut your hair, Martín. You're not in Paris any more,' she admonished me, as if I needed a reminder of the fact – particularly in the suffocating apartment where we lived, crammed with whatever furniture she had managed to keep from her old home years ago, the stage of her days of glory. Squeezed into rooms too small for them, the pseudo-Louis pieces made at the turn of the century to impress the eye were more likely to injure our shins. Their faded, chipped gilt and balding cut-velvet upholstery seemed to mirror my mother's stale hopes.

'Don't worry, my hair is fine,' I said, reaching for the newspaper.

'Lucas might not like it, and you can't miss this opportunity, darling. Your trip cost me money I could ill afford. You can't count on being kept forever, you know.'

The remark was typical of my mother. It was she who had insisted I should go to Europe in the first place. Now she was turning her undeniable generosity into yet another stage of her financial Via Crucis. Her approach was slightly different than usual, though; while her standard comments about our relative poverty merely demanded pity for herself, now there was an edge of recrimination that was unjustified, since I had told her I wanted to be financially independent as soon as possible. Perhaps she knew about Delia and me, had made assumptions about what she imagined my true motivation to be, and this was her discreet way of conveying her disapproval. Or I could be investing my mother's words with hidden meaning because of my own extreme susceptibility to anything that reminded me of Delia.

'I never counted on being kept,' I snapped back. 'If I'm offered a job, the first thing I'll do is rent an apartment. It will be much better for both of us.'

'Why? That's completely unnecessary. Aren't you happy here? It's hard enough for me with your brother living so far away . . .'

Her voice dripped self-pity, and I felt a too-familiar mixture of impatience, sorrow and love. She expected too much from my brother and me, or at least she expected a dedication we couldn't give her any more.

'Don't worry, I'm not planning to move to Patagonia like Miguel. I'll be round so often that you'll hardly notice the difference,' I offered in conciliation. It was enough to stop the crescendo of fretting; she seemed to relax, and reached for my hand to give it a brief, affectionate squeeze.

'You look much better now that you're eating properly. And you seem to move much more easily too,' she said, as if the benefits of being back home included my physical recovery.

'I'm not wearing the bandage this morning. The doctor said I should wear it only for one week.'

'Maybe you should have kept it a bit longer, just in case. It must have been a terrible fall. I can't understand what on earth made you ride a bicycle after so many years. Where were you? You haven't told me much about the accident.'

'I was in Normandy.' It was all I had told her when she first noticed the bulk of the bandage under my shirt, and now I felt obliged to expand. 'I was near . . . some village I can't remember, a few kilometres from the coast. It was nothing, really.'

'Your father and I were in Normandy a year before the war. We spent a few days in Deauville, where he was playing polo. It was so beautiful. I remember Dulce Liberal so well, we saw her at a garden party there. She was all in white, wearing the most wonderful hat I've ever seen. People really don't know how to dress any more . . .' Her eyes glazed over, and I recognized the symptoms. My mother was about to launch into one of her evocations of the past. I had heard the story before; any other time I might have listened patiently, but now my feelings about stories of the good life in France were too raw. I gulped down my coffee.

'Lucas is expecting me in half an hour. I'd better go,' I lied. Killing time in a café was a safer option than staying here with her.

'Good luck. I'll pray for you,' she said when I kissed her. It was hard to say if her religious beliefs were genuine or a social duty, something she felt was expected of her. Probably both, like a crumbling garden wall smothered by ivy that weakens its foundations while holding it upright.

I felt more relaxed as I rode on the bus to the centre of town, distracted from my own thoughts by the morning bustle around me. Ever since my humiliating parting from Delia, anger had been my dominant emotion. From a simmering, unfocused feeling of impatience at any time, to choking, blinding surges of rage when I relived that last scene with her, I experienced all gradations of anger. My moments of reprieve were outside, among the constant flow of anonymous faces and changing scenes in the streets that diverted my attention from the sizzling flow of my inner rage.

This morning, the imminent interview with Lucas Marquez, my awareness of its significance on my immediate future, overshadowed my thoughts of Paris, or at least pushed them into the back of my mind. For the first time since coming back I felt 'normal', my old self almost, but as soon as I walked into the broad, solemn stone building in the banking district where Marquez's offices were, and I looked up his name on the indicator board in the austere entrance hall, I experienced a familiar and yet nearly forgotten feeling, the kind of gut-knotting anxiety that used to come over me before an exam.

I hated exams; not so much the actual experience as the wait, having to stand in a corridor or a draughty anteroom until my name was called, the fear of prospective failure nearly as daunting as failure itself. My unease now was unjustified; when I phoned

Lucas Marquez to arrange our meeting, he made the prospects of a job in his firm sound more like a *fait accompli* than a possibility. However, I couldn't help reliving my old fears as I waited in an armchair outside his office. The dusty smell of horsehair rising through the cracks in the leather upholstery, the glass-fronted bookcases, and the fluorescent lights behind egg-crate diffusers created an atmosphere as sterile in its way as the Neo-Grecian loftiness of my old college building. Also, after months of casual clothes in Spain and France, I was wearing a suit again, another reminder of exams. However, I hadn't extended my adoption of the old ways to slicking my hair back into a hard crust, as was the custom for men in Buenos Aires then – and probably the reason behind my mother's disapproving remark.

A buzzer rang on the secretary's desk, a few steps away from my seat, and I sat up in full alert.

'Mr Marquez will see you now,' the girl said. She led the way down a corridor lined with leather tomes as imposing as if they held the Sinai tablets, although their bindings were more likely to conceal superannuated legal journals. She opened a door at the end and stepped aside.

'*Pero m'hijo, que gusto verte!*' Lucas Marquez's voice boomed his convivial greeting from the other end of the room. He patted my shoulder affectionately as he shook my hand in a whirlwind of bonhomie and English cologne, then led me towards a group of leather armchairs at the other end of his office, a less battered brethren to those in the waiting room, arranged around a low, glass-topped table. 'We'd like some coffee, Lavinia,' he told his secretary.

'You were this tall last time I saw you,' Lucas said once we sat down, his hand hovering at waist-height above the floor. 'I had a shock when you came in, you look so like your father. Poor Francis, such a good friend. How's your brother?'

He was certainly trying hard to put me at ease; his mention of my father had the opposite effect, but Lucas couldn't know that. His teeth gleamed almost as dazzlingly as his slicked-back dark hair, an irresistible smile aimed at me as evidence that I would be foolish not to like him. It was a lawyer's grin though, the kind that should carry a disclaimer.

'He's fine. Working very hard, I guess,' I said.

'He has to. That place was neglected for decades . . .'

Now Lucas was less loquacious than before, and I could understand why. After graduating as an agronomist, Miguel had persuaded our paternal uncle to let him manage what was left of the original family land in northern Patagonia. My great-great-grandfather was an Englishman from Leeds, who came to Argentina as a young man, and he bought a lot of land south of the Rio Negro. It wasn't a place for absentee landlords, which is what his descendants became, like many of their contemporaries. Unlike the Pampas, the land wasn't so fertile that it looked after itself. By my father's generation, successive sales had shrunk the original holding to a worthless fraction, which remained in the family only because nobody wanted to buy it. I was sure Lucas thought it unkind to remind me in any greater detail of my ancestors' approach to asset management.

'Isabel told me you were in Europe recently. My wife is driving me crazy about going there soon. She adores Paris. We haven't been there for two years . . .' He made it sound like a failing, as any of my mother's friends would. For them, an annual trip to Europe was both a necessity and a therapeutic experience.

'It's a very good idea for young men to see the world,' he went on approvingly. 'And have fun too. I hope you had fun, one must at your age. Tell me about Paris. Didn't you think it a fabulous city?'

'Paris was fun,' I said. It was the last word that would have come to my lips, but Lucas had used it. It was still there, floating in the air, and I threw it back at him in haste, to stop myself from having to think about Paris and getting mired in a choice of words, in editing my memories into acceptable trivia.

'I didn't stay there very long. I travelled around France, until I ran out of money. It's time to work now, and I look forward to it,' I said meaningfully.

'Ah, yes, Isabel called me about that. Of course Martín must work with us, I told her.' Lucas paused when his secretary came back with the coffee, so I had to wait to hear about my promising future until she had laid the cups on the table and left. 'I have spoken to Pedro Gonzalez, he's in charge of *Sucesiones* here. I will introduce you in a moment, after we've had our coffee. I also started there, when I joined my father in 1947 . . .'

Even as a neophyte, I had heard enough about professional life to know that Lucas wasn't taking any risks. The apportionment of estates among heirs was largely established by law. It was a routine task, involving mountains of paperwork and statutory formalities; anybody with a legal training could do it. The work was as dull for the people in charge as it was lucrative for the firm, since fees were a percentage of the value of the properties concerned. *Sucesiones* was a safe place to bury an inexperienced graduate.

'We have friends in Paris,' Lucas said proudly. 'Although she hasn't seen her for years, Susana is very fond of Delia Lagos. They were at school together, and Delia is a remarkable woman.'

I hoped I hadn't winced. His voice suggested nothing but a passing comment. Lucas's eyes might have revealed an edge to it, but I didn't see because I lowered my reddening face as soon as I heard Delia's name. I waited for a moment to look at him again, until the word stopped burning in my ears. His face seemed so guileless, his voice so devoid of any ulterior motives, that even in my hyper-sensitive mood I doubted that Lucas was being malicious. My mother's was a world where everybody knew, and knew about, everybody else. It was also customary to mention important friends abroad whenever possible. International connections were a badge of honour.

Nonetheless I doubted that his reference to Delia was inadvertent. Although she and I hadn't mixed with Argentines in Paris, people there must have talked about us, the kind of people friends of Lucas Marquez might cultivate. It would have taken only one traveller making a few phone calls once they were back in Buenos Aires for the story to spread. I wondered if this was to be the pattern from now on, that I would not only have to live trapped with my recurrent thoughts about Delia, but also be forced into dissecting everybody's words at the mention of her name, looking for hidden innuendo.

'I don't think I've met her. What will my salary be?' I asked bluntly. Like most people who need money badly, I hated discussing it. I only forced myself to mention the matter because, unpalatable as it was, it was preferable to hearing any further mention of Delia.

'I have no idea,' Lucas laughed. 'I think we pay beginners fifteen hundred pesos a month, but don't take my word for it. We'd better go and find Gonzalez,' he said, rising to his feet. The figure was barely adequate, but it was more or less what I knew friends of mine were earning at their first job. The possibility of bargaining didn't occur to me; all that mattered was that the subject of Delia had been dropped.

'Absence makes the heart grow fonder' is one of those pieces of popular wisdom printed on a thousand cards, but it wasn't true for me. It made my heart grow heavier, more unforgiving. I was glad to be away from Delia, from everything connected with her that had seemed so exhilarating at the time, although 'glad' is a convenient but imprecise description of my feeling. I felt a kind of resigned relief, a self-protecting cloud of numbness occasionally shredded by gusts of contempt for her, and I welcomed anything that stressed the change in my life – even the fact that it was late winter here, that the uncharacteristic grey sky and cold weather did not remind me of Paris in the cusp of summer. All my time there was free, while now I was in the office by nine o'clock, ploughing through deeds, valuations and death certificates for the rest of the day as if they mattered, and visiting possible apartments to rent in the early evening, which I marked in the paper during my bus journey to work. My eye did not linger on those streets or buildings that make tourist guides describe Buenos Aires as 'the Paris of South America'. In any case, successive real-estate booms were turning the townscape of slate mansard roofs and wrought-iron gates my parents had known into a jumble of high-rise blocks, or empty building plots where the party walls resembled melancholic jigsaw puzzles, geometric ghosts of the houses that had stood there. Shreds of damask wallpaper in red, gold, or green, and strips of wainscot punctuated by the black squares left by removed fireplaces were all that remained of the grandeur of the former rooms. Big white billboards spanned their empty frontages, announcing the forthcoming marvels of air conditioning, high-speed elevators, and sliding metal windows. The future was there, to fill in the void left by a crumbling past.

Whenever I thought about Delia, I forced myself to ponder her reasons for asking me to stay in her house while she was away. I needed an alibi for my shame. I told myself that she had known that I would pry into her private papers, and find out about her link with my father, a connection that might have bothered her as much during our affair as it troubled me now. I needed her to be party to a foolish, unjustifiable act that was really my own responsibility, in an attempt to mitigate my guilt at my discovery and its implications. That guilt, and the memory of Delia herself, had become one and the same.

'You'll never clean the place. Do you want Malisa to come in the afternoons? You won't have to pay her, I will,' my mother suggested, hovering around my room while I packed. I didn't want her maid coming into the apartment I had rented. I saw it as my own territory, a token of my newly acquired independence – which was the likely reason behind my mother's offer.

'The place is too small to swing a broom around, *mamá*. I'll manage myself.'

'Someone has to iron your shirts, Martín. You could bring your laundry here in the evenings – if you are not going out, of course.' She was trying to be understanding as well as helpful, when she didn't understand at all.

'I won't be having dinner here every day, *mamá*. I'm moving out.'

'Do you mean I'll never see you again then?'

It was typical of her to consider cohabitation or estrangement as the only possible alternatives, but her dispirited mood was not an act now, and it saddened me.

'You will see me often enough. And I have a phone, you know. You can call me whenever you want.' She didn't need my encouragement, but I wanted to give her hope, a crumb of consolation in what she considered a tragic turn in her life. In her way she was right, because she was facing loneliness, a feeling that pervaded my thoughts enough for me to understand how frightening it was. Unlike most of her friends, my mother couldn't afford to keep herself busy through constant shopping, or redecorating her home, and she had no other preoccupations. She wasn't stupid and she didn't lack drive either. What she lacked was a focus other than life as she had known it, and the flexibility of mind to imagine that any other option was possible.

Once Miguel and I became old enough to face the prospect with apparent equanimity, we teased her about the possibility of marrying again. She seemed shocked by the idea. 'I'd never find another man like your father,' she would say. Her vow of loyalty was a respite from our unspoken fears about some unknown man stepping into our father's role in her life and ours, and would smooth us into satisfied acquiescence. Even if she had wanted to marry again, the kind of man my mother would have considered marrying was not available. She was too old for a suitable single man, and too young for her male contemporaries to become widowers in the near future. Ten years later, half of her friends would be divorced; in those days only an American woman or a local Salome would have considered the possibility of stealing somebody else's husband. Divorce was unthinkable, as well as legally impossible. Quickie divorces arranged in Mexico were the only option available for those daring enough, but they meant social opprobrium, a kind of second-class citizenship.

I zipped up my suitcase and cast my eye around the room for the last time. I had moved my books and records earlier in the day. Although I had been looking forward to leaving home, the sadness of bare shelves and an open, empty closet hit me. In a flash, I saw myself in Delia's house again, throwing my things into a bag, eager to leave. I had learned about leave-taking. I could understand how my mother felt. I threw my arm around her shoulder as we walked out of the room.

'I'll come to dinner next Sunday,' I offered. I knew a full week was too far ahead for her expectations; less than that would have been too much of a concession for me.

We walked down the corridor in silence. Either side of her bedroom door stood a pair of half-oval console tables festooned in gilt garlands. Their tops were covered in knick-knacks and framed photographs, adding to their claustrophobia-inducing bulk. My favourite picture of my father was among them, a casual shot of him smiling at the camera, wearing an open-neck shirt. I stopped, and held it up.

'Do you mind if I take it?' I asked.

'No, of course not. Don't you want a photograph of me too?'

'Don't be a pain. I have lots of photographs of you, and you know it,' I replied. Her question made me feel less nostalgic about leaving my former home. My mother had become another element in that mix of memories, places and experiences that I wanted to leave behind me. Her main fault was being there, like a lightning conductor in a storm.

I had taken my chances by phoning Patricia soon after I came back. We had been going out for two or three months before I left for Europe, and we had slept together just before my departure. It had been more a token of commitment than an outburst of passion on either side, or that was how it seemed to me in retrospect, after I discovered that my interest in her was far less urgent once we'd had sex. As for Patricia, feigning coolness was part of the image she cultivated – and probably she didn't have to pretend too hard. I had written to her from Spain, and sent her a couple of postcards from Paris – until I met Delia.

Patricia sounded extremely unwelcoming at first, as might be expected after my long silence. I persevered. Eventually she said she was arranging a birthday celebration for a mutual friend, and she suggested I join them. I hadn't made contact with old friends yet; a group event was far preferable to one-to-one encounters, where I would have to talk about my trip time and time again. My lips would be threading words into amusing descriptions of places, while my mind would be full of images of Delia and me together.

Patricia asked me to collect her from her place. 'We'll meet here. Charlie and Fernando will bring their cars, so you don't need to bring yours,' she said. No car meant no chance of privacy, or a quick stop at the Acapulco Hotel to make love on the way back, but her suggestion suited me. Like her, I wanted to keep my options open, and there was the fact that 'your car' meant my mother's. It had been a linchpin of my past social life, but I didn't want to borrow it now.

Since Patricia told me to be at her apartment at ten o'clock, I knew I shouldn't be there until after eleven at the earliest. As I followed a maid into the drawing room, I could see the others through the open dining-room doors at the far end, sitting around the long table and having coffee. The animated group seemed to mirror the mythological banquet scene in the tapestry on the wall behind them. Clearly I was the only after-dinner guest, and the table was big enough for an extra place. Patricia could have asked me to dinner too. She was making a point, although she smiled warmly enough as she bounded across the drawing room towards me, the hem of her black dress swinging a couple of inches above the edge of her knee-high boots, her thick, glossy dark hair cut straight along her jaw-line. I realized once again how pretty she was. Then I remembered Delia gliding down the stairs the night of our big party in Paris; the contrast with Patricia's skin-deep prettiness, and with what had seemed her seductive poise when we first met, had struck me before I could prevent it. I forced myself to be impressed by Patricia again. I didn't want to compare them, because I didn't want to be reminded of Delia's uniqueness.

'What a shame I couldn't find you to ask you to come to dinner. I arranged it at the last minute.' Something like the small change from the bright smile I aimed at her glinted in Patricia's eyes; it wasn't enough to make her sound convincing. 'I phoned you at your mother's place, but the maid said she didn't have your new number.'

There was little point in mentioning the fact that I had given it to her when we spoke, and by then we had joined the rest of the group. On my way here, I wondered whether Patricia's mother's attitude towards me would be icy, as usual, or merely frosty now that the risk of her daughter and me becoming serious about each other had diminished. As we went into the dining room, I prepared myself for her bird-of-prey stare and a tight-lipped greeting, but Patricia's parents weren't there. She and her sister had been given free rein of their parents' home, and this was their own dinner party, which made my exclusion even more pointed. Perhaps at any other time I would have been less sensitive to what was nothing more than a symbolic slap on the wrist. It upset me because it made me feel rejected, although the rest of the company swamped me in greetings and congratulations, like a foreign legionnaire returning safely after a mission.

'What was it like, Martín?' 'Did you have a great time?' 'Tell us about it!' As soon as I started everybody else cut in, eager to tell about their own travelling experiences in Europe, so I didn't need to say much. I stared at them, at the group that had been my close friends before I left, and that now seemed so distant, so irrelevant to me. A maid began to clear the table, and then somebody said it was time to go. On the way there, six to a car, I was told that our destination was the hottest disco in town, recently opened.

'Don't tell him! Don't tell him!' was the chorus as someone tried to explain further about the place, on our way to the northern part of the city. Eventually we turned into what looked like a gas station, and drove into some sort of tunnel. 'Close the windows,' the driver warned us before going in; soon they were covered in thick foam spurting out from the sides of the tunnel. Everybody shrieked merrily as giant coloured brushes began to rub the car.

'It's an automatic car-wash. Isn't it amazing?' I was asked.

'Maybe not for Martín. He's been to Europe, remember.'

'We can imagine what you were up to,' someone cut in before I could reply, and everybody laughed – except me.

The feeling of a Brave New World continued once we got out of the cars and went upstairs, into the disco. It was going to be an expensive evening, and I regretted coming here. My moodiness lessened briefly after a spell of slow-dancing with Patricia, between long crescendos of pop songs played thunderously loud, an innovation as ground-breaking as the car-wash downstairs. However, she had a similar smooching session later with another guy from a group on a table near us. They were friends of Queenie's, Patricia's sister. The guy looked older than me – and he had to be very rich. Everybody else's Rolex watch was steel, while his was gold – I seemed to be almost the only person without a Rolex at all. I felt left out sitting on my own, and I couldn't be bothered to try to make conversation at the top of my voice in order to be heard over the deafening noise, so I decided to go to the rest room instead.

I found myself standing next to Queenie's boyfriend, an

arrogant bore who stood in front of the urinal, legs firmly apart, his head high and his chest puffed out, as if he was posing for immortality in bronze. He had been there when I joined him, and he was still there when I finished.

'Tell me, Martín,' he whispered as we zipped up in unison, 'everybody says you had a thing with Delia Lagos in Paris. Is it true? I hear she's quite something in the sack . . .'

Perhaps he was more curious than the rest, or bolder, or just drunk. The admiration in his voice didn't make me feel any better. I waited for him to turn and face me, his smug grin blazing across his face like a banner of macho complicity, then I aimed carefully and punched him hard on the chin.

I wasn't hitting him really. My punch was aimed at what Charlie Lascano, a self-satisfied fool, symbolized for me during those few seconds: my own ridicule in the eyes of others, and my anger. I was angry because he had implied that all that mattered was that I had screwed Delia; that all there was to it was that I, of all people, had laid the great legend.

'Fuck off, Charlie,' I said. I left him there, reeling against the tiled wall, too stunned to react, and walked out of that damned place. The stairs were next to the rest rooms, so I didn't even have to pass the others on my way out. Charlie could tell them I was gone. He was likely to invent some story about me not feeling well. He wasn't going to lose face by owning up to a brawl in which he hadn't left me bleeding on the floor.

The air outside was cold and fresh. At first I could think of nothing else other than the unexpected buzz in my ears, then I worried how I was going to get home. It was nearly two o'clock, and buses were few and far between. Luckily my stormy exit had spared me from my share of the bill. I had just enough money for the long cab ride.

The breeze from the river, only a couple of hundred yards away, felt chilly. I raised my collar, crossed my arms and tucked my hands under them, and scanned the traffic for an empty taxi with the red light on. Waiting in the winter night cooled my aggression. My self-justifying anger turned gradually into reluctant remorse, a kind of *vin triste* without the benefit of being drunk. I could find a number of reasons to justify hitting Charlie – but it dawned on me that I had hit him because what he said might be true. Maybe all there had been to it, all there was behind my glorious tale and its woeful end, was the fact that I had screwed Delia, something that meant so much to me and probably meant so little to her.

I didn't call Patricia again. Work kept me busy, and my spare time was filled by putting up shelves or similar chores in my apartment. I went to the movies to kill time, but it was hard, and not just because of being on my own. Before I could immerse myself totally in what happened on the screen, now my mind went blank, to be filled by images of Paris and of Delia. It was as if somebody else's fantasy, no matter how skilful, was not enough to cancel my own. At times, the images on the screen would turn into my own memories. A particular look, or a shot of a man holding a woman's face as he kissed her, the sight of a woman's hands on a man's naked back, became *my* eyes, *my* hands, *my* skin gazing at, touching, or feeling Delia close to me.

I thought a lot about my father too. After a few weeks in Buenos Aires, time and distance eroded my original revulsion into guilty acceptance, a more bearable emotion. I had placed his photograph in pride of place on the bookshelves in my room, like a silent companion. Perversely, Delia had provided me with something I had wanted for so long: a personal link with him. Everything else was blocked by the barrier of time: he had lived and died before I could know him. Love for Delia was something we had shared, a common experience. Agonizing as that knowledge was, it made him more real to me than anything else I knew about him.

I had envied my father when I found his letters, and I still envied him. Envy might be the wrong word though, because it implies resentment grudgingly qualified by admiration. My resentment was aimed only at Delia or myself, at her wanton wrecking of my life, and my own inability to deny her that power. I felt nothing but admiration for my father. He had succeeded in marriage, sports, in anything that mattered to him. God, luck, or whatever it is that determines such things, had given him the confidence, the self-assurance that was as evident in every photograph of his beaming face as his famous good looks.

I envied his parting from Delia most of all. He had left her. He had had the strength, or the wisdom, to drop her, to humiliate her by seeing through her game and calling her bluff. I couldn't deceive myself that I had left Delia by choice. I had forfeited that privilege. I had gone back to her house that night in a rage. I could have told her what I knew, and I could have asked her to confirm or deny my suspicions, but the truth was I didn't know what I wanted. I wanted the right to be angry, without the risk of finding out if my fears were really justified or not. She chose to throw me out instead – literally. No matter how hard I tried to invest my exit with the self-respect of the righteous, effectively Delia had claimed that territory first – she had got rid of me. Her expedience hurt me as much as her heartless indifference: Delia had pushed me down the stairs and out of her life without any concern for the consequences. I could have broken my neck for all she cared. I had done nothing to justify her spite, other than ask her about my father.

Perhaps she had made me the scapegoat for her rage at the fact that he had dumped her all those years ago. The glorious Delia Lagos hadn't been good enough for him, and she had never forgotten that. Maybe I had seen the real Delia that night. Smarting from my humiliation and unable to retaliate, I felt gratitude to my father, as if his action had avenged me in advance.

My apartment was in an old building facing the back of the cemetery, a neglected small apartment house that had gone from the bloom of youth into crumbling senility without the consolation of a dignified old age. Recoleta, the burial ground for most people of any consequence or means in Buenos Aires since colonial days, is now in the middle of the smart part of town, which surrounded it as the city grew along the river front, towards the north. The expensive buildings stopped one block away from the edges of the cemetery, giving way to a cheap hinterland, like well-dressed passengers on a bus keeping their distance from a tramp. I walked along the forbiddingly tall walls of the graveyard every day. The domes or pyramids crowning particularly large family vaults overshot the ramparts, and the marble angels at their top overlooked the stalls of the street market outside. These days the area has become a haven for antique dealers and expensive restaurants, the fair is gone, and the cobbled roads have been paved over. Then it was a refuge for people like me, who wanted to be in the district but couldn't afford to live in the good streets, or for activities that might offend the better-off neighbours – like the food market or the Acapulco Hotel.

When I was a child, my mother used to take us to our family vault on October 16th: the anniversary of my father's death. By the time I was old enough to understand, once my mother's reminiscences had crystallized into a feeling of love for him in me, the annual ritual had stopped. Neither Miguel nor I regretted the omission, or even questioned it. We didn't talk about it. In my case (and I suppose it applied to my brother as well), I couldn't associate those dour visits, the coldness of the place, with my own feelings.

One Sunday morning, as I walked past the cemetery gates on my way to buy the newspaper, the memory of those visits came back to me. Perhaps inspired by the sight of people going in with bunches of flowers, I decided to visit my father's grave. The decision came to me forcefully and unexpectedly. I knew it would be different now. Apart from any other consideration, I was on my own. At first I had trouble in finding my way along the maze of narrow streets and alleys, although I remembered the place well enough. After a couple of wrong turnings, I managed to locate the small granite building. I was in luck; the caretaker was a few doors away, letting some mourners into another vault. Once he finished, he came towards me, shaking his head and making much of his search for the key among the many on the ring chained to his belt. I couldn't understand the reason behind his mumbling, until he articulated loud and clear the difficulty of making ends meet on his meagre salary. His transparent request for a tip somehow sounded to me like my duty rather than his expectation, and I obliged him. He took my money, opened the iron and glass door while muttering what sounded like condolences if only I could understand a word he said, and then he left me alone.

The place was exactly as I remembered, other than that it had seemed small to my child's eyes, and now it felt stiflingly so. This oppressive feeling was compounded by the silence and the strong smell of damp, which rose from the crypts below through the bronze grating on which I stood, in front of the altar with its image of the Sacred Heart. The winter sunlight coming through the stained-glass dome bathed the white marble of the statue in water-colour shades of green and blue.

I needed some ritual to articulate my feelings, and give meaning to my presence here. I stood for a while, trying to remember the pattern of my childhood visits. Then we would lay flowers on the altar by the entrance, and say prayers afterwards. At least our mother would; my brother and I murmured the Lord's Prayer, our eyes cast down and our hands held together, but then I wasn't sure if any of the other prayers I knew were suitable for the occasion. Hail Marys seemed out of place in the circumstances because they were so full of feminine references, and the Creed was too terrifying.

I've never forgotten my feeling of uncertainty during those visits, my intuition as a child that something was expected of me to suit the solemnity of the occasion, without being able to tell what it could be. I sensed the need for grief even if it was an emotion unknown to me, because I saw my mother's sad face. Even so, I couldn't grieve for my father, because I had no memory of him. I had heard about him, and I knew about fathers because other children had them, but it was an abstract notion, particularly in the shrine-like atmosphere of a family vault, where nothing connected with my everyday life.

A milder version of that anxiety came over me now. I had given up praying long ago, and I hadn't brought flowers either. I leaned against the railing, where my eyes were drawn down to the dark void below. I knew my father's coffin was in the second crypt, the reason why my mother had restricted our visits to the ground-floor chapel, in fear that Miguel or I would fall down the steep stairs. I started to negotiate the narrow steps, which bent tightly around a corner. I could not only smell the damp now, I could feel it in the chilly air.

There were deep stone shelves on three sides of the crypt. Even the dim light filtering through the bronze grating above me was enough to turn the edges of the highly polished coffins on the slabs into gleaming black lines. My first thought was that I would be here one day too, among all these long-dead relations I had never met, and I rubbed my cold hands against the sleeves of my jacket. The soft, warm feel of the woollen fabric against my fingers broke the morbid spell. I went down the second flight of steps.

Light as grey as the stone walls dripped into the last crypt from high above, through the metal grille that formed the floor of the upper chamber. There were two coffins facing the stairs. The top shelf on that row was still empty, and so were the other niches in the room. I turned my back on the hollow spaces waiting to be filled, where my mother, my brother and I would be laid to rest eventually, and faced the coffins, trying to identify my father's. I had been a pall-bearer at my grandmother's funeral five years ago; now I recognized the elaborate silver handles on her coffin, which occupied the lower niche. I stared at the other coffin for a while, taking in the fact that I was standing in front of my father's coffin for the first time in my life. I felt my eyes prickling with tears. Then I noticed the name engraved on a small plate on the side. It was my grandfather's. My father's coffin wasn't there.

I felt cheated. I wanted my visit to flow easily, in unison with the strength of my feelings, unencumbered by the trivialities of practical detail, and now I had to confront the fact that I had no clue which among these anonymous black boxes held the remains of the father I had come to mourn. It was a smarting reminder that he remained as nebulous to me in death as he had been alive, and it reinforced my determination to find his coffin. I raised my head and unclasped my hands, ready to go back to the upper crypt, when I noticed that the top shelf wasn't empty as I had thought. There was a small casket at the back of the ledge, almost invisible in the shadows. It could have held a small baby, but all my cousins were alive, and none of my father's siblings had died in infancy. Anyone from an earlier generation would have been buried upstairs.

I was intrigued by my discovery, although not enough to stay there in the dank cold to try to work out an explanation. Once I was in the upper chamber again and ran my eyes over the niches, in an attempt to identify which one among those coffins held what was left of my father, I was struck by the realization that it made no difference. If I had come here in the hope that I would be able to feel closer to him, the anonymity of the coffins, the anonymity of death itself, had defeated me. I was overwhelmed by the futility of my search and the oppressiveness of the place. I climbed up the steps towards the light, like a diver eager to reach the surface.

Once outside, I slammed the door shut, and started to walk towards the gates. After the morbid bleakness of the vault, I enjoyed the warmth of the sun on my face. The noise of traffic on the other side of the cemetery wall was a welcome reminder of street life, but I didn't feel ready to join it yet. There was a stone bench ahead, on the sunny side of a line of cypresses. I sat on the hard slab, took my cigarettes out of my jacket pocket, and lit one. As I held the lighter to the cigarette, the sight of the flame brought back to me that afternoon in Paris, when I had burned my father's letters with this very same lighter.

Once again, I felt his presence both painfully close and impossibly remote. I knew too much and too little about him. I had come to the cemetery in the hope of making some contact, something that I couldn't define, let alone find. If I searched for a genuine memory of him in my head, I found nothing – only imperfect reflections of myself, as in a broken mirror. Like his body in the family vault, memories of him had to be somewhere in my head, but I didn't know where.

'I got ham, turkey breast, and Russian salad on my way back from mass, but you might like something hot instead. Or we could eat out,' my mother suggested. Our Sunday dinners were becoming customary, and so was the menu. Home-cooking was not an option during the maid's day off, when the kitchen became a treacherous territory for my mother, who had never cooked anything in her life. After three weeks, she had run through the cold food options available from El Aguila, a long-established tea-shop and delicatessen near her apartment, and it wouldn't have crossed her mind to try elsewhere. Her choice of shops was as qualified by self-imposed rules as every other aspect of her everyday routine. I would have accepted her suggestion of a restaurant, if it weren't that I hadn't been paid yet, and I didn't want her to pick up the check.

'Let's eat here, it's less trouble,' I said, following her to the dining room. She made herself busy laying the table, taking cutlery and plates from the solemn mahogany dresser topped in marble that now reminded me of the funerary monuments I had seen that morning. Then she darted in and out of the kitchen, to bring the food she had laid out on serving dishes. My mother seemed to enjoy the task, the ephemeral feeling of family life.

'Will you get the water and the wine, Martín?' she asked, and I went to the refrigerator. There was a half-full bottle of white wine, so I checked if there was another one on the shelf. My mother liked white wine.

'Help yourself, darling,' she said as we sat down at table, her hands busy with a number of medicine bottles in a small basket beside her plate.

'You take too many pills.' I knew my comments didn't make any difference. Hypochondria was one of her ersatz occupations.

'These are homeopathic medicines. Inés told me about this wonderful man, and I went to see him. They are quite harmless, you see.'

Probably they were, but there were enough pills in her room and her bathroom to fill a drug-store. She got them through a number of doctors, or through the local pharmacist, who turned a blind eye to regular customers without a prescription.

'You don't need them,' I insisted.

'Oh, leave me alone, Martín. Tell me, how is work?'

'Fine. I'm very busy at the moment. There's a lot to do.'

'I hear Lucas got the *sucesión* of Eduardo Ramos. He should do well out of that one.'

Eduardo Ramos was a very big landowner who had died recently. My boss was in charge of his estate, and I was assisting him, but I knew better than to tell my mother. Who owned what was a favourite topic during her canasta afternoons, and she would pester me for all the details if I gave her the chance. Any confidentiality would only last until her next phone call to a friend.

'There's something I want to ask you,' I said instead. 'I went to Recoleta today, to see our vault.'

'What an extraordinary thing to do. Why?'

'I just felt like it. There was a child's coffin there, and I can't work out whose it could be.'

'I don't know. Some child who died long ago, probably. Many did in those days.'

'It can't be that long ago,' I said. 'It's in the lower crypt.'

My mother raised her wine glass, but it was empty. I filled it again.

'Do you mean the casket there?' she asked abruptly.

'Yes.' I waited for her answer. My mother reached for her cigarettes instead, although she had hardly eaten anything. She fumbled at the packet, drew out a cigarette and lit it, then watched the smoke drift into the faceted drops of the chandelier lumbering above us.

'It's not a child's,' she said eventually. 'It contains your father's ashes.'

I was stunned. Cremation was unheard of among people like my parents. It wasn't done, and the Church forbade it.

'Francis wanted to be cremated, and I respected his wish. He didn't care for religion,' she explained. 'We had disagreements about it. We didn't see eye to eye on everything – but no couple ever does, I suppose. Your father wasn't someone who kept his views private, which made life difficult at times.'

For once, she wasn't slipping into hagiography.

'Did you have lots of arguments then?' I asked, to encourage her to continue.

'No, of course not, although Francis could be very possessive. He always made a great fuss if he saw me dancing or talking to another man for any length of time, even if he didn't really mean it. I suppose he thought that was what he should do. It must be hard for people your age to understand how trapped we could feel when we were young, because you are free to come and go as you please.'

Her last comment could have been a mild reproach to Miguel and me for moving away from home. I ignored it, because I was more interested in whatever she might say about her former life. My father's domestic idiosyncrasies were more significant to me than her usual accounts of worldly glory.

'Maybe you gave him reason to be jealous,' I said, hoping that my preposterous suggestion would flatter her, but it seemed to have the opposite effect.

'That's ridiculous!' she replied, obviously angry. Her face was slightly flushed. 'You can't understand, because things were very different in those days, Martín. I had to ask for permission to do anything before I married. It was nice to be able to talk, or be with friends without having to explain. Sometimes Francis couldn't accept that.'

'Did you have any other boyfriends before you married?' I had heard her mention names of boys she went out with in her youth, without making it very clear if they had mattered to her or not.

'Of course,' she said with pride. 'But they weren't that special to me, and then I met your father. I was nineteen when we married, so I didn't give the others much chance really.'

'What about him?'

'What do you mean?'

'Did *papá* have a serious girlfriend before he met you?' Nothing could be more natural than a son's good-natured curiosity about his father's youth, and yet I couldn't look my mother in the eye. I felt naked in front of her, as if the true reason behind my question was as obvious to her as it was to me.

'I suppose he did. One didn't talk about things like that. It wasn't necessary.'

I knew she was lying. It was frustrating to be so close to the question that I really wanted to ask, and yet not be able to ask it directly.

'I met someone in Paris, at the embassy, who said he knew *papá* many years ago, before you married,' I lied in turn. 'He told me they met at the time *papá* was in love with Delia Lagos, or so everybody thought.'

Her hand clenched her napkin, then she sat back and glared at me.

'*You* met Delia Lagos in Paris, Martín. Everybody knows about it. She must have told you that herself, and it's just the kind of story that whore would invent. I don't expect anything from some-one like her. But you . . . becoming a cheap gigolo . . . She's my age . . . It's filthy. How could you do it? That bitch!'

It was so unlike her to use rough language that I was dumb-founded; then, once I realized she had known about Delia and me all along, my rage rose to match hers. I had suspected it, and

Lucas's innocent remark and Charlie's blunt question should have been more than enough confirmation. *Everybody* knew. My anger was ignited by my embarrassment, and fanned by the realization that my mother – and the others – assumed I had fallen for Delia because of her money.

'Delia didn't tell me anything,' I ranted back. 'You hate her because she has everything and you have nothing. Or maybe because *papá* married you once he couldn't marry her . . .' I wanted to hurt my mother as much as she had hurt me, badly enough to bring up my father's love for Delia, something that would have been unthinkable a moment ago.

She jumped to her feet, her chair crashing to the floor.

'Only Delia could have invented that rubbish! That woman . . .' Words became trapped in her mouth in her rush to spit them out. '. . . that woman ruined my life, and now she wants to ruin yours! She's capable of anything! What did she tell you about me? It's all lies!'

My first reaction was to lash out at her with equal venom. Hating Delia was my own private right, not hers. My mother's anger made more sense to me than her words. My father had chosen her, not Delia; she hadn't been the aggrieved party. Nobody had ruined her life; bad luck and her own limitations were responsible for that. She was blaming Delia because she always blamed somebody else. I thought of telling her that I had found the letters, as proof of my father's love for Delia, only to realize I couldn't. It was too humiliating – for her *and* for me. I couldn't help my own confused feelings about Delia. I couldn't ignore them either. I didn't want to compound my misery by adding my mother's hysterical – and quite probably invented – accusations to my own grievances.

'I don't know what the hell you're talking about. Delia never told me anything about *papá* or you,' I said much more quietly.

Too engrossed in her own fury, my mother had not heard me, and she carried on talking without interruption. '. . . Delia always hated me, she hated that I was happy and she wasn't. She ruined everybody's life because she envied us! She only wanted you because she wanted to hurt me . . . !'

I couldn't make sense of anything she said, but I didn't want to ask for an explanation either. I had had enough; I would not listen to her for another moment. I stood up.

'It's better if I go now, *mamá*. I'm sorry I upset you.'

I could hear her sobbing quietly behind me as I left the room. I went to the entrance hall, put on my overcoat, and waited. I didn't want to leave without saying goodbye, but I wanted to give her time to calm down. Eventually she joined me.

'We must forget this conversation, Martín. We have both said ridiculous things.'

'I know. It's over anyway,' I replied, meaning Delia and me. I wanted her to know it.

'I suppose we all do things we regret when we are young,' my mother replied. 'Old stories should be left alone. Let's not mention it ever again. It's not worth it.'

It was sensible advice, and it was evident that she felt as spent and contrite about our argument as I did. My mother embraced me; I felt as safe and secure in her arms as if I was a child again. We stayed like that for a moment, then I kissed her good night, and left quickly.

Six

I tried to dismiss the whole episode as an inevitable emotional explosion on my side; my visit to the family vault had affected me more than I wanted to admit. As for my mother, '*What did she tell you about me? It's all lies!*' was the kind of melodramatic contradiction she was prone to when on emotional overdrive. I had incited her to talk about the past, when I should have sensed the danger myself. The letters in Paris should have been enough warning to leave it alone. My father had left Delia for her, and they were close friends at the time. There must have been anger and jealousy on both sides, even if my mother had won in the end. There were obvious reasons to explain them. Delia was not only far more beautiful, she had money, and an unassailable position in the world; all the things that mattered enormously to my mother, and that she had lost. Even when they were young, Delia was everything my mother had been trained to aspire to. Envy could never have been too far below the surface.

My maternal grandfather made crackers. And biscuits, too. For the last twenty years of his life, at some time of the day or other, most Argentines reached for the orange and bottle-green packets bearing his name, churned out in an incessant stream from a block-long factory in Barracas, the industrial suburb where he had settled when he arrived from Spain. He must have been a very driven man, and I had heard he was proud of all that he had achieved: his company, his grand house on Libertad Street, in the best part of town, and his wife, who died a few years after him, but not before she sold a business she didn't have the slightest interest in. At least she was sensible enough not to attempt to run it; whenever

I despaired of my mother's shallowness, I had to remind myself of stories she had told me about her own mother, whose relentless pursuit of 'the right people' was her lifetime's preoccupation. It still reached us from beyond the grave, like some B-movie curse.

My grandmother must have been pleased by her daughter's friendship with Delia and – had she still been alive then – I guess she would have enjoyed my parents' brief social glory, when my mother came into her money after her marriage, only to blow it away in a few, memorable years. Everything had been so short-lived, so fickle, and finally so irrelevant, that I didn't want to dwell on it again now. Whatever slights there had been between Delia and her *nouveau-riche* friend Isabel thirty years ago shouldn't concern me.

They affected me because Delia was involved. Delia had been selfish about my father, and equally selfish in her attitude towards me. She knew, while I was ignorant. If there was blame to be apportioned, it was hers, because she had refused to answer my questions, to either confirm or deny my fear that she and my father had been lovers.

'. . . The benefit of the Term is vested in the *Arrendatario* for all the residue thereof now unexpired subject to the payment of the rents reserved by and the performance and observance of the covenants on the part of the *Arrendatario* and the conditions contained in the Contract. Provided always . . .'

'Hang on . . . Read that again, Martín,' Gonzalez said, leaning back in his chair. His hands clasped behind his head, his feet on his desk, he had been listening to my reading of an old land tenancy arrangement for the last twenty minutes.

'. . . The benefit of the Term is vested in . . .' I started for the third time. I was bored enough by now to stop hearing my own voice inside my head. It came to me as if it were somebody else's voice in a restaurant, clear enough to be heard but not interesting enough to make me pay attention.

'. . . and the performance and observance of the covenants on the part . . .' I knew it was about to happen. I could see it coming. I couldn't do anything to stop it.

'You've started to read too quickly. Slow down,' Gonzalez said, and then I saw the image. It was inside my head, but as sharp as the typed papers in front of my eyes. A man's hand and wrist, caressing a woman's breast. The woman was Delia. The man was my father.

'In consideration of the covenants . . .' Now I saw my father's back, and Delia's fingertips clawing his shoulders as she bit his neck. '. . . During the whole of the said Term hereby granted . . .' His hands held her hips. Her flesh dimpled under his grip. Her legs and his became entangled as they rolled on the crumpled sheet. '. . . at the relevant date of review as determined in accordance with the foregoing provisions . . .'

'Not *so* fast,' Gonzalez snapped. 'You're mumbling. I want you to read loudly and clearly.'

The kaleidoscope of hands on hands, lips on lips, breasts, legs and arms whirled inside my head. The images crackled like lightning. I knew they would be gone long before my heart settled again into its normal rhythm. But those hands, those legs, the man's body I saw so clearly in those jumbled-up partial images, as if it were a rough-cut shown at speed, couldn't be my father's. I'd never seen them. I didn't know what they looked like. The watch on that wrist was mine. I was wearing it now. It had been his, but now it was mine. The way the skin creased over those knuckles, the dip between those shoulder blades, the shape of those fingers, were so clear to me because they were my own, and yet I knew it wasn't me making love to Delia. It was my father, and I was watching the scene through the illusion of my memory.

'. . . to the Owner and any tenant of the Owner and any other person for the time being entitled to the same and free uninterrupted passage . . .' I flung the papers on the desk.

'I'm sorry. I'll be back in a moment,' I said, rushing to the door. In the rest room, I locked myself in a cubicle, and lit a cigarette. It was the most private place around. I knew it from other times when these images had come to me. I was familiar with the cycle by now. I just needed a few moments on my own for the process of denial to start, when I would once again run over the dog-eared repertoire of reasons why it would have been impossible for them to have made love. Then I would be ready to carry on, hoping this would be the last time I would see those atrocious hallucinations.

I didn't want to know if they had been lovers. I didn't want to hate Delia. I didn't want to love her either. I wanted to forget the whole thing, to put her out of my mind forever. I wanted what I had taken for granted before: a life without pain.

'I missed you,' I said. Lying naked next to me in my bed, Patricia smiled.

'You don't need to lie, Martín,' she said. 'And you don't have to worry either, I'm on the pill now. My doctor just got it from America.' Patricia announced it in the kind of falsely casual tone she would have used to explain that whatever she wore was from one of those new, ultra-fashionable boutiques that had started to multiply in the best parts of the city.

Her candour should have pleased me. Patricia was letting me know that she didn't count on my commitment, or expect it. Frankness was an unwelcome guest, though, at least for me. I had gone through the motions to bring about our reconciliation, when in fact all I was trying to do was prove to myself that I was free from Delia. I had failed. Not in the physical sense, although it would have been more logical if I had. I had gone through sex with Patricia almost as an out-of-body experience, a spectator to my own pleasure, such as it was.

'I'm not lying,' I said feebly, trying to inveigle conviction from self-deception.

'You're a romantic, Martín, that's what's so nice and so boring about you.'

Patricia got out of bed and sat at the table, her back to me. After rummaging through her bag she produced a brush, a mirror, and a small bottle of white, thick liquid; her fingers were busy re-anchoring her cascading hairpiece. Then it took her some time to stick the corners of her fake eyelashes back in place, by careful application of the glue from the bottle. Once she had finished reinstating her Bardot-inspired, doll-like look, Patricia stood up and faced me.

'I might give you a proper mirror for Christmas, if you're still around,' she said.

'I'm not going anywhere,' I said.

She gave me a look. 'You certainly weren't here tonight,' she replied.

'We need to check the records in Rawson, even if it turns out to be a waste of time. Ask Amelia to book you a flight, Martín,' my boss said.

He was talking about an estate we were handling, which included a large parcel of land in Patagonia. The original property had been divided between our clients' father and his brothers. None of them had cared very much about it in their time because the land had been a wilderness, but now their descendants were arguing about the boundary lines agreed at the time of the subdivision. The government had announced that a large dam would be built nearby, and irrigation could turn the disputed area into valuable farming land.

My job included the kind of dreary tasks nobody else at the office would do if they could help it, and a trip to Rawson fell under that category. For once I didn't mind. The city was only three hundred kilometres away from the farm where my brother lived, a manageable distance in the vast spaces of the country, and I hadn't seen Miguel for more than a year. I had last written to him after I moved into my own place. To my surprise, he had written back, suggesting I visit him there. Now I decided to take up his offer.

Miguel seemed pleased by my call. We agreed that he would collect me from my hotel in Rawson on Friday afternoon. I phoned my mother next, and told her about my trip.

'You can give me whatever you want to send Miguel on Sunday,' I said. It was a good way of acknowledging that I would be coming to see her as usual, in spite of our argument, and I could hear the relief in her voice when she said she would put some things aside to give me.

'Do you want to borrow the car to go there?' my mother asked while we were having coffee. She had tried her best during dinner to make up for the fiasco of the previous Sunday, bombarding me with offers of help, but her understanding of distances on a national scale was on par with her sense of distances in town. Anything that was more than fifteen minutes away from her apartment was *terra incognita*.

'I can't drive two thousand kilometres both ways in three days, *mamá*. Thanks for the offer, but it's a crazy idea.'

'You haven't asked me for the car recently,' she insisted.

'Because I don't need it,' I lied. I missed the freedom a car gave me, and I was about to buy a beaten-up Renault from a secretary at the office, borrowing money from my bank at impossible rates, in the hope that inflation would take care of it.

'You need a car. I'll get you one, if you can find something that's not too expensive.'

It was so typical of her. One moment she would complain about the electricity bill with real anguish, the next she would come up with some ludicrous suggestion, as if she was still living in the days when, if in doubt whether to buy one fur coat or another, she would take both.

'You're more generous than you can afford,' I said. 'You've done enough for me, and I really don't need a car.'

'I have the money,' she insisted. 'One of my tenants offered to buy the apartment from me. He paid a good price.'

It was more likely that she had been ripped off, as usual. The only asset my mother had managed to save from her inheritance was an apartment building nearby. She had sold most of the apartments over the years, and by now she had only two or three left. The rents had been frozen when Perón changed the law, a long time ago. Although my mother never discussed her income in detail, I suspected that it had become a pittance over the years. I wondered what efforts of thrift and ingenuity she had employed to keep up appearances, and for how long she would be able to do so.

My concern for her surprised me. I had always seen my mother either as a source of love and comfort, or as an irritation. I had never *worried* about her. Now that I didn't live with her, I could see her vulnerability, her loneliness. If we hadn't been sitting at the table in her dining room, at the scene of our argument a week ago, I might have steered the conversation towards the wisdom of finding a suitable man and marrying again, but any reference to remarriage inevitably raised the spectre of her previous one, a subject that had become too sensitive. I felt as if echoes of our quarrel still lingered in the room.

'Keep the money. You'll need it,' I replied, more gently than usual.

Someone in the last century said that if a man wants to know how it feels to seriously consider suicide, he should spend a week in a rural town in Argentina. It was a view I could understand as night fell over Miguel's house, and we weren't even in a town. We were a hundred kilometres away from the nearest village, on the edge of the great Patagonian plain, turned by the Andes cordillera into a wind tunnel for the gales blowing from the distant ocean. During the drive from Rawson, I had plenty of time to stare at the arid landscape that family mythology had made sound as if once it had been ours from the mountains to the sea; a land harsh enough to justify never going there, received and lost without ever being seen. I admired my brother, with the indulgent admiration of those who know better than to involve themselves in mad enterprises. The wind made the house creak day and night, like a boat on a turbulent sea.

We sat by the fireplace after dinner; the burning coal glowed more brightly than the electric light, which was at the mercy of an unreliable generator in a shed outside. The large whiskies Miguel had poured were more effective than the fire in keeping us warm.

'You look good. There must be a bit of *indio* in you to be able to live here,' I said facetiously, but it was true that Miguel looked well. He had inherited our mother's narrow face, her sharp nose, and her dark brown-black hair, but there was something different about his eyes now, a calm unlike the nervous flickering stare I remembered.

My brother smiled in acknowledgement of my compliment, and I felt a jolt of recognition. The eyes in my dream were Miguel's. I was almost certain that the half-seen face didn't *feel* to me as if it had been Miguel's, and yet those eyes were unmistakably his. Not the expression though. I had witnessed Miguel's anger many times in the past: sometimes aimed at me, at our mother less frequently, but I never saw in his eyes that flash of pure, incandescent rage I had seen in my dream.

'I'm happy here. I like the place, crazy as it might sound,' he replied. 'I needed to get away.' He didn't add 'from her', because it wasn't necessary. In a way, Miguel had had an easier relationship with our mother than me: they never argued, but they never agreed, either. I used to think Miguel resented what he saw as her preference for me, the younger child, which wasn't true. She would have doted on him too, if he had given her the opportunity.

'How is *mamá*?'

It wasn't a question he would even have asked before. Certainly not during his last two or three years at home, when Miguel had been as circumspect during meals as if he had been a lodger, when my mother's monologue kept the semblance of family conversation at table, occasionally livened up by my own adolescent contributions. I found my mother unbearable at times; most of the time, in fact, as I got older. But there were moments when it was different, when I knew I loved her, and I suppose she knew it too. We *related* to each other, in our own imperfect way, while Miguel had an accommodation with her, like people forced to share a hotel table during holidays.

'She's fine. Or as fine as can be. She's sent you a sweater by the way, I've got it in my suitcase.'

'They're usually too small,' he smiled. 'I'm glad you're here, Martín.'

So was I, because I found it much easier to talk to him now. Distance had blunted the divisions between us. It seemed hard to imagine that there had been a time when Miguel had fitted a padlock on his closet doors to stop me from wearing his clothes. There was more to the change than distance or the mere passage of time: we had become different people. The old feeling of envy stirred fleetingly. There had been a sense of purpose to the new direction in Miguel's life: it had been his plan and his choice to come here. He had been in control, while my life seemed to drift along, shaped by people or events almost in spite of myself.

'I had an odd conversation with her,' I said, and told him about my visit to the cemetery. 'I was too young to remember anything about *papá*'s death. Did you know he was cremated?'

'No, because I didn't go to his funeral. They had been away, then one day *mamá* came back and told me that he had died in the country.'

'How did you feel?' Obvious as his answer would be, I wanted to hear Miguel talk about that time in our lives. The experience had been real for him, while I had always had to imagine it in retrospect. It had been one of many respects in which I had resented Miguel's age advantage over me. Those thirty months became insignificant once we grew up, but they had seemed such an unfair gulf before. He always had new school uniforms, which I had inherited. I envied him his dental braces as a badge of seniority, and then I envied that he was free of them by the time I got mine. Miguel owned or learned everything before I did. Best of all, he *remembered*. A goal he scored when we played football at somebody else's garden, his smirk when he was able to take both hands off the handlebar while I chased after him on my smaller bicycle, branded with the shame of stabilizers, none of this made me feel so insignificant, so incomplete during our childhood as his occasional, casual references to something our father might have said or done. The fact that our mother usually contradicted his memories, or dismissed them as imaginary, made little difference to me. He remembered our father, and I did not.

That feeling of admiration for his knowledge, and the inevitable sense of missed experience it triggered in me, was probably why, when we were small, I never asked him for information he didn't volunteer. Eventually, my affected lack of curiosity became spontaneous. Our mother's reminiscences of early family life seemed far more interesting than any of Miguel's occasional contributions. Now my small, almost trivial question threw me back to that time, and I felt a mixture of agitation and curiosity, as if we were in short trousers again, and he had agreed to disclose the facts of life.

'Desperately sad, and very angry. I felt he had gone by choice, as if he had opted out and left me. You're not very sensible at that age, I suppose. *Mamá* was very upset too.'

'Why do you sound as if she shouldn't have been?' I asked, and then wished I hadn't. I wasn't questioning my brother's accuracy; I was merely surprised by the edge I detected in his tone. However, many of our arguments in the past had been sparked by some remark of his about our mother, and my automatic defence of her.

Miguel stood up, scooped coal with a small shovel from a cut-down oil drum by his side, and dumped it in the fire, then he sat down again and reached for his glass.

'I didn't mean that. You were asking about how I felt. I remember her crying all the time,' he said, staring into his drink.

My curiosity was no longer strong enough to overcome my discomfort at a subject we'd never discussed before. Sharing confidences was too new an experience for both of us. As with pre-adolescent discussions on sex, perhaps it was preferable to stop once the gist of the information had been exchanged. I reached for the bottle of Chivas Regal and refilled our glasses.

'Good whisky. Where on earth do you get it here?' I said.

'We are south of the *paralelo*. You can get whatever you want. Didn't you notice the "boats" in Rawson when we drove through?'

The *paralelo* was the latest in the long series of sporadic – and doomed – attempts to entice people to move from Buenos Aires to Patagonia, this time by abolishing the prohibitive duties on imports to the area south of the forty-second parallel. Nobody had moved, but the availability of smuggled goods in the rest of the country had improved spectacularly. 'Boats', as American cars festooned in chrome and bristling with lights and fins were called in everyday language, had become a familiar sight in cities a long way north of the *paralelo*, and were no longer surrounded by admiring kids.

'There's something I want to tell you,' he said. 'I've met a girl in Rawson. She's called Margarita.'

Miguel had never talked about any girls before. When we lived together, our mother or I made our own assumptions on the frequency of phone calls from or to a particular girl, or their eventual tapering off, but he never mentioned anyone as special.

'Great. Who is she?'

'She's a trainee doctor at the local hospital. Don't say anything to *mamá*, OK? She'll drive me crazy with questions about her parents, and then she'll be horrified. I don't want her on the phone every day.'

'Are you getting married then?' I tried to sound enthusiastic. I knew I felt happy for Miguel. I didn't begrudge him his happiness, other than it heightened my own feeling of loss.

'We haven't talked about it, so there's no need to complicate anything – don't make too much of it. We are good together, and that's all that matters now. What about you? What have you been up to recently?'

It was a perfectly normal question to ask. For his standards, Miguel had been remarkably open with me. Now he was giving me the chance to reciprocate, to unburden myself of the misery of the last few weeks. 'There was someone, but it was a mistake,' I said. 'Luckily it didn't mean much.'

'Is she someone I know?'

'I don't think so . . .' I couldn't back out now. I had to give Miguel a name – and then I would have to tell him about Delia. I would have to tell him about the letters.

'Maybe you do,' I went on. 'It's Patricia, Queenie Rousselet's sister. You used to go out with a friend of Queenie's, didn't you?'

I managed to keep the conversation going. I don't think Miguel noticed how shabbily deceitful I felt. Like Delia, I had withheld the truth from somebody who trusted me. Shame had been my reason. For the first time I wondered if it had been hers too.

'But what did Miguel have to say? Don't tell me that you travelled all that way and then you said nothing to each other.' Even over the phone, I could hear my mother's impatient disappointment after my account of the visit. I had only been back in my apartment for ten minutes when she called me. She must have been trying before I came in.

'Didn't you ask him anything?' she insisted.

I wondered if she had some inkling because she had spoken to Miguel already. My mother was good at reading between the lines.

'About what?'

'About how he is, of course. Is he happy there?'

'He's fine, *mamá*. You know what he's like, he never says much. We just talked about old times, mainly. He asked about you, of course.'

'He did?' Now she sounded pleased. 'I hope he's happy there.

Sometimes I worry so much about him being all alone. I can't understand why he chose to bury himself in Patagonia, among all those sheep. It would have been so easy to find him a job at an *estancia* near Buenos Aires, I could have asked any of my friends. By the way, would you mind coming to dinner next Wednesday instead of Sunday? Pepe and Fina have invited me to the country. I'm leaving on Thursday, and I won't be back until Monday, so –'

'I can't,' I interrupted her. 'I'm busy that evening.' I didn't want to establish the precedent of variable dates for my visits. I would end up seeing her more often than I intended.

'You must have another evening free. I'd like to see you, darling,' she pleaded.

'I'm sorry. I'm really busy.' I knew I was hurting her, and yet I couldn't stop myself. I didn't want to own up to the fact that my life was even emptier than my mother's.

'I'll see you the following Sunday then. Bye, darling.' She tried to sound casual, which only made me feel worse.

'Second gear is a bit tricky to engage, but you'll get the hang of it after a while,' Cristina said. 'I never had any real trouble. If you ever need a garage, I use one near here that's very good. Their card is inside the manual,' she added ominously, although it didn't dent my enthusiasm. I wanted a car, and her price was all I could afford. With the papers in my pocket and keys in hand, I climbed into the driver's seat. The doors rattled slightly as I speeded down the quiet, cobbled streets of Palermo. The tramway tracks were still in place, adding to the torment of the shock absorbers.

Cristina lived in the older, humbler part of the district, far from *Jardín Zoológico* and the park. The traffic thickened around Plaza Italia, where conscripts from the nearby barracks milled about the statue of Garibaldi or gathered under the palm trees, in the dim hope of picking up girls for their day out. By the time I skirted the square, I had gone through enough stops and starts to master the gear-shift, as Cristina had predicted. It's going to be all right, I thought, my optimism enhanced by the sight of crowds jostling to get into the zoo, its gates flanked by the usual sellers of popcorn, toys, caramelized apples, and multi-coloured balloons from huge tricycles that were converted into mobile stalls. I lost sight of the Russian domes of the parrot house as I turned into Avenida Las Heras, where the crowns of the huge *tipas* trees formed a canopy over the wide road, and headed for my next appointment.

Ever since my trip to Patagonia, I was at work early every morning, stayed late every evening, and ate lunch at my desk. I wouldn't be able to replicate Miguel's perfect isolation, but I could try. I didn't want to see anyone from my usual circle. They knew about Delia, and I wasn't in the mood for sympathetic criticism, or locker-room curiosity. Their interest was a reminder of what I was trying to forget.

I had arranged to have lunch at a schoolfriend's home that Saturday. We hadn't seen each other since his wedding a year ago. Although we were in different classes at school, Raúl and I had played rugby in the same team, a temporary common purpose that had created a bond less deep but more enduring than interests or views, because it could survive on our very sporadic reunions. Raúl's family owned a couple of pasta shops, and his wife was training to be a dentist. They weren't the kind of people who would know or care about sentimental gossip concerning the glorious Delia Lagos and myself.

'You should think about marriage, Martín. You don't know what you're missing,' Raúl said, reaching for his wife's hand once she sat down, back from the kitchen, and had laid a large bowl on the table.

'I'd have to find somebody like Ana,' I said. She smiled, and began to serve chocolate mousse onto dessert plates.

'I can't be the only woman worth marrying. You must have met somebody you really like by now,' she said.

'It's never the right person. Or maybe I go about it in the wrong way,' I replied, glancing at my watch. The happiness of newly married couples forms an invisible wall around them, as flawless as the china on their table or the furniture in their rooms. You are not really there from their point of view, or at least that was how I felt.

'How's work?' I asked. We had talked about my job before lunch, so it was time to reciprocate. Raúl was an accountant, and he worked for a farming company. I wasn't going to hear anything that would interest me much.

'Very good. The company is doing well, and it's not a big office, so I have more responsibility than I would elsewhere. My plan is to stay with them for another year, and then I'll try to find a job with one of the car companies in Córdoba, or join one of the big American accountancy firms here. That's the way things are going, and –'

'I can't remember who owns your company,' I interrupted him before he could get too involved in the boring details. Raúl was the kind of man who planned his life well in advance.

'It's a *Sociedad Anónima*, but it's wholly owned by the Lagos family, in fact. You must have heard of them. Keep it quiet though, it's supposed to be a secret,' he reminded me, in the tones of someone who was divulging inside information for the sake of friendship.

'Of course.' I enjoyed the chance to talk about Delia casually, as if I was hearing about someone I didn't know, the pathetic fiction that there was an infinity of indifference between her and me. 'Are they the sons of Ambrosio Lagos?' I wasn't giving anything away. Ambrosio's name was too well known, even for people our age, but I used the word 'sons' deliberately, to avoid any suspicion that I knew Delia, or that I had even heard of her.

'There is a son called Sebastian. We don't deal with him at all though. His business affairs are handled by his sister Delia, who has his power of attorney.'

I remembered the handsome young boy in velvet breeches and a crisp white shirt, in the portrait at Delia's house. I hadn't asked her about the portrait in detail during our first morning together, because I was so eager to appear cool and worldly, and then it had become part of the background. I could have asked her a few weeks later, when we were watching TV that night, if I hadn't been so taken up by my own concerns. Now I wondered why she hadn't mentioned her brother – but then I hadn't mentioned Miguel either. Delia and I had entered into a silent pact to keep reality at bay.

'She lives in Europe,' Raúl went on. 'My boss talks to her on the phone, or goes to see her every once in a while. I hope it will be my turn soon, I wouldn't mind a free trip. He told me it's been like that ever since the old man died, and that nobody's seen Sebastian Lagos for twenty years. He had a very bad accident, a car crash I believe, and has stayed out of sight ever since.'

'Why? That's pretty unusual,' I said, struggling to sound no more than politely interested. Delia's silence was less explicable than I had thought.

'I don't know. Maybe he's badly disfigured, or he became a vegetable after the accident or something. My boss told me he was very weird anyway; didn't get on with his father at all. Lagos's wife was not all there,' Raúl explained, touching his temple. 'The old man was worried that his son took after her, and that Sebastian would blow the whole lot once he was gone. You have no idea how rich Ambrosio Lagos was; he owned any amount of land, and he invested abroad very cleverly. He arranged the power of attorney for his daughter a short while before he died.'

'Does Sebastian live in Europe too?' I asked, fumbling for any question that would keep Raúl talking. He seemed to enjoy the chance to show his knowledge, and I wanted him to carry on, to give me time for my own thoughts. I had justified Delia's silence about her brother because I hadn't talked about Miguel to her – but he wasn't a cripple. He wasn't dependent on me.

'My boss thought that he was abroad, in a clinic, then somebody else told me that Sebastian lived on one of the *estancias* where he had worked, at least while he was there. It's not one of the estates we manage, but then the Lagoses own more *estancias* than you have hairs on your head, or at least than I do.' Raúl patted his receding hairline. 'Why are you so interested in the guy? He's just a sucker who crashed his car.'

'I'm not that interested. You started the story in the first place,' I replied. I sounded casual enough, because my concern wasn't about Sebastian. I was struck by the fact that Delia hadn't mentioned him at all, and Raúl couldn't give me the answer.

'You always go on and on about your work, darling,' Ana intervened, then she reached for the bowl.

'Would you like some more mousse?' she offered.

*   *   *

I stayed for another half an hour or so before I left, exchanging promises of frequent reunions in the future that I had little intention of keeping. I was glad to be on my own again, to have the chance to digest what I had heard.

I wasn't worried about Sebastian Lagos. Tragic as his story might have been, I didn't know him. It was Delia's behaviour that really troubled me. She hadn't mentioned Sebastian in any way. Her attitude would have been reasonable if there had been nothing to say about Sebastian, if he had been a typical landowner, breeding cattle and children with equal enthusiasm. Now I wondered if she hadn't cared for or trusted me enough to tell me about him. I had admired Delia's openness about our affair, when it might be that it didn't matter very much to her. It is easy to be frank about the irrelevant. Maybe she was only secretive about important things. My only comfort in the slow, grinding process of turning our time together into a memory, day by day, was the thought that Delia could be sharing it. I couldn't bear the thought that I might have meant much less to her than she had meant to me.

Sundays were always tricky. When I got up the next morning, and saw the leaden sky and the rain pelting down, I faced the fact that I had an empty day ahead of me. Even the prospect of dinner with my mother would have made a difference, if she hadn't been away.

The ghostly morning light made my apartment look smaller and gloomier than usual, and the movie shows didn't start until two o'clock. It was raining too hard for me to bother to go to the kiosk and get a newspaper, so I checked the programmes in Saturday's edition instead. As I spread out the broadsheet pages, I noticed an envelope I had left on the table. Lucas Marquez had given it to me that week.

'I've got something for you, Martín,' he had said. 'It's for Isabel and you, in fact. I hope you can come. Susana asked me to bring the invitation here, you know what the post is like,' he sighed before rushing off. It was an invitation to a cocktail party at the *Museo de Arte Decorativo*, to be given by the Friends of the Museum the following week. Lucas's wife was on the committee. It was the kind of event my mother relished, and to which she tried to drag my brother or me, with little success. This time it would be difficult for me to back out. Although the invitation was largely a token of friendship towards my mother, Lucas was my boss.

I made a half-hearted attempt at tidying up the apartment by pushing things out of sight, then I showered and shaved. As I got my clothes out of the cupboard, I noticed that I was running out of shirts. There were only two left in the pile, and my laundry wouldn't be ready for collection at the *lavadero* until Thursday. One of the clean shirts had French cuffs, which was the reason I hardly ever wore it. I would have to now, and I had left my cufflinks at my mother's. I could stop there to retrieve them and leave her invitation, on my way to the movie house.

I arrived at her place just after midday. I had to turn the lights on, because all the windows were shuttered. Although she lived on a sixth floor, my mother worried about burglaries long before they became a fact of life in Buenos Aires. Her wall safe was in her bedroom, behind a picture. I turned the combination left and right until I heard the familiar click, and opened the door. There were only a few small jewellery boxes inside, holding pieces that had survived her financial débâcle either because they were not worth selling or because she cherished them especially. I removed the green leather box containing my father's cufflinks and studs, my share of his valuables when my mother divided them among us on Miguel's eighteenth birthday.

Once I had locked the safe, I rested the invitation against the telephone on my mother's bedside table, then I scribbled a message on her notepad, explaining that I would meet her at the museum. My eye fell on the books she kept by her bed, between bronze bookends in the shape of monkeys, which used to intrigue me as a child. They held a couple of romantic novels and the latest *Angelique*, as usual. There was also a small volume, bound in brown leatherette, perhaps more relevant to her than any of the others. It was the Social Guide, which my mother used as her telephone book.

I pulled it out and flicked quickly through the pages, until I reached the 'L'. There were only two Lagoses listed: *Lagos, Delia María – en Europa*, and *Lagos, Sebastian Ambrosio – Estancia*

'San Octavio', Estación Las Palmeras, Provincia de Buenos Aires.

Raúl had been right. Sebastian was living somewhere in the country; another piece of the past had fitted into place. However, my discovery seemed far less exciting than the sight of Delia's name in print. Those few words, those few letters on a page, conjured up a riot of images at once. I saw her smile across the breakfast table, her profile outlined by the light from the screen at the movies. I saw our shadows ahead of us as we walked in the dappled shade of the chestnuts in the Tuileries. I saw the iridescent drops of water running down her beaming face in the sun as we swam in Capri.

And then I saw her eyes, drilling into me as she pushed me down the stairs. That terrifying face was Delia's too.

Seven

'How marvellous!' 'It's really marvellous!'

I kept hearing that word as I moved around the rooms of the museum and caught snippets of conversation amongst the crowd. They could have been talking about the building, although I doubted it. Most of them had been here many times, and some when it had been a private house, before the crash in the 1930s. It was much more likely that they were discussing the minutiae of everyday life. I was surrounded by people to whom everything seemed 'marvellous'.

I had been there for nearly an hour, and I wanted to leave. My purpose for the evening was accomplished once I had greeted Lucas and his wife, but it was wise to see my mother briefly before leaving. Otherwise she would grumble, since I had told her I would be here.

She wasn't in the grey drawing room, so I moved to the ballroom. Thick red ropes formed a protective cordon around the gold and cream panelling and the furniture, and it took me some time to make my way through the throng gathered in the middle of the room. The only evidence of people in the small rotunda beyond was a few empty glasses on the base of a marble statue, and the noise of conversation from the dining room next door. The crowd was thinner here, perhaps because the solemnity of the echoing marble room was too stultifying for gossip. I headed for the main hall again. The enormous space was packed end to end: it would take me too long to check the crowd. I unhooked a rope, climbed up a few steps of the wooden spiral stair to the upper gallery, and inspected the sea of heads below. I couldn't see my mother. Even if she was there, I had had enough by now.

On my way out, I noticed a small painting on the stone wall next to the door, one of many similar pictures around the room. It was a religious scene, and the figures stood against a pale gold background; the deep blue of the Virgin's cloak was as luminous as a summer evening sky. I looked at it for a moment, then read the small brass plate screwed into the bottom of the carved frame: *Crucifixion – Siennese School, XIVth Century. Donated by Delia and Sebastian Lagos, 1959.*

Initially, the sight of her name struck me as sharply as when I had seen it in the Social Guide at my mother's apartment, but there I had been on my own. Now I was surrounded by hundreds of people, and their noise broke the spell. I kept my eyes on the engraved words. I read Delia's name again and again, as if I were inoculating myself against a hitherto incurable disease. After a while, something about the inscription struck me as odd. I couldn't tell what it was – perhaps my own feeling of relief at being able to read Delia's name without any consequences. I stared at the painting for a moment, as if I had no greater motive than admiration of a beautiful thing, and then I moved away.

I collected my coat from the cloakroom, went down the staircase, and left the building. It was only when I walked across the forecourt towards the gates that I realized why the inscription had struck me as odd, beyond the initial surprise of finding names that were so much on my mind. Sebastian's accident had crippled him enough for Delia to have his power of attorney. It couldn't be that Sebastian's limitations were merely physical. He would have handled his own affairs in that case. The donation of the picture, nearly twenty years after his accident, had to be Delia's decision alone, and yet she had chosen to make it in their joint names, as if Sebastian had a say in the matter. The gift in their joint names was an attempt to keep up the illusion of a human being whose views had to be considered. Delia's silence was her protection, a fiction of normality created for her own sake. She was good at that.

The fresh evidence of her willingness to deny or conceal unpleasant truths confirmed my own experience of Delia as double-faced and self-serving in her attitude towards me. However small, the unexpected token of her hypocrisy restored my flimsy equilibrium, so dependent upon a sense that hers was the much greater wrong. It allowed my more immediate concerns to return to the present. My mother had missed tonight's event, which was unlike her. Only ill health would have kept her away. The Automobile Club was across the street. I could phone from there, but a combination of principles and common sense made me reconsider the idea. My apartment was ten minutes away. I would call her once I was back home.

'Martín? Is that you?'

I could tell from her sluggish voice that my mother had been drinking, or had taken tranquillizers. Perhaps both.

'Yes, it's me. I thought I'd see you at the museum. I left the invitation on your bedside table.'

'I didn't feel like going, and I didn't know you would be there. Why didn't you tell me? Maybe I would have gone then. You never tell me anything these days.'

I had told her I would be at the museum, but her complaint made me less concerned. It was just like my mother to twist the facts to suit herself. Recrimination made her sound normal again.

'I've been calling you. I need to see you,' she went on.

'Are you all right?'

'Yes. No, I'm not all right. You . . .'

'I'll be there in half an hour,' I said, and put the phone down. Cutting her short was the only way to stop the conversation from becoming a drama. She usually got worked up more easily on the telephone than in person.

I heard noises in the kitchen when I let myself into my mother's apartment. The faint sound of a radio confirmed that the maid was going about her routine, as reassuring a sign of normality as the smell of cooking wafting through the closed door to the hall. Whatever was wrong with my mother wasn't serious enough to upset the pattern of activity in her home.

I saw her as soon as I walked into the drawing room, because she was sitting in a corner, by the only lit lamp in the room. A bottle of Scotch, a bowl of ice, and a half-full tumbler of whisky were on a tray on the coffee table, a further indication that everything was as usual. Even her appearance gave no reason for concern; she was wearing a smart, simple black dress, her string of pearls and her good brooch were in place, and she had been to the hairdresser. I had expected to find her in bed, or at least in her dressing gown, since taking to her bed was her habitual reaction when something really troubled her. However, her face contradicted all other evidence of calm, matching the despondency I had heard in her voice.

'I was about to leave for the museum when I called Miguel. He told me,' she said point-blank, without giving me time to kiss her, or even offering her cheek.

'He told you what?'

'That you asked him about Francis's cremation. I didn't know you could be so careless, Martín. Your brother needs little encouragement to berate me.'

'He didn't seem angry when I asked him. What did he tell you?'

'Nothing, he just mentioned it, but I could tell he was upset with me. I asked you never to repeat what we discussed that night.'

She had asked me not to mention Delia again, or at least that was what I had understood. I couldn't see why the rest of the conversation should be unmentionable too.

'I'm sorry. I didn't realize you didn't want me to tell Miguel.'

'I don't want you to tell *anyone*. It was a very difficult decision for me. People would have been shocked if they knew about the cremation, even when it had been your father's wish. Religion matters to me, Martín. What I did was against the faith. That's why I don't want it discussed at all.'

Although it was a preoccupation I didn't share, I could understand her conundrum, particularly on a matter at odds with religious dogma *and* social convention.

'I'm sorry,' I repeated. 'I'll never tell anyone again, don't worry. I understand now.'

'What else did Miguel tell you?'

'About what?' Her curiosity annoyed me. She wasn't really interested, it was her way not to feel left out.

'About your father's death. I know you, Martín, once you start asking about something, you don't stop. I can't understand your morbid curiosity about something you don't even remember, but I'd rather you asked me than anyone else.'

'I only asked him how he felt at the time,' I replied. 'You never said much about *papá*'s death when we were children. Now I'd like to know more.'

'Has it ever crossed your mind that it has nothing to do with you, that I might not like talking about it? It was the most terrible time in my life. I don't want to dwell on it.'

I had justified Delia's silence about Sebastian on similar grounds. Sebastian was alive, though; my father had died more than twenty years ago. Not only time made a difference. I was willing to accept her reticence to talk about Delia and my father, or her animosity towards anything connected with that time in her life, because I shared them. But her claim to a right to silence on the details of his death was both unexpected and unjustifiable, and it upset me.

'There's something you must understand,' I replied, perhaps more brusquely than she deserved. 'He was your husband, but he was my father too. Even if you don't like talking about it, you must accept my interest in his life – or his death. You've never told us much about his actual death, in fact. All I know is that you were in the country, and he had a stroke. You've never said if he died immediately, if he was in pain, or anything that would give me some idea of his last hours. In any case, I asked Miguel, not you. I wasn't expecting him to tell you about our conversation, although I can't see why it should be unmentionable.'

'You're right. Of course you are entitled to ask,' she said, in a quieter, more conciliatory tone. 'It's natural for you to want to know. It all happened very suddenly. We were on a friend's yacht, going up the Paraná river, when your father collapsed. We were hours away from the nearest hospital, and it was late at night. Nobody could do anything, so I watched him die, unable to do anything for him. I hope he wasn't in pain. I felt so impotent, and then so guilty . . .'

'Why should you have felt guilty? It wasn't your fault,' I said.

'Guilt doesn't work like that, Martín. You can't explain it away. We docked in the morning, and Francis's body was taken to Rosario. I couldn't bear the thought of coming back to Buenos Aires with his coffin, and having to go through a wake, and the funeral, with you and your brother around. He was cremated in Rosario, and I published an announcement in the paper once I was back, saying that his funeral had taken place in private. I decided to honour Francis's wish, because it was the best I could do for him. His parents would have tried to stop me if I had attempted to do it here, and I had doubts myself. It was hard enough as it was; they didn't speak to me for months afterwards. Neither did Harry and Teresa. It was as if we had ceased to exist for Francis's family. I wondered then if they really were so hurt by the cremation, or if it was just an excuse to avoid having to help us. By the time you and Miguel were old enough to be told the truth, I had lived with the deception for too long to own up, and I thought that saying nothing was the best solution. I hope you'll forgive me.'

The fluency of her speech was at odds with her face. I wondered if she had prepared herself for this moment over the years, in the knowledge that she might have to explain her decision one day. Her words sounded rehearsed but her eyes were improvising, and I felt sad for her, sad and moved by her self-imposed remorse. My mother remained trapped in rules and conventions that time had withered into irrelevance. Reasons that had seemed so overwhelming to my grandparents and her then, or even now, were meaningless from my point of view.

'I'm glad you told me. There's nothing to forgive.' I thought we had talked enough about a subject we both felt uncomfortable with.

'It's a pity you didn't come to the museum; lots of your friends were there,' I said.

'Why don't you tell me about it over dinner? I'll let Malisa know that you're staying.' She stood up and went to the kitchen, walking as briskly as she usually did. Her worries – and the effect of the Scotch – seemed to have vanished.

It was a morning like any other. Better than most, in fact; as I sat in the bus on my way to work, no thoughts of any kind came to my mind. I had been lucky to get a window seat, so I idly watched the moving scene.

The man sitting next to me left his seat, which was immediately taken by one of the passengers standing in the aisle. He apologized as he brushed my elbow when he opened the briefcase on his lap, and I glanced at him out of the corner of my eye. He was more or less my age, and wore a grey suit more or less like mine. At first sight, the most significant difference between us would have been the transistor radio he took out of his briefcase. He slipped the earphone into place, fiddled with the tuning dial, and sat back.

After a minute or two, I heard the sound spilling out of the tiny earphone. It wasn't much clearer than the buzz of some insect at first, which made me more aware of the faint noise. Then I heard music, fragments of melody I couldn't place. I began to hum the tune. I stopped.

The man was listening to Marvin Gaye singing 'Hitch Hike'. It was the record I had bought in Paris, and danced to it with Delia in her drawing room.

'Would you mind turning the radio off?' I asked. The man stared at me blankly. I repeated my question more loudly.

'I don't see why. It can't be bothering you,' he replied.

'Turn it off!'

People turned towards me. The man sighed, and twiddled the sound control.

'I can still hear it. Turn it off!'

'You can't hear it now,' he snapped. The guitar solo was banging in my head like a hammer.

'TURN IT OFF!'

I grabbed the radio and threw it to the floor. He tried to struggle, but we were too close, and too confined by the seat. His blow didn't hurt much. We rose to our feet, grabbing each other's lapels. I felt hands gripping my arms, and somebody pulled the man away from me. A woman screamed.

'It is disgraceful!'

'Hooligans, that's what they are!'

'It wasn't him, it's that one who's crazy!'

'He threw the radio on the floor!'

'Driver, stop!'

The chorus of furious disapproval grew more heated by the second. I shoved my way towards the door and jumped out of the bus in motion.

I reeled and stumbled onto the sidewalk, then leaned against a wall to steady myself and catch my breath. Once I started to calm down, shame at my loss of control overwhelmed me.

The tune was still pounding inside my head. I wondered if it would ever end.

The crowd of pedestrians on Calle Florida filled the street from kerb to kerb. I stopped outside the building of *La Nación* and joined the group of people standing in front of the windows, reading the latest news displayed on boards behind the glass. I was about to move on, when I remembered that my mother had shown me an obituary of my father years ago. I wasn't due back in the office for another half-hour. It wouldn't take me long to find it in the library.

The man behind the counter shook his head and clicked his tongue in disapproval when I told him I wanted to see the back copies for October 1942, then he disappeared through a swing door. I began to doubt he would ever come back, but eventually he did, and dropped an oversize folder on the counter. As I started to flick through the yellowing pages, I glanced at the headlines: *Door-to-door battle in Stalingrad, Brazil declares war on Germany, State of emergency extended in Norway, President Castillo defends Argentina's neutrality*. It was strange to see history side by side with everyday life, in the form of ads for shoes, cigarettes, or '*Virilinets' tablets for men, the remarkable potion prepared by Dr Weiss in Berlin, effective against impotence, depression, or amnesia*, the last two afflictions probably caused by the first. The naïveté of the copy and the images made the ads look even more archaic than the news.

I slowed down once I reached October 16th. Those mourned on that day included a pious matron, and an old gentleman who had excelled at bridge. The obituaries were cheek-by-jowl with the society column, pairing births, weddings and parties with the blunt finality of death, in an unintended *sic transit gloria mundi*. As I glanced at the account of the matron's virtuous works, the corner of my eye picked up something, a line that looked familiar, in the tight small print in the adjacent column. I focused on it instead, and saw my parents' names.

It was only a short paragraph in the 'Travellers' section,

detailing who was going where. A brief entry announced that my parents were travelling to the *estancia* San Octavio, as guests of Mr Sebastian and Miss Delia Lagos, on their yacht *Jupiter*.

I read the announcement again, slowly, not quite believing or understanding it. I had assumed that my mother had fallen out with Delia before her marriage, when in fact their friendship had continued – and she had flaunted it. Only my mother could have bothered to let the society columnist know about their trip; men didn't – or pretended not to – care about that sort of thing, and I couldn't imagine Delia would do so. *We were on a friend's yacht, going up the Paraná river, when your father collapsed* . . . My mother's voice rang in my ears.

But Delia had lied too. Not only about her connection with my father; I could justify that. Like my mother, she had given me the impression that their casual relationship had ended once my parents married, when in fact she had been with them when he died.

I turned the pages mechanically, until I came to my father's obituary. In the usual turgid prose, it mentioned his prowess at polo, his gift for friendship, and the tragic sudden ending of a young life before he had fulfilled his promise. I was about to return the papers when I remembered my mother's mention of the notice she published. As she had said, it had appeared on October 20th, the day before the obituary, announcing my father's death, the names of his wife and children, and that his funeral had already taken place. It was standard form, other than that there was one small mistake.

They had boarded the yacht on October 15th. My mother had said he died in the early hours of the next morning, and we always used to visit the cemetery on October 16th to lay flowers in the family crypt.

The notice gave the date of his death as October 17th.

My boss poked his head around the door.

'Is it ready, Martín? I need those papers by six at the latest,' he told me.

'Don't worry, I'm nearly finished,' I replied. My voice conveyed dedication as earnestly as the sight of my desk, covered in files and legal tomes, and there were several hand-written pages in front of me. I knew I could have finished the wretched thing earlier, if I had been able to concentrate.

The mistake about the date in the announcement might have been a typographical error. The small discrepancy wouldn't have bothered me if it hadn't been for my distress at the much larger lie fostered by both Delia and my mother.

I went back to the papers in front of me, my mind partly focused on the task, while sifting through my recollections of my last conversation with my mother. *What else did Miguel tell you?* Her question had sounded like an introduction to the real subject, her own difficulties in fulfilling my father's wish and the opposition of his family, when she could have been probing my knowledge. Miguel hadn't known about the cremation, and she had no reason to suspect he had found out on his own. There had to be something else, something my brother knew that she didn't want me to find out.

My jacket was hanging on the back of my chair. I reached for the inside pocket, pulled out my cheque-book, and looked at the balance. With a large dose of optimism, I had enough money to last until the end of the month. Just.

I handed the small green leather case through the semi-circular opening in the glass screen. The man glanced at the contents, then turned and slipped the box into an open hatch on the wall behind him.

'Next,' he said, nodding almost imperceptibly to one side. Although I had been completely unfamiliar with the workings of the *Banco Municipal* when I went in, after standing in a queue for nearly an hour I had learned. His nod meant I should move to the side and wait. I stayed there for longer than I would have liked, watching an assortment of trinkets and objects being handed over for valuation by people whose faces suggested varying degrees of despair. Eventually my box came back, with a form attached to it.

'Four thousand pesos,' the man told me after checking the paper. It was my turn to nod. He put the box back into the hatch, then handed me a piece of paper. As I walked towards the cashier's window to collect the money, I wondered if I shouldn't go back and cancel the transaction. I felt sullied by the whole thing, humiliated by the fact that I had turned my most precious possession into something handled and touched by people who cared nothing about it. I had no choice, though. I couldn't afford to go and see my brother otherwise.

Once I left the window, I folded the money and the redemption ticket, and put them away in my wallet. It was much more money than I needed for my plane ticket to Rawson. The balance would go into my bank account; if I was careful, I could save the amount in a couple of months, and recover my father's cufflinks and studs before they were auctioned. I had no intention of letting them go forever.

'I'd never have guessed you like the place so much,' Miguel said as he met me in the lounge of Rawson airport. 'Where's your luggage?'

'I'm taking the next flight back. I need to talk to you,' I replied.

'You made me drive all this way for a chat? What is it? You could have told me over the phone, Martín.'

I must have looked troubled enough, because the mild irritation in his voice had gone when he spoke next.

'Let's find somewhere to sit down,' he said, heading away from the passengers' exit.

'There must be a bar,' I suggested.

'You're pushing your luck,' my brother replied, in the tone of someone who knows better. He steered me towards a corner of the dingy hall, where a man stood behind a counter.

'Two double *grapas*,' Miguel ordered. Even inside the building, I could see his breath in the cold air. We collected our glasses, and moved to a forlorn row of chairs against a wall.

'I saw *mamá* earlier this week,' I said. 'She mentioned that you told her about our conversation, about the cremation.'

'You mean she gave you hell about it, and you're cross with me because of that. You've always been too quick to see her point of view, Martín. I don't see why I shouldn't have asked her. You were troubled enough by it to tell me . . .'

'I don't mind you telling her. That's not why I came here,' I interrupted him, before our meeting turned into the kind of argument we used to have in the past.

'What is it then?'

'I don't know. It's a long story. I met a woman in Paris, called Delia Lagos . . .'

'I know all that. *Mamá* told me,' Miguel interjected. 'She was very upset about it.'

'What did she say?' I asked.

'Nothing you wouldn't expect. "How could Martín get involved with a woman that age, it's so humiliating." You know what she's like once she starts . . .'

Miguel didn't know about Delia's relationship with our father. Relieved, I told him about my visit to the newspaper library.

'I can't understand why they make such a mystery of the fact they knew each other, or why *mamá* was so anxious about whatever she thought you told me,' I finished.

Miguel sat back. 'She's not worried about the cremation,' he said.

'What is it then?'

'Nothing . . . it's not worth bothering about now, Martín. It's too long ago.'

I didn't pause to think whether Miguel might be right, because his words were a throwback to the time when he knew everything and I didn't. I couldn't accept his evasions. I was entitled to know.

'You *must* tell me what you know,' I pressed him. 'You don't want me to pester *mamá* until she tells me, do you?'

Miguel lowered his head and stared at his hands which were clenched in his lap. 'Do you remember the old house?' he asked.

'Yes, of course,' I replied. Although I was too young to remember the house my mother had inherited from her parents and sold after my father's death, she had shown it to me whenever we walked past, before it had been demolished years ago.

'We were supposed to be in the nursery on the top floor all the time. You were a baby then, but I was old enough to have discovered that our nanny went to her room while we were having our afternoon sleep. I could hear if there were people downstairs, lingering after lunch. I would stay on the first floor, and explore *mamá* and *papá*'s rooms. I liked it there, and the maids didn't come to that floor until later in the day. One afternoon, the house was very quiet. I knew *papá* was away; he must have been playing polo, I guess, and I thought *mamá* was out too. I went to their bedroom, where I played for a while. When I was making my way back to our floor, I heard noises in one of the spare bedrooms. I tried to open the door, but it was locked. There was another way in, through the bathroom. I had discovered that. I went into the room. *Mamá* was there, in bed with a man. He wasn't *papá*, and they were naked. She screamed when she saw me. I ran away.'

Miguel drained his glass. 'She never said anything about it, and neither did I. Something was wrong, although I couldn't understand what. For a long time I thought I felt so bad about it because I had been doing something I shouldn't have, and the scene stayed with me. Eventually I was old enough to realize what I had seen.'

His words left me helplessly confused. Long ago I had accepted that our parents had sex, that they had done the same things as those ugly fat men in socks and women in rolled-up stockings in photographs that looked as old as they did themselves, and that we inspected in detail in some dark corner of school during break. But I accepted it in my head only. Occasionally during our teens, Miguel and I had considered the likelihood that this or that man who took our mother out to dinner might have been more than just a friend. Our sniggers had everything to do with our need to prove our own worldliness and the absurdity of our suppositions, not with actual belief in them. The notion of sexual need was imperatively obvious for us, ludicrous or simply inconceivable when it came to our mother.

My immediate response to Miguel's story now was revulsion; whether triggered by her infidelity to my father, or by the sheer fact of my mother's sexuality, I couldn't tell.

'Do you know who the man was?' I forced myself to ask after a long pause.

'He was Sebastian Lagos. I knew him because he and his sister were often in our house. That's why I couldn't stand those evenings with *mamá* sitting on the sofa telling us about her wonderful married life,' Miguel replied. 'The older I was, the more I knew it was a lie. And she knew it too.'

I was too astounded to say anything. The idea of my mother's infidelity was hard enough to accept. That her lover had been Delia's brother made it atrociously real. Had Miguel been unable to identify him, or named anybody else, a meaningless name, I might have tried to question his memory of the scene. Not now.

'She could have meant it. Maybe she was drunk that afternoon, and it happened only once. We don't know,' I said, in a pathetic attempt to justify our mother. I was trying to defend her because I was trying to save something, whatever I could, from the fantasy I had believed in so willingly. Miguel gave me a look, precariously balanced between pity and contempt.

'*Papá* was hardly ever there, Martín. Whenever he was, they would fight all the time. Not in front of us, because we didn't see them that often, but I remember our nanny and the butler talking about it. They must have thought I couldn't understand, as if I was a half-wit. That was the worst part for me. I had this knowledge that didn't make sense until I was old enough to understand, and none of it tallied with *mamá*'s version. Her lies about her wonderful marriage only drove those memories more deeply into my mind. They never went away.'

All I knew was what Miguel had told me, and it wasn't enough. I couldn't ask my mother without betraying his confidence, and she would deny everything anyway. I couldn't bring myself to ask relations or friends of the family about my parents' private life. They might not know anything about it, or at least I hoped they didn't. In that sense alone, I was willing to become my mother's partner in silence. Otherwise, I was haunted by the picture of her marriage as something very different to the gift-wrapped version she had presented to us for all these years, everything I had taken for granted about my father and her.

Delia was no longer ever-present in my thoughts. It was my mother who troubled me now, because of the ever-widening gap between her explanations and the facts I was coming to know. Miguel's words had turned what had been unshakeable certitudes – the bedrock that anchored everything I cherished about my parents – into quicksand. The realization only made me more eager to find out as much as I could. I was distraught at having been deceived by my mother all my life, but I still hoped that it was a mistake, that Miguel had imagined everything.

Since I couldn't confront her with the larger discrepancies in her account of her marriage, I decided to tackle the small one about the date of my father's death. It might have been a printer's error, and my mother might have published a correction afterwards. I wanted evidence, no matter how insignificant, that she wasn't hiding anything else from me.

I went back to the newspaper library as soon as I could get away from my office during the day. This time I took the bound copies to a table, and sat down.

It didn't take me long to check the *Avisos Fúnebres* for the second half of the month. I couldn't make much of the fact that no correction had been published. My mother might have missed the error in the first place, or been distraught enough not to bother about it. However, I was reluctant to leave, and I began to read the papers from the beginning of the month, out of curiosity.

The front page on Sunday October 4th announced Roosevelt's freeze of wages, rents and farm prices, and the relentless advance of the British Army in the direction of El Alamein. A smaller headline referred to the forthcoming visit of President Castillo to the Province of Santa Fe. Towards the back of the paper, the business section led with the news of record beef exports to Britain, a trend likely to continue during the war. The last pages were crammed with ads for cattle auctions, followed by more refined equivalents about forthcoming sales of paintings, furniture and *objets d'art*. The biggest announcement was about the imminent sale of the contents of my parents' house on Libertad Street, to be held on the premises. Aubusson tapestries, Persian carpets, Osler chandeliers, silver, French and English furniture, pictures: the list of items to be auctioned was comprehensive enough to suggest a distress sale. A partial clearance of unwanted items would have taken place at the auction rooms instead.

My mother had always said that she had run into financial trouble after she became a widow. If she had been forced to sell in 1942, the problem had become critical before my father died. Nothing less than that could have forced her to give up her grand setting then.

There were too many inconsistencies, evasions or outright lies for me to ignore any longer, or try to justify my mother's attitude. The cremation was an embarrassment for her, the mistake about the date in the newspaper could have been an oversight, and her affair with Sebastian was understandably taboo, but there was no conceivable reason for her to lie about the fact that financial troubles had hit her before my father's death, not after.

'When did you sell the big house?' I threw the question at her without any warning. My mother was catching her breath, in the wake of her detailed report about a wedding she had attended that week.

'After Francis died. You know that. Why do you ask me?'

'How soon afterwards? Six months? A year?'

'I can't remember exactly, and I can't imagine why you want to know so precisely.'

'I just wondered, because I walked past the site the other day. It must have been such a big house,' I prevaricated.

'It was. It's a pity you don't remember anything about it. The staircase was fabulous. Everything came from Paris. The parquet, the panelling, the door knobs, every single bit.' The alertness I had noticed in her eyes a second ago turned into a dreamy, out-of-focus look. 'But big houses became a nuisance, because it was impossible to find the staff to keep them going after we married. Francis and I had decided to sell it a few weeks before he died. It was much more sensible to move to an apartment, like most people our age. We even arranged to auction the contents, but I couldn't go through with it when he died, so I cancelled the sale at the last minute. However, I wasn't able to keep the house for very long afterwards.'

Her explanation fitted the facts as I knew them. It could have been accurate, and she sounded convincing enough, although my mother's guileful glance suggested she didn't expect me to believe her. We sat still in silence, like mirror images of distrust.

'I was very surprised when you called, Martín,' Aunt Teresa said. 'Harry and I have always been very fond of Miguel and you. It's a pity that Isabel –'

'I spoke to Miguel last week. He's doing a good job,' Uncle Harry cut in. His nickname was an acknowledgement of the family's English roots, and so was his effort to avoid unpleasantness.

'I saw him not that long ago,' I said. 'Miguel seems happy there.'

'The place needs a young man. It was too much for me,' Harry commented. My uncle wasn't *that* old; he was two or three years older than my father, so he must have been in his late fifties. Unlike his brother, Harry had gone to university and trained as an architect, which explained the modern pieces of furniture and abstract paintings awkwardly mingling with the inherited Victoriana around us. According to my mother, it had been both Harry's and his father's unwillingness to become involved in the running of the estate that had led to its decline, as if my father's penchant for the good life in Buenos Aires exonerated him from his share of responsibility.

'Would you like another drink?' he offered, reaching for my nearly empty glass.

'Yes, please,' I replied, with conviviality in mind. Another round of drinks would also take Harry away for a moment, and leave me alone with Teresa. I wanted to steer her back to her interrupted reproach.

'I know it's a pity that we haven't seen each other as often as we should have in the past. It wasn't my choice,' I said, guessing it would be what she wanted to hear. My mother had never concealed her dislike for her husband's family, and she was upset whenever Miguel came to see Harry.

'It's kind of you to say that. Every family has problems, but one shouldn't dwell on them after twenty years.'

Dwelling on the past was precisely what I had in mind, so I ignored her suggestion.

'You're right,' I said. 'No matter how distressing the cremation might have been for the family at the time, it doesn't make sense to avoid each other now.'

'What are you talking about?' Her perplexity sounded as genuine as my own. After her earlier comments, I wasn't expecting Teresa to persevere in the fiction.

'My father's cremation . . . *Mamá* told me how angry you all were about it . . .' I mumbled.

'Oh, that. Yes, of course. I see what you mean now.'

Harry came back with the drinks, and Teresa stood up.

'I'd better have a look in the kitchen. We have a new cook,' she said, leaving Harry and me alone. My aunt was the kind of woman who believed in men's conversation.

'I'm glad you are working with Lucas Marquez. Good opportunities are hard to find these days,' Harry said once he had sat down again. 'It is much more difficult for young people now . . .'

I couldn't allow him to slip back into small-talk.

'There's something I want to ask you, Harry,' I interrupted. 'Were my parents in financial trouble when *papá* died?'

He stared into his drink as if he expected to find something in it.

'I can't remember,' he said. 'I don't think so,' he added feebly.

'Try to remember. It's important,' I insisted.

'You should ask that question of your mother then.'

'I did, and she denied there were any problems at the time. I'm not sure she told me the truth,' I replied.

'What difference could it make now?'

It was what my mother had said. Everybody seemed to believe that time cancelled out my right to know.

'I wouldn't ask you if it didn't matter to me.'

Harry remained very still, looking out of the window as though he had spotted something of great interest in the dark garden.

'Isabel went to see your grandfather shortly before Francis died,' he said. 'She told him she couldn't afford to pay Francis's debts any more, and that my father should meet them this time. Isabel said that she would be forced to sell her house otherwise.'

'What debts?' I asked in disbelief. My mother had always extolled my father's wisdom in financial matters, and how helpless she had been once he was gone.

'Isabel said that Francis had spent a lot of her money, then he lost more through bad investments, and then he started gambling to make up the loss. My father was very distressed, because he couldn't do much to help. He wasn't a rich man. Isabel said she knew that Francis had married her for her money, and she would have no alternative but to ask for a separation, to save what she could from her inheritance,' Harry went on. 'My father felt she seemed keen on the idea, although she asked him not to say anything to Francis yet. Isabel wanted to discuss it with him first.'

There was something weird about the whole scene, my uncle and me sitting comfortably in his cosy drawing room, drinks in hand, me listening quietly to his calm voice as he reduced into rubble yet another line of defence in my mind. I had come here willing to blame my mother for whatever I found out, but I didn't expect the picture of a marriage falling apart, where my father had been as guilty as she was – or more so. If he had only been after her money, it would explain her falling in love with Sebastian.

'Shortly afterwards, we saw an announcement of the sale of Isabel's house, and Francis died a few days later.'

'What was the date of his death?' I asked, and Harry seemed surprised.

'October the seventeenth. You must know that,' he replied. 'Isabel didn't come back to Buenos Aires until the following week. Francis died on a Friday, and she called us as soon as she was back to tell us that your father's funeral would take place the next morning. That was the last time we saw her.'

'She told me it was because there was an argument about the cremation,' I said.

'There was no argument. Isabel said it had been Francis's wish, and my parents had no objection. They weren't religious people,' Harry replied.

His version of events was so at odds with my mother's that I questioned his motives. I was too keen to find ulterior motives in anything my mother said, when Harry might not be impartial either. He had his own reasons for transferring blame too.

'You could have tried to see Miguel and me, at least,' I said. I didn't care if I sounded reproachful. They were our family, but they had ignored us. They never made any effort to contact us, other than at inevitable family reunions, like weddings or funerals.

'It was your mother who made it plain she didn't want to see us. I asked her if she needed help when she called me about Francis. Isabel said the best help we could give was to leave her alone.'

'She might not have really meant it. Those must have been very distressing times for her,' I said. Harry looked down.

'It was all too credible, unfortunately. Isabel and Francis were at loggerheads during his last year, and it was possible that she didn't want any further contact with us. We thought it was better to let things be.'

Harry and Teresa were too well-mannered not to ask me to stay for dinner. Even if their invitation had been less perfunctory I would have declined, and I suppose they were glad of that. I was too distraught to be able to sit with them for the rest of the evening, labouring over casual conversation.

Belgrano was still an area of houses and big gardens; apartment towers and supermarkets were yet to arrive. The quiet, cobbled street left me alone with my thoughts. My mother had lied about everything. About her marriage, about my father's infallibility, about the reason for her self-imposed estrangement from his family. She had lied about the time of her financial crisis. She had lied about her closeness to Delia and Sebastian.

My father's death was at the heart of her inventions. Something had happened then, something she didn't want Miguel or me to know about. It could have been her affair with Sebastian, but that wouldn't explain her sudden break with my father's relations. She could have felt humiliated by her imminent financial ruin, but she had disclosed her difficulties to my grandfather, and people knew about her plans to auction her house.

Whatever it was, it had embarrassed or shamed her enough to justify twenty years of deception. Whether she lied or not was no longer the issue; what mattered to me now was the reason behind her lies. Yet I couldn't bring myself to despise my mother for being deceitful. In my innocent way, I had been party to many of her fabrications. There had been a time when I had enjoyed her breathless depiction of a world too perfect to be real, even if I was old enough by then to sense it. It had appealed to me precisely because she made everything sound so different to the flat drudgery of life around us, as if she had been my Scheherazade, whose limited imagination wouldn't go beyond what she knew.

I could comprehend the motive behind those exaggerations, or her silence about Sebastian or her marriage falling apart, but neither explained her ever-growing equivocations about my father's death. She had nothing to gain from them, and they baffled and saddened me. I felt a kind of weary, knowing disillusionment with her. I didn't want to hate her; I just needed to *understand.*

Eight

The sight of the entrance hall to my building in the morning should have depressed me, but by now I had learned to live with more disturbing facts than a narrow, cheerless corridor that smelled of cats. It didn't look depressing that morning, not with the sun casting the pattern of the wrought iron and glass door onto the tiled floor. I picked up the mail from the doormat without my usual trepidation: it was the second week of the month, and bills usually arrived at the beginning or the end. Distributing the mail was one of the many chores the caretaker should have carried out as part of his job, if he hadn't known where he stood with regard to Christmas tips from the other tenants. His intuition about my eventual compensation for his services wasn't misguided either. My mail remained on the floor, like everybody else's.

I checked through the pile and left it on the meter cupboard. Although there was only one envelope for me, its size and the quality of the paper made it stand out among the others. I tore it open and pulled out the stiff white card inside. *María Mercedes Solanas de Rousselet requests the pleasure of your company . . .* My eyes skimmed over the rest of the engraved copy because I knew what it was. Patricia's grandmother was giving a ball for her granddaughters, in a losing battle to maintain traditional standards. Queenie, Patricia's older sister, had become a model, and both girls were talked about too much, for no other reason than that they did openly what their friends did discreetly. This must have worried old Mrs Rousselet, particularly with regard to their chances of a good marriage. Soon the notion of 'reputation' would become as quaintly old-fashioned as black and white television, but the concept of 'marrying well' would survive the decade – and probably the next millennium too.

I knew about the ball because Patricia had asked me already. I had taken up with my old circle of friends again, perhaps an inevitable reaction after three months of self-imposed isolation, in an attempt to distract myself from my fixation with the links between Delia, Sebastian, and my parents, my frustration at my partial knowledge, and the fear – or the hope – that I had reached a dead end in my discoveries. Harry and Miguel had told me what they knew, and I couldn't bring myself to ask my mother for a full explanation. She would dismiss my misgivings in pained shock as aberrations – or she might lie.

Assuming that I would have been able (or wanted) to question her, Delia *would* lie. If I found myself day-dreaming occasionally about the possibility of challenging her with all I had found out since coming back, it was only because I longed for a chance to humiliate her with the evidence of her mendacity, and have the last word. I could see her so clearly in front of me – her eyes shifting away for a second, then focusing on me with such guileless sincerity while she told me I was wrong. I saw her *so* clearly, in fact, that I had to stop my imagination right there, without fade-outs.

I found it easier to accept my mother's failings, because they confirmed my expectations; I didn't need her to be perfect. I was less willing to discover my father's faults, or his share of responsibility in their marital troubles. Admiration for a fantasy is fragile, and I had already lost my faith in Delia. I couldn't despise him too. There would be nothing left.

'. . . I think they'll go to Givenchy. Queenie loves Saint Laurent though. She'll look fantastic, I'm sure. You're really a friend of Patricia's, aren't you?'

'Yes.' I knew I had made a mistake, but it was too late. Chantal Menendez, my date for the afternoon, was attractive in a Jackie Kennedy sort of way, a resemblance she encouraged through her plumped-up, glossy brown hair, and a pale blue coat so sharply tailored it could have stood up on its own. Otherwise, she was unusually and excruciatingly boring, something I had failed to notice when we met at the Rousselets' farewell party. Queenie and Patricia had been sent to Paris by their grandmother to buy their dresses for the ball, which clearly left Chantal gasping in a mixture of admiration and envy.

I was glad of my unintentional wisdom in agreeing to come with her to the cattle show at La Rural, rather than suggesting something else. It was cheap (which pleased me), a social must (which pleased her), and there was always something to watch when our conversation stalled, which was often. Now we were meandering along the aisles in the Shorthorn section of the show, where some relation of hers owned the winner in the two-year class. We stood in front of the creamy-white bull, its coat brushed to a wavy perfection not unlike meringue.

'The way he holds his head is rather marvellous, don't you think? And look at the line of the back . . .' Chantal ran through the bull's winning points, more for the sake of showing off her knowledge than to enlighten me. I nodded without really listening; the large exhibition hall, packed with people and cattle, felt hot, and I unbuttoned my coat. The sun coming through the roof lights and the strong smell of straw in the air created the illusion of a summer's day.

We turned, ready to move on, when I found myself facing Lucas and Susana Marquez. I should have been at the office, if I hadn't told Gonzalez that I had a dental appointment. Lucas gave me a look. His wife, in the blissful ignorance of another social afternoon, gave me a kiss.

'Martín, how lovely to see you!' she said.

'Lovely to see *you*. This is Chantal Menendez,' I said to Susana Marquez, with a vague wave of my left hand that encompassed Lucas too. I avoided his glare.

'Of course. You're Baby and Tuco's daughter. It seems *ages* since I saw you. My, have you changed!' Susana cooed.

'I had lunch with your father at the Jockey on Monday,' Lucas contributed. His displeasure seemed to have been replaced by bonhomie. We made small-talk for a couple of minutes, and then he took his wife's arm. 'There's Mario,' he said, his hand firmly steering his wife's elbow.

'We'd better leave you young people in peace,' she said.

'See you tomorrow – I hope . . .' were Lucas's parting words to me.

'Let's look at the Great Champion,' I suggested as soon as they moved away, eager to put distance between them and us. We strolled down the aisle, then Chantal stopped in front of one of the pens.

'That *is* a beautiful animal,' she commented. Perhaps it was; I didn't know, nor did I care. If I stood still in front of the creature as if it was a mesmerizing sight, it was because I had noticed a sign on the side of the pen announcing that this was the Reserve Great Champion. The exhibitors were Delia and Sebastian Lagos. Chantal also read the sign nailed onto the gatepost.

'Everybody says Delia Lagos is gorgeous still, in spite of her age,' she murmured.

The comment in itself was not unusual. It was what people would say about Delia, and Chantal delivered it in a tone that implied it had nothing to do with me, as if it was as inconsequential as what she said next.

'*Mamá* used to know Sebastian when she was young. She always says it would have been much better if he had died after that awful accident. Some people said Delia was driving, that's why she never came back. Can you imagine, poor guy, being a vegetable for life. It must be terrible for her.'

It was nearly two o'clock when I dropped my draft on Silvana's desk. Most people had left for lunch; the office was nearly empty, but she was still there. Silvana smiled at me beyond the call of office cordiality, and she had the kind of languidly voluptuous looks that brought to mind sleepless siestas in hot, airless rooms. I had started to linger at her desk for a minute or two whenever I took something for her to type, testing the ground just in case. Silvana mentioned her fiancé occasionally, and it could be that her interest in me didn't go beyond a desk-bound flirtation.

Her attitude now suggested I should be cautious, because she kept her eyes on the newspaper without acknowledging me at all. She seemed completely absorbed in the second page, the international news, although I couldn't imagine Silvana preoccupied by foreign affairs. I rested my hands on the back of her chair and leaned forward, as if I was trying to read over her shoulder. I could feel her body heat, trapped in the narrow gap between her back and my chest.

'What is that?' she asked sharply.

'What is what?' I asked back, my breath skimming her bouffant hair. Silvana didn't move.

'There's something on my back,' she complained, not very convincingly.

I looked down. 'It's my tie. Does it bother you?'

'This English thing is like a movie,' she said, neither acknowledging my question nor raising her eyes. 'Now the doctor has killed himself.'

'I don't know what you're talking about,' I replied. I moved my hands a fraction, until my fingers were trapped between her and the back of the chair. I felt the ridges of her bra hooks through the thin jersey of her top.

'Yes, you do. That minister in London and the call-girls, that's what I mean. The doctor was the guy who introduced the girls to him. He organized orgies with funny mirrors and people in masks, can you believe it? He looks as stuck-up as Marquez. Mind you, I wonder what *he* gets up to in his spare time. Or you, for that matter. My mother always says that men who look as if you can trust them are the worst.'

Silvana swivelled her chair round. I was forced to take my hands away and straighten up. Now the physical contact between us was broken. I couldn't complain though. Her eyes locked on mine, suggesting all kinds of possibilities, and she didn't do anything about the hem of her skirt, which was half-way up her thighs.

'Maybe you should find out if you can trust me, Silvana. Give me a chance.'

'You should be so lucky. Posh guys like you only want one thing.'

'What about the others then?'

'They don't lie so well. You know where you are with them.'

'You were telling me about the English doctor,' I said.

'He was going to be sent to jail, so he went home after the trial and took sleeping pills. He was alive when they found him, but he died in hospital later.'

'That's a daft thing to do,' I said. 'Even if he had gone to jail, he'd have got out one day.'

'That's a daft thing to say,' Silvana retorted in a huff. 'Try to put yourself in his place. He had lost everything, and he had no future. Sometimes suicide must seem like the only way out.'

'You could be right,' I said. There was no point in arguing about a newspaper story, not when the fullness of her mouth, glistening with pale pink lipstick, was far more captivating than anything she could tell me about yesterday's events at the other end of the world.

'How about having dinner one evening next week?' I suggested. 'I haven't been following the news. You can tell me all the details then.'

Silvana gave me a look from under her thick eyelashes. 'We don't need to go anywhere. I can tell you the details now,' she said.

'It's not the same. I won't listen so carefully here.'

She took a pencil from the desk and rolled it in her fingers, very slowly. 'What am I supposed to tell my fiancé?' she asked, as if it worried her. 'He's very jealous, you know.'

'You don't need to tell him anything, because there's nothing to tell. Having dinner with a friend from work is no crime. I can't imagine why it should worry you,' I replied.

'Lawyer's talk,' Silvana sighed, then thought for a moment. 'Let's leave it until next week,' she said. 'He has to go to Mendoza on Wednesday because of his work.'

'How about Thursday?' I suggested.

'Thursday suits me fine.'

'Thursday then.' Neither of us smiled, or gave any sign of excitement at the prospect, secretly enjoying our bogus indifference in the game of escalating flirtation. Only after I had walked away from Silvana's desk did I realize that our date was for the evening after Patricia's ball. I had been looking forward to that, but now I was far more interested in what might or might not happen with Silvana. I took this as a sign of returning normalcy, of my recovery from a bout of obsessive behaviour that had gone on for far too long.

* * *

I left with everybody else that evening, joining the great exodus at five-thirty, a recent change to my routine. I had come to accept the fact that I didn't like my work. I knew I had to gain experience, and eventually I might ask Lucas if I could be transferred to a more exciting department than *Sucesiones*. I could move to another office, or start on my own eventually. There were a number of options for the future, but none of them addressed my main worry. I didn't like my profession. I didn't want to become someone like Lucas or any of the other senior lawyers in the office, willing to argue any case or advance any argument for payment. The interminable paperwork, the need to complicate everything, irritated me. I wasn't cut out for the career I had chosen, and the fact was as impossible to ignore as a too-tight pair of shoes. Delia's premonition in that respect was a further irritant. I didn't want her to be right.

The rush-hour crowd flowed down the street and disappeared into the subway entrances, like water sucked into a drain, or swirled around the bus stops, trying to climb into the packed *colectivos*. I decided to walk back home, as I often did. I enjoyed the long walk, the change in feeling and texture from one district to the next. I headed along San Martín Street; as I left the banking area behind me, the mass of pedestrians began to thin out. I glanced at the windows of the money exchange bureaux along the street, but the intricate arrangements of foreign bank notes that decorated them during the day had already been removed to safety for the weekend. Only the cafés remained as busy as during working hours, with men in suits lined along the counters, drinking black coffee from small, thick white cups, and discussing business amongst clouds of cigarette smoke.

I had felt trapped in Buenos Aires when I came back from Paris. I only saw its ugly side then: the raw edges, the bazaar-like aspects of some of the streets, the brutal changes in scale from old to new. I hadn't noticed them before I went to Europe because I didn't know anything different. I couldn't compare. Besides, over the years I had developed the kind of tunnel vision through which we see places or people we love; I reacted only to those sights I enjoyed, and was blind to the others, or I had learned how to avoid them. When I came back, everything reached me with equal force, the beautiful and the ugly, the good and the bad. Now I had retrained myself to turn this corner rather than the next, to raise my head by a particular street lamp to look at the balcony opposite, to focus on the immediate and ignore what was next to it – as I did when I faced the Convent of Catalinas. At the time it had been built, two or three hundred years ago, it had been surrounded by open country, on the outskirts of the city. Nowadays the convent was encircled by office buildings and busy streets, and the tiled dome of the church was dwarfed by a multi-storey party wall, streaked with soot, behind it.

The tops of palm trees were visible over the old roofs. I had heard that the courtyard was very beautiful, one of the few remaining areas of the original building, but outsiders were not allowed to visit it. The Catalinas were *monjas de clausura*; their vows forbade them to see other people, or to speak to each other. The thought of these invisible women moving around the building in silence, like clockwork figures behind the forbiddingly tall walls and deeply set windows, in the middle of the busiest area of the city, came to my mind now, perhaps because the huge panelled door was opened for a second to let in a man carrying a basket of goods. I caught a glimpse of a veiled head, and the gloomy hall behind.

To counteract that melancholy image, my thoughts immediately shifted to Silvana and our forthcoming date. I was fairly sure we would sleep together, or at least I hoped we would, but it could take some time to go through the rituals of seduction. I didn't mind. We found each other attractive, and the fact that there might have been an element of calculation on Silvana's side added to her appeal for me. It made me feel important, in control. I was too young for Delia, and had felt powerless with her. As for Patricia, we could have tried harder, if we hadn't known that there was no point. She had to marry someone who was rich, and I didn't want to marry someone like her. I didn't want my parents' life.

Perhaps I was excited about the prospect of Silvana simply because she was someone new, different; the way she held her hands on her hips as she spoke, with her shoulders thrown slightly back to the advantage of her impressive breasts, made me restless. I remembered her face during our chat that afternoon, particularly when she pursed her succulent lips in mild annoyance because I contradicted her when she was telling me about the English doctor. *Try to put yourself in the guy's place. He had lost everything, and he had no future. Sometimes suicide must seem like the only way out*, she had said. Silvana had sounded so adamant, as if she was delivering the crucial line in the afternoon soap that she and the other girls took turns to follow on a transistor radio they smuggled into the office, the earphone concealed under their hair as they typed legal papers.

I stopped dead in my tracks, so abruptly that the man walking behind bumped into me. He complained, in the annoyed manner people adopt when nothing serious has happened, but I was so distracted by my own thoughts that by the time I apologized, he had stormed on. *Sometimes suicide must seem like the only way out.* I had examined my mother's increasing contradictions about what had happened at the time of my father's death, and yet I had never thought about the possibility of suicide. It was as likely a cause of death for a healthy, fit young man as any other.

The more I thought about it, the more plausible it seemed. If my father had been a handsome opportunist, instead of the perfect man of my mother's rose-tinted chronicles, I could imagine his terror when everything crashed around him. All he'd had was a gift for polo, at a time when no money could be made out of the sport. His wife's money was gone, and she was considering a separation from him. The debts were his responsibility. He wouldn't have been the first to kill himself when facing ruin.

His suicide would explain my mother's vagueness about the precise circumstances of his death, and her attempt to conceal their financial difficulties at that time, the reason behind his decision. Even the cremation ceased to be inexplicable; suicide was a mortal sin. Not to have honoured my father's choice would have made no difference: he was already damned from the point of view of the Catholic Church. My mother could have lied about the details of his death because she thought it would be best for all of us, not simply to protect herself.

A cold wind began to blow as I cut across Plaza San Martín, rustling the leaves on the *gomero* trees and the palm fronds, and I raised my collar. Delia, Sebastian, and my parents had been together when my father died. An unhappy coincidence if he had died of natural causes, it took on a far more tragic turn once suicide was a possibility. Perhaps it was then that my mother had said she was leaving him, confronting my father on Sebastian's home ground in an attempt to make it easier for them, only to find herself the catalyst of his death.

There could be a completely different – and justifiable – reason for Delia's silence. She must have known or suspected that I had been told my father died of natural causes. She had wanted to avoid any possibility of letting the truth slip out, of hurting me – but then she had kept quiet about knowing him at all, about their love for each other long before his death. My surge of relief was quickly swamped by exasperation at my anxiety to excuse her, always ready to strike at vulnerable moments.

I ran across Arenales Street, avoiding the traffic rushing down towards the river. A murderous taxi driver seemed to aim right at me with unusual zeal, so I had to sprint the last few yards to the safety of the sidewalk, and I only managed to stop just before the railings around the huge house at the corner, where the American Express building stands now. The lights in a room on the main floor were on; it was too far above the ground for me to see anything through the tall windows, other than the top of the panelled walls, the glimmer of gold mouldings on the ceiling, and the crystal drops and prisms of the big chandelier. One of the pictures of Delia with my mother had been taken at a party in that house, perhaps in that very same room. Sebastian must have been there, and my father too. I could imagine them, laughing and having a good time, the sound of a jazz band coming from some great hall beyond, mixed with the noise of voices and the clink of glasses.

The dark edge of the granite kerb ahead of me turned white in the light, and the number ten bus roared past. A few people waited at the stop, fifty yards away. I could try to catch it, to drag myself away from being left alone in the street. As I started to run, I saw Sebastian's face in the portrait in Delia's study again. I slowed down, and let the bus pass by.

I couldn't imagine my mother triggering a crisis in her marriage. Her way was to face the world as a victim, not to take charge of events. There were many alternatives I could think of, different roles for Delia, my mother or Sebastian during my father's last hours. None of them was impossible, all of them seemed unlikely. The only certainty I had was that, once my father was dead, she must have relied on Sebastian Lagos as her hope for the future.

That woman ruined my life, and now she wants to ruin yours! My mother's words had sounded like her usual melodramatic style, when perhaps she had been factual for once. If Delia had been responsible for Sebastian's accident, as Chantal had said, it was a much more likely reason for my mother's enduring hatred of her than a failed adolescent romance with my father.

Sebastian wasn't dead though. Even if he was, responsibility for an accident did not turn a driver into a murderer. But Delia had left the country, and Ambrosio's letter referred to guilt. The occasional mention of Sebastian's name in donations or public events could be a loving gesture from his sister – or a cover-up, if I took my mother's words at face value.

As usual, everything came back to Delia. The possibility that she might have killed her brother overshadowed any other speculation. At last I had found – or had reason to suspect – something shocking about her, something that didn't involve me or my father. The blame would be solely hers now. I would be free to despise her. I would be able to erase every trace of love for her from my head. My heart too, even if I had had plenty of evidence by now that I should consider it a double agent.

It was Friday night, and the weekend was ahead. I could try to find out if Sebastian was dead or alive.

'Can you tell me the way to San Octavio, please?'

'The way to San Octavio . . .'

The man at the gas station outside Las Palmeras repeated my question in order to gain time and to eye me carefully. He was reacting in the usual manner of country people when faced with an outsider, particularly one asking directions towards the big estate in the area. If something in my voice made the man suspicious, the tip I slipped across the counter restored his confidence.

'Drive through the town, then you'll come to the cemetery. There you'll see a turning on the right, by the *Virgen de Luján* shrine. Take that turning and keep going for about twenty kilometres, until you come to a gate,' he said.

I climbed back into my car and drove away into the town. I had left Buenos Aires nearly four hours ago, and by now Las Palmeras had slipped into the after-lunch stillness of provincial cities. Doors and shops were closed, and windows shuttered. A few surly teenagers milled around the flagpole in the main square; being awake at siesta time was probably the only way available to them to express their individuality. The avenue to one side of the square was called Ambrosio Lagos; the second or third road after that was Octavio Lagos Street. I was in Lagos country.

A long screen of tall eucalyptus trees marked the end of the town, then I was in open country again. Soon I saw the whitewashed walls of the cemetery, and a small obelisk with the image of the Madonna. I took the turning, as instructed, and slowed down to allow for the bumps of the usual dirt track. There was no need; the narrow road ahead, a straight line disappearing into the circular horizon, was paved. Pot-holes and crumbling edges showed that the tarmac was old. No road leading to a private estate would have been paved during the Perón years, so the work must have been done before then, in the thirties or forties. The road was a reminder of Ambrosio Lagos's influence in his time; even when landowners ruled the country, not many managed to have the roads to their *estancias* paved.

There was a gentle swell to the land around me; the final, almost imperceptible ripples of the *sierras* of Southern Brazil and Uruguay across the river, before they dwindle into the Argentine prairie. I wasn't near the river, and yet I could feel it in the landscape, in the damp richness of the soil, as black as the hides of the Aberdeen Angus cattle grazing in the fields, their lustrous coats highlighted white along their spines by the bright winter sun. There were clouds in the distance, but it was impossible to tell if they were five or fifty kilometres away. The constant sweep of birds across the sky, the hovering of hawks, the gliding of ibises, or the dart-like flight of scissor-tails, underlined the stillness of the big, empty land below them.

A long line of trees appeared on the horizon, the sign of the main access road to an *estancia*. It jolted me into impatience, and I accelerated. Five minutes later, I stopped, unhooked the white painted gate, and went over the cattle grid. I was in San Octavio.

I drove for about five or ten minutes more under the huge casuarina trees, their rustling, feathery foliage forming a dark mesh over the road. I didn't see anyone in the fields, which wasn't unusual. It was siesta time still. Half-way down the avenue, I noticed a cluster of houses and sheds to the right. There was no one about here either. Eventually I reached the edge of the park, and the unbroken expanse of open country beyond the casuarinas was replaced by pools of light and shadow, open areas of grass encircled by woods.

Occasionally I could see buildings through the trees, the standard appendages of a great *estancia*: paddocks and stables first, then a chapel. There were chains and padlocks on every door. I saw no signs of neglect, but no evidence of life either. By now the park began to acquire a pattern: avenues of mature trees, a sculpture or a gazebo forming a focus on the endless lawns. The road cut into a thick wood, and my eyes squinted in the abrupt darkness. There was a sharp bend ahead. A moment later the trees were behind me. I was on open ground again. Startled by the light and the scene facing me, I stopped the car.

The green of the grass was so intense here that I expected to see water drops on its blades, as if rain had stopped a moment ago. There was shimmering water in the distance instead, the broad, mile-wide ribbon of a river that formed a mirror for the sky above, curving down towards the earth. The colour match between water and sky made the land across the river look like a mirage island trapped between them, partly concealed from my sight by the clusters of cedars, palms and magnolia trees in the park.

The house stood four or five hundred yards ahead. At first glance, only the straight edges of towers, roofs and battlements made it recognizable from the dense foliage of the trees nearby. Every wall was covered in thick ivy, smothered in turn by bougainvillaea and jasmine around the base of the building. The frothy exuberance of the creepers blurred the lines of the castle-like structure, seemingly growing upwards from the ground like some colossal topiary. The foliage was neatly clipped back at the edges of the shuttered windows though. Somewhere, out of sight, were the many people who kept San Octavio in perfect condition.

I started the car again and drove slowly towards the house, when a tractor emerged from behind a large araucaria tree to my left. We drove in parallel for fifty yards or so, then the tractor turned towards me. I increased my speed slightly, to be out of his way by the time the driver reached the road, but he accelerated too. By now the tractor was close enough for me to see the driver's weather-beaten face under his black beret. I nodded and smiled, as custom demanded, without much success: the man didn't appear too concerned about keeping to form. The tractor turned sharply and blocked my way. I stopped abruptly as the great ribbed tyres loomed larger in my windscreen. It seemed unwise to leave the illusory protection of my car, so I rolled down the window and poked my head out.

'Good afternoon,' I said in a friendly tone, as if stopping there had been my intention all along.

'You are on private property. If you're not off the *estancia* in five minutes, I'll call the police,' the driver snapped. The see-saw lilt of his provincial accent did not hide his hostility.

'I am here to see Don Sebastian,' I explained.

The man hesitated for an instant. 'I'd turn back now, if I were you,' he said, starting the engine. 'Otherwise I'll push you off myself.'

'I am a friend of Delia Lagos,' I said. 'She asked me to come and see Sebastian.'

The man was confused. He turned off the engine, then he started it again and moved the tractor out of my way.

'Go to the house,' he mumbled, and I drove on. I could see him in my rear-view mirror, watching me.

I parked outside the main entrance. There were cobwebs on many of the louvred shutters, as if the windows in the house were never opened. A pair of stone griffins flanked the steps leading to the heavy oak doors, set deep into the wall. I pressed the bell and waited for some time, long enough for me to consider giving up. Eventually I heard the noise of bolts being pulled, and locks being turned on the other side of the door. It opened a crack, until I could half-see a face within.

'What do you want?' It was a woman's voice, hard and suspicious, unconcerned about sounding charming.

'I have come to see Sebastian,' I repeated, dropping the country-style 'Don Sebastian' I had used with the tractor driver. To appear to be on close terms with the Lagos family was my only hope. 'I am a friend of Delia's,' I added.

The door opened another inch, to allow the woman to have a better look at me.

'Who are you?'

I could feel her eyes registering my features one by one.

'I am Mar . . .' I realized I was about to make a bad mistake. It was one thing to *act* as if I had nothing to hide, but to behave openly was crazy. I didn't want Delia to know I had been snooping around her house, asking for her brother.

'I am Marcos Rodriguez Peña,' I said eventually. It was the name of the street where my mother lived, and as likely a surname as any other. It sounded pretty good, I thought. A bit of a mouthful, the important name of an important friend of the family. Or that was what I hoped this woman would think.

'Don Sebastian doesn't see anyone,' she snarled. Behind her, I could see the deep darkness of a large hall, and part of a chandelier shrouded in netting, floating in the penumbra like an upside-down air balloon. A life-size bronze nymph held up a candelabrum at the foot of massive stairs.

'I *am* a friend,' I insisted.

'I'll tell Don Sebastian you called. You must go now.' By the time the sentence registered, I found myself staring at the studded panels of the closed door again. Then I heard the bolts and the locks.

I walked back to my car, feeling both mystified and frustrated by the incident. I had travelled all this way only to be sent back empty-handed, which was predictable enough. I thought of parking the car among the trees by the side of the road, and going back towards the house on foot to keep watch, but I knew it was a mad idea. I had been asked to leave; someone would notice my car and call the police, who might charge me for trespassing.

I must have been driving for a couple of minutes when the corner of my eye caught some movement in the distance, beyond the trees, and I stopped. Less than a hundred yards away, a woman was pushing a wheelchair along an avenue through the park. A man sat in the chair, his legs covered by a rug, his head almost slumped to his chest. In spite of the golden afternoon light and the still beauty of the park, the scene reminded me of my sighting of the nun through the half-open door of the convent two days ago, and my momentary sorrow at her trapped life.

I had seen Sebastian at last, only to realize that it didn't change anything. I had fooled myself into believing that I would find an explanation by coming to San Octavio, the evidence of Delia's guilt. All I had instead was a fleeting vision of her tragically crippled brother, now forever joined to my recurrent memory of Delia's guileless smile.

Nine

'How did you know you'd find me here?' Silvana asked teasingly as I walked into the records office. She was standing by the table in the middle of the room, putting files back into a couple of cardboard boxes.

'I have my ways,' I replied. The records office was the grandiose name given to a couple of large storage rooms in the basement, where old documents were kept.

'I am sure you do,' she said. Her eyes didn't move from her task, and I started to look for the file I needed among the hundreds of boxes and binders on the shelves. They were arranged alphabetically, so it didn't take me that long to find the one I wanted. I had just pulled the file off the shelf when I heard Silvana's voice again.

'Martín, could you help me?' she asked. I saw her at the far end of the room, standing at the top of some folding steps, pointing at the boxes on the floor.

'These damn files need to be put back at the very top,' she moaned. 'Could you give me the boxes, and hold the steps while I put them back, please? They're very rickety.'

'Sure,' I said. I picked up a box and gave it to her. She leaned down, her glossy brown hair tumbling over her shoulders. Our fingers brushed as the box moved from my hands to hers. Silvana straightened herself up, then she seemed to lose her balance as she stood on her toes and lifted the box towards the shelf.

'Hold me!' she screamed. My hands gripped her knees, and held her steady. The hem of her knitted dress covered my knuckles. Silvana slipped the box into place, then she looked down.

'You should keep your eyes on the steps, not up my skirt,' she scolded me.

'Don't be silly. I need to see what you're doing,' I replied.

'Pass me the other box,' she said.

As I raised it from the floor, I noticed that Silvana's feet had changed their position. They stood apart, to improve her balance – giving me a better view of the soft skin inside her thighs, under the shimmering film of her stockings.

'Don't get ideas,' she said. I held her legs again. This time my hands went under her skirt, and my fingers dug softly into the stockinged flesh above her knees.

'I need to hold you steady,' I explained.

'Don't press too hard, you might bruise me,' Silvana said, busy with the box.

'You tell me. I only want to do what suits you,' I replied.

She gave me a thin-lipped smile, at odds with the twinkle in her eyes. 'Sounds as if you have the right approach,' she said slowly, then pulled out a box and held it with both arms.

'You have to watch out for me now,' she warned me. 'I can't hold on to anything on the way down, so I rely on you.'

My hands moved to her hips and then to her waist as she came down the steps. I let her go once her feet touched the ground, when she turned. I didn't step back, and Silvana didn't try to put any distance between us either. I felt the softness of her breasts pressed against my shirt.

'My boyfriend left this morning, earlier than planned. We can have dinner together tonight, if you want,' she suggested. She stood still, her face raised, waiting. I knew I could kiss her now, a perfect prelude that would weaken any obstacles later, once we went through the motions of dinner as a face-saving excuse to fall into bed on our first date. I was about to tighten my hold, eager to press my mouth on hers, when I cursed my luck.

Patricia's ball was that evening. I would have been willing to miss it for Silvana's sake, but I had run out of choices that lunchtime. I needed my cufflinks and my studs for the ball; after redeeming them from the *Banco Municipal* I was almost broke, and dinner would cost more than I could afford. The bank had closed by now, so I couldn't pawn my cufflinks again until tomorrow. All I could afford was a dirt-cheap restaurant, with shouting waiters and the sizzle of flies frying on the electric insect trap, which would hardly help towards creating an atmosphere of passion and romance. Silvana would think that I was treating her cheaply, as an easy lay. She would resent that more than anything. She could pay me back by going home as soon as dinner was over, and she could go on refusing a second date as my penance – perhaps indefinitely. I couldn't run the risk. I thought of borrowing money from my mother, but it would be an unpalatable humiliation after crowing so loudly about my need for independence, and there was something unseemly in borrowing from her to be able to take Silvana to bed. I couldn't borrow from anybody else in the office; those I was friendly with would be as broke as I was two days before pay-day.

In any case, our date was for tomorrow evening. If I stuck to the original arrangement, I would be able to pawn my cufflinks again. I could go to the party *and* have dinner with Silvana.

'I can't. I'm not free tonight,' I said. She broke away from me.

'Then maybe I shouldn't be free tomorrow night,' she replied tartly.

'It's not what you think. An old friend of mine is giving a party. I'm going on my own, not with another girl.'

'Why don't you take me then?' Silvana asked, and I didn't know what to say. The Rousselets' ball was not the kind of party people gate-crashed, but the truth was that I wouldn't have taken Silvana there in any case. I would have to explain her, and put up with amused looks. She wouldn't have the right sort of clothes, she wouldn't know the right things to say – and her accent would make eyebrows rise. I felt both annoyed with myself for the realization of my own snobbery, and ashamed by the knowledge that I wasn't prepared to do anything about it.

'It's a very formal party. You'd need a long dress,' I said.

'I don't have one. That's it then,' she sighed. Silvana held tight to the box and walked away, then she paused by the door.

'You *are* too posh for me, Martín,' she said. 'I should pay more attention to what my mother says about snooty guys.'

'Do you mean you want to cancel tomorrow night?' I asked. At that moment I was prepared to give up the ball if necessary.

I'd borrow from my mother rather than miss my chance with Silvana.

'I said I should, not I will,' Silvana replied. 'See you tomorrow.' She held my eye for a fraction of a second, and then whirled around. It could have been my imagination, but I was sure that her hips gave a little flick as she left.

I went to the table, and checked through the file until I found the papers I was looking for. I had been taking notes for a minute or two when I heard the door open behind me.

'What on earth are you doing here?'

I turned round. Lucas Marquez was glaring at me from the door, his keys still in his hand.

'Gonzalez asked me to check this file,' I explained.

'*He* should have come, not you. Juniors are not allowed in here.'

It was nonsense. Everybody came to the records room.

'I'm sorry. Nobody told me,' I replied.

'How did you get in?'

I strained to keep impatience out of my voice. I hadn't done anything wrong.

'I . . .' If the rule existed, Silvana wouldn't thank me for telling Lucas that she had let me in. 'I was told to ask Silvana for the key, but she wasn't at her desk, so I took it from her drawer.'

My explanation was close enough to the truth, and Lucas seemed satisfied.

'I suppose you can't have known. Don't do it again, though,' he said.

'It's your money, and if that's what you want, it's fine with me. I'm not going to complain about doing less work for the same pay, but you young people today . . .'

I was sure that if I opened my eyes and looked into the mirror facing me, I would see Armando shaking his head in disapproval, a feeling further accentuated by his pursed lips. He had cut my hair for the last twelve years, so I was familiar with his repertoire of facial expressions. The source of his disenchantment now was that I had asked him not to use clippers, only scissors, and that I wanted the hair at the back of my neck covering the top of my shirt collar. He gave me his arguments in favour of the *media americana*, the standard, less drastic version of the short-back-and-sides style to which it owed its name, until he realized I was a lost cause. He examined the pairs of scissors lined up on the marble top of the small chest of drawers between the mirrors, then began to snip away, the vehemence in his voice trailing off as he became more engrossed in his task.

It could also be that his opposition to my subversive request was moderated by the second part of my instructions, when I asked him to shave me. Although I had seen other men being shaved at the barber, I had never tried it. The ritual attracted me: the hot towels, the shaving cream whipped by the brush into a thickness akin to clotted cream, the silvery flash of steel as the barber sharpened the cut-throat razor on a thick leather strap. On the other hand, there was something quaintly old-fashioned about the whole ceremony; most of the customers undergoing it had balding heads, and a fold of flabby flesh rose against the edge of the barber's hand as he pulled the skin of their necks taut before running the blade over it, momentarily stopping their complaints about how much better things used to be.

But today I felt in the mood for dated self-indulgences. I was going to a big party, of the kind that was becoming rarer and rarer, like the people who could afford to give them, and I had felt my excitement building up during the day at work. I had left the office slightly early, to make sure I had time to collect my tuxedo from the dry cleaner and have my hair trimmed.

Although the invitation was for half past ten, guests were expected to arrive an hour later at the earliest. Nobody had asked me to any of the dinner parties given before the ball that night, which wasn't surprising. Patricia's mother must have been involved in the preparation of guest lists with her friends, and my rating with her ensured that I was excluded, so I had made plans for the few hours ahead. I would have something to eat, then I would go to the cinema for the first evening show. It finished at half past ten; I would be back home by eleven to change, and it would take me about half an hour to walk to Mrs Rousselet's house.

The metallic sound of the scissors snipping at the back of my head stopped. Armando took a small, square mirror and held it behind my head.

'That's excellent. Exactly what I wanted,' I said.

Armando's silence while he cut my hair had been intended to make his disapproval unmistakably clear, but now he relented. 'I can use scissors, you know. I haven't been in this business for nearly forty years for nothing.'

Armando opened the top compartment of the chromed steamer beside the mirror. He took out a couple of hot towels and laid them on my face, then I heard him press the pedals at the foot of the chair until I was tilted right back. I found myself staring at an immobile ceiling fan high above my head, then I closed my eyes.

'Those Negroes in America,' Armando said, his voice reaching me through the soggy layers of terry-cloth, 'they're going too far.' He removed the towels and started soaping my face before I could say anything. 'People don't know their place these days, that's the trouble. Everybody wants everything at once. They've had it too easy.'

It was the kind of theory my mother would come up with, and it was intended as innocuous small-talk. I rose to the challenge nonetheless, because I believed in the possibility – or the merit – of convincing others that their views were wrong.

'You don't understand . . .' I started, but Armando silenced me by pushing my chin up gently with his left thumb, followed by the sharp blade against my throat. It nearly caught my Adam's apple as I gulped. I felt the blade move up and down, and I thought of the skill and concentration needed to follow the hollows and dips of someone else's neck with a long, straight edge, and how easy it would be for the blade to slice through skin and draw blood. I relaxed in my seat, closed my eyes, and let the barber carry on his racist monologue unopposed. It was futile to argue with someone who holds you in their power.

I had chosen the Lorraine cinema because old classics were shown there, and I had seen all the new releases that interested me. Since my main purpose was to kill a couple of hours, any good movie would have suited me, but I knew I was going to enjoy *Double Indemnity* from the opening shots, which set a climate of harsh reflected light and deep shadow at night, and stifling heat during the day. Barbara Stanwyck and Fred MacMurray drank iced tea, exchanged blistering looks, and discussed murder in rooms where sunshine was turned into black and white stripes by the Venetian blinds. Pre-war America did not seem archaic in 1963. The cars, the telephones, the hair-styles, the clothes in the movie looked dated, but not the characters or the narrow choices available to them. In any case, a woman trapped in a loveless marriage, who involves her lover in a plot to kill her rich husband because it is the only way to have what she wants, is a timeless story, and one pictured so compellingly in the movie that I followed it intently, loving every minute of it. The movie house itself, with its ribbed glass wall-lights and plywood seats, was a leftover from the forties, making it hard to identify any break in time between the screen and its surroundings.

It was only after the murder had taken place, once the man's daughter questioned the circumstances of his death, and the insurance man literally felt in his gut that there was something wrong about the case, that I felt myself drawn into the story other than as a spectator. I could understand both the sixth-sense awareness of the man, and the girl's realization that disparate facts or incidents pointed to her stepmother's guilt – as I could share her ultimate reluctance to confront the facts, her wish to carry on with the life she knew.

The tale of a disintegrating marriage and a love affair in the 1940s wasn't fiction to me. Like the woman in the film, my mother's only chance to have what she wanted, to be able to marry Sebastian Lagos, would have been for my father to die. I was sure she wouldn't have killed him herself, but she could have encouraged Sebastian to do it – or not dissuaded him if Sebastian had come up with the idea in the first place.

The more I thought about this possibility in real life as I stared at the screen, the more extreme it seemed. And yet it would explain many things: the need to cremate the body to destroy the evidence, and Delia's reluctance to talk about her brother – or my parents. She had been with them that night. She had distanced herself from Sebastian and my mother ever since. I had brought myself to consider the possibility of suicide, when murder was a much better explanation for my mother's unlikely arrangements for the funeral, or her relentless glorification of my father ever since. I knew by now how unjustified it was – and she herself had mentioned her feelings of guilt.

Delia's knowledge of the murder would justify my mother's outburst during our argument. *What did she tell you? It's all lies!* At the time I assumed she meant my father's love for Delia, or his decision to marry her best friend instead. I had suspected an element of guilt in her anger, but probably for the wrong reason.

I felt as if the armrests of my seat were clamping me into my place. By now the action on the screen had gone back to Barbara Stanwyck's house, where both she and her lover try to kill each other, because the other's death is their only way out. I hardly heard the shots on the screen; my mind was somewhere else, on a yacht I had never seen, a spring night twenty-one years ago, almost exactly to the day.

'Who is it? Who is it?' my mother shrieked from her bedroom as she heard the front door shut, then I heard the bell ring in the kitchen. It was half past eleven, so Malisa must have been in her room, sound asleep.

'It's me, *mamá*,' I said, standing in the doorway to her bedroom.

'Martín? What are you doing here so late? Wait a minute, don't come in. Go and fix yourself a drink, darling. I'll be with you in a moment.'

I left her to her preparations for facing the world, even if that world consisted only of me. She wasn't making a special effort for my sake; my mother would check her lipstick in the nearest mirror whenever she heard the doorbell. Her delay suited me; I hoped it would give me time to steady myself, to overcome the knot of fear and anxiety that had gripped me ever since I left the cinema. I was afraid of what I might hear, afraid that my mother would lie again, and desperately anxious for her to come up with an explanation that would stop my wild suspicions.

I went to one of the intimidating cabinets looming in the corners of the sitting room like trapped giants, found the bottle of whisky and poured myself a glass. As I closed the door, I glanced at the oval medallion at its centre, framed in brass foliage pitted in black.

It was a reflex from years past, when my brother and I engraved our initials on the polished veneer with a pin. Once our excitement subsided, we were terrified of our mother's reaction when she saw it, and we obliterated the inscription with brown shoe-polish. It was still visible if you knew where to look.

I had time to have a sip or two before my mother came in. She had brushed her hair, and her lipstick matched the coral pink of her quilted dressing gown. The colour suited her, and she had managed to make herself look impeccable in five minutes, but for the first time I noticed that her face had changed. Her forty-fourth birthday was a couple of months away. Although she didn't look old yet, her jaw-line was softer than I remembered, and there were fine wrinkles near her mouth. I wondered whether, now that I didn't live with her, I had begun to see her as she really was.

'You look wonderful! It's such a pity that men don't wear black tie as often as they used to,' she said. 'Are you going to the Rousselets' party then? They are not as *comme il faut* as they'd like to be, but it's good of Minena to have sent the girls to Paris for their dresses. Everyone did when I was your age. I hear she's down to her last *estancia*, though. It's shocking; Pedro Rousselet was said to have thirty thousand hectares when he and Minena married. This country . . .' Her eyes rolled in her familiar gesture of dismay.

I stared at her in disbelief, and not only because of her snobbish remarks about the Rousselets and their unjustified belief in their own grandeur, when her own father had been a parvenu too, if judged by her own ludicrous standards. My mother was making small-talk, as if she couldn't sense the reasons that had brought me here. The tension in my face, the throbbing in my temples, were invisible to her.

'I'm glad you came to show me how handsome you look tonight,' she smiled, imagining me to be as self-absorbed as she was, coming here only to strut in my best clothes in front of her.

'That's not why I'm here,' I replied brusquely, in spite of my vow to keep calm.

'Why did you come then? It's nearly midnight,' she said warily, realizing that I had not come for a light-hearted filial chat.

'I looked up *papá*'s obituary at the archive of *La Nación*. I found out that he died on board the Lagos's yacht. Delia and Sebastian were there.'

My mother reached for the silvered box on the coffee table, and took a cigarette. She lit it with the Aladdin's-lamp lighter next to the box, but only after a few attempts. I made no effort to help her. I didn't want to move from my seat, to do anything that could crack my own teetering control over myself.

'I told you he died on board a friend's yacht. What are you hinting at?' she asked.

'I'm not hinting at anything, other than that you never said who the friends were.'

'I don't like to be reminded of that time in my life, Martín. You agreed we'd never speak about this again.'

If she wasn't willing to explain, I was going to tell her all that troubled me: the possibility of my father's suicide, or the horrifying option that he had been murdered – by her. I couldn't accuse her point-blank, but I knew the words would come to me once I started. All my feeling, my awareness of myself, centred on my tongue and my lips. I caught my breath, ready to speak, when I realized I couldn't. I couldn't bring myself to tell her, because I knew there would be no turning back. Once I had spoken, nothing could undo the consequences. I would hurt her beyond measure if I was wrong, and I would never be able to see her again if I wasn't. I had to be wrong. All of a sudden my theories, my seemingly imperative presumptions, became hollow, absurd even. Least of all could I say, 'I've come here tonight because I thought you might have killed my father to be free to marry Sebastian Lagos.' It was mad. My mother couldn't have done it, and yet she was hiding something from me. *You agreed we'd never speak about this again* meant that *this*, whatever it might be, was something I wasn't allowed to know.

'Your announcement in the paper said he died on the seventeenth of October, but you always said *papá* died on the sixteenth,' I replied, grasping at the single fact I was sure of. My mother raised her hand to her throat; her fingers reached for the string of pearls that would have been there during the day. In their absence, she stroked her skin instead.

'I didn't read the announcement when it was published,' she

said eventually. 'Even if I had, I wouldn't have bothered to do anything about some small mistake. Those who were close enough to care knew the true date.'

'Harry must have been close enough, and yet he thinks *papá* died on the seventeenth,' I retorted.

'You've been to see Harry?' My mother didn't sound shocked, or critical. She sounded mildly baffled instead, as if I had announced my decision to go on holiday to a place that was notorious for its bad weather.

'Why not? He's my uncle.'

'Harry and Teresa are trouble-makers. They never liked me, and they make things up. What did he tell you?'

'Nothing. Or not very much, in fact. We talked about this and that,' I said, knowing she wouldn't believe me. My mother was more likely to let her guard slip if she was exasperated.

'You asked him the date of Francis's death. That doesn't sound like casual conversation,' she said, her voice beginning to rise to its more usual pitch.

'The date came up during our conversation. I asked him what he knew about *papá*'s death.'

'But I've told you about it many times. You didn't have to ask Harry.'

'Why shouldn't I? Whenever I ask you, I find out that something you've said isn't quite right. The newspaper gave the wrong date. Harry told me they didn't mind the cremation at all, since it was *papá*'s decision. You didn't even mention that Sebastian and Delia Lagos were on board.'

My mother flinched. 'Sebastian Lagos was of no relevance whatsoever to your father's death. He happened to be there, that's all. Harry and that prissy wife of his were always trying to stir up trouble between your father and me. They were jealous, because they couldn't lead the kind of life we did. I wouldn't believe a word he said about Sebastian or anybody else, if I were you.'

I had made some kind of progress. However tentatively, we were discussing Sebastian Lagos.

'Neither Harry nor I mentioned Sebastian during our conversation.' I wanted my mother to be frank, and yet I couldn't bring myself to declare openly that I knew of her affair. I could live with that knowledge, but I wanted to leave the shell of her illusions intact. It was safer.

She drew deeply on her cigarette, let the smoke out slowly, and stared at me through the haze. 'I'd like to know exactly what's bothering you.'

My mother suspected I had found out about her and Sebastian. She believed Harry had told me, and I wasn't going to dissuade her. It was preferable to her finding out that Miguel had done so.

'I want to know what happened. I want to know how *papá* died.'

She seemed relieved. 'You know already. We were on the yacht when he fell ill. He lost consciousness, and there was nothing anybody could do. We were too far from anywhere to turn back, and San Octavio was closer than the nearest town up the river. I think somebody called the *estancia* on the radio, and asked for a doctor and an ambulance to be waiting for us when we arrived. Francis was taken to hospital in Rosario immediately, where he died later that day. It *was* October the sixteenth,' my mother said bitingly.

'But *why* did he die? What was the cause of his death?' I pressed her.

'You know that too. Must we go over this time and time again?'

'Yes, we do have to. I need to know that you are not covering up for Sebastian Lagos if he was responsible for . . . whatever happened.' I couldn't bring myself to use the word 'murder'. It would have sounded absurd, false, in this familiar room, my mother and I sitting with glasses in our hands as we had done hundreds of times before. The word would sound as unreal as Sebastian himself seemed to me – and unbearable if it concerned my mother, who looked at me in astonishment.

'You've gone mad. Are you suggesting that Sebastian killed your father? That's the most monstrous lie I've ever heard in my life. Is that what Harry told you? Has he told anyone else? Was Teresa there when he said that?' Her voice was brittle, and her words came out without a break, in the way my mother spoke when she was about to lose control completely. She stood up, her face slightly flushed.

'You might believe what I'll show you then, if you don't believe me,' she snapped, heading for the door. She came back a few moments later, and gave me a piece of paper, stained yellow by the years. I unfolded it carefully, and read my father's death certificate, issued in Rosario. The cause of death was a brain haemorrhage. The document was signed by a doctor and a witness, and stamped with the hospital seal. I was about to return it when something at the top of the page caught my attention.

'Can I have it back now?' she asked, holding out her hand.

I looked at my mother. 'It's dated October the seventeenth,' I said, without returning the sheet to her.

My mother looked over my shoulder. 'I'd never noticed before,' she said, with too much emphasis and not enough conviction. She wasn't surprised, or at least not surprised enough, as if she had known but forgotten about it.

'I remember now,' she said, taking back the paper and folding it. 'By the time your father died, on the evening of the sixteenth, the registrar had gone home and the office was closed. The certificate was issued the next day, so they must have muddled up the dates.'

'Then why does Harry believe his brother died on the seventeenth? You must have told him the true date, and yet he mentioned the wrong one too. It is too much of a coincidence for him to make the same mistake as the newspaper.'

My mother put the paper in her dressing-gown pocket. 'I'm sorry,' she said. 'The whole thing seems so silly now, but it didn't at the time. I was like a zombie when your father died. I was on my own, in Rosario, where I didn't know anybody, and I just wanted to deal with everything as quickly as I could. Only when I was back in Buenos Aires, and your father's ashes were in the vault, did I feel strong enough to call Harry and tell him what had happened, and publish the announcement of Francis's death. By then it was the nineteenth of October; I didn't know how to justify the fact I hadn't called them for three days. I noticed the error in the death certificate, and I thought that if I told Francis's family he had died one day later, I would look less indifferent towards them. I had to change the date in the announcement too. But I couldn't lie to Miguel and you; that's why you knew the right date.'

I didn't want to believe she'd had anything to do with my father's death, and her dismay when I accused Sebastian had been genuine. I felt certain of that, for the same reason I didn't quite believe my mother's explanation now. I knew her too well. On the other hand, it was improbable enough to be true, and my mother's horror of being seen to do the wrong thing was not to be underestimated. She had been more or less the age I was now. Acting on impulse, without giving it much thought, was not unknown to me. She could have lied for foolish reasons, and then become trapped in her own fabrication.

But I was too eager to exonerate her. I had seen the ad for the auction of her house. Harry had told me about her request for financial help to my grandfather, and that her marriage had been a shambles by then. She had explained the error about the date, but nothing else.

'You lied about *papá* though. All these years you told us how wonderful he was, when it wasn't true,' I said. I had endeavoured to keep Harry out of the conversation because I had forced him to talk. I felt a duty towards my uncle, but now my scruples were too weak to stop me. I told her everything he had said.

'*Papá* lost your money. That's why you had to sell the house – and you were arguing all the time. He wasn't the perfect man you pretended.'

As I spoke, my mother's expression shifted from incomprehension to shock, until it settled into an angry glare.

'Who told you all that rubbish?' she asked as soon as I had finished. I couldn't bring myself to tell her, until I realized she would think Delia was responsible.

'Harry did, but only because I pressed him.'

Her face went red. 'And you didn't question his motives for a second, did you? Let me tell you about your uncle Harry – and his family. By the time I married your father, they were living on hope. Your grandfather was useless when it came to money. Harry should have gone to live in Patagonia, to stop the rot, but he didn't want to. He convinced his father that Francis would be much better for the job. I wasn't going to bury myself there, and Francis didn't have to. It was their problem, not ours. Then your grandfather asked Francis for money, time and time again, and Francis gave it to him. I was very angry when I found out. Not so much with Francis, but with them. That's when I went to see your grandfather, to tell him that it had to stop. I *did* say that I was in financial trouble myself, to convince him that he couldn't count on us any longer, and I said I'd rather separate from your father than carry on subsidizing his relations. It was a threat, nothing more. People twist facts to their convenience, and your grandfather might have told Harry his own version of the conversation afterwards. Harry wasn't there. All he knows is what his father told him. He blames Francis because it's easier than blaming himself.'

I remembered my uncle, sitting in his armchair, his grey cardigan as rumpled as his face. I hadn't doubted him, perhaps because he hadn't lied – only repeated what he took to be accurate; a version of events that bypassed his father's or his own failures.

'Why were you trying to sell the house then, if you didn't need money?'

'We've been through this before. We weren't the only people trying to sell a big house at that time . . .' My mother launched into a list of gilt-edged names. 'Do you think they were all ruined too? I don't know what's come over you, Martín. You don't believe anything I tell you.'

I knew what had come over me. It was Delia. It was because of her that I doubted everything. The letters had shaken my faith in her, turned my father into a bad memory, and I wanted to drag everybody else into my own pit.

'Harry said you and *papá* argued all the time, that there was trouble in your marriage . . .'

She knew I was talking about Sebastian. I saw it in her eyes.

'We argued when we were with his family, because I couldn't stand them. That's why I didn't want to see them after Francis died. We might have argued at home occasionally because of them, but all couples argue at some time or other. As for trouble . . .' She hesitated. 'I don't know what you mean by that,' she said, although her tone suggested otherwise. 'All marriages go through bad patches, and there are things I regret very much about our last year together, things that meant nothing in the end. Your father was a wonderful man. That's how I want to remember him, and how I want you to remember him too. Never let anyone make you believe otherwise . . . Darling, why are you crying?'

I couldn't tell her, because I didn't know myself. Too many waves of relief converged on me; I couldn't choose which one had triggered my tears. My mother had come as close to owning up as I could expect. The tacit admission of her affair, difficult as it must have been for her, meant that she had been equally sincere about the rest of her explanations. She didn't know Miguel had told me about Sebastian; it would have been far easier to deny any blame at all. Her honesty had not only restored my faith in her; it had also given me back my faith in my father, which was burnished bright again.

My mother came up to me, sat on the arm of my seat, and put her arm on my shaking shoulders. 'You must leave other people's past alone, Martín. You'll have your own one day. It's complicated enough to live with that, I promise you. Don't invent something you don't need.'

We sat together for a while, until I felt calm enough.

'It's getting late. I'd better go,' I said.

'Have a lovely time tonight, darling,' she said as we walked towards the door. 'You must tell me everything about the ball next Sunday. There's nothing like a really big party at your age. I remember . . .' She kept talking while I waited for the elevator, my eyes focused on the red light as if hypnotized by its glow. I opened the gates and faced her.

'Good night.' I really wanted to say 'Thank you', if it hadn't meant going back, however tenuously, to a conversation we were both glad to leave behind.

It had rained while I'd been with my mother. The rain had turned to drizzle now, so I was glad I had changed my plans for the sake of speed, and had driven here instead of walking as I had intended. The street shone black under the lights, and the air smelled of wet asphalt, but it felt clean to breathe after the suffocating stillness of her apartment. I got into my car and drove away. Familiar sights like the corner pharmacy, or the news-stand where I used to buy Mexican comics during my childhood helped me surface back into normality.

My immediate reaction was exasperation. I had trapped myself into chasing ghosts because of Delia. I had been living in memories, recollecting her, and prying into the part of her life I couldn't have. I wasn't going to dwell on anybody's past any more. I was going to change.

My resolution energized me. I could be free of Delia. I *was* free of her, in fact. She wasn't part of my life any more. She was on my mind only because I kept her memory alive, because I had refused to let it go, to sink into irrelevance. When I turned into Avenida Santa Fe, the perspective of white glass lamps on gilded metal posts turned the straight road ahead into a sedate version of an airport runway, as if I was about to take off for new, exciting territory. The avenue was quiet at this time; a few people walked idly along the sidewalks, perhaps going home from the movies, or window-shopping after meeting friends at a café, their faces lit by the luminosity spilling out of the displays behind plate glass.

The realization that I loved the city, that I could be happy here if I tried, hit me abruptly. All I had to do was leave the memory of Delia behind me, and I had nearly achieved that. I no longer missed *her*; I missed what we had, or at least what I had had, how I felt when we were together. I could find that again, through somebody I could love in the knowledge that I wouldn't be hurt.

I turned into Libertad Street and drove past the site of my mother's former house. I glanced at the apartment building now standing there. The shutters on the windows and the stone-like render on the front looked a pearly shade of white in the dark, made starker by the deep green of the magnolia tree in the forecourt of the old building next door, its branches spreading above the tall railings. The building was there, a real, tangible presence. It was a fact, unlike the fading image of the vanished old house in my mind, which meant nothing to me. One day I would be able to look back at my memories of Delia with equal detachment.

I crossed Avenida Alvear, and found a parking space. I guessed that was as good a place as I was likely to get so late in the evening. I walked down the steep slope and turned right into Posadas Street. Mrs Rousselet lived on one of my favourite corners of the area, in the small square at the end of the road. It was almost a cul-de-sac, an anomaly in the rectilinear grid of the city.

There was an air of suspended life in those few blocks. They had been earmarked for demolition thirty years earlier, to open up the huge 9 de Julio Avenue, which would cut across the whole of the city from south to north. The municipality had run out of money when the works reached the edge of the richest district in town, and some of the inhabitants had enough clout to delay the works even longer. The road would reach the River Plate one day, but nobody knew when. In a city constantly being rebuilt, nothing new had been erected on those blocks for three decades. They were frozen into an illusory permanence by the threat of eventual expropriation, a metropolitan version of Sleeping Beauty's castle, untouched by scaffolding and cement mixers.

I walked into the square. The steps down into Pasaje Seaver, a bohemian alleyway of modest buildings leading to the roaring traffic of Avenida Libertador a hundred yards away, introduced an element of surprise into the ring of grand houses and apartments. Beyond the trees, I could see a crowd of people in evening clothes through the lit windows of the Rousselet house. The doors to the house were open, and a man in a white collarless jacket stood guard just inside. He asked my name; after checking the list in his hand, he stood aside and let me in.

I checked my cuffs, smoothed down my jacket (my father's name was still legible on the label from his London tailor), and walked up the marble stairs. As I stepped into the hall, the first thing I saw was Patricia's grandmother, almost slumped on a throne-like armchair, and I remembered my mother's comments about Mrs Rousselet's precarious finances. She looked so frail that whatever money she had left was bound to prove more long-lived than its owner. Her shoulders stooping under the black silk of her long dress, her gnarled hand clutching her ebony cane, the hard sparkle of her diamonds throwing light onto her papery old skin like candles illuminating a church relic, Mrs Rousselet was a *memento mori*. Flanked by some of her relations, she seemed more likely to want to spend the evening in bed than amongst the din of her granddaughters' three hundred friends.

Patricia's parents introduced me to the doyenne as perfunctorily as possible. Their daughters' weakness for people like me, who did not fit the canons of suitability, was one of the reasons for this extravagant ball, to the detriment of Mrs Rousselet's shrinking estates. However, the old woman must have been more alert than I thought, or just bored, because she screwed her watery eyes around onto me.

'Who is this young man?' she asked, her voice crackling like a badly tuned radio.

'He is Francis and Isabel's son, Minena. They used to come to the *estancia* before I married,' one of her daughters explained.

'Ah, yes, your father . . . so good looking . . . I remember . . . You look like him . . .' It was hard to say if her voice faltered because of the effort of looking back over the years, or merely because of the exertion of speech.

Other arrivals caught my hosts' attention and I moved on. I had been told I looked like my father many times. I was used to the comparison, but in the aftermath of my visit to my mother, it gave me a feeling of confidence. On my way to the main drawing room I took a glass of champagne from a passing waiter and caught sight of myself in a large mirror. The image could have been any of the many photographs in my mother's album: same looks, same clothes, same background of a grand party in a grand house. For an instant I saw Delia standing by my side, in one of those fluid long white dresses she wore in those pictures. The sound of the band burst through open doors, shattering the illusion, and I moved away.

I didn't want to aim straight for the heart of the party yet. In the dining room across the hall, waiters were busy at the long supper tables, straightening cutlery and squaring up rows of glasses among huge pyramids of white peonies, but no guests were there. I noticed Patricia in a smaller drawing room next door. She was being photographed surrounded by friends, against the background of a red damask wall.

The Paris couturier in charge of the much-mentioned dress had done a good job. Her pale pink, floor-length silk sheath, sparkling with crystal drops, flattered her narrow frame. The simplicity of the dress balanced the intricacy of her coiffure: Patricia's blue-black hair was pulled up into a tall arrangement of flowing curls that rivalled the furbelows of the chandelier above us. Long ear-rings, long white gloves, and a forest of eyelashes completed the effect. She looked lovely, and I told her so after I had kissed her cheek, which she offered with some anxiety for her make-up.

'You're not angry, are you?' she asked, moving away from her group.

'Why should I be?'

'I couldn't help it, Martín. I should have called you when I came back, to explain, but then I thought that you wouldn't mind . . .'

I was flattered by Patricia's retroactive guilt, although it was unimportant now. We had always known we had no future together: Patricia was bound to marry someone with a lot of land, or a lot of money, or both. There was no need for a post-mortem, least of all at her own party.

'You're being silly. Come on, let's dance,' I said, taking her arm and leading her away.

We joined the crowd in the main drawing room, their elbows pumping and knees bending in the final throes of 'Let's Twist Again'. The lighting changed to a moody blue, and a trumpet solo played the first notes of 'Moon River'. I held Patricia's waist, she rested her gloved hand on my shoulder, and we started to slow-dance across the floor.

There's something particularly comfortable about dancing with an ex-girlfriend: there's no need to say anything, nothing to prove. My thoughts and my feet just drifted to the music. I felt secure in a world I knew, and which was still there to be enjoyed. I should stop hankering after some imaginary better option. I could make a go of my profession; I could try to become a successful, money-making lawyer like Lucas Marquez; I could marry one of the girls here tonight – not all of them were as guilelessly practical as Patricia, or as vapid as Chantal Menendez. Or I could follow in Miguel's footsteps. I could move to another city in the country, marry someone like Silvana, and start a new, different life, a life as blissfully uneventful as a Sunday afternoon.

Even in my reverie, the last possibility seemed so unlikely that I focused again on the immediate scene. The song was about to end when Patricia stopped dancing, just a fraction too soon for the music. She seemed to be staring at someone behind me, someone who must have been very near. A hand rested gently on my shoulder. As I turned, I caught a glimpse of long fingers, the flash of a jewelled bracelet, the edge of a black lace sleeve.

Then I saw Delia's face. She took my breath away. She looked as magically beautiful as I remembered her, something I would have thought impossible a moment ago. Now she was here. Nothing had changed. Nothing at all.

We moved closer to each other. I couldn't think, I couldn't see anything other than the wonder of her eyes, her lips, the perfection of that face I knew by heart – and yet still it stunned me.

After what could have been ten minutes or ten seconds, I realized we were dancing together, because a photographer's flash nearby shook me out of my spell. I can't remember the music, or anything else around me. I was deaf, I was blind, I was mute. My only feeling was in my hands that held her waist, in my fingertips touching her skin beneath the flimsy layer of black lace that felt as intrusive as a wire mesh fence, my thighs brushing against hers through our clothing.

Her black-gloved hands rested on my shoulders, and her temple was against my cheek. I closed my eyes. The scent of jasmine rising from her skin reminded me of summer nights, when the air feels warm and moist, clinging to one's chest like a damp shirt.

It took me a while to realize that the music had stopped. Delia and I opened our eyes and we looked at each other. I took her hand and led her out of the ballroom. We walked across the hall; I noticed out of the corner of my eye that the Rousselets were still there. When we reached the stairs, Delia took off her black satin pumps. We raced down the marble steps as if the house were on fire.

Ten

The shrill sound of the alarm clock startled me into wakefulness. For a split second, I thought I was in Paris again, because Delia was here, and we were in bed, naked. The sheets were entangled around our legs, roping us together.

My arm reached over her head and turned off the damned thing. The prospect of a day in the office was unbearable; if I went to work, life would become 'normal'. We would be apart for several hours. It would be enough time to think, to be sensible, to feel the need for explanations. I didn't want that.

'You could do with a double bed,' Delia murmured, her face buried in the pillow.

'Unfortunately, what you see is what you get,' I mumbled, sitting on the edge of the bed, my eyes itching with tiredness. It must have been four or five in the morning when we'd finally gone to sleep.

Her finger ran along my spine. 'A double bed would be nice at any rate. Why are we up at this ridiculous hour?' she asked.

'I have to go to work.' In spite of my numb exhaustion, I could sense the significance of this trivial exchange. Delia and I could be together without having to dwell on the past. Impossible as it had seemed, I had imagined our reunion at times during those long, dreary months of loneliness. I had envisaged it as an explosive quarrel where I would confront Delia with the overwhelming shame of her affair with my father and her lies. Damning words would burst out of my mouth as soon as I saw her. Now it seemed so unreal, so insignificant against the fact that we were together again, that I could stretch out my hand and touch her.

'Can't you be ill for once?' Delia's eyes showed such eagerness for me to agree that I had no trouble in obliging her.

'I suppose I could,' I replied. 'Ill enough to stay in bed all day, you mean.'

'That's the general idea,' Delia smiled, holding up the bedclothes so I could snuggle up to her again. 'I have to stay in bed until the evening anyway, so you'd better keep me company. I'd look pretty odd out in the street wearing that during the day,' she said, nodding towards her evening gown, which was crumpled on the floor.

I held her tight against me, and I shut my mind to any other thought. The past or the future didn't matter.

We didn't stay in bed all day. Later that morning, I made coffee and we made love. We fell asleep again, then at some point I called my office to say I had a temperature. It wasn't a complete lie; there was something feverish about my perception of those first hours together: the warmth of our bodies, the luscious cycle of arousal, satisfaction, sweet tiredness, and renewed desire; the softness of Delia's face in contented sleep, the glint in her eyes when she was awake.

By one o'clock I was hungry. Heady as it was, the smell of sex was not enough to make up for the absence of central heating, and the air felt icy on my bare skin. I got out of bed and switched on the electric heater in the futile hope that it would make a difference.

'We could have lunch,' I suggested.

'Do you have any food?' Delia asked. She had judged the situation accurately.

'No, and I'll have to go to the bank later. All I can offer you is coffee and a sandwich in the café round the corner in the meantime.'

'Sounds perfect,' Delia said. It could be that she didn't have any money in her evening bag, or perhaps she'd guessed that I wouldn't want her to pay. Things seemed to have changed.

'I have no plans for the day, other than being with you – if that's what you want, of course,' she added quickly.

There *was* something different in her attitude. During our first time together I had felt she'd tried to humour me as a matter of tactfulness, an extension of her impeccable manners. Now there was an uncharacteristic eagerness to please about her, as if, in spite of the last few hours, Delia wasn't sure of my true feelings. The thought that I could have been the cause of her unexpected return to Argentina after twenty years flashed through my mind, a notion so satisfying that I was about to ask why she had come back, but I couldn't bring myself to. Delia might say she was here because of business, or any other reason but me, and I didn't want to hear that.

'I don't have other plans either. Don't forget I'm ill,' I said, and she smiled.

'I'm sure you'll feel better after lunch. I have to find something to wear though.'

She got out of bed, wrapped the blanket around her, went to my closet and opened it. After a quick inspection, she collected a few things and went into the bathroom. She came out ten minutes later, her hair still wet from the shower, dressed in my jeans, shirt and sweater. Wide turn-ups, pulled-up sleeves, and the length of the sweater concealing the rumpled waistline of the jeans, made her look endearingly absurd and beautiful at the same time, half-way between a too-elegant clown and a ballet dancer fallen on hard times. Delia took one look in the small wall mirror I had bought recently, and laughed out loud.

'I'd better wear your raincoat as well,' she said.

I had loved that side of Delia in Paris, her willingness to adapt to the inequalities of our affair, to see their funny side. But there she had been on her territory, in full control, and I suspected an element of elegant slumming in her attitude, like the fearful excitement of the rich when abnormal circumstances force them to use public transport. I didn't have that feeling now, perhaps because I felt more confident on my own ground, or simply because those were first days again, and nothing goes wrong during the first days between people in love. We would have to talk about our parting in Paris sooner or later, but for now neither of us mentioned it. Reality finally impinged when I found an oversize box of analgesic suppositories on my desk when I went back to my office on Friday.

'I'm glad you recovered so quickly,' Silvana spat out when I came across her in the corridor later that morning. 'I left something that might help you on your desk. I suggest you use them all at once.'

'I'm sorry I stood you up. I should have called you, but I was feeling awful,' I lied.

'I heard you were ill, and I was worried about you, so I went to your apartment after work. The caretaker told me he had seen you leave a few minutes earlier, with some "gorgeous broad", as he called her.'

She must have called while I'd been taking Delia back to the Plaza Hotel. Perhaps there was some divine retribution in Silvana's managing to find the usually invisible caretaker, who had made up for my lack of tips by giving her too much information.

'He said the woman wasn't that young. I suppose she was your mother.' Silvana had a way with words.

'No,' I replied. 'She is a friend who turned up unexpectedly. She lives abroad.' I saw Lucas Marquez coming out of his office at the far end of the corridor and walking towards us.

'I must go,' I said before Silvana could expand on her grievances. Lucas's uncanny ability to overhear conversations was much discussed around the office, and his daughter had been at the Rousselet ball. She must have seen me there, dancing with Delia. If she hadn't, she must have heard about it as soon as we left.

My suspicions were confirmed when I called my mother that afternoon to say I wouldn't be having dinner with her on Sunday.

'I guessed you might be busy this weekend,' she said coolly. 'I was looking forward to hearing all about the Rousselet ball. I have probably heard enough already, though. It was really quite amazing, apparently,' she said. Her tone made it plain that what she called *amazing* had little to do with the party itself.

'I'm sorry, I must go. Lucas needs me,' I cut her short. I didn't know what she might say to stop me from seeing Delia again. Another lie, or perhaps she could tell me the truth. I was afraid of either possibility.

I spent the weekend with Delia, and it was as good a time as ever we'd had. She even seemed to enjoy the lack of comfort in my squalid apartment. We had been to her suite at the Plaza only for a moment, for her to change clothes and pack a small bag. She did not suggest I stay there; she said she was glad to be able to stay with me, because she didn't like hotels.

We walked a lot that weekend. Those were the first days of September, when the short winter in Buenos Aires finally gives up, and the sunlight seems as transparently bright and new as the budding leaves on the trees. The air was warm already, but it was too early for the oppressive heat and damp that could fall on the city like a blanket in a few weeks. Delia preferred to walk around the old centre of town, where the city stopped trying to be Paris and let its true nature show, like guests after a formal party, shedding their shoes as soon as they are in their cars on their way home.

Delia wanted to see everything. Because she had been away for so long, in some ways she looked at the city with the eyes of a newcomer. It gave me pleasure to act as her guide, to be able to show or explain sights that surprised her, as she had once unveiled magical corners of Paris for me. I still wondered why she had come back, and I still found it hard to ask, now for reasons that had nothing to do with my pride. If Delia was here temporarily, then she would return to Paris: tomorrow, or next week, or next month, but some time. I didn't want to know, because the prospect of losing her again was crushing.

If she were to say that she was in Buenos Aires because of me, living with her meant confronting difficult options I couldn't resolve. I would have to live with the fusillades of my mother's rage, and with a thousand little pin-pricks from everybody else. I'd be seen as Delia's dependant, her officially sanctioned gigolo; at best, I'd become a curiosity, someone like those little turbaned black boys beside grand ladies in Venetian paintings. That was how people would see me, how I would come to see myself. To ask her anything at all meant bringing reality into our lives, opening the way to considering the future, when the present seemed too precious, too short, and too fragile to be challenged.

In fact Delia's eventual explanation of her reason for coming back came without prompting, while we were at the old Tortoni café for a break during one of our walks. The wall panelling next to her chair framed a mirror, and she checked her make-up. I loved it whenever she did that, because it allowed me to stare at the beauty of her face in peaceful contemplation, without the crackling of eye-to-eye contact, too heady to be maintained for long. She knew I was watching her, but she had to concentrate on her task, her lipstick following the contours of her mouth as slowly and as precisely as if it had been the tip of my finger.

'I didn't know you were *such* a close friend of Patricia Rousselet's,' she said, once she'd put the lipstick away and faced me again. 'Her sister told me when I saw them in Paris.'

Flattering as Delia's implicit jealousy was, I was bothered by Queenie's indiscretion, particularly since she must have known how things stood between her sister and me.

'I didn't know you were a close friend of theirs either,' I replied.

'I only met them recently, when they called me in Paris out of the blue.' Delia didn't elaborate on the connection. 'They said Minena was giving them the dresses for their party, and they asked for my help. I arranged for them to see a few collections, and we had fun together. They are very lively. Then they asked me to their party, and I thought it was as good a reason as any to come back after so long.'

Delia was a sort of honorary ambassador in Paris for Argentine people *comme il faut*; I could understand Patricia and Queenie calling her. The sisters *were* fun, so it was possible that Delia had enjoyed spending time with them. What seemed much less likely was that Delia would have decided to come back so suddenly, after twenty years, for the sake of a ball, when she must have been to so many. Even if jet planes had just come into service, it was doubtful that she cared so passionately about any party to make a sixteen-hour flight at short notice. An all-too-familiar feeling of injured incredulity came over me, and Delia must have sensed it.

'That's not why I came back,' she added quietly. 'I'm sorry about the way things happened between us in Paris. I overreacted, and ever since I've wished I hadn't, but your accusation about your father was so unexpected, and *so* unjustified that I lost control of myself. I couldn't understand what on earth could have put such a mad idea in your head, until I realized you had found the letters. Did you take them with you when you left?'

'No. I burned them.'

'That's what I should have done myself years ago,' she said. There was not a hint of regret or condemnation in her voice. She seemed pleased, in fact. 'I can imagine how you must have felt when you read them. But you made too much out of nothing.'

'You can't expect me to be *that* reasonable. I was very angry when I found them.'

'It was such an insignificant event in my life,' she said. 'You judged my friendship with your father as if it had happened now. Things were very different then. We met at parties occasionally and we flirted a bit. We weren't serious. It was just a game, without real meaning. We never even kissed, and there were quite a few other girls who your father flirted with at the same time. You might have assumed something completely different from his silly letters, when they were just part of the game. We all sent ridiculously passionate letters to each other, because it was the only way we could feel daring, as if we were breaking the rules. I was seventeen or eighteen. Don't tell me you didn't do silly things yourself at that age.'

Although I didn't contradict Delia, I didn't believe her either. I had read the letters. They were not a game. But I had destroyed them, and she knew it. I couldn't prove her wrong. It would be her word against mine. There was something else too, far more significant than any other consideration. Having Delia again had shown me how much I had missed her, how empty my life had been without her. If she was sincere, and nothing had happened between her and my father, I would hurt her unnecessarily by disbelieving her – or I could force her to save face if my doubts were accurate. Either way, she could react as she had in Paris, and leave me – this time for good. I couldn't bear that.

'You must believe me,' she said. 'I owed you an explanation, but now we'll put it all behind us without ever mentioning it again.'

Delia was using my mother's words. There was a difference though: this time I had no qualms about being a partner in silence. It suited me too.

'I missed you terribly,' she murmured. It was the right thing to say, even as an afterthought, but she had lied a moment ago, I was sure. Or at least it was the first time I suspected Delia of lying to me deliberately, rather than merely avoiding the truth.

'I have an idea,' she said, bubbling with excitement that sounded forced to me. 'Let's go and have a drink at La París before lunch. I haven't been there for God knows how long. It was such a wonderfully old-fashioned place even then. I wonder what it must look like now.'

'But it was demolished ages ago!' I said, almost as astonished as if Delia had suggested an audience with the King of Spain's viceroy. The París's *salon-de-thé* had been a fashionable place for people of my parents' generation, until it had closed four or five years ago – maybe six. It had been gone for a really long time. I wondered why Delia had thought of the place. She must have been there with my father, and now she wanted to . . . I stopped the train of thought immediately. I had allowed my imagination to ruin everything in Paris. It wouldn't happen again.

'It's no longer there,' I said in a calmer voice.

'Oh . . .' Delia seemed at a loss, then she looked at herself in the mirror again and fluffed up her hair with her fingertips.

'Let's forget about it,' she said too briskly, probably bothered by her self-sprung trap about the passage of time. I thought she had blushed, but then she pulled out her compact from her bag, and began to powder her face and I couldn't be sure. By the time she faced me again, Delia looked as calm as ever.

'Martín?' Patricia's voice sounded perplexed. Maybe she had just got out of bed. It was half past eleven on a Monday morning.

'I wanted to thank you for the party. It was great,' I said.

'I'm glad you enjoyed it. God, you are *so* formal,' she laughed.

Only very punctilious people of our parents' generation would phone to say thank you for a party in Buenos Aires, but I wasn't calling her for the sake of politeness: that was my excuse to find out why Delia had been at the ball. I didn't know how to raise the subject casually, and there was no reason for Patricia to have Delia's confidence. Nonetheless, I couldn't stop myself from making the call. I needed to know for sure that Delia had come back because of me. It meant so much to my pride.

'You must have left early though. I didn't see you again after our dance,' Patricia went on.

'Didn't you? I was here and there. It must have been quite late when I left. You were too busy with your other friends, that's why I didn't say goodbye,' I replied.

'Don't worry, I understand. Now, tell me the truth. Was the party a bore?'

'No, of course not. Why?'

'Well, my parents saw Delia Lagos leave quite early, and she didn't say goodbye either. The next morning Minena's butler found the most gorgeous evening coat in the cloakroom. Then someone from the Plaza rang to say it belonged to Delia, and they would send someone to collect it. She must have been desperate to leave, so I can only imagine that the party might have been really dreadful . . .'

I didn't fall for Patricia's worries over her party for a second. She knew what had happened. Her parents had seen Delia and me leave together, and now she was trying to tease the rest of the story out of me.

'No, don't be silly. The party was great, but some people are very absent-minded, you know. I only danced with Delia once, so I can't tell you how she felt about the party. Is she a great friend of your parents? She said she'd come back specially for the evening.'

I tried to sound as casual as possible, but it was so manifest to me that this was the real reason for my call that I was sure Patricia guessed it. She remained silent for a beat. God knows what she had heard about my parting with Delia in Paris, which must have been the reason for her strange apology at the ball. It had nothing to do with us: she had been worried about how I would react to seeing Delia there.

'They know her a bit, but I never expected her to turn up,' she said eventually. '*Mamá* said we should call her in Paris, and Delia was very nice to us. We asked her to the party before we left, because it would have been beastly not to after all she'd done for us. She said there was no way she could come. I knew she hadn't been back for years. I wonder what made her change her mind?'

'Don't ask me. I don't know any more about Delia Lagos than

you do.' I had a feeling my answer had sounded as unconvincing to her as it did to me.

I loved the fact that Delia shared my life during those first days in Buenos Aires, and seemed to enjoy herself so much. She only went back to her room at the Plaza in the mornings, after I had gone to work. Her clothes were there, and she made or received calls at the hotel. Then she met me again at lunchtime, to eat at any of the cheap but reliable restaurants near my office where, dressed in her Paris clothes, she stood out among the men in grey suits. A couple in love was an unusual sight in the banking district; a couple like Delia and me would have been unusual anywhere. Sometimes people stared at us. Delia didn't seem to notice, or if she noticed she didn't care. Her indifference to others had nothing to do with the fact that they were people she'd never see again, as I found out a few days later.

'It is my turn to take you out to lunch today,' she said one morning. I knew Delia wouldn't choose the kind of place where steak and French fries were the house's best effort, and the notion of her settling the check was far more upsetting for me now than it had been in Paris. I could envisage the kind of scathingly patronizing looks I would get here.

'I am expecting a call from Paris around midday, so I'll be at the hotel,' she added. 'We can have lunch at the Grill. There will be no unpleasant surprises there, you see,' she smiled, and I had to smile too. Delia hadn't forgotten the arrival of the bill after our first lunch together in Barbizon, and she was trying to spare my feelings. 'Meet me at one o'clock in the foyer,' she added.

We didn't kiss when we met again, in the opulent quiet of the hotel foyer. A peck on her cheek would have been a ludicrous compromise, and I couldn't have brought myself to kiss her on the lips in full public view. Delia didn't expect it either. She stood very straight, her stance as elegant as everything else about her. It was Delia facing the world, not the Delia I saw when we were alone.

I had never been to the Plaza Grill before, and I wanted to appear as if I was entirely familiar with the surroundings. The maître d' came to us as soon as he noticed Delia, and led the way to one of the tables by the windows. He fussed over her, pulling out her chair in a movement that blended practical assistance with a conceptual genuflection, beckoned a waiter nearby to come over, and moved on in a swirl of polite niceties.

'Do you do *Soufflé Furstenberg*?' Delia asked the waiter after inspecting the menu. The man looked non-plussed.

'No, *señora*, I'm sorry.' The waiter's professionalism stopped him from asking Delia what it was, as insecurity stopped me too. He took our orders, and then left us alone.

'Don't look so grim,' Delia teased me. 'Nobody is going to come and arrest you. You're not a criminal, you know.'

For a second I wondered if she had guessed my recent worries. It was unlikely, but my present discomfort was real enough. The Plaza Grill was the kind of place where friends of my mother's or Lucas Marquez's came for lunch. Even Lucas himself might turn up. I hadn't felt self-conscious in any way when I had been around town with Delia, and I was annoyed by my pusillanimity now. I didn't even feel free enough to be really angry; my feeling was a kind of belligerent discomfiture. I didn't so much mind people remarking on her age or mine. What I couldn't stand was being seen as Delia's kept man, her 'toy-boy', if the expression had existed then, which was the obvious assumption to make when people saw us at a place like this. I had been paying my own way for months, and Delia had been my guest ever since she came back. Even so, being perceived as dependent on her rankled all the same, because it was true in every respect other than money. I was willing to believe that Delia had come back because she needed me. However, once we were together, she was in control again. Her power was in her presence; the only power I had was to give her up, to make her suffer – which was the last thing I wanted.

'What on earth is *Soufflé Furstenberg*?' I asked once the waiter was out of ear-shot. I preferred to reveal my ignorance rather than my misgivings.

'My cook makes it, so you must have had it in Paris. It's a spinach soufflé with a soft poached egg inside. It's difficult to find in restaurants outside France,' Delia explained. A middle-aged couple at a table in the distance had been trying to attract her attention, and they succeeded at last. Delia smiled with her lips only, then turned back to me.

'I've been arranging a few things this morning,' she said. 'Keep Saturday afternoon free, I want to show you something.'

'What?'

'I won't tell you. It's a surprise.'

I pressed her to disclose what it was, but she refused. Then she talked about something else, something as light and inconsequential as the mysterious *Soufflé Furstenberg*, and lunch didn't turn out to be the dismal experience I had feared. I have forgotten her words, but I still can see Delia in front of me now, leaning back in her leather chair, her fingers undoing the brass buttons on the sleeves of her jacket and turning them up with slow precision; the cream silk lining made the suntan on her wrists look a deeper shade of golden brown. I remember her eyes, changing from smoky blue to bluish grey in the light, and her smile. I remember staring at the half-circle of golden skin at the base of her neck, exposed by the soft shirt that rose in a smooth, gentle slope to the curve of her breasts. The faint change in the texture of the thin silk suggested the tracery of the lace cups of her bra underneath.

'I want to take you home, tear off all your clothes as we run up the stairs, kick the door down, and fall into bed with you forever. I don't want to be here,' I said, my knee pressed against hers under the table. By now the waiter had cleared our plates, and we were waiting for coffee. Something distracted her for a split second, then she leaned towards me and took my hand.

'I forgot to tell you something,' she said. Her voice was unusually loud. 'I saw in the paper today that they are showing *The Birds*. We could go tonight.'

I was suggesting an afternoon of passionate love, and yet she chose to talk about the movies. I was about to become angry at her indifference, when I noticed that someone was standing next to me, looking at Delia, who had let go of my hand. She must have noticed our visitor approaching.

The woman was about my age. She was quite good looking in her own right, and had turned herself into a striking beauty by intensive grooming and the kind of clothes sleek magazines photograph as if they belonged in an art gallery. I recognized her because her picture was constantly in the papers. She was Dolores de la Force, the very young wife of the richest man in the country. Delia's non-sequitur about the movie, which had irritated me so much a second ago, must have been because Dolores had been close enough to overhear us.

'Delia, darling, how lovely to see you!' she cooed after they kissed. 'I'm going to Paris next week to get a few things, but you won't be there, I gather. *Je suis desolée.* I *must* travel now, because soon I won't be able to. I'm expecting a baby. Simón is so happy,' she announced proudly.

'How marvellous. I'm so glad for you both. This is –'

Dolores took off again before Delia had time to finish. 'It is *so* tiresome though,' she sighed. 'There are millions of things to buy or think about when you are pregnant.'

'I wouldn't know,' Delia said tersely, then she took advantage of Dolores's temporary silence to introduce me.

'Your name sounds terribly familiar.' Dolores was either being polite, or it was her subtle way of announcing she had heard plenty about us, although she looked too vacuously good-natured to be malevolent.

'Why don't you join us for coffee?' Dolores suggested. 'I'm with Delfina Méndez and her mother, who'd love to see you. Sarita Méndez says she was at school with you.'

Delia turned her face towards Dolores's table, and I followed her gaze. One of the women there was young, a friend of Queenie Rousselet's. The other was firmly ensconced in middle age.

'I don't remember her. She must have been ahead of me,' Delia said.

'I'm sorry. I don't have time for coffee. I have to go back to work,' I cut in. I couldn't stand the prospect of small-talk at a table of rich women, who would inspect me surreptitiously – and call my mother later.

'I have some things to do too. What a shame,' Delia said. Dolores kissed her goodbye, acknowledged me with the embers of her smile and a nod, and went back to her table.

'Let's go,' I said impatiently. I could see Dolores de la Force and her friends were deep in conversation, and I guessed what the subject was likely to be. I wanted to get out of there at once.

'You seem to be in a terrible rush all of a sudden. There's no hurry. Let's have another coffee,' Delia replied.

'I told you I've got to get back to work.'

'It's not *that* late, you know.'

She opened her bag, took out her gloves and put them on, stretching the soft kid leather over each finger, one by one, until the gloves fitted her hands like a second skin. Then she untied the silk scarf knotted to the straps of her bag, and re-knotted it. Delia always took trouble over her appearance; even so, it seemed to me as if she was trying to delay us – or to contradict me.

At last she stood up. We were half-way across the restaurant when she stopped. 'Actually I've got a little time. I might as well have a coffee with Dolores,' she said. I was startled by her change of mind.

'Well, goodbye then.' I leaned forward to kiss her, but I, too, changed my mind. I turned away and headed towards the door. Behind me, I heard the fluttering of greetings as Delia joined her friends.

I wondered if she was trying to prove something to them – or to me.

'You are famous, Mr Posh,' Silvana said as I walked past her desk, handing me the magazine she had been reading, open at a double-page spread on the Rousselet ball. There was a big picture of Queenie and Patricia, standing stiff and solemnly elegant in their finery in front of a monumental Chinese screen, and smaller photographs of scenes of the party. One of them showed me dancing with Delia. The caption read 'Delia Lagos and a guest', a symbolic depiction of my predicament in print.

'I can see why you were ill the following day,' Silvana added.

In the picture, Delia and I stared into each other's eyes, our faces very close. We weren't smiling or talking; her fingers gripped my shoulder as strongly as mine clasped her hand. In a way, the picture was as revealing or as intrusive as if it had been taken when we were naked in bed.

'I've got your mother on the line, Martín.'

My first instinct was to ask the receptionist to say that I was out. It was Friday afternoon, and I didn't feel like having an argument. More accurately, I didn't feel like hearing my mother rant. She must have seen the magazine too.

On the other hand, she was unpredictable. Worse, she was obsessive. If I refused to take her call, she could come to see me at my apartment, or even wait outside until I talked to her. The prospect of my mother and Delia coming face to face was unthinkable. My boss was out, with the other junior who shared my office; it would be easier to talk now that I was alone here.

'Put her through,' I said. There was a click on the line, and I waited.

My mother didn't let me down. There was no 'Hello', no attempt whatsoever at small-talk.

'You must know why I'm calling you,' she shot at me.

I had a fairly good idea.

'Is it about dinner on Sunday?' I asked, giving her a chance to cool down.

'You promised me you would never see Delia Lagos again, Martín.'

I hadn't promised her anything of the sort, and it would have been a meaningless pledge. I had believed I would never see Delia again after I left Paris.

'Sarita Méndez just called me. She saw you at the Plaza today. You know what I think of that –'

'Who I see is none of your business, *mamá*,' I interrupted her, 'and I'm not interested in your opinion of Delia. It has –'

'Listen to me! You're making a fool of yourself. Everybody says you are being kept by her, that you are her boy of the week. She's already been to bed with half of Paris, and I can't believe you could be so stupid. Why her? You could have any girl . . .'

My hand crumpled a sheet of paper lying on my desk. I was enraged by my mother's viperous accusations against Delia – and the realization that, for an instant, I had believed them.

'I don't know what makes you think I want a moral lecture from you. Or that you have any right to judge Delia,' I snarled.

I could have predicted the outcome. My mother became hysterical. 'How can you say that? I've sacrificed everything for Miguel and you. I've lived for both of you, nobody else, and now you make a fool of yourself with that woman of all women . . .'

As usual, the combination of wrath, accusation and self-pity which she handled so deftly infuriated me. 'And you made a fool of yourself with her brother. Maybe the attraction to the family is genetic!' I blurted out.

I knew I shouldn't have said it. We had talked about Sebastian before, on the night of the Rousselet party, but there is a difference between tacit acknowledgement and open accusation. I knew it, and yet I couldn't stop myself. The line went dead.

'Something's bothering you.'

I didn't turn towards Delia. I kept staring at the ceiling.

'You weren't your usual self last night either,' she insisted.

'I don't think I'm acting any differently from usual,' I said in hollow defence.

'I'm talking about your head, not the rest of you,' she said.

I hadn't mentioned the incident with my mother, and I didn't intend to. I knew how things stood between them, and animosity is seldom unilateral. I didn't trust myself enough not to ask Delia for the reason my mother hated her so if the subject came up, but I didn't want to get trapped again in a past that wasn't mine.

'It's work,' I said. 'I had an argument with my boss. I don't like him.'

'Why? Lucas is a very able man.'

I couldn't help being amused by Delia's business-like tone. Here was something she knew how to handle.

'I'm not senior enough to deal with Lucas himself. I only see him occasionally. My actual boss is somebody else, and I don't like him.'

'Then you must change jobs.'

I had felt awkward enough during my first interview with Lucas, because I knew he was seeing me only because I was my parents' son. To be interviewed by some stuffed shirt on the strength of my connection with Delia was out of the question.

'It's not as bad as all that,' I said quickly.

Eleven

Arroyo Street had the beauty of the unusual. In a townscape of straight roads, it meandered along the ridge of the steep old river bank, the greatest geographical luxury imaginable in a city where the nearest hill is two hundred miles away. Unlike the arrow-straight perspective of most streets in Buenos Aires, the curving screen of façades blocked the views beyond the next hundred yards, and the fractured vista of windows at different levels on the sloping side streets contributed to the air of mystery. It was Saturday, and most of the people in this rich corner of town were away for the weekend; there was nobody about. Even the doormen were out of sight, having their siestas, and the great polished doors were closed, adding to the aura of protected privacy around the stone-faced apartment buildings. It was a street meant to make passers-by feel like outsiders, and it succeeded, particularly in the final stretch before it reached the square. There the tone was set by the awesome railings of the French embassy, only dwarfed by the monumental building itself.

Delia had asked me to meet her here at three o'clock to show me her announced surprise. She was having lunch with some distant cousin or uncle. The man was stone-deaf, according to her, and therefore not worth wasting my time on. After our lunch at the Plaza, I thought she might have decided to avoid being seen in public with me in the future.

I crossed the road and waited in the portal of the nearest apartment building. After a while, I saw a taxi approaching. Delia got out, her jacket casually slipped over her shoulders. She greeted me with a smile, opened her bag, and pulled out a set of keys as she came across the road. I joined her outside a house I had noticed many times before: it was one of the few left on the street that hadn't become an embassy or an institution. Its shutters had been closed for as long as I could remember; combined with the dour grey of the soot-streaked façade, its stone garlands and mouldings splashed dirty-white by pigeon droppings, this gave the elegant building a melancholic, haunted air. Built to look like an eighteenth-century French house, neglect had achieved the authenticity of history more successfully than craftsmanship. Delia slipped a key into the great oak door.

'I don't want to ring the bell, because Américo might be upstairs,' she explained. Delia's manservant spent his life going up and down stairs, and I had never heard her worry about it before. The remark had to be a casual way of letting me know the butler had come with her to Argentina, something she hadn't mentioned before.

Once inside the house, I followed her up a flight of marble steps leading to the main storey. We stood in the double-height hall, under the bleached daylight filtering through the oval skylight high above us. Open double doors on three sides of the hall led to empty, shuttered rooms.

I was expecting the usual would-be Louis décor of the 1910s. Instead I found myself in something akin to the interior of the great liners I had visited with my mother as a child, when we went to say goodbye to friends on their way to Europe. There were walls clad in parchment, or dark lustrous woods as figured as marble. Floor-to-ceiling lacquer panels showed exotic scenes in lush, fantastic landscapes, where men with bows and arrows and loincloths returned to impossibly slender women in diaphanous tunics, carrying the quarry of the hunt on their broad shoulders. Fluted lights in frosted crystal reflected in misty mirrors. On one side of the hall, a wide black marble staircase led upstairs.

Delia noticed my astonishment. 'My father asked me to redecorate the house after my mother died,' she said. 'I was quite proud of the result at the time, but it looks rather odd now.'

It was unlikely that Ambrosio Lagos, the man who built an Ivanhoe-style castle in the country and a neo-Louis house in town, would have liked these then ultra-modern rooms, let alone felt comfortable in them. He must have been willing to indulge Delia's whims, even to the extent of living in a house that was so obviously not to his taste, any more than it was to mine. I didn't find the style 'odd', as Delia thought, or intolerably avant-garde, as Ambrosio might have done. I found it ugly. Now I would find the rooms magnificent, and I fight cheque-book battles at auctions for pieces like those; then I found the late-thirties style suffocatingly old-fashioned, out of date, neither excitingly new nor evocatively old.

Delia went up the stairs, her heels clicking *staccato* on the bare marble. The furniture on the upper floor was covered in dust sheets. Américo was in one of the rooms, supervising the work of a couple of cleaning women and a team of painters on ladders, cleaning and retouching the ceilings. He reported progress to Delia; I couldn't say that he ignored me exactly, but his greeting was the barest acknowledgement of my presence. I had the feeling that Américo and my mother would have found common ground where Delia and I were concerned.

'The hot water and the central heating are working,' he reported to his mistress. 'The boiler has been well maintained, so there was no trouble getting it started.'

I imagined a team of men regularly sent by someone in the Lagos organization, a wheel of typists and managers and bankers, secretaries and handymen, *gauchos* and blue-collar workers, accountants and lawyers, with Delia at its hub, keeping San Octavio, this house, and other places I didn't know about ready for her return, whenever that might be.

'The painters say they could finish the house in a couple of weeks,' Américo added. He never addressed Delia as '*señora*', as a servant would, but he didn't call her by her Christian name either.

'I want these rooms ready as soon as possible,' Delia said.

'They know that, and I'll make sure they work non-stop. They've finished the rooms you wanted ready by today.'

'Good,' Delia approved, then she turned round and walked along the gallery, towards the back of the house, overlooking the garden. The smell of fresh paint was very strong here. We went into a suite of rooms; the one nearest the door was a bathroom in white and grey marble. It had been cleaned and polished, but it looked as dead and inhospitable as the rest of the house. Delia turned on the multi-faceted faucets. Steam rose from the gushing spout, misting up the mirrored wall.

There was a dressing room next door, lined with wall-to-wall closets. Delia's luggage was piled high in a corner; even for someone to whom the notion of excess luggage was meaningless, there were far too many pieces for a short visit. She didn't pause until she reached the last room. A double bed stood against the wall facing the windows, its sensuously curved, shiny wood glistening in the big, empty space. There was a large tree in the garden, the buds of new leaves at the tip of every twig. When in full foliage, it would hide the party walls and light-wells of the adjacent apartment buildings, but now their sight added to the claustrophobic atmosphere of the house. Claustrophobia was the wrong word, though, because my oppressive feeling here had the opposite cause; the loftiness of rooms too large for ordinary human life.

'Well, what do you think? Do you like the place or not?' Delia asked. 'I'm in two minds myself. We can't stay in your apartment indefinitely, and you know I hate hotels. I suppose I could sell it and find somewhere else, but I wanted to consult you first, of course.'

Delia hadn't brought me here to show me a curiosity from pre-war days. The pile of luggage made clear that she was planning to stay in Buenos Aires, and she wanted us to live here. She had decided it all without consulting me, counting on my agreement, or perhaps thinking that a *fait accompli* would make it more difficult for me to object. Her apparent delight in slumming at my apartment hadn't lasted long. Although it hurt me, I could understand that; my irritation was because of her automatic assumption that I would move wherever she decided, even if we went through the pretence of a shared choice.

'I don't want to live in this house, or in any other place you can afford but I can't,' I said. 'I have my own apartment. It's good enough for me.'

'You misunderstand me.' Delia seemed confused, or discomfited at least. 'I never thought for a moment that you would live here, but I can't stay indefinitely in your place either. There's just enough room for your clothes. I spend most of my time rushing from your apartment to the hotel, and I never know where my things are. I also need my own home.'

Romantic as it seemed to me, it was true that she couldn't stay in my apartment for any length of time, and yet it was disingenuous to equalize our respective positions. Delia was free to come and go, to choose, and I wasn't. Insisting on my need for my own territory had, a moment ago, seemed a show of my strength. Now that she had made an identical claim, it became starkly clear how precarious my position was. It wasn't Delia who felt uncomfortable when we lived together. She had been happy to do so in Paris. I was the one who worried about others – a thought that made me consider who 'others' were. I could invoke Lucas, or my mother, or their friends staring at us in restaurants; but they weren't the real problem. I was my own problem. I couldn't bring myself to live here openly with Delia. Now she was solving the impasse by stating her need for independence, and that worried me too. I didn't want to be in her power, but I couldn't ignore the fact that she had it.

'You can do whatever you like. You don't have to stay with me unless you want to,' she added, starting to unpack her cosmetics and placing them on the mirrored dressing table.

Delia stirred when my alarm clock went off, then she turned over without waking up. I left the room quietly. In the bathroom, my shaving things were lined up on the glass and chrome shelf under the circular mirror. After a shower, I went to the dressing room, where I had left my overnight bag with a couple of shirts and some underwear. I had brought it here on Friday evening when Delia had asked if I wanted to spend the weekend with her.

The word 'weekend' added to my insecurity. For the first time since we had been together, Delia was defining boundaries between her time and mine. As I walked into the dressing room, the sight of my small bag and her mountain of suitcases, standing side by side in a corner of the room, seemed like a symbol of our respective positions.

Once I was dressed, I went back to her bedroom and kissed Delia goodbye. I enjoyed the conventional domesticity of the situation, a man in a suit and tie kissing a woman before going off to work, a typical scene in so many movies. But in the movies the heroes didn't walk down the stairs quietly to prepare their own breakfast, like an interloper. I was quite sure Delia had never made breakfast, for herself or anyone else, and Américo had been away over the weekend. I assumed he had come back on Sunday night, but he wouldn't know I was there that morning. Even if he did, I doubt he would have gone out of his way to make my life less uncomfortable.

'Let's go out to dinner,' Delia said. We were in the drawing room, finishing our drinks. 'Think of some place that's fun,' she added.

Ever since she had moved here, Delia had been less keen on going out in the evenings. Unlike me, she seemed to find the warmth of home in this silver-leafed folly, but perhaps it was beginning to feel oppressive to her too. I guessed she wasn't leaving the choice of restaurant to me only because of the bill. Most of the restaurants she knew must have closed down, or fallen out of fashion. After her failed proposal of a drink at La París, she had avoided mentioning any place by name, unless we had been there together.

'How about Edelweiss?' I suggested. It was a landmark, so Delia might at least have heard of it.

'What a good idea,' she said enthusiastically – and ambiguously. I wasn't clear if she'd been to the place or not, but she was bound to like it. The Opera House was very near, so young dancers and singers came to the restaurant every night. The food was good and cheap, while the *frisson* of elegant slumming brought in some of the performers' smart audience too. The buzz of a place open all night in the middle of town attracted casual passers-by who couldn't care less about art; they added to the sense of adventure of those who did. But it was only eight o'clock; far too early for dinner.

'It's a beautiful evening, so we could walk there. You said you wanted to look at the windows of the antique shops on Libertad. Or we could go to a movie,' I said.

'Yes, let's . . .' She stopped and turned her head towards the door to the hall.

'Are you expecting someone?' I asked.

'No. Why?'

'Because you keep turning towards the door all the time.'

'*All the time?* You are rather hyper-sensitive tonight,' she said lightly, as if she found my comment amusing. 'I turned towards the door because I heard Américo in the hall, that's all.'

Delia had turned towards the door *every* time Américo's footsteps had echoed in the hall, in fact. I had noticed her action, without linking it to the familiar sound of the butler going about his chores. I had also noticed an unusual nervousness in her manner, an almost imperceptible change in the tempo of her movements.

'I'll go upstairs to get my bag. I'll be back in a minute,' she said. For once, it was true. As we went through the hall, Delia looked into the study.

'Goodbye, Américo. Please tell Dionisia we won't be here for dinner,' she said.

The telephone on a side table near me rang. I was about to pick it up, but Delia cut in front of me.

'Oh, hello . . . No, it's all right, but I thought I told your secretary not to call me after six. You caught me on my way out in fact . . .' It sounded like an ordinary business conversation, but I noticed she glanced at me a couple of times, as if she wanted to check to see if I was reacting in any way.

'No, I can't speak now. Call me tomorrow morning. Bye.' Delia put the phone down, and we left.

We had begun walking towards the square, when she must have noticed my sullen silence.

'How's work?' she asked.

Delia wasn't interested in my work, and she knew I didn't care for it myself. Her question was such a transparent attempt at small-talk that I couldn't but suspect she wanted to take my mind away from whatever she thought was troubling me – her telephone conversation. I was positive Delia hadn't wanted me to hear the voice on the phone.

'My work is fine. Who were you talking to just now?'

'Oh, nobody you know. Someone from the company. Why?'

'Because you were in such a hurry to take the call, that's all.'

She seemed at a loss for a second. 'Don't be . . .' she started, and then paused. 'You're right. I didn't want you to take that call – or any other call. I had forgotten what this city's like. I can't bear all the tittle-tattle about us, and you answering my phone would only make it worse. I wish I didn't mind, but I do.'

I knew how she felt. The fact that under her aloofness Delia could be troubled by exactly the same problems I was made me feel very close to her.

We were in time for the early evening show at the movies, and then we went to Edelweiss. Delia loved the place. We lingered after coffee, finishing our wine, whispering sweet nothings, or just staring into each other's eyes and saying nothing at all.

Occasionally she nodded at someone in the restaurant. She seemed so relaxed in public, so oblivious of anything other than our being together, that it seemed impossible she could be vulnerable to what others might say about us. I wondered if she had made it all up, but she had no reason to do that. I *was* being over-sensitive.

'Would you mind trying to make that wretched thing work, darling? It would be nice to have music,' Delia said. There was a massive piece of furniture on one side of the drawing room. It was a combined RCA radio and record-player, its huge speaker concealed by silky cream fabric stretched taut behind a rising-sun motif. The dark red-brown wood was varnished to such a high gloss that it looked as if the whole cabinet had been dipped in syrup. At the time it had been brought to the house it must have clashed badly with the muted silver and greys of the lacquered furniture around, but now they harmonized because it all looked equally antiquated.

I turned the ribbed crystal knob on the controls. There was a whirring sound, then a crackle, and a dim yellow light shone behind the tuning dial. I tried the record-player next. I was startled by its speed. It had been three or four years at least since singles had changed to 45 r.p.m., and I never played my old 78s these days.

'It works,' I said.

'Good. Choose whatever you want. There are some records there.'

I pulled out one of the albums. The tooled-leather spine cracked as I opened it, and the dusty smell of old dry paper rose up as I turned the brown sleeves gingerly. Through the paper, the records felt heavy and fragile, like discs of thin glass. I glanced at the names on the labels: I recognized Paul Whiteman, Al Jolson and Sophie Tucker because my mother had a few records by them. On the very rare occasions she'd put one on, Miguel and I had roared with laughter at those boring relics we thought almost prehistoric. From a coin-size photograph above the spindle hole in one of the records, Maurice Chevalier beamed a toothsome smile. There were other French records, by singers whose names meant nothing to me.

I put the album back on the shelf and pulled out another, and then another. I came across some Glenn Miller records. I knew who he was, because my mother had taken me as a child to see the movie about his life starring James Stewart and June Allyson. Some records were marked 'Delia' on the label, others were inscribed 'Sebastian'. I recognized her handwriting, less assertive than it was now, but already distinctive. Her brother's was completely different, a rather childish, weak scrawl where the stroke across the 't' looked like an after-thought, a half-hearted attempt at boldness.

'Your brother's records are still here,' I said.

'Oh, really . . .'

I waited for some further comment, but there was none.

'Where does he live now?' I tried to sound as if I didn't much care, but felt obliged to ask for the sake of courtesy.

'In the country. He had a bad accident years ago, and he's chosen to live there ever since. Haven't you found anything you'd like to listen to yet? If we're going to be waiting forever, I'd rather go upstairs and have my bath instead.'

I kept flicking through the albums. I decided that the more obscure records must have been bought by Delia's parents. Some of the songs were embarrassing because they were historical pieces, and most of them I didn't know at all. I chose a record at random, laid it carefully at the top of the spindle so that the eroded hole would sit on the catch, rested the balancing arm on it, and turned the winged switch on.

A woman with a velvet voice started singing. My English wasn't that good then, so I could only make out the words 'all through the night'. It sounded soft and pleasant, and I stretched myself out on the sofa next to Delia. I slipped my arm under her back and held her tight, her head resting on my shoulder. My free hand followed the contour of her face and her neck, then glided over the flimsy barrier of her silk top and caressed her breasts as I leaned over her and kissed her lips. It was a movie-like kiss at first, passionate but controlled, the kind of kiss that comes to an end neatly, but then it became something else.

Delia pushed me away gently and got up. 'I think I'd better have my bath,' she said.

There's something wonderful about intimacy, about knowing someone so well that you can make allowances for their idiosyncrasies. I knew Delia wanted me as urgently as I wanted her. We had shared times when ripped clothes, a hard floor, or the risk of public places meant nothing against the imperative of making love without delay.

But there is pleasure in delay too, and occasionally she played a teasing game and made me wait. Like now. I closed my eyes and imagined her upstairs, taking off her clothes, pushing the straps of her slip off her shoulders and letting it drop into a soft heap on the marble floor, unhooking her bra and pulling down her panties as the mist of steam building up in the bathroom swirled around her. Then she would get into the bath and relax in the soothing warmth of the water that covered her.

I stretched on the sofa, which was too long for my feet to reach the further arm, and let myself sink in the softness of the down-filled cushions, still trapping her jasmine scent, as if I too were luxuriating in a steaming, scented bath. Now I saw Delia reach for the soap and the sponge. She worked up a thick, frothy lather, and rubbed the sponge slowly all over her, squeezing it so that foam oozed over her fingers. White rivulets streamed from her breasts to her belly, and flowed down her thighs, her wet skin gleaming as if it was oiled.

I could see her so clearly in my head, more clearly than if I were there, with her, as if I could stretch out my hand and touch her. Now I saw her naked in front of the mirror, rubbing herself dry with a towel. I took in the beauty of her gently sloping shoulders, the play of light and shadow on the planes and hollows of her back, and then my eyes dwelt on her buttocks, smooth and firm, ready to fill the hollow of my hands. Her nipples hardened as her eyes caught mine in the glass.

Restrained by my clothes, my prick pressed against my thigh. The rest of my body had become irrelevant. Those endless miles of veins, arteries and nerves, my wilful heart that would beat whether I was asleep or awake, the miracle of my brain, capable of understanding the universe, the chemical prodigy required for my cells to replicate themselves day after day; all these had only one purpose: to take me to Delia. I wanted her immediately, so intensely that I felt I might choke. I *had* to fuck her. Now.

I climbed the stairs. I pushed the bedroom door open. Delia was standing in front of the mirror, rubbing herself dry with a fluffy white towel. I smelled the soap on her skin. I felt her back against my chest. I felt the warmth of her naked body reaching me through my clothes, until my fingertips hijacked my senses. They followed the slope of her chest, the curves of her breast, the hollow of her navel, and then they reached the swelling of her labia. I caught her teasing smile in the mirror, then she reached for my hand and took it to her lips, brushing my fingers with a kiss that felt as light as breath.

I lifted her off her feet, and carried her towards the bed. I was ready to shed my clothes in an instant. Both of us naked, we would fall onto the bed. The thought that I would be inside her soon was so overwhelming that I bit my lip. I could anticipate Delia's moans when she finally lost control of herself. During that instant, nothing would make any difference, and nothing, other than our pleasure, would make sense.

I let go of her and fumbled at my shirt buttons with impatient fingers. I felt her hands on mine, and I smiled. Delia wanted to undress me herself.

'Don't get too carried away, please,' she said. 'I'd rather we went to sleep, if you don't mind. I'm feeling so tired . . .'

I didn't understand at first, then I couldn't believe what she had said. Delia had never refused me before. It couldn't be that she didn't want me – not when I wanted her so badly. We couldn't be so out of tune with each other.

I realized that she meant it. She wasn't excited, or even interested. The benign indifference in her face shrivelled my prick more effectively than cold water.

'Don't look so miserable,' she smiled as she leaned down to pick up her nightdress. 'There's always tomorrow, you know.'

I lay in bed next to her, after she had kissed me good night and rolled over, her back to me. I thought that tomorrow was an unbearably long time away.

It was a beautiful evening, that time just before sunset when the sky glows a peachy pink, and Avenida Santa Fe seemed full of lovely girls. I didn't notice any in particular: I noticed them all. My gaze wandered from one to the next, taking in the beautiful lips of a blonde coming out of a shop, or a voluptuous brunette staring at a store window, the thin, pale blue knit of her sweater following the shape of her breasts as lovingly as if it were my own hands.

As I came across those passing women, I undressed them all in my mind. The bright light of the street turned into the penumbra of the foyers I walked past, those cavernous dark spaces where they would spread themselves naked on the hard cold floor and wait for me to lean over them, to fuck them one by one, one after the other . . .

A loud, gong-like sound brought me out of my reverie, and I felt a pain in my hand, which was closed into a fist. Only then did I realize I had thumped one of the cast-iron poster displays, crowned by the municipal crest, that stood along the road. People stared at me in worried curiosity. They might have suspected that the reason for my outburst was that I was mad, or at least not all there. They couldn't know that Delia had not allowed me to make love to her since that night.

It would have been easier, or at least more straightforward, if she had said, 'I don't want to sleep with you any more.' On the contrary. Delia had asked me to stay with her every night. She would cling to me after we turned off the light. She held my face lovingly when she kissed me. She asked me to hold her in my arms before she went to sleep.

But when I had tried to make love to her the morning after her first refusal, Delia had said she had asked Américo to bring us breakfast upstairs. Sure enough, there had been a knock at the door a moment later. She'd opened it and taken the tray, and then made such a performance about the need to have breakfast quickly, and an early appointment with her company lawyers, that any eroticism was snuffed out. That night I had waited until we were in bed, then I'd held her tight, our bodies pressed together. I'd kissed her, and she had seemed to respond, but when I'd tried to slip my hands under her nightdress, Delia had moved away.

'I'm sorry,' she had said. 'I hate doing this to you, but there are too many things on my mind at the moment: boring, practical problems that have nothing to do with you – I'm sure you understand.'

Ever since she had remained as loving, as tender towards me as usual – but sex between us had come to an abrupt end.

I pretended to understand, because I had no choice. The notion of not wanting sex was beyond my comprehension. I forced myself to lie next to her every night out of fear, without bringing up the subject again. I didn't trust myself to keep calm; her refusal angered and hurt me too much. An argument could lead her to suggest we parted for a few days, to cool down.

The only reason I could imagine for her sudden coolness was another man. I had heard her on the telephone when she had cut her caller short. It could be that it was a business call, but it could also be that she had thrown in the reference to his secretary to fool me. So I lay next to Delia every night without touching her, listening to her calm breathing in the dark, as she rested and I struggled to stop the panic in my head and the turmoil in my body long enough so that I could sleep.

I smoked in those days. Everybody did; even Delia. She smoked very rarely though, so I was surprised one evening when she asked me for a cigarette after dinner. We were sitting in the drawing room downstairs, where she had rearranged some furniture and culled pieces she didn't like. I had heard her on the phone talking to decorators or antique dealers.

It seemed that this was going to be home for her for some time, but still I didn't ask her about her plans – probably because my own were so unclear. I had been afraid of the future, of facing life with Delia in Buenos Aires – until the turn in our affair, when my fear of losing her obliterated any other worry.

'Sorry, I've run out,' I said after checking my packet.

Delia walked to the door. 'Américo,' she called. I could hear his footsteps on the marble floor of the hall.

'Would you go up to my room and bring me a packet of cigarettes,' she said. A few minutes later, Américo came back holding a small silver tray with an open packet of cigarettes on it.

'Thank you,' Delia smiled. I was about to offer her a light when Américo beat me to it.

'I noticed there are only eight packets in the carton,' he said. 'You have only asked me for cigarettes once since we arrived.'

It would be just like Américo to imagine that I had taken the cigarettes on the quiet, and to bring the fact to Delia's attention, as though I was some petty thief. She had given them to me herself when I had run out over the weekend.

'I took them myself, Américo, don't worry,' she said.

'One has to be vigilant these days, with so many people coming and going in the house,' he explained tersely as he left the room.

I felt angry. The butler was probably trying to incriminate me in his stupid way, or perhaps he was genuinely concerned about the painters or the cleaners helping themselves to Delia's things. My anger was more to do with feeling that I was at school again, constantly afraid of being caught doing something I shouldn't. I didn't like having Américo floating around like a ghost, any more than I liked staying in this museum-like house, a symbol of Delia's power and a reminder of all the reasons why we were so ill-matched. I hated the atmosphere here, a throwback to a time that was Delia's, not mine. None of this would have been more than a fleeting irritation if I hadn't been so on edge. Now everything came together, and my annoyance became rage.

I stubbed out my cigarette and stood up. 'I'm going home,' I announced.

Delia seemed astonished. 'Why?' she asked.

'I have things to do.'

'You're angry. Is it because of Américo and the cigarettes? That's ridiculous.'

'No, of course not,' I said in the emphatic tone bad liars use when they are caught out.

'You shouldn't take any notice of Américo. He's been with me for more than twenty years, and he has his peculiarities, like everybody else. He over-protects me, that's all.'

'Maybe that's why he makes it so obvious that he doesn't like me. He watches me as if he were expecting me to break the furniture.'

'Quite often you look as if you are about to. Américo can only judge from what he sees.'

'That makes two of us.'

'Something *is* bothering you, then. What is it?'

She couldn't be so disingenuous. Delia slept next to me every night. She had seen my frustration. She had witnessed my unhappiness. There had to be a reason behind a question she didn't need to ask.

'I need to go to my own place, that's all. I can't get used to being here. I'll call you tomorrow,' I said. I knew I would be miserable there, on my own, but I needed to challenge Delia's supremacy in some way – without losing her.

'Come here,' she said, reaching for my hand. I stepped back. I was about to open the door and leave the room when she spoke.

'Why did you go to San Octavio, Martín?' she asked, as casually as if the question didn't concern her much. I stopped dead in my tracks.

'Clara told me a young man came to the house. From her description, it had to be you.'

I remembered the grim-faced housekeeper at the *estancia*. I had gone there shortly before the ball, just after Patricia and her sister had left Paris, when Delia had refused their invitation to come back to Buenos Aires. If she had heard about my visit to San Octavio then, it could have been the real reason for her sudden change of mind.

'I wanted to see your brother,' I said.

'Why did you want to do that?'

'Because – ' I didn't want to tell Delia everything – 'my mother was very upset when I came back. She had heard about you and me, and she implied you had been responsible for Sebastian's accident. I was told you were driving the car when it happened, and that nobody had seen Sebastian since. That's why I wanted to check for myself if he was alive.'

Delia seemed to accept my explanation, or at least she didn't seem surprised. 'There was no car. Sebastian had a very bad fall when he was riding, and he was alone when it happened. You can check the police report, if it matters that much to you. He has lived in San Octavio ever since. Your mother is talking nonsense.'

'You never mentioned him in Paris. I thought there had to be a reason for your silence.'

Delia reached for the cigarettes again and lit another one. She wasn't so at ease as she pretended to be.

'It's pointless to talk about something that hurts you and can't be changed. Sebastian is a sorry sight. I don't like to talk about him. I'm sorry if that upsets you, but he's my brother, not yours.'

It was the same as when I had asked her about my father in Paris, and Delia's reminder that I had no right to pry into her life irritated me anew. If I decided to be more cautious now, it was only because I knew the risk of another confrontation.

'I'd better go,' I said, turning towards the door. I caught a reflection of Delia in the highly polished wood, staring at me. The image was too blurred, a faceless outline in which I couldn't read any expression at all.

Although I had said I would call her, Delia phoned me at the office the next day. She hadn't done so ever since she had been in Buenos Aires, but then the pattern had been that I would call her during the day, and for once I hadn't.

'I'm sorry to bother you at work,' she said. The mundane apology was unnecessary, and further proof of the coolness I suspected in her.

'Are you planning to come here this evening?' she asked casually. Her question made me realize how foolish I had been a moment ago. Delia must have been as worried as I was by the turn in our relationship. She needed my reassurance after our conversation the night before.

'I don't know yet. I have a lot to do here. I'll call you later,' I replied, making the most of my new-found ascendancy.

'It might be better if we saw each other tomorrow then. I've arranged to meet someone for a drink this evening, to discuss business. It could take rather a long time, so we might have dinner if it gets too late. I'm really sorry about this. I hope you don't mind,' Delia said. She sounded contrite enough, but I was alarmed. We had been together every evening until now.

'Of course not. Let's talk tomorrow then,' I said.

I sat for a while after I put down the phone. I couldn't expect Delia to be available for me at all times. Reasonable as her explanation was, it did nothing to mollify me, because reason has little to do with love. I might have felt less apprehensive if she hadn't brought up my visit to the *estancia*, planting doubts in my mind about her true reason for returning. She might not have come back just because she missed me. By now I was wary of explanations that relied largely upon my willingness to believe them.

The phone rang again. I picked it up immediately, in the expectation that Delia had changed her mind.

'It's your mother, Martín,' the receptionist said, and I remembered the message on my desk, which I had ignored when I'd come in that morning. My mother wanted me to call her.

'Put her through,' I said, resigning myself to listening to her usual accusations, although I wondered what could have triggered her this time. Nothing had changed since we'd last spoken. I wasn't living with Delia, and we hadn't been seen together in public either.

'How are you, darling?' my mother said in a chirpy voice, and I realized immediately that this was her effort at conciliation.

'I'm very well, thank you. How are you?'

After confirming she was fine too, my mother launched into chatting about a recent letter from Miguel, and her usual round of social activities. She didn't dwell on it though; she got to the point quickly.

'I haven't seen you for a while. I wondered if you were free to come to dinner with me any evening this week.'

Her invitation was so open-ended that it was hard to refuse without deliberately upsetting her, and I had enough trouble in my life already. I still couldn't believe that she didn't want to admonish me about Delia. If I avoided her now, she would try again. I might as well go through it sooner rather than later.

'I'd love to. I'm free tonight, in fact,' I replied.

'That's lovely. Be here at nine then.'

Delia came out just after seven o'clock. I had been keeping watch on her door for the last half-hour, half-hiding behind a pillar of the *porte-cochère* of the house at the end of the block. I hadn't considered what I would do if she were to walk in my direction, but luckily she didn't. She headed the other way instead. I waited until she was sufficiently far from me, and only then did I follow her.

Spring, frequently as short in Buenos Aires as a cease-fire between old enemies, was turning into early summer. The evening was warm, and Delia wasn't wearing a coat. Her narrow dress showed off her slim figure and her long legs. I was unsettled by the sight of her walking alone, seemingly without any concern other than reaching her destination on time. A taxi approached. I feared she would call it and I would lose track of her in a second, but she kept walking. Wherever she was going, it had to be close enough to her house.

We came to the end of the road, where she headed right once she was past the fountain, and I hurried to catch up. As I turned the corner, I saw Delia walking up Esmeralda Street. My task was easier now that we were in a busier area; cars on the road and people on the sidewalks would hide me from view if she were to look back suddenly, without warning, as if she had sensed my presence. I almost wanted her to do that. It was painful to be so aware of her, of every movement she made, while she was completely unconscious of me.

I followed her across Plaza San Martín. I guessed her destination once she went past the monument. Delia was heading for the Plaza Hotel. I couldn't follow her there; I watched her go in from the other side of the wide road, where I took cover under the trees.

I was ashamed, angry at my own obsession. There was nothing

suspicious in what Delia was doing. She had told me she would be having a drink with someone to discuss business, and she was clearly going to meet him at the Plaza Bar. Only my distrustful frame of mind could find anything questionable in that – and it did soon enough. Delia had her own house. It would have been simpler to ask her guest to come and see her at home.

For all I knew, she still had her suite at the hotel. Delia could be asking for the key at the desk now, then she would nod discreetly at a man standing idly in the foyer, who would follow her into the waiting elevator. I only turned away when I imagined them inside the room, kissing hungrily, his hand unzipping the back of that elegant dress I had been watching so intently until a moment ago. It was an image as crushing as my wish to wipe it out of my mind.

'Do you remember that movie camera I gave you for your birthday years ago?' My mother had been working hard at keeping our conversation going, and I had tried to appear at ease without succeeding. I had been thinking about Delia all evening.

'Yes, I do. I still have it, although it doesn't work any more. They can't get the part to fix it,' I said.

'I always regret not having helped you when you wanted to study movie-making. That's what you really wanted to do, wasn't it?'

It was the last subject I expected her to bring up.

'It doesn't matter any more, *mamá*. That was years ago.'

'You are too young to know what "years" means. There's always time to put things right. I remember you saying that the school was somewhere in America.'

'That's the place I knew about at the time, but since then I've found out there are others.'

'Are you still interested then?'

She wasn't making idle talk, and I wondered what the reason was for this sudden concern.

'Even if I were, it wouldn't make any difference. I can't afford the fees.'

'I could help you.'

Now I understood. My mother was trying to make amends for

our recent friction, and she must have thought hard about something she could offer that would please me. As usual, she was acting as if money didn't really matter, as if she had a divine right to some inexhaustible supply.

'Don't be silly. You know you can't, and I wouldn't want you to,' I said.

'I could sell one of the apartments,' she insisted.

'That's crazy. You don't have that many left anyway.'

My words must have given her pause for thought.

'Probably not,' she said eventually. 'But I have some jewellery I never wear. I could sell it. Or I could sell that.' She nodded towards the still-life painting on the wall opposite me. I had heard her say many times that it used to hang in the dining room of her former house, and how valuable it was, but I had reason to suspect the accuracy of the valuations she put on whatever she had left from better days. They were based more on sentiment than on fact.

'I don't want you to sell anything for my sake. In any case, American schools are far too expensive,' I said.

'You said there are other places.'

'There's a film school in Paris. That's the only other one I know about.'

'I don't think that one would be so good. You ought to go to America really.'

At last we had reached the true reason behind her offer. She was trying to separate me from Delia in the only way she could think of, the way of her rich friends. I had often heard her mention someone or other who was sending their silly daughter abroad, in the hope that she would forget some persistent boyfriend who was suspected of being more interested in the girl's fortune than in her; but I wasn't a naïve young thing, and my mother wasn't rich. Her upside-down logic made me smile for the first time that evening.

'I don't want to go anywhere,' I said. 'It's good of you to offer, but I'm happy as I am. Tell me about Miguel instead.'

It was just after half past ten when I left my mother's apartment. As soon as I was on my own, I began to think about Delia and the man she was with. There was a public telephone at a café nearby. I dialled the Plaza Hotel number and asked for Delia's suite. I heard the extension ring many times, then the operator came back on the line.

'There's no reply,' she said.

I didn't move away when I put the phone down. It could be that Delia wasn't there – or it could be that she and her anonymous lover were too busy to bother to reach for the phone. Images of her in bed, of her face flushed in pleasure, rolled through my mind. I *had* to prove myself wrong. Delia had said she might have dinner with her companion, so perhaps they were still in the hotel dining room. I hoped so, with the fervent anxiety of the unconvinced.

I needed to know what she was doing, and I needed to see the man with her, to flesh out his phantom image. I thought of going to the Plaza to check the restaurant myself. Delia might see me though; her eye could be caught by the small flurry of activity at the door when the maître d' came to me. My fingers clenched the receiver. I could call the Plaza Grill and ask for her, but that wouldn't be enough. Still I wouldn't know if she was with a man or a woman. I should ask for him, make him come to the phone and hear his voice at least, anything that would make him real. I didn't know his name, though, and I couldn't ask for 'the gentleman having dinner with Delia Lagos'. Staff at hotels like the Plaza wouldn't keep their jobs if they were dumb enough to fall for that line; dealing with jealous husbands or lovers had to be part of their everyday routine. I needed some unimpeachable excuse, a credible reason not to mention him by name, and yet be put through to him.

I dialled again, and asked for the Grill.

'My father is having dinner with Delia Lagos. I need to talk to him urgently, please.'

Sweat trickled down my forehead as I waited.

'What's wrong, darling?' said a male voice at the other end, as anxious as any father receiving an unexpected, urgent call from his son. No man had called me 'darling' since my teens, or spoken to me in that concerned tone. Trapped by my own fabrication, the voice rang in my ears as if it were my own father's. I didn't know what he had sounded like. Every feature, every expression in his face was familiar to me from photographs, but this voice could have been his for all I knew, and for a moment it was. Unexpected tears stung my eyes.

I slammed down the phone. It was only when I was out of the noise and sticky air of the café that I began to think that I had heard that voice before. I played it back in my head again and again, until I decided that it could have been the voice of any middle-aged, upper-class Buenos Aires man, the type who would be Delia's invisible lover – or who occupied a high enough position within the Lagos organization to merit dinner with the owner to discuss business.

I walked towards my car. The night air felt almost as damp as my shirt, which was clinging to my back. I took off my jacket and loosened my tie. The incident underlined my irrationality in doubting Delia, although there was a kind of frustrated discernment behind it. The possibility of another lover was a more acceptable focus for my underlying suspicions of her; it could be easily disproved. I didn't really feel threatened by her supposed infidelity, because I didn't really believe it.

Ever since Delia had come back, I had shunned any mention of the circumstances of my father's death, or my mother's involvement with Sebastian. They didn't concern *us*. If the questions had tugged at some corner of my mind occasionally, I had dismissed them as quickly as they sprang up, because I told myself I didn't care any more. Now Sebastian had come between Delia and me. My visit to San Octavio had troubled her for some reason. She was better than my mother at concealing her true feelings, and yet I had sensed the same anxiety in both of them, a similar eagerness to find out what I knew. But the knowledge was theirs, not mine.

My suspicions weren't unfounded. If I had tried so hard to ignore them at first, it was because I sensed that my mother was lying. I sensed that Delia was lying too. I didn't dare choose between the truth and her love.

Delia was out when I called her late the following morning. I called her again mid-afternoon, and I tried yet again before leaving the office. It could have been my imagination that made me hear a note of irony in Américo's voice whenever he asked me if I wanted to leave a message, but it was enough to add to my distress, and my need to hear from her.

I went back to my apartment, wondering what to do next. I had been there for twenty interminable minutes when someone knocked at the door. It was her, looking as cool and unruffled as usual.

'I'm sorry I couldn't call you back earlier. I had meetings all day,' Delia said. 'Nobody seems able to decide anything by themselves now that I'm here.'

She came closer. 'I'd better kiss you myself, since you seem so unresponsive,' she smiled.

As soon as I felt her lips on mine, I realized how silly I had been over the last two days. Delia was here. She had come to me. Anything else was just my own nightmares, my terror of losing her.

The rest of the week only confirmed my new-found certainty of Delia's love. We spent every night together, and there were no further reminders of her independence. We were in her bedroom that Friday evening, enjoying the hazy calm of post-coital satisfaction, when Delia broke the silence.

'What's the time?' she asked without raising her head from my shoulder. Her arm lay across my bare chest, like a sash of office.

'Quarter to eight,' I replied. I began to kiss her. I moved from her lips to her neck and her shoulder, but Delia gently pushed me away and got out of bed.

'Come on, we must hurry.' She led me to the bathroom, and turned on the shower.

'I thought we had all the time in the world,' I protested, less harshly than I meant to, because Delia stood in the shower with me, her body pressed to mine. Then she began to soap me; there was purpose to her motions, not just pleasure.

'The *Vapor de la Carrera* leaves at nine o'clock,' she said. 'If we are out of here by eight, we'll just make it.' She threw a towel at me and started to dry herself. Delia's suggestion was crazy – and irresistibly tempting. The night boat to Montevideo was a creaky old steamer, all brass and polished mahogany, made in

Liverpool before the First World War, as the small plates on the companionways and funnels reminded its passengers. We could have dinner on board, watch the moon from the deck afterwards, and sleep in each other's arms, rolled by the slow waves of the River Plate. It would take us away from Buenos Aires over the weekend.

In a stimulating feeling of shared urgency, we dried ourselves quickly on our way back to the bedroom. Delia took a small bag from the pile of empty luggage in the adjacent dressing room, and dropped a few things she took from her cupboard into it as she got dressed. I added a change of underwear and a spare shirt from my meagre stock which was now housed in the chest of drawers. Some of the large trunks were open, already half-full. Américo must have started packing that afternoon, before Delia gave him the evening off. She knew I felt uncomfortable when the butler was around.

'I like your idea of packing for the weekend. You're not expecting me to cart those trunks downstairs and load them into a taxi, I hope.'

'Don't be ridiculous. I'm taking very little,' she replied. 'Pack a sweater and your cords,' she added. 'I thought we could go to Punta Ballena, and come back on Sunday. It's beautiful at this time of the year when there's nobody about, but it can get cold. I have a house there. You'll love it.'

The brass edge of the porthole framed a rectangle of dark sky, and the lights of Buenos Aires, blinking into invisibility in the far distance as the ship moved away from the shore.

'I hope you won't burst into song,' Delia said, and I gave her a blank, puzzled look.

'*Volver*,' she explained. 'You know, when Gardel is on the boat, and he sees the city lights at the end of the journey.'

Carlos Gardel had been the foremost tango singer in Argentina, a hero in the national pantheon after he died in a plane crash some time in the thirties. But the tango was out of fashion by the time I grew up. People my age did not bother to learn how to dance to that old-fashioned music. I had seen bits of Gardel movies because they were shown occasionally very late at night, but I always switched them off because I found them grotesquely stilted in their saccharine sentimentality.

'Oh, yes, I know what you mean.' It took me a couple of seconds to come up with the comment; it was enough for a pause to develop in what had started as cheerful banter, like a passing cloud turning sunshine into dullness. Delia couldn't care about Gardel any more than I cared about The Platters; I felt uneasy because we had fallen into the ever-open trap of the difference in age between us. She raised her cup, only then noticed it was empty, and put it down again.

'Would you like another coffee?' I asked.

'No, I want to get out of here. It's too stuffy,' she replied, almost toppling her chair as she stood up. I caught up with her by the door.

'Let's go outside,' I said.

Most of the other passengers were still having dinner, and the deck was empty. We leaned on the rail, side by side. Moonlight glossed the brown, muddy waters into a deceptive sheen; the lights of Buenos Aires had turned into a faint, nearly invisible glow in the night sky, but we were still too far away to see the Uruguayan coast. We could have been in the middle of the ocean, and I thought how easy everything would be if we could remain like this, Delia and I travelling indefinitely, never seeing the shore, in a succession of happy, sunny days. I took her hand.

'I love you,' I said for the first time, using those words that sound artificial or trite when read or overheard – and mean so much that I hadn't been able to bring myself to utter them until now. I noticed that there were tears in her eyes.

'It's the wind,' she said, wiping them with the edge of her hand, then she faced me.

'I love you too,' she murmured. I thought I detected the faintest trace of melancholy in her voice. Then she kissed me, so eagerly that it was hard to say whether she felt passion or despair.

Twelve

I still have a sense of wonder at beautiful landscapes. Part of their magic for me then was their feeling of permanence, as though they had been there since time immemorial and would remain unchanged, but now that feeling is qualified by an awareness of transience. There are places I don't want to see again, to preserve my original memory intact. I gather that these days Punta Ballena is studded with apartment buildings and millionaires' villas as white as the yachts bobbing in the bay, their roofs bristling with satellite dishes; that the wooded strip between the road and the beach to one side of the peninsula has been tamed into lawns, and that holiday homes encircled by hydrangeas stand at the top of the dunes.

None was there when I saw the place with Delia. The silver and white bus we took from Montevideo was a replica of a Greyhound coach, even to the white whippet painted on the ribbed steel. I had only seen buses like these in American movies; being on one of them added to my feeling of adventure, a feeling augmented once the bus began to climb the coastal edge of the sierras, their rounded contours fading into a hazy lavender blue on the horizon. The road skirted the ocean, the horizon rolling back in front of my eyes as we went higher and higher. The engine revved hoarsely until we reached the top of the cliff, where the bus slowed down, as if catching its breath after the long ascent.

Although it was off-season, and there were only five or six people on board, the driver was probably following his standard routine to allow the passengers to admire the panorama. A long way below us, a wide beach stretched in an arc of pale sand, ending abruptly in the rocky cliffs of a small peninsula that rose gently towards its blunt tip, like the spine of a giant stone whale. The sea was not quite ocean yet, its tidal force softened by the River Plate estuary, and shallow breakers formed a broad carpet of white foam before reaching the sand. The long sweep of white and yellow contrasted with the deep green of the pine forest along the coastal plain; only a couple of buildings facing the beach broke the thick cover of foliage.

As the bus started to move down the hill, Delia walked up to the driver. 'Stop at the next crossing, there should be someone waiting,' she said.

I could see a gig on the side of the road. As we got off the bus, the thick-set man with glasses standing next to the carriage came up to us.

'Good morning, *señora*. I'm Zenón,' he said, touching his *gaucho*'s beret as a sign of respect. The man took our bag, and we climbed onto the seat at the back. A smell of old leather and warm hay rose from the padded upholstery as we sat down. The horse, gently lashed by the reins, broke into a half-hearted trot along the dirt track up the hill. Delia and I slid against each other on the seat as we hit pot-holes or bumps, and I threw my arm around her shoulders when the tall plumage of pampas grass on the sides of the road closed around us. I held Delia tightly, to keep us both warm in the crisp, invigorating sea air. The bright spring sunshine made the landscape glow, but it wasn't strong enough yet to dispel the morning chill.

The road became steeper. We were well into the side of the sierra by now. Rocky outcrops burst through the cover of shrubs, weeds, and wild, bell-shaped flowers in white, pink and blue. Eventually the ground levelled, and then we stopped. A cluster of fig trees blocked the view of the house, which stood against the hillside. Rough slate slabs laid on the ground as steps led to a small terrace where a woman waited, her light-brown hair streaked blonde by the sun. She was wearing a white kitchen apron over her bright blue dress.

The house wasn't large: a white, bold prism with square windows set in the thick masonry. At one end, the front wall formed the side of a shallow staircase. I followed Delia up onto the flat roof, where the square terracotta tiles reflected the heat of the sun. We could see the horizon in every direction: the sea in front, the hills and a lagoon to one side, and the bay to the other. I had been to Punta del Este for a few days a couple of summers ago; I recognized the skyline of the small town on a peninsula miles away, its lighthouse marking the end of the land.

'It *is* beautiful,' Delia murmured.

'You sound as if you've never seen it before,' I said.

'I hadn't. My father and I came to Punta del Este the last summer he was alive, and I fell in love with the place. It was very wild in those days. We were asked to an *estancia* nearby for the day, and I found this spot when we were riding after lunch. I asked my father to buy it for me; he thought I was crazy, but he obliged me. I asked Jean Michel Frank, who was living in Buenos Aires during the war, to design the house. I never saw it finished, because I left before then. Someone from the office has looked after it ever since. I suppose they use it for holidays.'

Delia's passing reference to her departure from Buenos Aires at the time intrigued me. It was as if she had bolted rather than simply left.

'Let's go inside,' she said. 'We'd better make sure we can stay here. There might not be any furniture, for all I know.'

There *was* furniture, and lunch waited for us. For once I felt comfortable in one of Delia's houses, perhaps because it was new territory to both of us. The housekeeper and her husband acted as if they weren't quite sure who we were, and Delia did nothing to enlighten them. Throughout lunch, she praised the simple food with the enthusiasm of a polite guest, balanced by the ease of manner more suited to the owner of the place. The housekeeper managed to keep her curiosity at bay until the end of our meal.

'Are you friends of Mr Rivera then?' she asked when she brought us coffee.

'I know him fairly well,' Delia replied. 'Have you worked for him long?'

'Five years. We used to work for Don Simón de la Force before, on the other side of the hill, but he was impossible,' the woman replied dryly.

'I'm glad you find Mr Rivera a better employer,' Delia said courteously. The woman nodded, and went back to the kitchen.

'Who is Mr Rivera? I thought that the house was yours,' I said.

'He is in Maldonado, and he manages holiday homes in the area. He deals with my people in Buenos Aires. I'm sure he's led the caretakers to believe he owns this place. Probably he uses it in the summer.' Delia replied quietly, to avoid being overheard.

'You must tell them who you are then,' I said, with the pomposity of those who have reason to question their own standing.

'Why? I'm sure they'll take much better care of the place if they believe Rivera is the owner rather than someone who only comes here every twenty years.'

Delia's deceit was small, inconsequential, probably wise in the circumstances. There was an amusing, farce-like side to it, and yet it made me uncomfortable. If I hadn't known the facts, I would have fallen for her act as readily as the housekeeper.

Delia didn't need to tell Zenón and his wife that she was their employer to get them to do whatever she wanted. Her charm and her tips took care of that. After lunch, Zenón departed on foot for a farm on the other side of the hill, where he assured Delia one of his friends could lend him a pick-up truck for us to use during our stay. He said he would be back in about an hour.

Once he left, Delia went into the kitchen. Through the door, I could hear the noise of pans and crockery being put away.

'Lunch was perfect, Manuela,' she said. 'You know, I was here many years ago, but I still remember how delicious the local mussels are. Do you find them difficult to cook?'

'No, not at all,' Manuela replied, rising to the implicit challenge.

'You are such a good cook. What are we having for dinner?'

'Mr Rivera asked me to get *lomo*. I've already bought it,' the woman said.

'What a shame,' Delia commented in a mild lament. 'Any chance of you getting mussels this afternoon? You could keep the beef for yourself. I hope fifty pesos will be enough. Keep the change, if there's any,' she said, laying a bank note on the kitchen table.

I appreciated Delia's velvet-glove approach to bribery. Even she had to know that fifty pesos would buy enough mussels to feed us for days.

'I'll manage,' Manuela replied. 'I'd have to go to Maldonado in the gig, though. It would take me at least an hour to get there. I should leave now, if I'm to be back in time to prepare dinner,' Manuela moaned.

'Oh, I wouldn't want to disturb you at all. Let's forget about it. I'm sure the beef will be perfect.'

'No, no, it's no trouble, *señora*,' Manuela said hastily, worried about missing out on such a good deal, and the chance of a trip to town.

I left Delia to her negotiations and went to the terrace, where I stretched myself out on a deck-chair. The combination of sun on my face and wine during lunch made me drowsy, and I was sleepily aware of the sound of the carriage driving away. Delia was behind me, stroking my hair.

'They've gone,' she said. 'They won't be back for an hour at least.'

I jumped to my feet. 'Time for siesta then.' My drowsiness was suddenly gone.

We walked into the house. Manuela had closed the shutters before she left. I was blinded by the cool penumbra at first, until my eyes forgot the white light outside. I followed Delia into the bedroom in the state of heightened arousal brought on by new, unknown places, more powerful than new sensations. The room smelled of wax polish, and eucalyptus from the wood outside. We stood face to face and stared at each other. Her eyes glistened brighter than her mouth, brighter than anything else. There was no hurry. Both of us knew this was the best, volatile moment, when anticipation makes the memory real again, when we rediscover what we know so well.

We didn't kiss until we were naked, once our clothes cluttered the floor. The tip of my tongue pressed against hers hard, as hard as her fingers clenched my buttocks and pulled me close to her. There was no air, no void between Delia and me, and yet we weren't sufficiently close. Our hands and mouths ran over the other's body in blind recognition, feeling and holding, coming together and parting again, grappling at their own focused satisfaction only to move on in pleasure that couldn't please enough.

The smell of lavender on the fresh sheets seemed intrusive when we fell on the bed because it distracted me briefly from the headier warm scent of Delia's skin. Her hands rose to my face, framing it for her gaze that held a kind of innocent irony, as if she too were astonished at the fact that our eyes, untouching, unfeeling, could rope us together more strongly than our arms.

Her thighs gripped my hips. I reared up a little, just enough not to enter her. I didn't want to yet, or I wanted it too much not to relish the thrill of delay, of holding back while my fingertips explored her skin like unmapped territory. I didn't want my own pleasure to mask hers for me. I wanted to see her wince, moan in enjoyment, and only then take her and forget everything but my own release, my own power, until I opened my eyes to find myself spent, dazed and subdued within the shelter of her embrace.

I watched her face soften. The edge of her teeth dug into her lower lip. Her hands clutched the sheet. I heard her call my name in sweet despair. Suddenly, Delia pushed me back and rolled on top of me. She kissed my brow and my eyelids with small, flickering kisses. A moment later her lips moved to my chest, skimmed over my belly, and circled my navel. I had just closed my eyes in anticipation when she raised her head and moved forward, her legs still pressed against my flanks. Her weight was no longer on me, while her fingers gripped my prick and guided it inside her. She raised herself up and down very slowly, deliberately, as if she wanted to stay on this bed, in this room, making love for the rest of our lives.

I'd been in love at other times, in places at least as beautiful as that coast was then, and it would be untrue to say that I felt less contented, less exhilarated than I felt that day with Delia. There is some inner measure of emotions, and we know its range. We can gauge happiness, in the sense of knowing when we have reached its apex. I had been in love before. There had been other sunsets by the sea, my arm around the shoulders of a woman I thought was like no other, while the horizon changed from orange to a lilac shade of pink.

None like that evening, though. I could see how happy Delia was, as happy as I felt myself. We had driven to Punta del Este later in the afternoon, once Zenón returned with the pick-up truck. Delia wanted to see the harbour. It was too early in the season for yachts, and the fish market was closed, as were most of the shops in town. After a stroll along the empty piers, we made our way towards the tip of the peninsula, along silent streets lined with short, robust palm trees, catching views of the sea around us on both sides as we approached the lighthouse. It was the heart of the old fishing village, long out of fashion with people who built holiday homes there: they preferred to be closer to the beaches and the pine forests. The white- or cream-rendered fronts and the wooden shutters showed the scars of winter in the salty air. We reached the end of the land and sat on the rocks, waiting for the twilight. The breakers foamed against the reefs. In the distance, a large dark object rolled in the waves and then disappeared in the surf on its slow progress towards the shore. The disc of the sun was touching the sea. I knew it was a mirage, that the sun was already below the horizon, but it seemed clearer, more sharp-edged than ever, as the best illusions are.

Delia raised the collar of her jacket. 'This is what we should do, live on our own somewhere like this,' she said.

It was a Saturday afternoon thought. By Monday she would be back in her real life, making long-distance calls to her banker or her broker, consulting her lawyer or discussing figures with someone like my friend Raúl's boss. Even if Delia was prepared to consider a new life away from everything, I wasn't. There was so little I could call my own. I didn't feel I had experienced enough. I couldn't give up what I hadn't yet had.

'Let's not make plans now,' I said. Sitting there with her, in the soft clarity of a fairy tale, 'now' seemed as permanent as eternity.

'We *have* to make plans, Martín. I don't like what's happening to us any more than you do. We can't stay in Buenos Aires. I thought it would be easier for both of us there, but it isn't. Was it you who phoned while I was having dinner at the Plaza last week?'

Delia knew it was me; it would have been as childish to try to deny it as it would be cowardly to pretend her instinct wasn't right. We had to leave. I had wanted it myself, although it was easier to cherish the prospect than face the certainty.

'Yes, it was me. It was a stupid thing to do, but I was desperately jealous. I thought there was somebody else.'

'I suppose I should be flattered,' Delia smiled. 'I'm glad you told me. There's nothing worse than lying to each other.'

'In that case you must tell me everything about my father's death.' I was surprised I could ask that question so calmly, without apprehension.

Delia edged away from me. 'We've talked enough about your father already. I've told you there was nothing between us,' she said. 'Are you still worried about those letters?'

'No, but I've found out so many things since I came back,' I replied. 'You were on the yacht when my father died, and yet you said nothing about it in Paris.'

Delia sat very straight, her hands in her lap. She stared at them, then she raised her head. 'I didn't want to talk about your father in Paris. Not because of him or me; I've told you it was a meaningless flirtation. It meant little then, and even less now. If I didn't want to mention your father it was because of us. I don't need to be reminded of my age, least of all by . . .'

She pronounced the word 'age' very quickly, like a runner sprinting over a hurdle, and then her voice trailed away. I knew I was hurting her, and yet I couldn't avoid it.

'I understand that, but I'm talking about my father's death now. My mother is angry with you, as if you had something to do with it. She told us he died on October the sixteenth. The notice and the obituary said he died the following day. There has to be a reason for the discrepancy.'

'Isabel would blame me for anything she can think of. You must stop listening to her, otherwise she will make you destroy what we have,' Delia snapped. She seemed upset for the first time. 'She tells you whatever she wants to believe, and you assume that everybody hides the truth from you for sinister reasons. Luckily, the motive behind most lies is some blunder or error of judgement, not deviousness. You are right: your father's death was on October the sixteenth, but it was announced as if it had happened on the seventeenth. I'll tell you why, if you promise me that you'll never discuss this with Isabel. It was a very unhappy time for all of us, and she is entitled to blame my family. There's nothing sinister about it, only stupid motives that led to bad decisions.'

My first reaction was mild elation, a kind of relief. My suspicions had not been the result of some neurotic obsession. Delia was going to tell me what I wanted to know. What I *needed* to know.

'You must promise,' Delia insisted.

'I promise I won't say anything,' I assured her. There was something brittle about her composure, in the stillness of her posture, when she started to talk.

'I had been friends with your mother since we were at school together, and Sebastian knew your father. The four of us saw a lot of each other at the time, as people do at that age. My father had arranged a big lunch in San Octavio, and he wanted us there. He suggested we brought some friends along, so we wouldn't be bored. Sebastian asked Francis and Isabel to come with us on the yacht. We boarded early on the fifteenth, and we were due in San Octavio the following morning. That night, your mother and I went to bed after midnight, and Sebastian and Francis stayed in the sitting room; I think they were playing cards. The next morning, I found Sebastian on deck after breakfast. We were about to dock, but there was no sign of Isabel or your father. We sent someone to their cabins to let them know that they should get ready. There was no reply when the man knocked at Francis's door. Sebastian and I went downstairs. Isabel was fast asleep. She hardly stirred when I tried to wake her up. There was a bottle of sleeping pills on her bedside table, and she had drunk quite a lot the night before.'

That sounded like my mother, and the trivial detail made Delia's story more real to me.

'Francis's bed was untouched, so Sebastian asked the steward to look everywhere on board. My brother had gone to bed around one o'clock, and Francis had stayed behind: he had said he wanted to go outside to get some fresh air. We checked the other cabins ourselves, but Francis wasn't there. Then someone found him somewhere on the top deck. A few moments later, Sebastian came back and told me that Francis was dead. An ambulance took

Francis's body to a hospital in Rosario. The autopsy showed he had had a stroke.'

'The reason we went to San Octavio that day was that the President had been touring the province of Santa Fe, and he was going to stop at our *estancia* for lunch on his way back to Buenos Aires. The visit was very important, a great honour for my father, who wanted his family around him. It was a public sign of Castillo's favour, and the Conservative candidate for the next presidential election was to be announced in a few months' time. My father had been working hard behind the scenes because he wanted to be the President's choice. Elections were invariably rigged then, so being the official candidate was as good as getting elected. The presidency was the peak of my father's ambitions; there was nothing else he wanted. His chance of getting the nomination was good, but he couldn't afford anything going wrong.

'Now he found himself with a dead man on his property, a close friend of his children. He wasn't prepared to cancel the lunch at short notice. Ministers, senators and congressmen coming from Buenos Aires were already on their way, and the President would arrive soon. On the other hand, he could hardly appear to be hosting a great social and political event when one of his guests had died on his yacht that very morning. My father decided to play for time, and by then Isabel had appeared on deck. He told her that Francis had fallen ill, and been taken to hospital. Isabel was hysterical. She was driven to the house, where she was kept under sedation.'

Delia paused. I remained silent, because I wanted her to continue her account. My questions could wait.

'Sebastian and I didn't attend the lunch either. We were too shocked to act as if nothing had happened. My father sent the yacht away; I suppose he must have told people we hadn't arrived because of some technical trouble, although I doubt anyone would have noticed we weren't there. That evening we heard from the hospital. The autopsy showed that the cause of death was a burst aneurysm, a congenital defect, apparently. My father pulled strings, and kept the story quiet until the next day, when Francis's death was announced. The public explanation was that the yacht had arrived late on the sixteenth, after the President had left; your father fell ill on the *estancia* that evening and was taken to hospital, where he died the following morning. That's why the notice you saw in the paper gave the date of his death as October the seventeenth. Eventually my father spoke to Isabel, and she agreed to the lie. It would have been very embarrassing for him otherwise, and it didn't make much difference to the tragic fact of Francis's death. Isabel didn't want to cause trouble for my father, but I think she saw us as responsible for his misfortune in some way, as if we had brought Francis bad luck. She distanced herself, certainly from me. She didn't call me, or try to make contact with me at all. At first I decided it was better to leave her alone, and then I moved to New York and lost touch with many people.'

Delia's explanation had shifted the blame to my mother, who was likely to see herself as a victim of fate. She would take out her resentment at her failed life on Delia, who had everything my mother had lost. She had distanced herself from my father's family too.

'Why was my father cremated?' I threw the question at Delia as suddenly as it came to my mind. She was absorbed in her own thoughts now, and it took her a second to respond.

'I didn't know he was. Isabel was in charge of his funeral, but I didn't attend.'

'I'd rather not ask her,' I lied. 'That's why I'm asking you.'

'So you are worried about upsetting her.'

'I don't want to give her the chance to say something I wouldn't like to hear.'

'What are you suggesting, Martín? What is it that you suspect, and yet you can't bring yourself to say? Why can't you be open for once?'

'That's what I think about you . . .' It was my turn to face unbreachable hurdles, for my voice to falter. 'I'm sorry, I don't know who to believe any more,' I said. 'I feel you're hiding something from me.'

Delia took my hand. 'It's me who should be sorry,' she said. 'You were right to feel cheated once you suspected something odd had happened. Please believe me when I say there's nothing else to the facts of Francis's death. It was a stupid fabrication by my father. It seemed so important to him at the time, and yet it became meaningless less than a year later, once Perón came to power. But he couldn't have known that. My father always got people to do what he wanted, and we all agreed to his lie. It makes no difference that he's been dead for twenty years; you can't stop lying once you start. That's why I left in the first place, and that's why I find it so hard to be here again. These old stories are like mud on a dirt road, you can't get out of it once you let it trap you.'

The breeze was strengthening. Delia held her jacket tight about her.

'Let's go back,' she said. 'Let's go back to Paris now. You can start your film course, and everything will be fine. Let's leave as soon as possible.'

Delia hadn't mentioned that Sebastian and my mother were lovers – but then I hadn't mentioned it either. She didn't know I had found out, so she had no reason to reveal something she could assume would upset me greatly. Whatever had happened between my mother and him was in the past, and I appreciated Delia's tact. It had nothing to do with my life. I didn't want to discuss my mother with her, and give her the chance to reciprocate unpleasantness. She was right about old stories: it was better to stay away from them. Going away with Delia was not only what I wanted, it would give me the chance to leave the past behind. It wasn't an easy option though.

'I don't want to depend on you. You know that.'

'I knew it would come to money sooner or later,' she sighed. 'You're being silly, but there must be a way. You can apply for a scholarship. I'll talk to people in Paris who can help you. We *must* go, Martín. We'll never be happy in Buenos Aires. We know how we feel there.'

I remembered our recent misery: Delia's sudden coldness, my irrational jealousy. I knew we should go – but I was frightened. Depending on her financially was not my only worry. I would have to trust her too.

'I can't drop my job from one day to the next,' I said.

'You can tell Lucas on Monday that you want to leave. That'll be a start at least.'

Delia stood up. 'It's getting cold. Let's go,' she said.

I helped her keep her balance as we climbed over the slippery stones, varnished by the water and encrusted with mussel shells and a grey honeycomb of barnacles. The dark object in the sea was very near the shore now, rolling backwards and forwards in the tide. It was a sea-lion cub, and he was dead. Soaked by the sea, his light grey pelt had become a murky, blackish shade of charcoal, as dark as the rocks.

Thirteen

It wasn't unusual in those days for people in Buenos Aires to mention the great earthquake that had destroyed San Juan in 1944. Although the city was a thousand miles away from the capital, they would reminisce about their fear when chandeliers swung over their heads and glasses rattled on their tables, as the ground rippled across the country from the Andes to the sea, through the great plain. It was fear of the unknown, of something both inexplicable and unexpected that was beyond their control, something that could shatter their lives instantly. They didn't know what had happened until emergency bulletins were broadcast on the radio. The news was reassuring because the danger was too far away to affect them, yet disquieting because it made the unimaginable closer.

It was how I felt after my conversation by the sea with Delia. Her words reassured me in many ways. Social convention still mattered a great deal then; Mrs Rousselet had not been considered foolish for jeopardizing her crumbling fortune for the sake of her granddaughters' standing among their friends, so I could imagine what it must have been like twenty years earlier. The presidency was within Ambrosio Lagos's grasp. He would have been forced to cancel his great event if news of my father's death had emerged that day, so he had played for time and hushed it up.

My mother's agreement to the deception didn't surprise me either. She abided by the rules, so she would not have wanted to cause embarrassment, and there could have been more to her decision than worldly *savoir-faire*. She was about to lose everything, and she must have considered the possibility that Sebastian might marry her now that she was free. But the fact that she was a widow with two children would have made her far from the ideal wife for his son as far as Ambrosio Lagos was concerned. To contradict and upset her potential father-in-law would not have done much for her chances.

She had lied to Miguel and me, though. Her reasons were understandable as far as the rest of the world was concerned, but not us. She hadn't trusted me enough when I asked her for an explanation, long after the reason behind the lie had ceased to be relevant. The ramblings of the old story affected me now because – inadvertently or not – Delia's explanation only reinforced my disillusionment. I had tried hard to justify my mother's affair with Sebastian; my goodwill had nearly run out.

I hadn't been entirely convinced when Delia had said that leaving Buenos Aires was our only chance, but I came round to it hour by hour, so I was glad to be back in my office on Monday morning. I wanted to ascertain work in progress and establish the earliest possible cut-off point before I spoke to my boss. I hadn't been at my desk for long when the internal phone rang.

'Martín, could you come and see me now, please?' It was Lucas Marquez.

I was perplexed. None of the estates I was working on was either big enough or complicated enough to deserve his personal attention.

'Yes, of course. Should I bring any papers?' I asked.

'No, I just want to have a word with you.' Lucas rang off. I walked up the stairs, then along the book-lined corridors, and reached the anteroom to Lucas's office.

Lavinia, his secretary, smiled at me. 'Please go in, Martín. Mr Marquez is waiting for you.'

Lucas heard the door, and put aside the papers he was reading. I had been to his office sporadically since I had started to work here. Unusually, he stood up to greet me, something he hadn't done since I came for my interview. However, his face wasn't emblazoned with the resplendent, welcoming smile of my first day, nor set into the everyday business-like expression I had become used to. There was an air of amiable concern about him as he led me to the more convivial part of the room, to the comfortable armchairs where we had sat during my job interview.

'Our daughters had a party at home last night,' he said, stifling a yawn as we sat down. 'I don't understand why they need to have the music so loud, but I suppose I shouldn't complain to someone their age,' he added jovially. Like most very good lawyers or doctors, Lucas Marquez had the art of making people feel at ease at will. 'It's a great thing to be young, Martín.'

I wasn't expecting small-talk, so I remained silent.

'You have to make the most of it. You won't get it back. Time wasted is time lost. You need to plan your future.' Lucas's truisms followed each other like well-disciplined troops on their way to battle.

'Isabel called me last week. She asked me to talk to you.'

I should have expected my mother not to remain idle after I had turned down her offer. She wanted Delia out of my life, and she must have thought that Lucas, in the role of 'masculine authority', might succeed where she had failed. I braced myself for a lecture on my private life, although I assumed that the prospect was as unpalatable for him as it was for me.

'She said you'd like to go abroad to study . . .' Lucas must have forgotten the specific subject, and his voice waned slightly, missing a beat. 'I gather you'd like to go to America, and Isabel wants to help you,' he added.

My impulse was to deny it, to claim that my mother had made too much of a casual conversation. I didn't like Lucas being dragged into the issue, however well-meaning his intentions. More relevant, although less easy to face, was that my future could be decided over the next few moments, once I admitted that I was planning to leave. The decision had seemed so painless, so inevitable when I was with Delia, and yet I found myself leaning towards equivocation now. Impatient at my pusillanimity, I forced myself to own up.

'This is all a misunderstanding,' I said. 'I don't want to go to America. I'd like to go to Paris, in fact, because there's a very good film school there, but I don't want my mother to help me. She can't afford it.'

Lucas took off his glasses and put them on the low table between us, then rubbed the bridge of his nose. Short-sighted people without their glasses look either vulnerable and friendly, or distantly aloof. In his case I couldn't make up my mind which it was.

'You see, Martín, I've known you and Miguel since you were born. You are almost like sons to me, and at my age one begins to look back a lot. When I see someone like you, a young man finding his way, I see myself as I once was. I remember my own mistakes. One of the few advantages of making mistakes is that you can warn others about the risks they are taking, because you know the signs.'

I wondered if we were heading for tango territory, a wise older man warning a foolish youth about the dangers of a bad woman who would ruin his life.

'Let me tell you a bit about myself,' Lucas went on. 'I didn't start this office, as you know. My father did, and he was very successful . . .'

I knew about Lucas's father from my mother. He had been a friend of my grandfather's. Both men must have been fairly similar types, ready to make the most of their opportunities at a time when the country resembled a conjurer's top hat out of which a dazzling array of tricks could be pulled.

'My father expected me to take over from him eventually. Although I wanted to be a doctor, I didn't ever mention it to him. From my career to my marriage or even my opinions, I always did what was expected of me. It's a good recipe for success, but it does have its drawbacks.'

Lucas wasn't lecturing me, as I had feared, and he didn't seem to be criticizing me either.

'You are bright enough to earn your living as a lawyer, even if you are not cut out for the profession. You could be successful at it, in fact, and that's the problem. Twenty or thirty years from now you might find out that you've made a big mistake, when it will be too late to do anything about it.'

I had to assume Lucas was talking about himself, and I was astonished. It was impossible to infer from his everyday performance as a man in command of everything around him that he wasn't pleased with himself or his life. He reached for a cigarette and offered me one.

'It would be a shame for you not to be able to do something you want so badly. There are enough lawyers already, and there's no point in wasting your time here. You should accept your mother's offer. When would you like to leave? I suppose the sooner the better. Gonzalez knows a young lawyer, a relation of his wife's, I believe, who can start a week from now.'

It took me a couple of seconds to realize that Lucas was firing me. In a very tactful way, undoubtedly, he was telling me to go. I wondered if it was part of his agreement with my mother, to force me to accept her help and do as she wanted, or if it was merely a manoeuvre to please my boss by giving my job to his relative. My lack of interest in my work had been plain to see, and Gonzalez might have used it to put pressure on Lucas. My mother's request gave him the opportunity to please both of them.

'I'll leave on Friday then,' I told him. I stood up and headed for the door, with the hollow dignity of someone beaten by a power much greater than his own.

I had planned to resign. I didn't care for my job. Being fired made no real difference, and yet a feeling of humiliation knotted my stomach when I left Lucas's office. Or I took it to be humiliation at first; once I was back in my office, I realized it was downright anxiety. I had counted on time to adapt to the idea that I would leave with Delia and give up the life I knew for good, to accept the implications, but everything was happening too quickly for me.

I still wondered if my mother was behind Lucas's shock tactics, in order to force me to accept her offer and go away. Delia had given plenty of evidence of her intention to settle in Buenos Aires; my mother couldn't know about her sudden change of mind. I reached for the phone and called Delia.

'I've spoken to Lucas. I told him I want to leave, and we agreed I should go on Friday.'

'That's marvellous. We can fly out on Saturday then. I'll arrange the tickets. There might even be a flight on Friday night.'

It was Delia's style to brush aside any difficulties as insignificant, but she was rushing me now. Long-distance travelling was different thirty years ago. There was no urgency, nobody travelled from one day to the next. It was a leisurely activity, a kind of slow-motion pleasure that started at the travel agent, where posters with words like 'Clipper' and 'Stratocruiser' emblazoned across them were pictures of smiling air hostesses in pencil-line skirts, army-style berets and high heels, or passengers blissfully asleep in their sleeping berths. In any case, I had to pack and clear my apartment. I wanted to speak to my brother before I left, and to say goodbye to a few friends.

Most of all, I needed time to brace myself for saying goodbye to my mother. I couldn't believe she would have asked Lucas to fire me, but her intervention had given him the excuse. I minded her meddling in my life more than the outcome, which would infuriate *her*. Another scene about Delia was inevitable once she knew about my decision, and the prospect made me yearn to leave right away, without explanations. But it was impossible, as well as cowardly, so I had to find a way to deal with her.

'Why are you in such a hurry?' I asked.

'I'm sorry,' she said. 'I'm so eager for us to go that I'm not making sense. Of course you can't leave so quickly. When would *you* like to travel?'

The change in her tone mollified me. 'I'd rather go on Monday instead. It would give me time to sort things out over the weekend.'

'Let's fly out on Monday then,' Delia agreed. 'What time will you be here this evening?' Her casual tone didn't fool me. I could hear in her voice that she was as keen to see me as I was to see her.

'I'll come straight from work,' I said. It felt good to sound so routine, like a real couple. Hearing Delia's voice restored my sense of balance. As soon as I put the phone down, the preparations for the trip, even the trip itself – my actual wrenching-away from all I knew other than Delia herself – seemed to become less daunting, less fearsome. Lucas's sanctimonious concern for my future as an excuse for my curt dismissal had been infuriating, but it had forced me into the right decision, and now I felt almost grateful to him.

I could even bring myself to think about my mother with some equanimity. She had tried to bribe me away from Buenos Aires because she must have been terrified of the inevitable alternative outcome. She knew I would go away with Delia sooner or later. She had lost my father, then Miguel, and she was about to lose me. The fear of loneliness was what drove her, touching every aspect of her life. It made Delia's explanation about the change in the date of my father's death far more credible than her own. My mother had agreed to the lie for the sake of her shallow priorities, in solidarity with the rules of a club that would throw her out when she could no longer afford the membership fee. She had used my father's family as an excuse for my sake, because she knew I would find the real one unworthy of her.

She would be on her own now, having to fend for herself, and I felt sad about that. I wasn't worried about her health – she wasn't old. She was fairly clueless about practical matters though, particularly money, and her offer of help was yet another sign of her ineptitude. Her standard of living was Spartan from her point of view, and she always moaned about it, and yet Miguel and I had been educated in private schools, we went on summer vacations, new clothes were bought when needed, and she had paid for our trips abroad when we graduated. Her way of balancing her accounts every few years had been to sell one of those apartments in the building she had managed to save from her financial débâcle. I wondered what she had left to see her through her old age.

I picked up one of the box files in my room and went to see Silvana. The file was my alibi in case she asked why I needed to go to the archive, but she wasn't at her desk, so I opened her drawer and took the key. I couldn't hear any noise when I reached the basement: nobody was about. I let myself into the records room and switched on the light. The air smelled of damp and musty old paper.

It wasn't long before I found my mother's name on a label. Her files occupied a whole box. I took it to the table in the middle of the room and opened it. Most of the files went back to my grandfather's time, during the days when Lucas's father was in charge of the practice, and our family business was worth handling. From 1931 onwards, my grandmother's name appeared on the correspondence headings until 1936, the year of her death. Then it was replaced by the name of my mother's uncle, her guardian until 1938, when she came of age after her marriage.

From 1940 onwards the correspondence started to include copies of letters between Lucas's father and a notary about the escalating sale of properties on behalf of my parents. I found a copy of a letter to my father, dated 1941, warning him about the need for more prudent administration. Early in 1942, the tone of the letters became sharper on both sides, my father protesting that they were being cheated by unscrupulous administrators, his lawyer replying that a drastic control of expenditure was necessary. The next letter was dated November 3rd, 1942, and addressed to my mother. After a paragraph of condolences on the death of her husband, the subject of probate of my father's estate was raised. Since there were no assets, no tax would be due.

There were a few letters about the formalities in connection with her custody of Miguel and me, and other legalities arising from her new status as a widow. Filed among them was a much shorter note, confirming the sale of all properties in my mother's name to Ambrosio Lagos, as instructed. The price agreed was a thousand pesos – a pitifully small sum even in those days before inflation. It had to be a legal fiction, concocted to disguise an outright transfer as a sale. Attached to the letter was a schedule of the assets in question: there was land in Azul, and several valuable properties in Buenos Aires. The inventory confirmed my scepticism about the agreed price, but there was something else. Included on the list was the apartment building that was now supposed to be my mother's only source of income.

I went back to my office. Luckily Gonzalez was out that morning, so I didn't have to struggle to put up a front of normality. I sat at my desk, staring blankly at the ceiling, unable to think. All I could do was wait until my thoughts had had time to catch up with my crushing feeling of dejection.

There was no conceivable reason for the deal between my mother and Ambrosio Lagos – unless she was bribing him. It seemed ludicrous at first. Ambrosio was enormously rich himself. He didn't need more money. However, one thing I had learned during my time at Lucas's office had been that sometimes money matters much more to those who have it than to those who don't. Ambrosio Lagos had turned a sizeable family fortune into an enormous one; he could have been the type of man for whom a good deal was irresistible, regardless of the circumstances.

My mother's reasons were far more relevant to me than Ambrosio's. She had justified the cremation as if it had been my father's request. Even when I had no reason to doubt her, the explanation had astonished me. It had seemed so unlikely that my father would worry about funeral arrangements at his age. The thought that she might have killed him in anger that night on the yacht had crossed my mind before, but I had discarded it as ludicrous – because I couldn't face it.

I had to confront it now. It explained everything: the need to destroy my father's body, and her subsequent deal with Ambrosio Lagos to buy his silence. A murder on board his yacht was a far more credible reason for the need to conceal what had happened from his guests and the President. Ambrosio had the power to arrange a cover-up, and he had used it to manipulate my mother into a desperate bargain.

What did she tell you? It's all lies! My mother had panicked when I had asked her about the cremation, because she'd assumed Delia had told me everything in Paris – as I believed she had told me the truth two days ago. Delia knew what had really happened. She had been on the yacht that night. I dialled her number.

'I thought you were busy. Don't tell me you miss me so much you need to call me every half-hour,' she said jovially.

'I need to . . .' I started, only to stop. My determination to tell her what I had found out faltered because I was no longer sure I wanted to know about my mother. Not because of her, but because of Delia and me. Delia had lied to protect us, to spare me knowledge that would ruin my life. Even if I didn't see my mother ever again, it wouldn't alter the fact that she had killed my father.

'I need to work late, so I won't be coming this evening. I'll see you tomorrow,' I said instead. I couldn't count on Delia not noticing something if she saw me today; I didn't trust myself enough to hold back if she asked me why I was upset.

'Come whenever you want. I'll be here,' she said.

'Did you find out if there's a flight on Friday night?' I would have gone now, if I had had the choice.

'You are impossible,' Delia sighed in mock annoyance. '*You* told me you couldn't leave on Friday.'

Because of my own turmoil, I was astounded she could sound so detached, so *normal*. But then Delia had known all along, ever since we met. She had had twenty years to distance herself from the knowledge; like an innocent bystander learning to live with the memory of an accident witnessed by chance, she had learned to put it out of her mind. I hoped one day I could put it out of my mind too.

It would take time though. I wondered if I would be able to live with Delia now, never mentioning my father's murder in order not to lose her. I had only to consider the possibility of life without her to know I had no alternative. I had nothing else.

'I've changed my mind. Why don't you find out if there's a flight on Friday after all?' I insisted, ending the call before she had time to ask me why. I sat there in a silence which had become an insidious reminder of my isolation, so I was glad when the phone rang.

'It's your brother,' the receptionist announced.

'Put him through.' I had been planning to call Miguel that evening anyway, to say goodbye.

'I phoned you this weekend but you weren't there,' he said.

'I was away. I have something to tell you. I'm going to study film-making in Paris. It's a three-year course, and I am very excited . . .' I heard myself describe my plans, and my enthusiasm seemed to make a tentative return.

'Has this got anything to do with Delia Lagos?' Miguel interrupted me.

'Yes. Why?'

'*Mamá* called me on Saturday. That's why I was trying to get in touch with you.'

'What did she have to say?'

'A lot of things about Delia Lagos, none very nice, and then she said she couldn't cope with all this, that it would be better if she were dead. I told her she was being ridiculous, but she sounded really upset this time, so I called Malisa and asked her to stay in the apartment over the weekend, just in case.'

My brother didn't need to elaborate. We both remembered the

sleeping pills episode about two years ago, after Miguel had announced his decision to work in the country. Our mother had been taken to hospital, where they had pumped out her stomach. She claimed it had been an accident, that she had taken sleeping pills at night on top of tranquillizers during the day. We knew different, although her doctor said she hadn't taken a lethal dose.

'You should talk to *mamá* yourself though, and tell her you're going.'

For a second, the chance to tell her I knew seemed irresistible, the best possible revenge, but then I saw how futile it would be. My mother had embraced me on the night of the Rousselet ball, cooing words of comfort about how wonderful my father had been. If she was capable of such brazen hypocrisy then, all I would find now were further reasons to hate her.

'I don't want to. I can't bear another argument with her. I might write to her once I get to Paris,' I said.

'What do I do if she calls again before you go? She phoned me yesterday too.'

I couldn't explain why I didn't want to see or speak to our mother. I envied Miguel's ignorance, but it must have been hard enough for him to live all those years with his memory of Sebastian and our mother together. He had mentioned it only when he could bring himself to face it, once it had stopped mattering to him. I couldn't leave him with the suspicion that our mother had murdered our father as my parting gift.

'Do whatever you want. I don't mind if you tell her I'm going.'

We talked for a while about my plans. Neither of us wanted to ring off; I wondered when I would meet my brother again.

'See you when I see you then. Good luck,' he said eventually.

'You too. Take care. I'll miss you.' The words came out of my lips sounding quite meaningless, because I was struggling so hard to hold back my tears. Saying goodbye to my brother made it brutally clear to me that leaving now would not be as painless as the first time, because I had no intention of coming back.

I began to sort out papers, then I noticed that the key to the archive was still on my desk. I ought to return it to Silvana. It would be a good opportunity to tell her I was leaving, although she might have heard already through the office grapevine. I found her at her desk, seemingly quite busy at a new, large grey typewriter, of a kind I hadn't seen before, an instruction manual open beside her.

'What a surprise,' she remarked when she raised her eyes from the sheet of paper.

'Don't say anything you might regret later. I wanted to ask you to lunch to apologize – and to talk,' I said, slipping the key back into the drawer. I felt in need of company, and lunch with Silvana seemed a far preferable option to being alone.

'I'm too busy to have lunch,' she replied irritably.

'Come on, give me a chance to make amends.'

'I don't care about you either way, Martín. I'm getting married next month. We're moving to Mendoza,' she replied, brushing off some invisible fluff from her sleeve with her left hand, so that I could see the full glory of her engagement ring.

'That's great. The more reason to celebrate then. Don't be difficult,' I said.

'Why should I bother to be difficult? I just want to learn to use this thing. If you want to help me, get me a sandwich from downstairs,' she said, without taking her eyes away from the typewriter. A silver ball covered in signs seemed to float over its central opening, like a NASA satellite.

'It looks very impressive,' I said.

'It's a golf-ball. We got them from America yesterday afternoon,' Silvana announced proudly. 'Marquez needs some work done in a hurry, and Lavinia asked me to give her a hand.'

'Must be something very urgent then,' I said.

'You should know. You choose your dancing partners well.'

'What are you talking about?'

'That friend of yours in the magazine picture. Lavinia told me she's incredibly rich. She asked Lucas to act as her lawyer last week, because she's selling everything she owns in Argentina. He was more or less jumping in the air afterwards, apparently. You are a clever guy, Martín. With friends like that, you'll be Lucas's partner soon.'

Delia hadn't told me anything about becoming a client of Lucas's.

'It's got nothing to do with me,' I said. 'In fact I'm leaving at the end of the week.'

'That's even cleverer of you,' Silvana said with a smirk. 'Why bother to work, if you've found something easier?'

I didn't reply. Her previous words had made me realize something far more disquieting. It had been Lucas's voice that I'd heard on the phone when I called the Plaza Grill. I was sure now. He and Delia had been having dinner together. Afterwards Delia had wanted me to leave with her. My dismissal could have been her way of ensuring I would be willing to go without delay. I had assumed Lucas was acting at my mother's behest, but he didn't owe her any favours. He wouldn't fire me just to humour her.

Delia was another matter. Lucas would have done anything to secure her as a client, although I was sure neither of them had discussed anything as crude as a trade-off. He would have mentioned my name in passing, suggesting that I might deal with her business in the belief that Delia's real motive would be to improve my position within the firm. Very casually, of course, a passing remark about Francis and Isabel's son working for him, to which she would have replied equally casually, 'Oh, yes, I met him in Paris. I gather he's very keen on studying film there. I don't think he really likes the law as a career, but he might need some encouragement in the right direction. He's wasting his time as a lawyer . . .' Lucas would know what was expected of him, and my mother's call would have given him the perfect excuse.

I didn't like any of it. Delia didn't need to intervene. I would have gone with her in my own time.

Silvana was watching me, either waiting for my reply, or merely enjoying my discomfiture.

'I'll have to eat on my own then. Would you like me to bring something back for you?' I asked her.

'A very rich lover. You seem to know how to find them,' Silvana replied with a glass-etched smile.

I spent the rest of the day tidying papers and drafting documents; it kept my hands busy, even if my mind was elsewhere. Delia must have thought I'd never find out about Lucas – who had to be the mysterious caller that evening, when Delia had been so evasive and I had suspected a secret lover. She hadn't taken any risks by involving him. His firm was one of the few in Buenos Aires big enough to handle her affairs. Having me fired into the bargain was merely a convenient bonus for her.

I found myself in a position I hated, at the whim of others more powerful than myself: Delia, Lucas – even my mother. Delia's manoeuvres hurt me most, because I didn't expect her to be so manipulative. Not after our talk in Punta del Este, when I had asked her – and she had apparently endeavoured – to be as open as she could. I had taken her urgency to leave as little more than another of her imperious whims, the reluctance of a pampered woman to waste any time once her mind was made up, just as she would say 'tomorrow' when a shop-keeper suggested that something she wanted would be available next week. She had dealt with me in the same way, using Lucas without much thought about what it would mean for me. *There's nothing worse than lying to each other.* Her words came back to me, and her vulnerable expression when she had said them, the setting sun in her eyes.

At five o'clock my phone rang. 'Delia Lagos called, Martín,' the receptionist said.

'Tell her I'm out if she calls again,' I replied, as sharply as if I were speaking to Delia herself.

'She left a message for you. She wanted to meet you at your apartment at six. She said it's *very* urgent.'

The smell of cigarette smoke struck me as soon as I opened the door. It wasn't a stale smell, and it added to my bafflement at Delia's peremptory message. She never smoked during the day; more intriguingly, she didn't have a key to my apartment. Neither could I understand why she had chosen to meet me here.

Some of these enigmas were solved immediately. It wasn't Delia who was sitting in my solitary armchair: it was my mother, who volunteered another clue as soon as she saw me.

'I told the caretaker that I was your mother, and he very kindly let me in with his key,' she explained. I supposed that his kindness might have been elicited by a few pesos.

'What the hell are you doing here?' I asked brusquely. Delia would appear any minute now. 'Are you on your way somewhere else? I can drop you off in my car,' I offered, eager to get her out of my apartment.

'No, I'm not. I came especially because I wanted to talk to you. I'm sorry I tricked the girl at your office,' she said. 'I doubt you would have come to see me if I'd asked you, Martín. I know you're living with Delia, and I guessed you'd come if you thought it was that harpy calling.'

'*You* left the message then?'

My mother nodded.

'You're mad,' I said. 'How could you do something like that?'

'Don't sound so shocked. You must be used to lies by now. Delia lives by them,' she retorted. 'Aren't you going to offer me a drink at least?'

My obsession with Delia had pushed any further thoughts about my mother and her deal with Ambrosio to the back of my mind. They came forward now, as suddenly, as overwhelmingly as the realization that I had come to hate her. The fine points of hospitality were the last thing on my mind, but the distraction would give me the chance to calm down. I removed the ice tray from the refrigerator and emptied it into a dish, took the bottle of Old Smuggler and poured two glasses.

'I can't imagine Delia drinks Argentine whisky. Too cheap for her,' my mother said, noticing the label. She hadn't come here to make amends.

'I'm glad I found you. I called you over the weekend, and I tried Delia's house too. I heard at the hairdresser that she's planning to leave. I was worried sick that you might have been foolish enough to have gone to Paris with her by now.'

In my turmoil over Delia that afternoon, I had contemplated staying here after all as my revenge, a way of hurting her as much as she had hurt me. My mother's words, her patent hatred of the idea, made clear to me what I should do.

'We're leaving on Friday,' I said. 'I love her, she loves me, and there's nothing you can do about it.'

'I don't think you will find her so lovable once you've heard what I have to say. I've thought a lot since we spoke on the night of the Rousselets' party.' My mother took a cautious sip followed by a more eager one, like a parched traveller across a desert finally reaching an oasis. 'You have only yourself to blame if you don't like what I am going to tell you. I can't let you ruin your life.'

'Cut the crap. You've come here to find out how much I know, haven't you?'

My mother seemed taken aback by my rudeness, by the hostility I couldn't be bothered to hide any more.

'Maybe Delia likes you talking like that, but I don't. You won't get far as a gigolo if you don't watch your words,' she snapped back.

'I'd rather be a gigolo than a murderer, although I'm sure you don't agree. So, tell me how it feels. I want to know.'

My mother reached for her glass. 'What exactly do you mean?' she asked, sounding less sure of herself.

'That you've run out of lies. I know about you and Sebastian. It was you who had *papá*'s body cremated. You lied about the date of his death – and you didn't *lose* everything. You gave whatever you owned to Ambrosio Lagos, to keep him quiet and get him to cover up the murder for you.'

I felt breathless when I'd finished, as if those few words had drained all my energy. She sat still, her legs crossed, her hand resting on her knee. She seemed as composed as usual, but her nails were digging into her flesh.

'So she even told you about the money. Perhaps I should read her ghastly books; she must be good at twisting her stories to suit her inventions.'

'Don't blame Delia, because she told me nothing. She lied, in fact, to stop me from finding out about you,' I rejoined.

'That's funny . . . I like the idea of Delia protecting *me*. And you are besotted enough, or stupid enough, to believe that Ambrosio Lagos could be bribed. He never did anything for anyone other than himself. Or his precious Delia. If you know I have nothing, how do you think we've managed until now?'

I had been so struck by the fact that my mother had given Ambrosio everything she owned, that I hadn't thought about the consequences.

'Ambrosio Lagos came to see me the morning after Francis died, when I was still in shock. He told me that the autopsy showed that Francis had died of a brain haemorrhage, but then he explained that he hadn't mentioned his death to anyone yet, because of the President being there the day before. The visit meant so much to Ambrosio that it would have been unthinkable to cancel it, or jeopardize it in any way. "I hope you'll support me," he said, adding that it would be much easier for him if we were to say that Francis had died a day later, on October the seventeenth. I was desperately sad and confused; nothing mattered much to me, so I agreed. Then he said he knew about my money problems, and that he wanted to help me. 'I'll pay all your debts, and settle a fair monthly income on you for life.' I had heard so many times that Ambrosio wasn't a saint, and yet he was solving all my problems at once . . .'

'Why?' I interrupted her.

'That's what I would have asked myself, if he hadn't told me himself before I had time to wonder. He gushed on about what a marvellous man Francis had been, and how much he had enjoyed his company whenever they met. I can still see his face, as if he could hardly contain his grief. "He came to San Octavio a few years ago, to play polo. He hadn't married you then," Ambrosio said. "We had a strange conversation. Francis told me he had a premonition he wouldn't live long. 'You are a powerful man, Don Ambrosio. If I were to die young, promise me that you will tell my wife I want to be cremated, even if my family opposes it.' " Ambrosio said he had been deeply touched by Francis's trust, and had given his word. "Now you can help me keep my pledge to your husband, in the same way I can help you with your problems. Helping each other is the best we can do at such a tragic time," he told me.'

My mother paused. 'Don't look so amazed. Of course I didn't believe him for a second. He wanted me to cremate Francis's body. Although I hadn't suspected anything until then, there had to be a reason, and it didn't take me long to work it out. He was protecting Delia. He wanted to help her, not me.'

All my mother had said so far made sense, and yet I didn't trust her. She had come here to drive Delia and me apart.

'How could he be bribing you, when you'd transferred everything you owned to him?' I asked.

'Ambrosio wanted it that way, to make it look like a sale. "Everything" was nothing much at all. Whatever I owned had been mortgaged ten times over by your father. Effectively, Ambrosio took over my debts and settled them.'

My predominant reaction to her explanation was revulsion. 'You used *papá*'s death to make money then,' I said.

'I had no alternative,' she retorted. 'It wasn't me who cheated in the first place – no, don't say anything yet. I know you're thinking about Sebastian. It's easy to lay blame when you don't know the circumstances. I took up with him because I was desperate, fed up with your father's infidelities. Francis cheated on me from the moment we got married. You can't imagine what it's like to be younger than you are now, and to find out that your marriage is a sham, that someone you love married you for your money. He didn't love me. At first I told myself that it wasn't happening, or that it didn't matter; then I made scenes. But my anger made no difference because he couldn't care less. All I could do was get even.'

'You could have left him,' I said.

'In Buenos Aires? In 1940? You don't know what you're talking about. Someone like Delia might have got away with it, but not me. I would have spent the rest of my life shunned by everybody. If the war hadn't started, and I hadn't lost my money, I could have moved to Paris with you and Miguel. Things were different there.'

There was something poignant about my mother, sitting in her pseudo-Chanel suit, her gloves resting between the straps of her bag, her legs elegantly crossed, dressed as if she was ready to take part in some canasta tournament, but instead owning up at last to a pathetically empty life. She had lied to us about her perfect marriage, as she had lied to me about everything else, but my new-found hatred of her was gone. Instead I found myself staring at her in pity. My love for her didn't change the fact that there had been nothing to salvage from those seemingly perfect years of her marriage, nothing left but poisonous memories.

'Then Sebastian and I fell in love. He cared for me, not for my money. That meant nothing to him – he would have more than enough of his own. Ambrosio Lagos had a heart attack soon after his wife died. He kept it a secret, because it would have meant the end of his chance at the presidency. His doctors didn't expect him to live long; then Sebastian would be independent at last, and he said we could get married then. Not here, of course; we were going to move to New York, or to Europe if the war was over.

'Sebastian was worried about his father finding out about us. He had always been close to Delia. He thought it would help obscure what was going on if the four of us were seen together as often as possible. I suppose Delia must have been shrewd enough to notice something – or Sebastian could have been naïve enough to confide in her. Either way, I'm certain Delia knew we were in love. I should have known she would cause trouble; I had had plenty of reason to mistrust her before.'

'Why do you say that? *Papá* left Delia for you, not the other way round.'

'So that's what Delia told you . . . How convenient for her. The fact is that Francis had already started courting me when Delia met him. Through *me*. She was a great flirt. Delia didn't care about anyone other than herself, but she would stare at men when they talked as if she had never heard anyone so clever in her life, and they always fell for it. It wasn't difficult; she was stunning, and her father was *so* rich. She tried it with Francis too. Delia must have been furious when he proposed to me instead.'

My mother's account was completely at odds with the letters I read in Paris. If she was telling me the truth, my father must have played a double game, keeping my mother as a fall-back position in case he couldn't get Delia, the big prize. I listened to my mother's sordid tale in stunned silence, slowly swirling the whisky in my glass like an automaton, as if I needed to prove to myself that I was able to move my hand, that the feeling of paralysis numbing my limbs was not real.

'Then Sebastian and Delia asked us to go to San Octavio on the yacht with them. Ambrosio was giving a big lunch for the President, and there were going to be hundreds of people there. Francis insisted we should go. We were in real financial trouble by then; I was going to have to sell the house and everything I owned to pay our debts. Francis thought he might meet someone useful at the lunch, someone who would help us turn things around. He was always counting on something miraculous happening. As soon as the yacht left Buenos Aires, I realized the trip was a ghastly mistake. We had been together many times before, but never on our own. There had always been other people around, or we had gone to the theatre or to a show; Sebastian and I had only had to pretend for a few hours. Now we were just the four of us on that damned boat, trapped there for a whole day. When we finished lunch I said I wanted to rest. The sun was on that side of the yacht, and our cabin was very hot. After a while I found the place stifling, so I went on deck again. Delia and Francis were at the stern, leaning on the rail, their backs to me. He was listening to whatever she was saying so earnestly, his head down. Delia must have heard my steps, because she turned. She stopped mid-sentence as soon as she saw me; from her face you'd have thought they were making small-talk, but Francis wasn't so good at dissimulation. He gave me a venomous look – I'd never seen him look like that before. Then he went inside.

'Sebastian appeared, and suggested a game of cards. Delia excused herself, so we ended up playing on our own, just the two of us, as the boat sailed up the river, among those endless islands in the delta. All that water, the willows . . . I hated the landscape, the sickening smell of plants rotting in the mud. Soon Sebastian got bored with our game, and he started to shoot at some birds. I couldn't stand the sight of the damned creatures falling out of the sky, shedding guts and feathers, so I went back to my room. We had intercommunicating cabins. Francis had locked himself in his, which I found a relief, because I knew he was having one of his moods.

'We dressed for dinner. Delia had the sense to say it was ludicrous, but Sebastian insisted. There we were, in our evening clothes, with the portholes and the doors closed to keep out the mosquitoes, gasping for air in that candle-lit dining room that looked like a funerary chapel. At the time she had decorated the house in Buenos Aires, Delia had had the yacht done up too. She fancied herself as daring, avant-garde, when she was just ridiculous, but Ambrosio let her do whatever she wanted. She even smoked in front of him. Francis was in such a foul mood that the conversation started and died several times during dinner. I spent most of the time staring at the ceiling fan, while Delia chattered away, as if she hadn't noticed anything. Francis was drinking a lot. He helped himself to wine during dinner, and he kept the decanter of brandy by his side once the coffee had been served. The staff left us alone after they had cleared the table; Delia suggested going on deck to look at the stars. "I don't give a shit about the stars," your father said, and Sebastian told him off for speaking like that in front of his sister and me. "You weren't so careful about manners when you started fucking my wife, were you?" Francis snapped back.

'Sebastian was stunned, and I was so ashamed I wanted to die there and then. For once I wished Delia would come up with one of those inane remarks of hers, or lead Francis out of the room. Instead she just sat still, staring at him as if he had been telling us about a game of polo, smirking at my humiliation. Sebastian said Francis was mad, that he ought to apologize for his crazy accusation, but he was so shaken that he wouldn't have convinced anyone. Francis told him that at least he ought to have the courage to own up.'

My mother reached for the bottle, and topped up her glass. 'All I could think about was how had Francis found out? I had been so careful. I couldn't bear it . . .'

I remembered my conversation with Miguel at the airport, when he told me about finding Sebastian and her in bed. She could have assumed that it had been Miguel who had told our father, and the possibility must have mortified her. My father had given her enough reason; he was guiltier than she was. I wanted to feel sorry for my mother, but at best I could only *understand* why she fell for Sebastian, and understanding did not temper my feeling of rejection. She expected my compassion when I couldn't give it to her, for the same reason that I hadn't been able to bring myself to speak frankly when I'd seen her on the night of the Rousselet ball: I didn't want to face the prospect of *her* guilt squarely. To absolve her now implied accepting unequivocally that my father, whom I had worshipped for so long, had been a worthless man.

'Then I understood,' she went on. 'Delia had told Francis that afternoon, when I'd found them on deck, and now she was putting on a show of innocence, as if what was happening had nothing to do with her. All of a sudden, Sebastian was furious. He told Francis he was getting what he deserved, because he had treated me so badly, then he said there was a way out for all of us. We would be able to move to Europe once the war was over, and there would be no scandal that way. Francis went into a rage. "What do you expect me to do in the meantime: look the other way while you two carry on? I'm not going to be made to look a fool," he bellowed. He said there was no need to wait to solve the matter. He would speak to Ambrosio the next day, who would be keener than anybody to avoid a scandal: he would know how to deal with the problem. Sebastian would end up running a cotton plantation in the north, not living in Europe with me. Otherwise he would tell everybody, and ask for a separation on the grounds of my adultery with Sebastian; not even Ambrosio would be able to keep that one out of the papers.

'Delia intervened at last. She told Francis that there was no point in ruining Sebastian's life – and everybody else's as well. I suppose she thought she could get him now. Francis said he hated her; none of this would have happened if it weren't for her. She had ruined *his* life. I knew then that she had told him. Delia didn't seem troubled at all; she took his arm and led him out of the room, onto the deck, talking quietly, as if Francis was a child. He was very drunk, and he stumbled as he walked. I couldn't stand the scene any longer. I went downstairs to see Sebastian, who was in his cabin. He was as dismayed as I was; he said he would never leave me, no matter what, and that Francis didn't want a scandal any more than we did. The best we could do was to go to sleep and wait for the morning. I went to my cabin and took a couple of sleeping pills. I was about to fall asleep when I thought I heard a loud noise. It could have been a scream, but I wasn't sure and I was so tired . . .

'The following morning I woke up after the yacht had moored. I called for breakfast. The steward said everybody else had disembarked earlier. I couldn't believe they'd all gone and just left me behind. I got ready as quickly as I could and left the boat. Ambrosio Lagos was on the pier. A car was waiting nearby; I supposed it would take us to the house. He asked me where Francis was. I said I hadn't seen him since last night, so he suggested we went back on board to find him. Two men got out of the car and followed us onto the yacht. Francis's cabin was empty. Ambrosio made a great show of asking the steward to search everywhere. Once it was obvious that Francis was missing, Ambrosio announced he would alert the river patrol. I broke down. I was confused and distraught, because I didn't know what was going on. Ambrosio called one of the two men, who told me he was a doctor, and that he would look after me. As soon as we were in the house he said I needed a sedative. He gave me an injection, and I passed out.

'It wasn't until the next day that Ambrosio came to see me. He said that Francis's body had been found on the shore, a few miles downstream from San Octavio, and it had been taken to Rosario. After asking me to cremate the body, he gave me the autopsy report and the death certificate, confirming that Francis had died on the seventeenth. There was nothing I could do – and by then Ambrosio had offered to save us from ruin. I couldn't fight him, even if it meant Delia getting away with what she did. No lawyer would have touched the case, let alone the police –'

'Why Delia?' I interrupted her. Disbelief was all I could feel, and alarm at my mother's tone. I was confronting twenty years of hatred and half-baked suspicions which were bursting like an infected wound.

'Who else? I've thought about it over and over again ever since. She was with Francis on deck, and he was drunk. That afternoon Sebastian had warned them to be careful, when she and Francis were leaning on the rail at the stern, because the gate there had a faulty catch. Delia had more or less thrown herself at Francis that night, but instead he had told her he hated her. She couldn't have him, and he had threatened to ruin Sebastian's life – and Ambrosio's career as well. They were the only people Delia really cared about. With Francis out of the way, there would be no scandal. She would have everything the way she wanted it. She must have told Ambrosio that Francis's death was an accident, and he did the rest . . .'

'All you know is that Ambrosio bribed you,' I cut in, sickened by her deranged assumptions. 'He was obsessed with his political future, and he wanted to protect it, that's all.'

'He didn't need to cremate Francis to achieve that, did he?' My mother's shriek blistered my ears, but still I refused to give ground.

'It could have been much simpler than you think – or maybe you don't want to face the fact that *papá* killed himself that night. He had lost you, and he had lost your money. He had nothing left. He could have jumped overboard. It would have been much more difficult to hush up a suicide than a natural death. Ambrosio didn't want a scandal, so he wanted the evidence destroyed. He was protecting himself, not anyone else,' I said, as if justifying Ambrosio Lagos was my priority.

My mother sat back, savouring the moment. She ran her fingers through her hair. It wasn't her usual careful caress that would coax a few rebel strands into submission: she clawed through the helmet of hair lacquer and artfully teased locks, wrecking it.

'I told you that part of my deal with him was that I would have an income for life. There was nothing in writing though. Why do you think Delia agreed to continue the payments once Ambrosio died? She didn't need to worry about his political future by then . . .'

My mother couldn't be lying now. I knew she had nothing. We had lived on Delia's money all the time. I squirmed in my seat as if it had become a bed of coals burning through my skin. Like my mother's words.

'She wanted my silence because she killed your father, and now you –'

I stood up. 'Get out!' I shouted. I wanted her gone. I couldn't get rid of what she had said, but I could get rid of her. I would hit her if she didn't go at once. My mother must have sensed it; the expression in her eyes shifted from a trance-like blankness to panic. She grabbed her bag. A second later I heard the door slam shut.

I stood still, then I punched the wall as hard as I could. The pain in my fist brought me back to some sense of reality. I sat down and filled my glass. I welcomed the bite of undiluted bad whisky in my mouth, as if it were some kind of disinfectant. I shouldn't believe anything I'd heard, I told myself. My mother was a hysterical woman, full of spite. She hated Delia because she envied her. Delia could have whatever she wanted, and my mother couldn't. Her accusation of murder was based on suppositions, not on fact. She hadn't seen my father die. Her hysterical inventions only confirmed my wisdom in leaving everything behind me. I wasn't going to spend the rest of my life like her, yearning after what I had lost, after some dream that reality had turned to dust.

My eyes drifted towards the photograph of my father which rested between my books, only to fall on an empty space. I had put the picture away when Delia moved in. The gap on the shelves matched the gap in my heart. I couldn't believe my mother's accusations because they denied what I knew. The woman I loved couldn't be a calculating murderess. I couldn't be so wrong about her, because then I couldn't trust anything about myself. My father was different; all I knew about him was what my mother had told me, and what I had imagined about him. There was no such man as 'my father': all I had was an image, a vision conjured up by my mother and fleshed out by fading photographs. She had given it to me, and now she had taken it away. There had been nothing remarkable about the man other than his looks. There was nothing to admire, nothing to love.

My mother's portrayal of my father as a grasping opportunist, her open admission of her infidelity, her avowal that she had been bribed into silence by Ambrosio Lagos, everything else she said had to be true, because it tarnished her too. She could have denied it all, insisting on her earlier explanations. She could have explained the deal with Ambrosio Lagos as nothing more than a business transaction to settle her debts. Even if I hadn't believed her, at least she would have preserved her own image of herself. Her hatred of Delia couldn't be so overwhelming that she would be willing to destroy herself in my eyes to explain it – unless she really believed her own version.

Much as I wanted to, I couldn't pick and choose. I couldn't accept only those parts of my mother's account that suited me, but discard her accusation of murder because it was at the core of my present agony. My love for Delia was all that stood between me and acceptance of what I had heard. It should have protected me like some great, unbreachable wall if I hadn't had evidence of Delia's duplicity that very afternoon. Murder was likelier to be the cause of sudden death at my father's age than an unknown congenital defect. Ambrosio's efforts to cover up the facts were far more understandable if he had been protecting Delia. Murder also explained the need to cremate my father's body. I had considered the possibility of murder myself – but with my mother and Sebastian as the guilty parties. She wasn't the only one to attribute blame to suit herself.

Ambrosio had mentioned the corrosive power of guilt in his letter to Delia. *'Why did you go to San Octavio, Martín?'* At the time I thought she was worried about what I might have found, when there was nothing to find there, nothing to hide. I had seen Sebastian. What really worried her was what I could have discovered *before* my visit. She had asked Lucas to fire me to hasten our departure, and to stop me from finding out more than I might have done already. I remembered her half-full trunks the evening we left for Punta Ballena, when I had made the stupid assumption that Delia had been packing for the weekend. She was getting ready to leave for good, taking me with her to stop me from finding out more before it was too late. She had refused to have sex, until I could hardly think about anything else. Then she had become as passionate, as loving as usual, once I had realized how much I needed her. By the time Delia made that moving plea by the sea, entreating me to go to Paris with her, she had already made certain that I would.

Images of Delia went through my mind: her eyes sparkling like fireflies in the candlelight during our first dinner together, her blissful smile when we met again at the Rousselets' ball, the sunset on her face in Punta del Este, all snapshots of perfection, of my love for her. Then I imagined her that night twenty-one years ago, leading my father to the same place where they had spoken during the afternoon, making him stand against the gate, the same smile on her face while her hand reached for the bolt, the water below churning into murky foam. Her hands rested on his chest, as if she were feeling the beat of his heart, her eyes holding his – and then her smile turned into the mask of rage I had seen when Delia had pushed me down the stairs. I heard her voice, her beautiful voice, addressing me for the first time at that party in Paris: *'Are you a relation of Francis's?'* I saw myself holding her, skin to skin, kissing her, making love to her.

The acrid taste of vomit filled my mouth and my nostrils. I stumbled to the kitchen sink and spewed it all out, a caustic, burning mess of cheap whisky and unbearable memories.

The phone rang around half past nine. By now it was night outside. I hadn't bothered to turn the lights on.

'What are you doing there? I was getting worried. There was no reply when I called your office,' I heard Delia say.

'My mother came to see me,' I replied. The sound of her voice, so calm, sent my pulse racing as usual, but this time it was abhorrence instead of desire that made my heart beat faster.

'Oh . . . I thought you might come for dinner, but I'd better not wait for you then. Is everything all right?'

If I gave Delia any hint of my feelings now, she would come here. I didn't want to see her in my apartment, among my things, ever again. I felt an animal sense of territory, of my own space, because it was my only shield from her. But I had to see her and tell her what I knew. Not because I expected her to prove me wrong. I had had enough of Delia's denials. Nothing she could say would make a difference. If I felt driven to confront her it was for my sake, not hers.

'I'll be there in about an hour,' I said.

The road outside my building was very quiet at night; only cats roamed, sniffing at the debris around the boarded-up market stalls, or darting after prey too quick for my eyes. Gently rocked by the wind, the street lights swung on their wires, casting a changing pattern of light and shadow on the black-red brickwork of the cemetery wall.

It was nearly midnight by the time I let myself in to Delia's house. It needn't have taken so long to walk there from my apartment: half an hour had been plenty when excitement had quickened my feet. I closed the front door as quietly as I could, and yet it sounded like a detonation in my ears. The house was still; beyond the marble vestibule, a solitary lamp on one of the consoles was not enough to light the recesses of the main hall. Américo would leave that lamp on all night, once Delia had gone to bed. I wondered if she was waiting for me upstairs, in her bedroom.

The thought of seeing her there again, lying in that bed where we had made love, repulsed me. Then I noticed that a light was on in the drawing room too.

Delia was sitting in one of the huge suede sofas by the fireplace, her legs gathered under her, reading one of those white-bound French novels that were as unmistakably a sign of her presence in a room as her scent. Her eyes were on the book, but I knew she was putting on an act for my benefit. She must have heard me coming in.

I stayed near the door, waiting. Only then did she look at me. Her face gave a passable imitation of amiable surprise, and she put the book aside.

'What took you so long?' she asked. 'I hope you've had something to eat, but I asked Américo to leave a few things in the pantry just in case.'

Her attempt at domestic routine, at everyday happiness, was enough to trigger the words I had rehearsed on the way here. They came to me easily, as though I was an automaton.

'My mother told me what happened on the yacht,' I said. 'She told me about Sebastian and her, about the argument, about you telling my father . . .' Still I couldn't bring myself to accuse Delia. 'She told me about what went on that night, and the following morning. Don't worry,' I added, noticing Delia's alarm, 'it's more than twenty years ago, so nobody can do anything about it. It's a closed case. You are safe.'

'What do you mean, Martín? What am I safe from?'

'I'd rather you were honest this time. You should try for my sake, because I'm being honest with you,' I said, then I repeated everything my mother had said. 'Did you kill my father? You know I can't do anything about it, even if I wanted to. But you *must* tell me,' I finished.

Delia stood up and went round the room, turning on a few lights. I remembered her in Paris a few months ago, checking the details in her drawing room before her friends came for a drink, ensuring that the atmosphere pleased her – or suited her image of herself.

'At least let's see each other properly,' she said. 'I'm surprised your mother could come up with such an unbelievably ludicrous story,' she said, going back to her seat. The calm elegance of the room matched Delia's manner and jarred with my overwrought mood. I followed her and sat down facing her, almost unaware of my own movements.

'I told you before that I don't see the point in going over what happened. The real tragedy was Francis's accident, and nobody can change that. I don't blame Isabel. She was very unhappy, and she was desperate. I don't judge her, any more than you should appoint yourself as my judge now.'

'Are you saying she killed my father then?' I barked. I wasn't going to let Delia get away with innuendo; half-said things that gave her some excuse.

'*Nobody* killed your father, can't you understand that? I lied to you the first time you asked, when I said his body was found on board the next morning, because I was trying to avoid you making this kind of absurd assumption. Other than her ridiculous fantasy about murder, what really happened then was exactly as Isabel told you. Sebastian and I weren't on board by the time she woke up. The steward had told us that morning that Francis was missing. He'd noticed it when he took breakfast to his cabin, because the bed hadn't been slept in. As soon as the yacht docked, we rushed to the house to ask for help, and my father went to the pier. Once Isabel appeared on deck, he told her about Francis, and she was brought to the house, where a doctor looked after her. I can't tell you the precise circumstances of Francis's death any more than Isabel can.'

Delia spoke very carefully, as if she was choosing her words.

'You're avoiding the issue,' I said. 'I want to know what happened that night, not the morning after. You went on deck with him, and he was never seen again. The whole thing was covered up by your father. He must have had a very good reason to do that.'

'Why can't you accept that my father overreacted because of his own worries while the President was there? It might sound petty now, but for him it was *everything*. I told you not to listen to Isabel. She gave you her own version, which she has nurtured over years of bitterness, and you take it as gospel.'

I felt trapped. I wanted to go to the window, to catch a glimpse of the world outside, to look beyond the suffocating confines of this room designed for measured social conversation, like a stage-set. Delia seemed so at ease here, her arm casually resting on the back of the sofa. I didn't want to appear less in control than she was.

'You paid her. All these years you paid for her silence. Don't tell me it had nothing to do with you,' I said, my words rasping in my throat.

'I wish Isabel hadn't told you that,' Delia replied. 'I can imagine how it looks to you, but I knew nothing about her arrangement with my father until he died, when I had to deal with his affairs. Isabel contacted my lawyers about the monthly payments she had agreed with my father, which he had made as long as he was alive. There was nothing in writing. They had a verbal agreement, she said. The money meant nothing to me, and I didn't want to enter into unpleasant arguments. Perón was effectively in power by then. Everything my father represented had become the enemy to be destroyed; there were plenty of people who would have loved the chance to blacken his name.'

'He must have been protecting someone he cared about a lot to take so much trouble. If it wasn't you, it had to be Sebastian.' I spoke more easily now. My self-control pleased me, until I realized it was only because I was tacitly acknowledging Delia's innocence. She was steering the conversation the way she wanted.

'Sebastian was too foolish to need protection. He was always somehow beyond it,' Delia replied dryly. 'And what would have been the point after his accident? I don't know why my father struck a deal with Isabel. I'd guess he was protecting himself. He was good at that.'

I had come here expecting Delia to crumble as soon as she heard me, but my words seemed to float past her like moths, while hers lingered in my ears, nibbling at my conviction.

'Then tell me all that happened that day. Your version,' I said.

'So you can go back to Isabel and cross-examine her? You have to stop doing this, Martín. There's nothing to find out and nothing to gain.'

'I don't want to cross-examine my mother. I want to believe

you, but I can't unless you tell me your side of the story. Why did you tell my father about Sebastian?'

'What do you mean?'

'Don't pretend you don't understand. I know he and my mother were having an affair.'

'I didn't tell him anything,' Delia retorted.

'My mother saw you talking that afternoon. He was listening to you, and he seemed very upset.'

'If she had arrived ten minutes earlier, she would have heard Francis telling *me* about the affair. I knew nothing before. I was trying to talk him out of doing something stupid when Isabel came on deck.'

I had asked for it. Delia could turn whatever I said around with impunity. I would never break through the bubble of smooth self-confidence that protected her. She was in control, as always.

'Someone must have told him.'

'It doesn't matter how Francis found out. If he told me, I don't remember.'

'I thought you wouldn't.' I left my seat and headed for the door.

Delia stood up and came after me, blocking my way out. 'I didn't kill Francis. Whatever you might think, I didn't kill him.' She seemed on the verge of tears. It could be that I was seeing the real Delia at last – or the final touch in a convincing performance. She was standing in front of a mirrored screen that reflected her head and the room from many different angles, a jumble of fragmented images and splinters of brightness. The tall, cone-shaped bronze urns in the corners threw circles of pale light onto the silver-leaf ceiling that shimmered like water, like the drops of rain now sliding down the dark window-panes.

'Nobody killed Francis,' she insisted. 'Please believe that. Isabel might have thought otherwise, or over the years she might have come to believe that's how it happened; even she admits it is her supposition, nothing else. The least you can do is hear me out, and then draw your own conclusions.'

It would have been a fair plea, but Delia had tried to deceive me before. If she were to convince me now, I would never know if it was because of her sincerity – or her hold on me; my impossible longing for the woman I had once believed her to be.

'Why should I trust you now? You could have been honest the first time I asked you.'

'So could Isabel, and yet you are prepared to accept what she told you.'

Delia came closer, as if she might attempt to touch me. My hands turned into fists, ready to hit her, but she walked past me and went to sit down instead.

'That afternoon, Francis told me he had found out about Isabel and Sebastian. I advised him to act as if he knew nothing. I would speak to Sebastian myself when we were back. I was sure he would stop seeing Isabel once he knew he had been found out. Sebastian would never challenge our father, or risk losing the life he knew. No matter how much he cared for Isabel, he wouldn't have done that for anyone. I wish Francis had listened to me, instead of confronting them during dinner, when Sebastian went to pieces. He was terrified of our father, and he could imagine his reaction to any scandal. He left the room immediately; it was Isabel who tried to appease Francis by suggesting that she and Sebastian would move to Europe as soon as the war was over. Francis reacted very badly. He hit her and she started to cry, so I took him outside. I talked to him until he calmed down. I suggested he should go to bed; he said he wanted to stay on deck, and I left him there. The others had gone to their cabins by then. The rest you know. The body was found later that day. My father wanted everything hushed up, but not because there had been a murder. There was no murder to hide.'

The clock on the mantelpiece struck midnight. It was as rare an object as everything else in that room, a crystal prism on a black enamel base, the diamond hands and numbers seemingly floating on a transparent block. It kept time apparently by magic, since it seemed to have no mechanism, but it was a trick, an ingenious piece of deception. The workings were cleverly hidden out of sight, and that's how I felt about Delia's explanation.

'If everything is as you say, my mother wouldn't hate you as she does,' I said.

'That's because she imagines far more than she knows.' Delia seemed exasperated now. 'Once he heard about Sebastian and Isabel, my father was adamant that their affair had to stop. He didn't want the slightest chance of gossip or scandal that could reflect on his political future. Sebastian wouldn't have opposed him in any case, least of all after what had happened. Whatever he might have told Isabel, he wouldn't have married her against my father's wishes. When she tried to contact Sebastian once she was back in Buenos Aires, her calls weren't put through, on my father's orders. She called me then, to ask for my help. I told her I couldn't do anything; it was a matter between Sebastian and her. I guess Isabel realized she couldn't fight my father, because she depended on him now, so she must have found it easier to blame me, and make me responsible for Sebastian's attitude. She's had twenty years to embroider her fictions, to convince herself that I was to blame for everything that happened that night.'

Delia stared at me, as if she expected me to agree.

'Still you aren't satisfied,' she said. 'I can't convince you unless you are prepared to use your reason.'

'I don't know what to think,' I replied.

'*You* tell *me* what happened then,' she said angrily. 'I want you to say what's on your mind. Spell it out, Martín.'

'My mother says you pushed him overboard, once you were alone. It is her word against yours.'

'Why would I want to kill Francis? Don't use Isabel as an alibi for your own suspicions.'

'I don't need alibis,' I retorted. 'He said he hated you, that none of this would have happened if it weren't for you. You might have told him about the affair because you wanted him back, and you killed him in anger when he turned you down, or maybe you wanted to protect your family. My father had threatened to tell Ambrosio, and make as big a scandal as possible.'

Delia sat back and gave me a pitying look. 'I don't think you could describe me as someone who is too worried about scandal,' she commented. 'I didn't tell him about Isabel, and he said that afternoon that he wished he had married me, not her. I suppose that's what he meant when he said he hated me later because I had ruined his life. I had no reason to kill him, and how am I supposed to have done it anyway? Have I really seemed like a murderer to you for all these months we've been together?'

The appeal to my love for her only reinforced my scepticism at whatever she said. 'He was very drunk. You could have pushed him overboard.'

She stayed silent for a moment, as if she couldn't quite believe what she'd heard. 'Francis was a very tall, big man. No matter how drunk he might have been, surely you can't imagine I would have been able to lift him over the rail. It's ludicrous,' she replied eventually.

A scene that had occurred only a few months before suddenly came back to me. 'You had no trouble pushing me off the yacht in Capri.'

Delia was perplexed, then she remembered. 'You didn't see me open the side gate there because it was behind you, and it took a silly kissing game to lead you there with your back to the rail. Do you think that a man whose life is falling apart is in the mood for games? The gate on our yacht was near the stern, and the door to the dining room was half-way along the deck. According to you, I took Francis out, opened the gate on our way to the stern while talking to him, and then I managed to bring him back to that precise spot without Francis noticing anything. No matter how keen you might be to blame me, you must realize it is impossible.'

Her argument didn't stop me, because I had figured it all out at last. 'You didn't need to. Sebastian had warned you that the gate had a faulty catch. All you had to do was take him to the gate, wait until he was leaning on it, talking to you, and then push it open.'

Delia reached for the box on the table and took out a cigarette. 'Your father had a stroke. That's what the doctors said, and that's what happened. You might make a good script-writer one day, but you would be a very bad detective. Can't you see your theory doesn't work? Gates on boats are built so that people can't fall through them so easily. They open inwards. Sebastian was hopeless about practical details, and apparently so are you.'

I sat still, bewildered by the conviction in Delia's voice.

'I hope you're satisfied now,' she said. 'Unless you want me to be guilty. If so, this is one thing I can't help you with, Martín.'

I didn't *want* her to be guilty, but neither did I want to feel as empty-handed as I did. I couldn't accept that I was wrong. Delia could be telling me the truth, but not all of it.

'You didn't tell my father about Sebastian and my mother. Who did then?'

'You've asked me that question already. I don't know.'

'He must have told you,' I insisted.

'If he did, I've forgotten. It was twenty-one years ago.'

'You seem to remember everything else very clearly. It would be better if you admit you told him.'

'But that's the problem, don't you see? You keep saying, "If you tell me this, I will believe you", and then you don't. It is as if you want to dwell on this, rather than leave it behind us so we can get on with our lives.'

Her mention of 'us' astonished me. I wondered if Delia could really assume we still had a future together. I stood up. 'This is pointless. I've had enough,' I said.

'Where are you going?' she asked anxiously, stubbing out her cigarette.

'That's no longer your problem,' I replied.

'Don't throw everything away, Martín. Please stay with me. You can sleep in another room if you want, but don't go. Not tonight. Would you stay if I told you how Francis found out?' she pleaded.

'Maybe, but you're never going to, are you?' I began to walk away.

'*You* told him,' I heard her say. Delia must have been desperate to try to implicate me as her last line of defence.

'Don't be ridiculous. I was two years old at the time.'

'I'm sorry,' she said, 'but that's what happened. The morning Francis and Isabel were leaving for our yacht, you and your brother were taken to their room to say goodbye. Isabel was still in the bathroom. You started to rummage through her bag, which was on a chair. You found a letter inside, and you gave it to your father. It was from Sebastian. That's how Francis found out.'

I don't need to recall my feeling after hearing Delia's words, because that shock never entirely went away, the realization that I had changed the course of their lives and mine through a single, fleeting act for which I had no real responsibility. I couldn't blame myself for what I had done that morning, twenty-one years ago. I imagined myself as a small child, my clumsy fingers rifling through the contents of my mother's handbag – both exciting and meaningless to me – until they clutched a folded sheet of paper, then tottering towards my father and giving it to him. I didn't know, or understand. I couldn't be blamed for what I'd done, so I couldn't feel guilty. My father would have found out eventually. But the end of their marriage and his death had been triggered by that single action of mine, and I had been the unknowing agent of fate.

I have wondered many times if I shouldn't have stayed with Delia that night, if my life could have been completely different if I had trusted her then. I don't believe she wanted to hurt me when she told me about the letter. She did what I had asked her to do, because she was desperate, and she thought it would make me change my mind. Delia wanted me to stay with her, and I wanted to expunge her from my life.

She failed – but so did I.

Fourteen

I couldn't tell the difference between thoughts and dreams that night. Both came to me in a continuous stream as I tossed and turned in my bed, where the sheets felt as hot as thick blankets. A relentless jumble of words and faces went through my head. I must have closed my eyes occasionally, perhaps slept for a few minutes, because the darkness became less threatening at times, like a soothing void that couldn't last. They were merely moments of passage between nightmares, memories and premonitions.

Sometimes I heard Delia's words as clearly as if she were next to me, at others I could see soundless images, like in a silent movie. I pieced those scenes together with disjointed fragments of memories churning in my head. I saw my father on the yacht, but dressed in his polo clothes, struggling with Sebastian as I had seen him in San Octavio, frail and crippled in his wheelchair. I saw Delia sitting down to dinner that night, wearing the black lace dress she'd worn at the Rousselet ball, and smiling at my father across the table. And I saw my small child's hand opening my mother's bag and taking out a folded sheet. I saw a man reaching for me. Sharply creased grey trousers, then a black belt with a silver buckle, then a pale blue shirt with white mother-of-pearl buttons passed in front of my eyes as his hands lifted me off the ground. My father smiled at me as I was held in his arms, offering him the folded sheet. I saw his face so clearly. I knew it was his real face at last, not an animated photograph. I watched him scan the page. Then he looked up and I saw the eyes in my dream again, the eyes I had seen from below as they glared at something or someone behind me. They were my father's eyes.

My dream startled me awake, into a drowsy consciousness. I sat up in my bed, shivering in the clamminess of my own sweat. I could still see my father's eyes, but his face had receded into the fog again.

Daylight came, transforming the shadows around me into familiar shapes and objects again, and forcing me into a semblance of alertness, as if the rituals of showering, shaving and getting dressed would bring back my sense of purpose. I knew what I wouldn't do. I wouldn't go to work this morning, and I wouldn't go to Paris. I would never see Delia again. Everything else was a blank, an ache that only heightened my urgency to leave my apartment without delay.

I was about to reach the front door downstairs when I saw the silhouette of a man through the frosted glass panel, then an envelope dropped through the letter box, although it was too early for the mailman. I recognized the pale grey on sight, the colour of Delia's stationery; it was addressed to me in her boldly angular script. I rushed outside, where Américo was opening the door of a car. I caught up with him.

'Take this back, please,' I said. The envelope felt thick in my hand. I didn't want to read whatever it said. I had heard enough justifications from Delia.

'She's gone,' Américo replied, without taking the letter from me. 'She left this morning.'

Sometimes a wish fulfilled becomes an unwanted gift. During my vigil I had thought how much easier things would be for me once Delia was out of my life.

'I heard you talking last night,' Américo said. 'She told you the truth. You shouldn't doubt her.'

My first thought was that he was relaying Delia's message on her instructions, in an awkward, rash attempt to convince me by whatever means, but it was too clumsy for her, and I had caught Américo by chance – he hadn't waited for me.

'I was on the yacht when it all happened. I was the steward,' he went on. 'You mustn't tell *Niña* Delia I told you, but she had nothing to do with the accident.'

'How do you know it was an accident? Did you see it?' I

prompted him, but Américo climbed into the car instead, turned on the engine, and drove quickly away.

It was the time of the morning in Buenos Aires when caretakers more energetic than mine hosed the sidewalk outside their front door. The wet tiles shone under the rising sun. The sight usually added to my sense of a fresh start, a feeling that seemed beyond my reach now. I pushed the glass door open and went into the café. The billiard table was still under its green oilskin cover, which would remain in place until later in the morning, when spotty boys playing truant from the high school nearby would walk in, their jackets folded over their books or their bags, as I myself had walked into similar cafés years ago. They all smoked *Particulares*, the local version of *Gitanes* cigarettes, without removing them from their lips, in a bad imitation of Jean-Paul Belmondo in a *Nouvelle Vague* movie turned into farce by their reluctance to smile under any circumstances. They would kill time in the café, playing billiards and drinking Cokes and espressos until it was safe to go back home. But it was too early for them yet, so the only customers were people like me, for whom the smell of hot coffee and frothy boiled milk in heavy metal percolators, the crackling skin of lard croissants and the droplets of water on the ribbed curls of butter created a fictitious homely atmosphere, which was as short-lived as the plumes of smoke rising from the first cigarettes of the day. There was something atrociously disquieting in those images of normality as they fought for my attention with my private obsessions.

I ordered breakfast as I walked past the waiter on my way to my usual table, and tore open the envelope before I sat down. It wasn't a long letter; all I found inside was a small, folded sheet of paper, and an Air France ticket in my name. Delia's message was very short.

Dear Martín,
I'm leaving today. I hope you will not change your mind, and you will come to Paris on Friday. It will be different there. Love,
Delia

Whatever illusion of distance I had managed to create between us during the night was gone. For an instant I felt as if Delia was sitting across the table from me, as if I was hearing her words, as if this was another of those long mornings together, drinking black coffee and ambling around the city before going back to fall into bed together and make love. The short message, a few terse words from her, was enough to throw me back into another time, when everything had seemed possible.

It was still possible, if only I could believe that she hadn't killed my father, if it weren't for my instinct that Delia still hadn't told me the truth about his death. Ambrosio Lagos's political ambitions might have forced her to lie in 1942, but they didn't justify her lies now. Guilt would, though: if not her own, then someone else's.

I tried to look at the options as dispassionately as I could, like a lawyer examining conflicting evidence. My mother could have murdered my father, and accused Delia once she feared I suspected her – but then Ambrosio Lagos wouldn't have needed to pay for her silence. If Sebastian had killed my father, Delia would have continued to bribe my mother to protect him, but I refused to accept she could be willing to give me up rather than admit it, that she would be prepared to sacrifice us for his sake. Sebastian couldn't be charged after twenty years. As for Delia herself, she had denied her guilt convincingly enough. Once again, my suspicions were like the ball on a roulette wheel, tumbling into one slot only to jump to a different one.

An all-too-familiar feeling of powerlessness came over me. I would never find out the full story. I had been through the rack of questions, accusations and denials with my mother and Delia; I couldn't endure that again. The idea seemed as intolerable as the likelihood of future reunions with my mother in her fusty apartment, to tell her about my work or hear about parties she had been to. I had to leave *now*. I would sell my car, my cufflinks, my father's watch, the few things I owned, and move to Venezuela or Mexico or Spain, to a place as far away as I could get on the money I would raise. Somewhere nobody had heard of Delia Lagos, a place where I had no memories.

There was no such place. Wherever I went, my doubts would

travel with me. I could put distance between myself and everybody else, but I couldn't shed my own knowledge. Worse than that, I didn't really *know* anything. Knowledge eventually brings acceptance. I could only suspect instead, and I would be damned to suspect forever.

I had to find out. There had to be a way. Ambrosio, Sebastian, Delia, and my mother were cogwheels and pinions in a mechanism they had constructed in partnership, for their own different reasons. It wouldn't have worked without any of the separate components. I had to break it down to find out who had killed my father, to wrap up all the loose ends in the hope that knowledge would bring an end to my troubles. I wouldn't discover what had happened that night through Delia or my mother. Both were trying to justify themselves. I would have to find the secondary characters, the circumstantial witnesses, people who had drifted away from centre-stage to the edges.

Américo was an obvious choice, but he was too loyal to Delia to be of any use to me. His only motivation was to convince me of her innocence. I needed less partial witnesses, people to whom Delia or Ambrosio Lagos meant little or nothing now.

I threw some money on the table and walked out of the café, into the rising heat of a new day.

I had listened to the radio in my parked car for nearly two hours, keeping watch on my mother's building from a safe distance, when I saw her maid come out of the staff entrance. Malisa was wearing a dress, not her uniform, and she was carrying a small suitcase. My immediate thought was that my mother had fired her, although it was unlikely. Malisa had been with her for nearly ten years. I leaned forward and checked the windows of the apartment. The shutters were still closed; it hadn't surprised me earlier, but it was unusual so late in the morning.

I had been prepared to wait until I saw my mother leave for her morning errands. Now I remembered Miguel's mention of the sedatives. I left the car, went to the café, and dialled her number. There was no reply.

I slowed down as I approached the building, adjusting my pace to a casual stride because Marcial, the caretaker, was outside, polishing the brass fittings on the door, a tin of Brasso in one hand, a yellow dust-cloth in the other.

'Hello, Martín! Haven't seen you for a long time. I hear you're living on your own now, boy,' he greeted me with his usual familiarity, in a flurry of Spanish s's and c's. Forty years in Argentina hadn't made him lose his accent. The affection in his voice was as genuine as usual. He had seen me grow up, and I had seen him grow old.

'Are you coming to see your mother?'

'Yes. Is she at home?'

'Didn't she tell you? She left last night, to stay with friends.' Marcial gave me an inquisitive look. He always had a sixth sense for possible trouble within his territory.

'Of course she did,' I said, feigning annoyance at my supposed forgetfulness, and concealing my relief. I had braced myself for whatever scene could be waiting for me upstairs. 'I'm not coming to see her actually. I need to get something I left behind,' I replied, knowing my rating with Marcial had slipped a few notches. Dutiful sons did not forget what their parents were doing; certainly not in his ancestral Galicia.

'Malisa has gone away too. Your mother gave her the time off. I'll let you in,' Marcial offered, always eager to be involved in whatever happened in his building. He rested the tin and the cloth on a marble shelf near the door and produced a large ring of keys from his pocket. I was certain he would come into the apartment with me if I gave him the chance, to check what I was doing there and then impress my mother with his knowledge later.

'You don't need to bother, Marcial. I've got the key,' I said. Disappointment showed in his face, soon replaced by a knowing look.

'And what are you up to these days?' he asked. 'I can imagine, living on your own. It's about time you and Miguel settled down, you know.'

'I'd better go,' I said, walking away before he could find additional advice for me. Luckily the elevator was there, so he couldn't ambush me by the door while I waited and continue the conversation. I was in a hurry, eager to move on.

I let myself into the apartment, headed for my mother's bedroom and opened the safe. There, under the boxes of jewellery on the lower shelf, I found my father's death certificate. I wrote down the name of the doctor who had signed it, and the name of the hospital that had issued it.

By the time I went down to the entrance hall again, Marcial wasn't there. I left the building, jumped into my car and headed for Rosario.

Domingo Cullen Hospital stood by the city's river front, near the port. As I went up the steps leading to the main door, I turned for a moment and watched the broad water of the Paraná, shining in the early morning sun. Corseted by embankment walls, depots and cranes, the river looked different here than in San Octavio, unable to compete for space with the sky above.

Once inside the hospital, I went to the enquiries desk. There was a queue, as could be expected in any public building. A woman of indeterminate age was in charge, her dyed blonde hair pulled back into a tight, flat chignon at the nape of her neck, in the style Evita had made her own more than a decade before. It was a safe way to publicly show her sympathies without putting her job at risk.

'I'm looking for Dr Medina,' I told her when my turn came.

'Dr Saúl Medina?'

'No, his name is Oscar,' I replied. Medina wasn't an unusual surname.

'There is nobody called Oscar Medina here,' she said, her eyes shifting to the man behind me.

'He worked here in 1942, and I must find him. It is very important.'

'If he was here then, he must be dead by now,' she scoffed. 'Next!' she added, and the man didn't miss his chance now. The flow of the queue shunted me aside like a piece of driftwood, and I knew better than to expect a second opportunity from a harassed receptionist.

I felt more impotent than tired after a bad night in a cheap hotel nearby. By the time I had arrived in Rosario the day before, the hospital was closed. I tried the emergency unit just in case, where nobody had heard of Dr Medina either. Now, after meandering around the huge hall, eventually I came across an archway into a side corridor; a sheet of paper was stuck on the wall with adhesive tape. Scribbled on it in ball-point pen was the word 'Records', and an arrow pointing down the corridor.

My confidence strengthened as I headed in that direction, away from the hustle and bustle of the main hall. Triplicate forms, log books and registers had been an essential ingredient of official bureaucracy in Argentina ever since colonial days. Perhaps something, a detail no matter how small, had escaped Ambrosio Lagos's efforts. 'Records' was the last office along the corridor; I knocked at the door and went in.

An old woman sat at a battered metal desk under a fluorescent light. A vista of filing cabinets and shelves bursting with papers tied with ribbons opened behind her, partially blocking the grimy windows at the back of the room. Her eyes lit up behind her metal-framed glasses when she saw me come in. I was an unexpected respite in the relentless boredom of her job.

'*Sí?*' she asked eagerly. It was a standard, meaningless affirmation in itself, but a more promising start than the more usual '*What do you want?*' of most bureaucrats.

'Perhaps you can help me,' I said. 'My father was brought here years ago, after an accident. He's very old now, and he would like to trace those who helped him. I believe that the doctor in charge was Oscar Medina.'

'I remember him,' she said. 'Very nice man, but he died long ago. When did this happen?'

'On October the sixteenth, 1942.'

'That *is* a long time ago,' she muttered, turning towards the mountain of paper behind her. 'And Dr Medina is dead, so there isn't much I can do for you.'

'There were others, though. My father remembers his nurse very well. An ambulance was sent from here to San Octavio, near Las Palmeras, to pick him up, so there must have been a driver involved too.'

The woman thought for a moment. She was eager to be helpful. 'We keep records of ambulance movements, and the staff on duty.'

She left her desk and headed for the depths of the archive. I saw her pull out a huge bound register from a shelf, then she came back.

'All ambulance journeys during 1942 are recorded here,' she announced proudly. 'October the sixteenth, you said . . .' She turned over the pages until she found the date, then ran her finger down the entries. 'Yes, here it is. The ambulance left at six p.m. The destination was Las Palmeras clinic. The team was Dr Medina and his nurse, Emilia Duarte. I remember her too. Emilia was a very dedicated nurse . . .'

'Where can I find her?' I asked.

'I don't know. She left the hospital many years ago. I hope this is the information you need, *Señor* García.'

'I'm sorry, but my name is not García.'

'Then the patient can't have been your father. His name was Pascual García. Look for yourself,' she said, turning the book towards me to let me see the evidence for myself. I glanced over the other entries for that date. There was none under my father's name.

'Are you sure he was brought here?' she asked. 'He might have been taken to the *Policlinico*, or another hospital in Rosario.'

'You must be right,' I said. 'Perhaps Pascual García was the driver in the other car. Could you check why he was brought to this hospital? There couldn't have been many accidents in Las Palmeras that day.'

The woman hesitated. 'I would have to look in his admission sheet, and that's confidential information,' she said. 'I'm not allowed to tell you.'

'It would be a great help for me if you did though,' I entreated her. 'I've come all the way from Buenos Aires, you see, and it would be such a waste of time for me otherwise. I believe my father was unconscious after the accident, and he was alone; someone might have made a mistake about his name. It would make all the difference if I knew for sure that this has nothing to do with my father.'

I could see her struggle between duty and the combined forces of kindness and boredom.

'I suppose it doesn't matter after all this time,' she said eventually. 'Wait here. It will take me some time to find the card.'

I paced the room many times, forcing myself to read the notices on the wall, checking the clock with increasing pessimism as the minutes ticked away. Eventually she came back, wiping the dust off her hands with a handkerchief.

'It couldn't have been your father,' the woman announced. 'Pascual García was drowned. By the time the ambulance arrived, he was already dead.'

I sat in my car outside the hospital for a while. Turmoil had become such a familiar feeling by now that it didn't stop me from considering my findings dispassionately. Ambrosio Lagos had tried hard to cover every angle. He had arranged for my father's body to be collected from Las Palmeras, once it had been found, and brought to Rosario under a false name. Then he had made Dr Medina sign the death certificate in the real name, either by bribery or coercion, and then my mother had arranged the cremation. A coffin had left hospital under one name, but reached the crematorium under a different one. Even if he had been alive, Dr Medina would not have owned up to any of this.

The woman at the records office had mentioned his nurse. She had been there too. I left the car and went back into the hospital, walking fast. I would ask the woman to look up Emilia Duarte's address, and I would find her.

My certainty decreased as I approached the entrance to the corridor. Having agreed minutes ago that the dead man had nothing to do with my father, it would be difficult to justify why I was so keen to meet the nurse on duty at the time of Pascual García's death. Staff addresses had to be confidential, to avoid disgruntled patients pestering them at home. If she gave the address to me, the woman would be infringing the privacy of a fellow hospital worker, not some man who died more than twenty years before. In any case, she had mentioned that Emilia Duarte retired long ago. Her address on the records could be out of date.

A young nurse walked past.

'Excuse me,' I approached her. 'Would you know the address of your trade union, please?'

* * *

It was late in the afternoon by the time I found Santo Tomé, a small village a hundred kilometres south of Rosario. There was nothing to distinguish it from other villages I drove through on my way there: a cluster of low, modest buildings surrounded by fields of sunflower and maize that reached the horizon. A few streets led into the central square, most of them unpaved. The black earth was baked by the sun, and milled by tractor and car wheels into grey dust.

Enriqueta Berry was the second street south of the square. Number 358, the address I had obtained from the trade union in Rosario, was near the edge of the village. There the houses were devoid of cement render imitating stone, mouldings, or any other sign of aspirations; their owners clearly contented themselves with the fact that the modest cubes of brick roofed by corrugated tin kept the rain out. A chicken-wire fence separated the road from the front yard, where a line of cement frogs marked the path to the door.

I could hear the noise of children inside as I rang the bell, then a boy opened the door. He must have been eleven at most, but his eyes showed he was used to being in charge.

'I'm looking for Emilia Duarte,' I said, and he seemed baffled by my words.

'I met Emilia years ago, when she worked at the hospital,' I added, counting on the chance that the boy might not realize it was impossible. I was a grown-up, an old man from his point of view.

'Does she live here?' I insisted.

'Yes.' The boy moved aside and let me in. There were two younger children in the modest front room, wrestling on the plastic-tiled floor. 'Stop it! You're going to break the TV!' he shouted.

'Grandmother is at the back,' he told me, nodding towards the rear of the room. A passage led to an open door, and I could see the evening sky beyond. In the rear garden, a few hens strutted around the rusting tins of cooking oil used as planters, pecking at whatever they found in the sporadic patches of yellow grass. Emilia Duarte was sitting on a kitchen chair, her back to the house. Her feet seemed rooted to the ground.

'I've come to see you. My name is Martín Lagos,' I told her.

'I don't know you . . .' Emilia murmured. The left side of her mouth barely moved when she spoke, other than the occasional twitch, and it became a downward line when she was silent. Her left arm hung limply by her side.

'I am a nephew of Ambrosio Lagos. Do you remember him? You met him at Las Palmeras, many years ago.'

'I saw Don Ambrosio many times,' she said proudly. 'I worked for him. And *Niña* Delia. She was very kind to me.'

'Did you know them before the accident, before you went to Las Palmeras with Dr Medina?'

'Dr Medina was a very good man too. The President was there. It's a beautiful afternoon. I don't think it will rain. I don't like rain.'

'I don't like rain either,' I agreed. 'What did you do for Don Ambrosio and Delia?'

She gave me a stern look. 'I looked after Don Sebastian. Poor Don Sebastian. Clara and the young girl look after him now. I'm sure he misses me.'

The name jolted my memory. Delia had mentioned Clara when she told me she knew about my visit to San Octavio. She had to be the woman who had refused to let me into the house.

'So you took care of Sebastian after his accident. That was many years ago. Do you remember how it happened?' I asked.

'I don't remember anything,' she said. 'Are you *Niña* Delia's son then?'

'No, I'm not. I told you we are cousins.' I wondered if anything I said really registered in her mind.

'I miss Sebastian. I couldn't look after him any more, and yet he needed me. It wasn't fair. Carlos is taking me to the movies on Saturday. He promised.'

I had no idea who Carlos was. I wanted to keep her talking about Sebastian.

'What wasn't fair?'

'I like the movies. I hope we'll see something that will cheer me up. Carlos promised . . .'

'I'll take you, if he doesn't,' I offered.

'Let's go now then,' she said.

'The movie house will be closed now. But we can go on Saturday. You were saying that what happened to Sebastian wasn't fair.'

'Accidents shouldn't happen. A young man who had everything, and then he shoots himself cleaning a gun. It's stupid. Dr Medina couldn't do anything. *Niña* Delia and I stayed up all night looking after him.'

'You stayed up all night at the clinic in Las Palmeras?'

'The house is beautiful though. So quiet. We used to sit outside for hours, watching the river. Who are you?'

'I told you. Did you see the drowned man?'

'I don't remember a drowned man, and I don't like you. You won't take me to the cinema. You're a liar. Carlitos!' she called. The boy came out.

'I don't like this man. Tell him to go,' the old woman said.

'I'll get *papá*,' the boy growled.

'Don't bother, I'm leaving,' I said. I rushed into the house, heading for the door as fast as I could. There was a photograph on the corridor wall. Emilia sat at the centre of the picture, surrounded by thc three boys, looking much smaller than they were now. A young couple stood behind her, and I recognized the woman. It was Clara.

Night had fallen by the time I stopped the car, once I was well away from Santo Tomé. I checked for lights behind me in the rear-view mirror, but there were none. I turned off the engine, and began to piece together the dotty old woman's words, extricating those that made sense from her disjointed non-sequiturs.

Emilia had gone to San Octavio with Dr Medina – and the ambulance must have gone to the clinic to collect my father's body, which had been taken back to Rosario and registered under a false name. When she had spoken about Sebastian's accident, she had said the President had been there, and mentioned the house. She and the doctor had come to look after Sebastian, who was badly injured. The cleaning of a gun must have been Ambrosio's excuse. There had been no riding accident. Sebastian had been shot on the yacht, and he had been kept in the house ever since. Ambrosio Lagos had hushed up the 'accident' for a few weeks, until there was no link with the President's visit. By then my father's funeral had taken place, and nobody could relate the two events.

What had happened *after* the shot was clear to me, but the actual incident remained as nebulous as before. I rearranged the facts like coloured fragments in a kaleidoscope. I couldn't imagine Delia or my mother shooting Sebastian in cold blood. My father was a much more likely candidate, driven by rage, jealousy, or despair. Delia had not contradicted my mother's account of her movements that evening. She had gone to her cabin after the initial argument, and taken sleeping tablets.

My father had been on deck with Delia; her brother must have come back and confronted him. Sebastian had been shooting birds that afternoon. He might have left his gun there, within my father's reach. If he had shot Sebastian in front of Delia, her anger and her horror could have given her the strength to push my father overboard. Or it could have been that Sebastian had pushed my father himself, and Delia had shot him in revenge. Ambrosio Lagos wouldn't have bribed my mother and arranged the cremation and the death certificate unless it was imperative to protect his children.

Impossible as that might have seemed at the beginning of my journey, I confronted a prospect as distressing as Delia's guilt. My father could have shot Sebastian. By now I had nearly resigned myself to whatever she might have done that night. If Delia was guilty, at least I could challenge her with my knowledge – or I would have the alibi of forgiveness. But my father was dead. His guilt was beyond reach. I would have to live the rest of my life with my vision of that moment on a yacht I had never seen, when the man in the photographs came alive in my mind, a gun in his hand, and turned Sebastian Lagos, the golden boy in the Sargent portrait, into the pitiable wreck in a wheelchair I had watched being pushed around the park of San Octavio. My father's life had been a failure; I didn't want his death to shame me too.

There was no moon. The scraping of the crickets in the fields grated on my ears, its loudness amplified in the dark. Whether Sebastian or my father had been the first victim, Delia had avenged him. I could feel a sort of compassion if she had wanted to hide from me that Sebastian had killed my father, and her own desperate revenge. If she had murdered my father in anger, hating her was a poor substitute for the fact that she had walked away from the hell she made for others.

I was allowing myself the luxury of clear-cut solutions though. Delia had drowned my father because he had shot her brother. He had been a murderer too, in intention at least. The fact that he had failed at murder only added to a long list of his failures; it didn't cancel his crime. If Delia was guilty, so was he. I couldn't blame one and absolve the other. They stood together, either in innocence or in guilt.

I had to find out, otherwise I would be cursed to run over and over the events of that night in my mind for the rest of my life, like watching an endless spool of film, always circling the truth without ever coming to a conclusion. Delia was gone, and my mother had not witnessed what really happened. Only Sebastian could tell me – assuming he was able to speak. I turned on the interior light, and unfolded a map. Las Palmeras was about an hour away from here, if I drove very fast.

Fifteen

I dipped the headlights soon after turning into the road to San Octavio, although the main house and the staff bungalows were a long way away. Distance was meaningless in the Pampas at night. I had been able to see the glow in the sky from small towns along my way twenty or thirty miles before I reached them. Only empty land stood between my car and my destination, and somebody on the *estancia* would notice the lights of my car approaching across the open fields.

The dimmed lights forced me to slow down. After a few interminable minutes of staring at the hollow blackness ahead, my hands and arms set into immobility by the dead-straight road, my neck and shoulders went numb. The back of my trousers and my shirt seemed bonded to the hot plastic fabric on the seat. I hadn't opened the window on my way here, to keep out the powdery dust that rose in clouds from under the wheels. I rolled it down now. The night air felt fresh on my face at first, until I got used to it. Then it became lukewarm, clammy, as unclean as I felt myself. The last two days seemed to roll into a continuum; the tiredness in my eyes battled with the self-perpetuating commotion in my head. Ever since leaving Emilia's house, I had juggled thoughts and possibilities into a never-ending re-run, editing and refining it every time.

On the evidence of my first visit it was unlikely that I would be allowed to see Sebastian. I knew nothing about his daily routine, and he was probably asleep now. It would have been much more sensible to spend the night at some hotel in Las Palmeras, and try my luck tomorrow morning, but sense was beyond me. I couldn't stop now. Even if I had the chance to challenge Sebastian, the image of a decrepit man wheeled around the park was fresh in my mind, and Delia's despondency at his condition had seemed heartfelt. The accident had left him unable to speak or communicate in any way.

But I didn't trust anything Delia said; Sebastian's physical condition might have been the perfect excuse to keep him out of sight, where it wouldn't matter if he broke down and spoke about what happened on the yacht. Emilia and Dr Medina had become accomplices to the cover-up; Clara was obviously Emilia's daughter. If they ever found out what had happened, people working on the estate were bound to silence too: those who had been there when it happened because of loyalty or fear of Ambrosio Lagos, those who came later because they were presented with a *fait accompli*. A job in a place like San Octavio was not an opportunity to be thrown away for the sake of gossip about the crippled son of a former owner. By keeping Sebastian invisible within the tight little world of the *estancia*, Ambrosio and Delia had safeguarded the endurance of their deceit. Everybody was bound tight into a common cause by guilt or interest.

It was just after nine o'clock when I reached the gate. As I started up the long drive, I turned off the car lights entirely. The moon was breaking through the clouds, and I could just make out the road ahead. After a while, I glimpsed a few lit windows in the distance, where the staff lived. People would be getting ready to go to bed now. I wondered for a second if someone could hear the clatter of the engine and the hiss of the wheels on the road; to my ears, they reverberated as loudly as voices in the still of the night. Soon afterwards I approached the copse I remembered from my first time here, the last turning before the lawns that surrounded the house. I pulled to one side and left my car. Not being expected was my only, feeble chance of success.

The breeze coming from the river had blown away the clouds. The towers and crenellations were sharply outlined against the velvet-blue sky, and the sweep of stars of the Milky Way glittered like spilt sugar on a dark floor. As I got nearer to the house, I caught a glint of light in the ground floor, filtering through the shutters. I climbed the steps to the front terrace, the rustle of the creeper in the wind muffling the sound of my feet on the stone. I pressed the white porcelain bell, and waited.

I must have been there for a minute or two when I heard the lock turn and the door opened. My carefully prepared speech, aimed at the nurse and mentioning her mother's name, died on my lips. Américo, not Clara, had opened the door.

'What are you doing here?' I asked before he could address the same question to me. I held the high ground this time. Unlike Clara, Américo knew why I had come here tonight. He was on the defensive.

'*Niña* Delia asked me to collect a few things for her before I went back,' he explained.

'I've come to see her,' I said, moving forward as I sensed his confusion, so unlike his usual aplomb. Delia had to be here too. She couldn't refuse to let me see Sebastian; not once she heard about the hospital, my visit to Emilia, and what the old woman had told me.

'I told you she went back to Paris two days ago,' Américo replied.

'Let me in, Américo,' I insisted. 'I know Delia is here, and I want to see her. And Sebastian too. I'm not leaving until I've seen them. I'll go to the police at Las Palmeras if necessary. If they won't help me, I'll get a search warrant in Buenos Aires.'

Américo pulled the door open and stood aside.

'You're wasting your time,' he said as I entered the hall. 'There's only me here. The house is empty.' He sounded slightly impatient, like someone facing an obstinate child and trying to use quiet persuasion, when his inclination would have been to smack the bothersome pest.

'I don't believe you. I want to see for myself,' I said. Américo shrugged, as if he was no longer obliged to keep up a polite façade.

'Suit yourself,' he muttered, then turned round and left through the double doors on one side of the hall. I was alone, free to roam around at my leisure, if I had known where to start. The monumental staircase seemed to drag me towards the murky darkness upstairs, but Américo could have gone to warn Delia, to give her a chance to slip away while I fumbled my way through the unknown house. I went after him, and found myself in a long, broad gallery, dimly lit by a vapour of moonlight coming through the mullioned bow window at the end. The panelling on the walls was carved into shallow pointed arches, repeating the pattern of the groin vaults soaring into the dark above my head. Suspended from gargoyle-shaped brackets on the walls, glass lanterns hung over the doors, but I couldn't find a switch anywhere.

I headed for the rectangle of light cast by an open door in the distance and barged in, expecting to find Sebastian or Delia. Only Américo was there, sitting on a chair and polishing his shoes by the light of a paraffin lamp; he didn't stop, or even raise his eyes. A camp bed in a corner and his open suitcase on a chair next to it heightened the desolation of a huge room empty of any other furniture. Lighter areas of pile showed where pictures or cabinets had stood against the wine-coloured cut velvet on the walls, which was now coming away at the seams.

I went back to the gallery, and I threw open door after door. The noise reverberated in the emptiness: the succession of reception halls were as bare as Américo's makeshift bedroom. There at least the air did not smell musty, as it did in these shuttered chambers which people had not entered since they had lost their purpose long ago. I could guess what some of the rooms had been during the great days of the house: the adjacent pantry was the clue to what had once been the dining room, the empty, ornate bookcases to the library. The rest of the rooms were a meaningless accumulation of gilded mouldings, coffered ceilings, frayed silks or cracked embossed leather, fading heraldic shields and chipped plaster cherubs, all waiting under their even coating of dust for life to return.

A huge portrait of Ambrosio Lagos hung in one of the rooms. It showed him standing in the park, the house in the background, a man in control of all he surveyed. I stared at the picture of the man that had changed the course of so many lives: Delia's, Sebastian's, my mother's and my own, as if I was confronting the real Ambrosio who could give me the answer I needed, instead of a shallow illusion created by deft brushwork and poor light. The once-vibrant depiction of his power seemed as hauntingly hollow now as the pomp of the stage he had built for himself.

Américo was still in his room when I went back to the hall; I could see his shadow dancing on the gallery floor through the open door. I began to climb the stairs, although I knew I wouldn't find anything on the upper floor either. Sebastian had been in a wheelchair, and there was no elevator in the house. At first the darkness, the emptiness, and the shabbiness of neglect made me see the rooms upstairs as identical to those in the main floor, but they were different. They had been built for family life, not for show; they were meant for people to sleep in or children to play in. The wainscot was painted pink in one of the bedroom suites, and the wallpaper pattern combined swags of pale pink roses with pastel-blue ribbons. I wondered if it had once been Delia's room. I sensed or imagined some distant echo of her presence there, the faintest, musty trace of a floral scent, and I nearly called her name. A whisper-like noise behind me, something like soft, weightless footsteps, made me turn. I expected to see Delia standing by the door; instead I caught sight of a small, fleeting shadow, and the whip-like tail of a rat in flight.

The octagonal room at the corner of the house must have been the master bedroom. There were dents and scratches on the parquet, where the legs of a double bed had stood long ago. I unfastened the shutters on one of the windows, and threw them open. Beyond the park, the moonlight coated the water with the same silvery sheen as the tree-tops. I wondered if Ambrosio Lagos had died in this room, if this view had been the last image in his eyes before he closed them.

I didn't bother to shut the window before I went back downstairs. Américo was still in his room.

'Where is Sebastian then?' I asked impatiently.

'I told you he's not here. You should listen for a change,' Américo replied tersely.

'And you should answer my question. Where is he?'

'I have no idea. He might be dead, for all I know.'

There was no point in countering that I had seen Sebastian here only a few months before. Probably Delia had arranged for her brother to be moved elsewhere as soon as she heard I had been to San Octavio. She had come back to organize the move, then she had done her best to take me away with her. I hadn't found Sebastian. Instead I had succeeded in destroying the last vestige of my illusion that there had been a time, however short, when Delia had come back for no other reason than her love for me.

I left the house and headed for my car, across the silent park. The smell of those fusty rooms was still with me, as if my clothes had been dipped in it; I didn't want to drive away breathing that insidious odour. I needed to stay outside for a while longer. The open air seemed hot and still, the strength of the river breeze abated by screens of trees. An avenue of tall eucalyptuses led towards the shore. I followed it until I came to a belvedere. The render was crumbling off the columns and the shallow dome, and the tiled floor was covered in dead leaves.

I rested against one of the pillars. The summer house was at the top of a small hill, overlooking the wide river that lapped the blanket of reeds covering the shore. I could see a pier some three hundred yards to my left; eerily still, glowing the same shade of chalky white as the moon, a yacht was moored next to it.

I walked down the slope until I realized it would be impossible to reach the boat that way. I turned back and followed the contour of the tree-lined shore, catching glimpses of the yacht through the clearings every now and then, as unreachable as a mirage, until I came to a broad path cutting across the grass towards the river. A few moments later, the mouldy, split boards of the pier creaked under my feet, and I faced the bow of the abandoned ship. Painted in black letters over the anchor was the name 'Jupiter'. The past had ceased to be unreal. It was there, in front of my eyes, within reach of my touch.

What had seemed pristine white metal from the belvedere, close to was streaked with rust, the paint blistering away. I tried to look through the portholes, but the dirty glass and the darkness inside made it impossible to see anything. Near the stern, a gangplank bridged the gap over the water. As soon as I climbed it I checked the gate, folded back against the rail. It opened inwards, just as Delia had said.

I tried the door facing me. The glass panel was split, and the varnish on the wood had turned into a scaly, murky film. The corroded hinges creaked as I pushed hard, until the door gave. Once inside, it took a while for my eyes to adapt to the dark.

Moonlight, so bright outside, was turned to spectral clarity by the grimy windows.

Unlike the house, everything on the yacht had remained in place. There were sofas and armchairs, rugs on the floor and pictures on the walls. Ashtrays and boxes were still on the low tables. There were cigarette stubs in a silver dish, hardened by time into gnarled sticks. Traces of lipstick remained on some of the untipped ends. Nothing seemed to have been touched since that night.

Sliding doors at one end of the cabin led into the dining room. The oval table and the leather chairs around it were covered in dust, curdled by the damp into a sticky membrane. I imagined the scene twenty-one years ago, when Delia, Sebastian and my parents had sat around this table, my father suddenly changing their stilted conversation into the angry confrontation that had led to his death.

The foul air was hard to breathe. The catches on the windows had rusted solid, so I went outside, to inhale the clean wind from the river deep into my lungs. I headed for the stern and leaned over the rail, staring vacantly at the shimmering water.

'It's *you*,' a voice said behind me. I turned round and there was Delia, her startled face pale in the moonlight, as if she had been expecting somebody else.

'It isn't safe here any more. You shouldn't have come,' she added. 'Stay where you are. Please.'

Delia moved towards me. I was leaning on the rusting rail, which vibrated slightly as she stood against it a few steps away from me, her back to the water, holding tight to the splintery old wood. She stared at me with such concentration, as if she still found it hard to accept I was here, when it was *she* who was supposed to have gone away.

'Américo told me you had left for Paris two days ago,' I said.

'I asked him to. You mustn't blame him.'

'I'm not interested in Américo. I'm more concerned about the fact that everything you've ever said to me has been a lie.'

'I came to see Sebastian. I might never see him again,' Delia explained, as if she hadn't heard me. 'I'd rather you had gone to Paris. I can't imagine what you expected to find here.'

'An explanation. All this time I've been searching for an

explanation,' I said. 'I've found out about Pascual García, the drowned man found on the same day my father disappeared. I've found out about Dr Medina and Emilia, who cared for Sebastian after he was shot that same day. By accident, she told me. You could have helped me find the answers, but you chose to deceive me every time.'

'Not everything in life has an explanation, Martín. Nothing you accuse me of was my fault.' Even now, when it was pointless, Delia was trying to redeem herself. She had lied to me. We both knew it.

'You lied out of kindness, I suppose.'

'Still you don't understand,' she sighed. 'The deal was made to protect Sebastian and my father, not me.'

'I don't believe you. Either you or Sebastian killed my father. I need to know which of you it was.'

'Has it ever occurred to you that I might have been trying to protect you?' Delia asked. 'Please at least believe that I love you.' She leaned on the rail, still at arm's length from me. I shifted away instinctively, just a fraction, but enough for her to notice.

'Francis and I were talking here, after the argument, when Sebastian appeared,' she said, her eyes fixed on thee horizon. 'He was holding a gun. He said he would kill Francis unless he agreed to keep quiet and to allow Isabel to leave with the children. Francis said he wouldn't, and Sebastian didn't have the guts to shoot him anyway. Francis walked towards my brother and grabbed the barrel of the gun, trying to pull it away from him. In the struggle the gun went off, and Sebastian was shot in the head. I was petrified, and so was Francis. He stared at Sebastian bleeding on the floor, then he flung the gun overboard and dived into the river.'

Delia was speaking so quietly now that I had to lean towards her to catch her words.

'Francis might have wanted to kill himself after what he did, or maybe he was trying to get away. I'll never know what went through his mind. Then I saw Américo. He had been tidying up the dining room, and he had come out when he heard the shot. We didn't dare move Sebastian, so I stayed on deck with him while Américo radioed my father at the *estancia*. By the time we arrived the next morning, a specialist had been brought by plane from Buenos Aires; he said that Sebastian's condition was too delicate for him to be driven to hospital, and the bullet had gone clear through his skull. Surgery would make no difference to his chances of survival. He was taken to the old house and put in an oxygen tent.'

I kept staring at the river as Delia spoke. I didn't want to look at her face.

'My father notified the *Prefectura* about Francis, and one of their patrol boats found his body later that afternoon. Once the President had left, my father must have arranged for Francis's body to be taken to Rosario. I didn't know about the changed name. Isabel was driven there the next day, and she made the arrangements for the funeral. I don't know whether Francis or Sebastian fired the shot. I've never known. I didn't want you to find out what happened, because you might have believed Francis was guilty, no matter what I said, and I wanted to save you from all the miserable details. It was all so long ago. I was haunted by that night for years, and then I met you. I thought I would be able to put it all behind me at last.'

It could be that Delia had been trying to protect me, as she claimed. I had considered the possibility of my father shooting Sebastian before coming here. The fact that the gun might have been fired unwittingly, that it could have been an accident after all, made a small difference, but it didn't alter my abhorrence for the cover-up. I hated the dishonesty behind it – and my own naïveté.

'Ever since you started to ask me about Francis, I dreaded that it would come to this, but I was wrong. There are no secrets any more. We can think only of the future now.'

I stepped back, away from her. 'You don't understand anything,' I said. 'It's over.'

'Don't be rash, Martín. It will be different in Paris. None of this will seem the same there. Time makes a difference too, I promise. You can study, or we can travel. We'll do whatever you want.'

I felt numb, choking in rage and despair. I couldn't think beyond the next minute, while Delia talked about the future, as if there was one.

'You must be mad. Do you think that you can explain everything, and then we can carry on as if nothing had changed? I don't want to see you ever again.'

'It wasn't my fault,' she sobbed. 'I'm a victim of all of this, like you. Blaming me won't change what happened. You will just be making both of us miserable.'

I had never seen Delia so desperately sad, and for a second I felt myself respond. My impulse was to put my arms around her to comfort her – until I thought that was what she wanted. My coming here might have been what she had planned too. Over the last two days I had seen myself as a free agent, driven by my wish to know, when it had been Américo who had steered me into finding an explanation that would vindicate Delia. He could have been waiting outside my door until he saw me approaching through the glass, and only then pushed the envelope through the letter box. Delia could have mapped out the whole charade, to make me believe she was talking openly at last. She had waited for me here, where the whole setting would invest her words with the trappings of a confession. She could have used Américo as she could be using me at this very moment.

'It won't work,' I said, turning towards the gangplank. Delia came towards me and grabbed my arm.

'You can't go. You've got what you came here for,' she pleaded.

'I didn't,' I replied. 'I came here to see Sebastian; all I got instead were your words. I've heard it all before. Each time it's a bit different, each time you admit deceiving me, but there's always a reason for your previous lies – and you are always blameless. It doesn't matter if you're telling the truth this time, because I know now that I can't trust you.'

I had left the yacht, and started the long walk across the park towards my car, when I heard Delia call my name. She had run after me.

'Why do you want to see Sebastian?' she asked. 'He can't talk. He can't hear. Nothing reaches him. There's nothing he can tell you.'

'That's what you say. If it's true, then you shouldn't be so worried about me seeing him.'

Delia stood there, her arms tightly crossed, as if she was protecting herself from the cold.

'I'll take you to Sebastian, if that's what you want,' she said eventually. 'Come with me.'

I followed her into the park, where she turned onto a small path cutting across the shrubbery. I saw a glimmer of light, and the outline of a building partly concealed by trees. The path led to a garden surrounding a low, square colonial house, its walls painted a deep shade of pink.

'This was the main house on the estate, until my father built that monstrosity you saw. I hate that house. I sold the furniture to make sure I never had to stay there again. I should have had it demolished,' Delia said quietly. She walked onto the veranda, and stopped near one of the barred windows.

The room was lit by a lamp on a table, too small to illuminate the whole space, and far less bright than the TV screen that also glimmered there. A woman was watching it. It was Clara. Next to her, his legs covered by a rug, was Sebastian, sitting in a wheelchair. His skeletal frame was wrapped in a tartan dressing gown, and his head was slumped to one side. His wispy hair was cut very short, a touch of false youth to a vacant face that seemed impossibly old. His eyes were fixed on the screen, but they were like glass beads, registering nothing. If his chair had been pushed a fraction to one side, he would have stared at the wall with equal intensity. Every now and then Clara turned towards him and wiped the saliva dribbling down his chin with a handkerchief in her lap.

Confronted with that dismal sight, I knew at once that Delia had outwitted me again, by feigning great reluctance to do what presented no real threat to her in the end.

'Are you satisfied now? Let's go,' she whispered, trying to lead me away from the window.

'No, I want to go in.' I wasn't going to allow her to decide what I should do.

'Very well then,' Delia replied angrily. She walked towards the front door. The nurse must have heard us go into the house, because she came through a door at the end of the room as soon as Delia turned on the light.

'It's me, Clara,' Delia said. 'Américo got Sebastian's medicines from Las Palmeras, but I left them in the house. Would you mind going to get them now? We'll stay with him until you're back.'

Delia saw Clara out, then headed towards Sebastian's room as impassively as if she was on her own, as if I had vanished into the night like the nurse.

Sebastian didn't move when we went in. Delia stood to the side of the door, out of my way. I moved towards the wheelchair until I was in front of Sebastian, close enough to touch him. My body blocked his view of the TV screen, and yet nothing changed in his vacant eyes. The only sign of life was his laboured breath, the slow heaving of the sickeningly pale triangle of withered skin framed by the collar of his pyjamas. There was an old, vertical scar in the hollow of his wrinkled neck.

I couldn't help feeling sickened by the sight of this wreck who had been someone like me once, someone for whom life wasn't just a matter of waiting for death as a liberation. I felt pity too, and yet sorrow or compassion are puny antidotes to visceral revulsion. I had forced Delia to bring me here. I wanted to leave now, but I didn't want to appear as cowardly in her eyes as I felt myself to be. I had to do something, anything that would justify my stupid insistence on seeing Sebastian. I brought myself to rest my fingers on his shoulder very gently, as if it could break under their weight.

'Sebastian, can you hear me?' I asked. His face remained blank, motionless, empty of any emotion, and I raised my eyes towards Delia. She was standing against the wall, her hands pressed flat to it. Her lips were parted and her chest rose and fell rapidly, as if the air she inhaled couldn't reach her lungs.

'Let's go,' I said.

'No, you can't go now. Can't you see it?' she asked hoarsely. 'Can't you see the resemblance?'

I had never seen Sebastian before. I wondered if the sight of her brother was as shocking for her as it was for me, and she was unable to make sense.

'It's not Sebastian,' Delia whispered so quietly that I thought I had misheard her. 'It's Francis. That's your father.'

* * *

Later – hours, days, or weeks afterwards – I would come to realize that it was this single fact that explained everything else. Then, all I could think of was that my father wasn't dead. I looked at his face again, trying to reconcile this wretched cripple with the hero I had worshipped all through my childhood, the bronzed champion of my mother's eulogies, the young man whose passionate love letters I had read in Paris. I tried to find something, anything, of the face I knew so well, the face I loved so much, among the wrecked features permanently arranged into a ghastly mask. I saw nothing but a mirror of my own horror, and then I heard Delia speak. She sounded as if she was far, far away from me.

'Sebastian shot Francis when he tried to grab the gun away from him. I'll never forget the terror in his face as soon as he realized what he had done. It was Sebastian who dived into the river and was swept away by the current. I don't know if he wanted to kill himself or just tried to get away in a panic. He was always mad, and pathetic in the end. I was about your age, Martín. All I had done was go to parties. I didn't know anything, and suddenly I found myself at midnight, in the middle of nowhere, with Francis dying before my eyes, and Sebastian gone.

'Américo said he would call my father on the radio. I was sure that if he knew what had happened, my father would order the skipper to turn back. He would concentrate on keeping Sebastian's disappearance quiet until the President had gone. Francis was irrelevant to him, but I knew he would die unless a doctor saw him quickly, and we were only a few hours away from the *estancia*. If my father thought it was Sebastian who was wounded on board, he would use his power to do something for him, so that's what I told him over the radio. I couldn't help Sebastian, but I could try to save Francis's life – that mattered more than anything to me. I didn't care how my father would react once he found out.

'At first he was furious with me; then Sebastian was found dead, and he must have thought that my lie gave him a temporary way out of his predicament. Francis's death would attract far less attention than Sebastian's. The doctor and the nurse from Rosario had no reason to doubt my father when he told them that the wounded man was his son. The doctor said it was very unlikely that he would live more than a couple of days anyway, a week at most.

By then there would be no journalists around San Octavio, because they would all go back to Buenos Aires with the President. Sebastian's body was taken to Rosario, and cremated quietly as if he had been Francis, who would be buried in Sebastian's place when he died. But Francis didn't die. It became impossible to hand him over to Isabel. She believed he was dead, and so did everybody else.'

Delia's voice froze me to the ground, as if I would never be able to remove my fingers from my father's shoulder, as if I was bonded forever to the sharp ridges of that bone I was feeling through fabric as thin as his flesh. She spoke continuously, in a trance-like monotone I'd never heard before.

'I wouldn't have wanted him to go in any case, because I loved him. I had always loved Francis. I should have married him. I thought he wasn't serious about me, or that he only wanted my money. And then it was too late. His life would have been different if he had married me – and mine too. I denied us both a chance to be happy, so I *had* to take care of him after the accident – I felt it was my duty. At first I believed he would pull through; I wanted it so desperately. I thought I could will him to recover. I stayed here with Emilia for months, until it became obvious he'd never get better. He didn't even recognize me, or anybody else. The man in this house wasn't Francis, it was just his body hanging on to life – but it wasn't the man I loved.

'It became unbearable to see him like this, having to pretend to Emilia all the time that he was my brother, watching every word I said not to give the truth away, so I returned to Buenos Aires. Frank Malden had come to lecture at *Amigos del Arte*. I met him there. I loved his books, and I thought I might fall in love with him in time, although now I suppose I saw him as an escape from a life I loathed. Frank asked me to go back to New York with him, and my father didn't try to stop me. By then he was a broken man. He had lost his son. Politics didn't matter to him any more. He and I became estranged. What had happened here crippled us both, in different ways.'

Delia stopped abruptly and left the room. I remained still, until everything she had said unscrambled in my head, her words turning into meaning. My immediate reaction was panic. She had walked away; I was alone with my father. There was nothing to distract me from the rasp of his breathing, no one to make me feel that this horror was not my responsibility now, that I was free to leave too.

The small cushion behind his neck had shifted slightly. His head lolled to one side, resting on my hand, and trapping it. I forced myself to straighten his head, to touch his face in a gesture that might have been loving if his skin hadn't felt so searingly alien to mine, if I had been able to recognize something of me in him, no matter how slight. I tried. I tried as hard as I could, raking my memories for anything that would bring this spectre in front of me alive; not memories I had fleshed out of photographs, but real ones. There must have been times when my father sat me on his lap, or held my hand as I tottered around with unsteady steps, or leaned over my cot to kiss me good night, a time when I smiled in delight at the sight of his face. He must have shown me the awesome immensity of the sea, or the fragile wonder of a butterfly. There must have been words I said that made him laugh, and words he said that made me understand. Those memories had to be somewhere in my head. They *were* there; they couldn't have vanished without trace.

But there was nothing, only a blank as empty, as meaningless as his eyes which didn't move, didn't focus. My father was the hero who had died long ago, when he was young and splendidly alive, not this dribbling wreck of a man. Whatever he was now, he couldn't be my father. He was somebody else. I couldn't make myself love him. His memories had stopped when mine began. All we had in common now was the impossibility of love between us.

Struggling against my revulsion, I took his hand. It felt cold and inert, weightless, like a dead bird. His face didn't change. Nothing I could do would make him notice me. I stood there, petrified into an inertia that seemed eternal, until a loud burst of applause from the TV audience shook me back to my senses. I let go of his hand, and stepped back. I wished I had never come here, that I had never come into this room. I closed my eyes before I turned; I didn't want to see him again, because I couldn't run the risk of doubting my decision. I had to leave.

I made my way out of the house like an automaton. All I could see was the door coming closer. I paused outside, until the surrounding darkness broke into shapes and colours again. Delia was waiting in the garden. She came to me. Her eyes were too bright, her face too pale.

'Now you know why I didn't want to talk about Francis in Paris. When I saw you there for the first time, it was as if he was back. I thought I had been given a second chance.'

Until a moment ago, I would have found it inconceivable that anything Delia could say by now would hurt me, although physical pain would have been preferable to the actual effect of her words on me. I felt breathless, as if a vacuum had formed around us.

'I was only a stand-in for him. That's all I was for you,' I managed to say.

'That's not true. I love you. It might have been as you say at first, but there was a difference. I couldn't have married Francis as he was. It's not the same with us. You and I, as we were, we could have been happy together. I don't know for how long, but long enough. We would have had a chance if you had listened to me, if you hadn't been so eager to know the truth, when it wasn't worth knowing. In that respect alone, I wish you were like him. Francis knew how to protect himself from unpleasant facts, to see only what suited him.'

We could have been happy together . . . Delia was wrong. She was using the past tense, as if there was no hope, as if my coming here had meant the end for us, when in fact it meant the opposite. Now I knew she wasn't guilty of anything. She had nothing to do with what had happened. We could leave.

'We *are* happy,' I said. 'I've got my car here. Let's go back to Buenos Aires and fly out tomorrow. A moment ago you said to me that it would all seem different in Paris. You were right. We can leave it all behind. I love you, and you've just said you love me. I don't care about the rest.'

Delia stood still, saying nothing. She looked so small suddenly, as though she had been hollowed out by grief.

'That was ten minutes ago,' she said. 'You didn't know then. You were different, and this was mine alone. I share the past with him, not with you. It's *my* past and *my* guilt, not yours. You must go.'

'That's mad,' I retorted. 'You can't stay here. I won't let you.'

'Don't take me so literally. Of course I can't stay here,' Delia said with a tired, melancholy ring to her voice. 'Doesn't make much difference though. I hadn't been here for twenty years until now, but I came back every day in my head. You don't need a ticket or luggage for that. Besides, I won't be able to stay away for another twenty years. Clara wants to leave. I'll have to find someone else – who might not last. Why would you want to share this? Would you come here with me every time I have to? Or would you ask me for details when I'm back? Or won't we talk about him at all? If we did, what would we call him? The man in that house *is* Sebastian. Everybody knows him as "Don Sebastian". "It's time for your soup, Don Sebastian." "Now let me get you into your bed, Don Sebastian." "Don Sebastian looks much better today, don't you think, *Niña* Delia?" Is he going to become part of your life, but you'll never tell your mother or your brother . . . ?'

I saw myself again in front of that horrible sight, in that forlorn room with the television on. I didn't want that. I didn't want him.

'I want you. That's all I want,' I said. 'Let's go.'

Delia stared at me so lovingly, so intensely, and then she shook her head slowly.

'No. You don't want *me*,' she said. 'You want me as you knew me before. You want a second chance, as I wanted it too when we met. It doesn't work, I promise you. There are no second chances. You must go.'

Perhaps it was what she was really trying to say without hurting me, perhaps not. What became irrevocably clear to me that instant was that I couldn't have Delia without having my father in my life again. As he was. On my own, never sharing my knowledge, my grief or my weariness with anybody else. I might lose Delia, or I might part from her one day, but I'd never be free of him as he was. I preferred my own version, my own dream. It wasn't a choice between Delia and him. I had to give both of them up. I kept my eyes on the ground for a while, and then eventually I looked at her.

'I'm glad you agree,' she said very quietly. I wished I could say something, anything, but my throat was frozen. I kept staring at her. The stars above us seemed to be in my eyes too; the image of her face dissolved into sparks through my tears.

'I . . .'

My words never came. I turned away and left her alone in the garden, surrounded by the song of the crickets, a little figure under a big dark sky.

Sixteen

I went back to my life, or at least to the sequence of everyday actions and habits that keep us seemingly sane when everything we treasure has been shattered beyond repair, and we are sinking into the debris. I found myself another job, with a small firm of lawyers that handled whatever work they were lucky enough to find. Even if I had been able to go back to Lucas's office, the idea was intolerable. The place had become as contaminated by corrosive memories for me as everywhere else I had been over the last few months.

I didn't try to see my mother. I didn't want to, and I couldn't trust myself to keep quiet if I were to meet her. She didn't attempt to contact me either. In the end she had tried to save what she could from the disaster, as I myself was trying to do now. Tempting as it was to concentrate my anger on her, it would have been a poor, ineffectual remedy for my sense of loss – which at least I could confront, unlike my shame.

For once, I couldn't fool myself about my claims to the high moral ground. Delia had led me to my father, and I had rejected him. I couldn't accept him into my life because all I had really cared about in the end had been my dream – not the real man. I had run away because I couldn't face the knowledge or the responsibility. Like Sebastian Lagos, I had jumped into a void rather than stay with the consequences of my actions. I had denied my father. At least my mother didn't know what had happened to him, or what he had become. I envied her ignorance.

I wondered if the need to justify herself had been Delia's ultimate reason for what she did that night at San Octavio. I always assumed her to be in control of her reactions and mine, to have lied by choice. If her motive had been to make me share her guilt, it didn't show in the letter I got from her two or three weeks later, when she was back in Paris.

I didn't keep that letter. Although it was short, I'm not sure I read it word by word; I just took it in, my eyes skimming over her writing. Delia asked me to forgive her for the damage she had caused me, and hoped I would believe her at last. But I remember every word of her closing paragraph:

> *Please forget me and all that has happened; think only about your future. I hope you'll be able to do what you want in the end, and I know that you'll have a charmed and happy life ahead of you.*

Her good wishes were as much as my remorse would allow me to accept from Delia. They seemed so unlikely to become true that I saw them as a sort of perverse – and well-deserved – punishment.

The next couple of months were more miserable than any. I was at home one evening when the phone rang.

'Martín? It's Miguel. I'm calling from the café at the corner. Have you had dinner yet?'

'I was cooking something, and there's enough for both of us. I'll come downstairs to let you in.'

I hadn't seen Miguel for what seemed like an eternity. 'You must have good news, you look remarkably cheerful,' I said when we greeted each other in the entrance hall.

'I arrived this afternoon, because I wanted to talk to *mamá* and you. When I called your office from the airport, they told me you weren't there any more. I'm here to tell you that Margarita and I are getting married,' he announced as we climbed the stairs.

'That's great,' I said. At least my brother had sorted his life out.

'We are planning to come to Buenos Aires next month, and you'll meet her then. Her parents live in Rawson, so we'll get married there next year.'

The thought of having any kind of plan for the future sounded impossible to me.

'No risk of getting lost here,' I said as we walked into my apartment. I laid the table, took the foil tray out of the oven, and ladled the food onto the plates.

'What's that?' Miguel asked, inspecting the unrecognizable mince smothered in a lumpy, creamy sauce.

'It's frozen lasagne, a new thing I saw advertised on TV. I decided to try it tonight,' I explained.

I had used my severance pay to buy a TV set. The idea of seeing other people had become almost as obnoxious as the fact of going out on my own, to sit in a cinema surrounded by strangers. I preferred to spend my evenings at home, staring at the flickering screen, often unaware of the actual image. Occasionally, at the most unexpected moments, like the evening news, even the safety of television was illusory: the fleeting sight of the riderless horse at Kennedy's funeral, the empty boots in the stirrups, came back in my dreams for weeks.

'You'd better try it some other time. Come on, I'll buy you dinner,' Miguel said. He took my jacket from the back of my chair and gave it to me. 'But I'd rather leave this with you before we go out,' he added, handing me a rectangular leather box. 'When I went to see *mamá* this afternoon, she said she wanted me to have a brooch for Margarita that had belonged to our grandmother. She said she wouldn't mind if we sold it, if the money would help us to get started. Then she said she had something for you too. She wants us to have these things now, when we could do with a little financial help.'

I put the box in a drawer.

'Is everything all right between you two?' Miguel asked.

'We had an argument some time ago. I'll tell you about it later,' I replied.

I told Miguel as little as possible. I said our mother had been furious when she heard I was seeing Delia again, but Delia had returned to Paris, so the argument had been pointless. Then we talked about many other subjects, or at least Miguel did. He seemed more confident and happy than I could ever remember. We said goodbye outside the restaurant, because he wanted to catch an early morning flight the next day.

When I got home again, I switched on the TV. That week's

episode of *Peyton Place* was nearly over. As the credits rolled, I remembered the box Miguel had given me. I took it out of the drawer and opened it. I expected to find a piece of jewellery inside, but nothing as valuable as what I saw: a broad diamond bracelet forming a geometric pattern around big, square stones.

Probably it was the last remnant from that golden past my mother thought about every day. I had thought about the past every day too; it had changed from something precious and shimmering like the bracelet into a tarnished, worthless burden that I would never be able to give away.

NOW

'I'M SORRY. I wasn't trying to make a pun,' the banker's wife said with a smile as we stood in front of Delia's portrait. The sound of her voice broke my absorption.

'I don't follow you,' I replied.

'*Unforgettable*. You must be tired of hearing that word by now. It was such a good movie.'

'Oh, I see. That was a long time ago, my first big break. I even wrote the script,' I said. It would mean little to her, but I'm proud of that movie.

'I loved it,' she gushed. 'It was wonderful, so atmospheric! You must have such a vivid imagination to be able to invent a story like that: two women in love with the same man, the murder on the yacht . . .' Her description of the plot was so detailed that I assumed she must have watched the video to refresh her memory before coming to Los Angeles. My companion was the kind of New York hostess who would ask fashionable writers to her dinner parties, and then rapidly scan their latest novel at the hairdresser's the afternoon before so she could say the right things. 'I was glad that the detective proved she was innocent in the end though. I only like happy endings; life is depressing enough as it is.'

'You're so right. I like happy endings myself,' I replied.

It is ironic that I have been able to live better than most people by selling them the notion that such a thing is possible, by creating two-hour illusions where life and all its good things rise from the ashes of tragedies that are never more than temporary, as if there could be fresh starts and new beginnings.

'You won an Oscar for *Unforgettable*, didn't you?'

'It was nominated for Best Picture, but it didn't win. Deborah won the Oscar for Best Actress though.'

'Of course,' she said, in the hushed tone of someone who broaches a risky subject by mistake. Her leading role in the picture had turned Deborah Conway from an unknown actress into a great star, in the same way that the movie changed my career from struggling tyro into a big-league director. Our marriage, soon after the movie was finished, had been news; not as big as our divorce six years ago though, when Deborah bolted with a young actor.

Some people in the same predicament would have remarked on the lateness of the hour and left immediately, but the banker's wife was too accomplished in social skills for that. She wanted to end our little chat on an upbeat note, a prelude to her graceful exit. People who care about form take trouble over their exits.

'You've had a brilliant career. How did you get started?' she asked eagerly, as if she really wanted to know.

'I came into some money in Argentina when I was in my twenties, and I used it to study cinematography at the University of Southern California,' I said. It was my standard explanation for the turning point in my life, when I had sold the diamond bracelet and used the money to support myself through college. 'I worked as a camera-man first, then I became a second-unit director, met people, learned the business, and here I am.'

'Do you ever go back to South America?' She wasn't taking risks. We were into standard-issue small-talk again.

'Not very often. My brother and his family used to come to Los Angeles on holiday, when his children were young enough to enjoy Disneyland. Now I always seem to be working, so it's difficult for both of us to get together as much as we'd like.' There was no need to say I had been back a couple of years ago, when my mother died. Neither of us wanted another depressing turn in the conversation to hold up her departure.

'I'm sure your next movie will be your biggest success yet. It really has been a wonderful evening,' she said – and only then noticed how late it was, and remarked that her husband would complain at being kept waiting. I saw them to their car, and I stood in the drive until their tail-lights disappeared.

I went back inside. The party would be coming to an end soon. The caterers would be busy in the kitchen, putting their equipment away, and the waiters would have made their final round, offering drinks or a last coffee to the lingering guests – Kelly among them. I knew she wanted to stay with me tonight, and that I'd let her. We met a year ago, when she was editing my last movie, and now we pretend work makes it difficult for us to see each other more often than we do.

Weekends are tricky enough, and she has started going to some place in the valley on Saturdays, where a Greek woman helps kindred spirits to get in touch with their inner selves. Kelly would like me to come with her, but I indulge in enough introspection without assistance.

Sometimes I fly to San Francisco to see Julia, my daughter. Not too often though. She is at Berkeley, and she has her own life. She wants to move to New York after graduation. We pretend I don't know, because her mother lives there, and Julia doesn't want me to think that's the reason behind her decision. I've learned the danger of trying to clarify blurred issues, so we don't talk about it. We love each other, and we leave it at that.

It would be foolish to describe my life as 'charmed', and I don't think Delia expected it to be when she wrote her letter. Like most lovely sayings, 'a charmed life' can't be a true fact. She must have meant it as an encouragement, as an expression of genuine hope. But I would be ungrateful if I were to say that my life hasn't been a happy one. It's not that different to my job. At times the script needs a bit of retouching, but the real secret is in the editing. If you cut at the right frame, discard the bad footage, and believe in the result, you have a good movie. Nobody needs or wants to see what's left on the cutting floor.

I started towards the living room, then I stopped. After my conversation with the banker's wife, I wanted a few moments on my own; not because of her mention of Deborah, which had mortified her more than it upset me, nor because of my passing thoughts about my mother either. We had made our peace after I came to California, initially by letter and then face to face, when I went back for the christening of Francisco, Miguel's first child, who is my godson. His name, suggested by my mother, met with general approval. There had been Franciscos in almost every generation of our family – and of course it had been my father's name.

Making peace is an inaccurate description of our rapprochement, because it implies the notion of war, when in fact my mother and I had avoided the slightest mention of anything that had led to our breach. I thanked her for her generous gift of the diamond bracelet, and she seemed genuinely interested in my budding career. I paid for her ticket to come to my wedding, and she came to Julia's christening two years later. I'm glad I managed to see her one last time after her stroke, although she was unconscious by then. I held her hand and sat with her. I believe she knew that I was there.

I didn't bother to turn on the lights when I returned to my study. The glow from the illuminated pool outside was enough to see by, and it suited Delia's portrait. It brought out the highlights in the print: her eyes, her cheekbones – and the broad diamond bracelet on her wrist. When I came across that portrait by chance, at a Sotheby's auction, I thought my eyes were playing a trick on me. I was sure it was the bracelet my mother gave me. At first I couldn't understand how Delia could have owned it in 1953, when the photograph was taken.

Eventually I figured it out. Delia knew I would refuse help from her after we parted. She must have asked my mother to pass on the bracelet to me, as if it was a family heirloom. Since she still depended financially on Delia, my mother couldn't refuse. Miguel's unexpected visit to tell her about his engagement gave her an opportunity to fulfil Delia's last instructions.

Maybe it's just a coincidence. Delia might have owned a similar bracelet, and tricks of memory make me see them as one and the same. I remembered the flash of diamonds on Delia's wrist when she touched my shoulder at the Rousselet ball, but I had no reason to pay attention to her jewellery. Delia owned plenty of diamonds; it could have been any of her many bracelets. The fact that I never saw my mother wear the one she gave me doesn't mean she didn't own it. It is conceivable that she simply didn't like it.

By the time I found the portrait, my mother had died, so I couldn't ask her. I prefer my own explanation, the idea that Delia helped me. I hated her for a long time, because it was the easiest way out, but you can't fool yourself indefinitely. I never loved another woman as I loved her, perhaps because I knew it was impossible. It's safe to love her now. She can't hurt me any more.

Delia broke my heart, and she created my life. In her letter, she asked me to think only of the future, and her gift ensured I would have one. She had more faith in me then than I had in myself.

I had lied to the banker's wife. I had been to Buenos Aires a few months ago. The last time I had gone there, when our mother died, I heard through various people that Delia was back in Argentina. When I bought her portrait, and worked out that she must have given me the bracelet, I went back in the hope that I would be able to trace her. But her house in Buenos Aires had been pulled down to make room for the avenue, in a final wave of demolition that also erased the Rousselet house. Eight lanes of traffic rode over the ground where that house once was. I stood on the central island, among the passing cars, staring up as if I expected to see Delia and me dancing across that gleaming floor again, her lace skirt swirling around my legs, but there was nothing, only air.

I thought she might have gone back to San Octavio, to my father's side. I couldn't follow her there. Not again. I hope she didn't, or that he wasn't alive by then. Ever since that night I have wished my father dead and out of his misery. I comfort myself with the expectation that he must have died long ago, as if that could alleviate my relentless guilt ever since I left him in that room. The thought of Delia sitting beside him in their old age, day after day, watching that wide river flow past, haunts me still.

But I am deceiving myself even now. I could have traced Delia. I could have tried to make contact with her. If I haven't, it is because I dread the sight of her as she must be now. Once in my life I went to any length to find out the truth, only to wish I had never started. It won't happen again. My Delia is that glorious face on my wall. I don't want her image erased by what time does to all of us. I want her as she was, as she remains in my memory.

Once, long ago, I had something I cherished that came to an end before its time, something I destroyed unknowingly, something I will never have again. Like Delia, at times I have found myself drawn to the mirage of a second chance, of what might have been.

So we have become equals at last. Neither of us had a second chance. And neither of us could ever forget.